# BEYOND DEATH

### A NOVEL
### BY MICHAEL ATAMANOV

*Wishing you safe travels on your fantasy journey,*

## PERIMETER DEFENSE
## BOOK#2

MAGIC DOME BOOKS

Beyond Death
Perimeter Defense, Book # 2
Second Edition
Published by Magic Dome Books, 2017
Copyright © M. Atamanov 2016
Cover Art © V. Manyukhin 2016
Translator © Andrew Schmitt 2016
All Rights Reserved
ISBN: 978-80-88231-14-1

# All books
# by Michael Atamanov:

*Reality Benders* LitRPG series
*Countdown*
*External Threat*
*Game Changer*
*Web of Worlds*
*A Jump into the Unknown*
*Aces High*

*The Dark Herbalist* LitRPG series
*Video Game Plotline Tester*
*Stay on the Wing*
*A Trap for the Potentate*
*Finding a Body*

*Perimeter Defense* LitRPG series
*Sector Eight*
*Beyond Death*
*New Contract*
*A Game with No Rules*

*League of Losers* LitRPG Series
*A Cat and His Human*

*You're in Game!*
(LitRPG Stories from Bestselling Authors)

*You're in Game-2!*
(More LitRPG stories set in your favorite worlds)

# Table of Contents:

# STOPPING THE INVASION

WHAT HAVE I done?! In my attempt to delay an untimely call to the Emperor's court, I ended up inviting an honest-to-God Alien invasion to my own system! It's like burning your own house down to keep your strict parents from noticing that you broke a vase. Tearing my gaze with great difficulty from the scattering of red markers on the tactical map, I tried to gather myself and spoke into the microphone in the confident voice of a commander:

"Extinguish the beacon! I need information on the enemy!"

"Distance to target: six hundred miles. There are multiple targets! I have nineteen marks on the radar. Identification by radar signature: Five *Sledgehammer* cruisers, four *Ascetic* destroyers, four *Hermit* destroyers, five *Meteor* frigates, and a big guy..."

I laughed with marked happiness into the microphone:

"That 'big guy' is an Alien battleship. Humanity has yet to come across one. I suggest, as its discoverer, that it be called 'Behemoth.' It's a big fat mythical creature that supposedly lived on humanity's far-off homeworld."

Admiral Kheraisss Vej intervened in the conversation and clarified:

"My Princcce, the Swarm already see thisss shiip. But not one remainsss who that could inform you of the tactical and technical characterisssticsss of such a big *Behemoth.*"

"So then, the Iseyek do not object to the name. And as for the battleship's capabilities, we can figure that out during the battle."

I was trying to hide my worry behind stirring speeches and showy enthusiasm. For the first time since I entered the game, I wasn't at all sure I would win. In fact, if I were playing for the Alien team, I would say quite the opposite: I'd consider this a done deal. Five *Sledgehammers* working together could make themselves into a real "ball of death," destroying any ship that gets too close to them. Even my battleship wouldn't survive two of their combined volleys. The many Alien destroyers and frigates would make absolutely sure that none of my light ships could get close to the *Sledgehammers.* It would have looked like a sticky situation, even if the enemy didn't have the *Behemoth* that we still knew nothing about. But with the enemy having a *Behemoth,* our chances of winning were so slim as to be transparent.

For a second, the cowardly thought to command the fleet to retreat and warp back to Unatari crossed my mind, but I chased it off. First, we haven't been beaten yet! Second, I couldn't throw the eight thousand inhabitants of the Hnelle station to the dogs. As far as I was concerned, their lives were completely dependent on our ability to defend them.

All the same, I couldn't show my apprehension before my subjects. Also, the Aliens had never shown any particular tactical skill in previous battles. Instead, they just stupidly crawl forward and put all their hope in the crushing power of their cannons and their instantly regenerating shields. So, I ended up calming myself down. We'll see yet who will take the day!

"Alright, fun's over. We've got a serious mission ahead of us. Let's get to work. *Pyro-1*: first receiver, *Pyro-2*: second. A squad of frigates will cover each of you. Be especially cautious – those *Meteors* are significantly faster than any of our ships. If one of them approaches you, do not engage. Retreat back to our heavies."

"The enemy has begun maneuvers!" reported Nicole. "The destroyers and frigates are approaching quickly. The *Sledgehammers* and *Behemoth* are lagging behind."

"All ships, at the ready! For now, we wait and see how they act... The enemy ignored our receivers. That is very good. So, first two frigate squads, your mission is to hold the *Behemoth* under webs. There's no way in hell we want him getting close to us. Nicole, you're in charge of that operation. The rest of the frigates, we're gonna need your webs. Work on the drones while you're at it. Anti-support, split up into groups of five. Your first mission is to give the *Meteors* a haircut. After that, work on the *Hermits*. Electronic warfare, turn the most dangerous *Ascetics* off. Attention! They're entering the combat zone! Frigates, advance! Release drones!"

A huge swarm of little green dots roared off toward the red ones on the tactical screen. As our heavies delivered a cloud of combat drones, the battle began.

"*Warhawk-4* here, I've got a *Meteor* under web. I've marked it in the overview!"

With a resounding boom, first Alien ship dissolved to atoms after a combined volley from forty destroyers.

"*Tusk-1* here, *Ascetic* under web!"

I heard two more blasts! And if the first of the double explosions was the *Ascetic* getting blown apart, then the second was one of ours.

"*Warhawk-1* here, I need help! These drones are eating me alive!!!"

"Warp out!" I screamed, but it was too late. Another fiery bloom erupted in the cosmos.

"Heavies, the marked *Ascetic* is primary. The secondary is that *Hermit* there. Fire on the targets under double web at will."

Another two Alien ships popped into clouds of tiny fragments after a combined volley from twenty heavy cruisers. After that, another explosion let us know that a *Meteor* had been shot down by my destroyers.

"My Prince! I can die happy!" This parting scream came from *Pyro-10*, after it was already too late to respond.

"*Warhawk-4* here, I'm holding a *Meteor* with web and disruptor. He's got me too! It looks like this is the end..."

"Anti-support, save *Warhawk-4*!!!"

An explosion was heard. And another! The tactics officer took two *Meteors* from the map.

"*Warhawk-4* here, we escaped by the skin of our

teeth! Thanks for the help! I owe you all a beer!" came the familiar voice of the female captain.

"*Warhawk-4*, warp out to the *Tria*. Your luck's just about run out for the day. So, I need webs on the last *Meteor*! *Pyro-11*, don't break off from the others! *Safa-4*, the same goes for you. Get back into formation. You'll be eaten whole if they catch you alone. Heavies, the primary is that *Ascetic* that's crawling away from you under two webs."

Boom! Boom! Boom! Hearing the blasts, I took a look at the tactical screen. The enemy's support ships had been totally wiped out, but the group of five *Sledgehammers* had already come to within one hundred twenty miles of us. The *Behemoth* was still far behind though. I could breathe a bit easier. The enemy had lost all light ships, charitably giving us an advantage in maneuverability on the battlefield. Now, my frigates could get close to the *Sledgehammers* and split them up, which would greatly simplify the situation.

"Third and fourth *Pyro* squads, hold the *Sledgehammer* I've marked on the map! Don't let it get any closer to us! *Tusks* and *Safas*, place webs and take point on that *Sledgehammer*. Let the other three come to us. *Bride of Chaos*, make a short advance! Heavies, stay twenty miles behind the battleship."

The *Sledgehammers* shot first, letting fly a combined volley from three ships. *Bride of Chaos*'s energy shield fell by half, but quickly recharged when ten heavy cruisers turned on their remote shield-charging modules.

"Primary is marked. Battleship and all heavies, get ready. Shoot only on my command. On the count of three... One. Two. Three!"

The targeted *Sledgehammer* went out like a candle in the wind. The combined volley from my battleship and twenty-two heavy cruisers pulverized the Alien ship into atoms.

"My good soldiers, you're some real beasts! Excellent. I've targeted a new ship."

The return fire came back at *Joan the Fatty*. The ship shook hard. The light flickered in the room. Some of the devices switched over to emergency power sources.

"Our shield is at just eleven percent. Shall we prepare for evacuation?" asked Captain Oorast Pohl.

"Recharge the *Fatty*!" I ordered on the fleet channel and, after removing my earphones, I answered the captain that there was no reason whatsoever for evacuation.

In fact, this was a critical moment. The enemy had given up shooting at the impenetrable battleship and was now focusing its fire on the cruiser where the fleet was being commanded from. It wasn't clear if the last volley had been intentional, or whether the choice of precisely *Joan the Fatty* from among twenty-two cruisers had just been random. But in any case, the ship wouldn't survive another volley from two *Sledgehammers* all on its own.

"Have you reloaded? On the count of three. One, two, three!"

Another *Sledgehammer* gave way to an orange and white blossom. Only one enemy remained nearby.

"Let's target the last one. Reload. And another thing: one of the cruisers shot before the command last time. If that happens again, whoever does it will be the fleet's next target. How much shield do we have left?"

"Thirty-seven percent. We're recharging slowly!" the captain answered.

"The *Sledgehammer* will get a shot off in nine seconds. We need forty-five percent shield to survive the attack..."

The ship shook again, but everyone around me perceived the strike with clear relief. "The shield held out!" The officers already understood that the ship would escape, as it would be able to restore shield before the next strike.

"We've just got four percent shield left!" Oorast Pohl said in a calm tone, before suddenly smiling. "We'll shoot it first."

"Fire!" I commanded, and the enemy ship was no more.

The two remaining *Sledgehammers* we swept up using the same tactic. But when it came time to deal with the *Behemoth*, complications arose immediately. When the fleet was trying to get within two hundred miles of the huge Alien ship, *Jeanne the Star Traveler* suddenly exploded. The heavy assault cruiser of the newest design was destroyed by just one volley directly through its reinforced front shields! I ordered the remaining ships to immediately warp out to the *Tria* at a safe distance.

"My Prince, two rescue shuttles have been observed from *Jeanne*."

I sighed bitterly. Two shuttles means that at most twenty-four were rescued out of four hundred crew members.

***Global fame increase. Current value +11***

***Global standing increase. Current value -20***

The message came in totally unexpectedly, and I got slightly upset, not having understood the reason for the positive changes. But I met with the happy eyes of Katerina ton Mesfelle and immediately guessed what was up. My advisor came closer and explained:

"Georg, we've just made the first emergency broadcast about the Alien invasion in the Hnelle system. Nineteen ships, a flood of panic and all that. There are scenes with good resolution – a huge battleship, the terrifying *Sledgehammers*, which already have a ghastly reputation among Imperial soldiers, and the destroyers. Well, and, at the end, a word about how the Sector Eight Fleet is prepared to engage in battle with enemies and a request to wish luck to the defenders of humanity. The only thing is, I was planning to draw out the story with five or seven broadcasts, but the enemy fleet is already gone. What am I supposed to talk about in the next one?"

I pointed to the huge red dot on the tactical screen:

"It's still too soon to talk about victory. I think we'll be able to destroy the *Behemoth*, but only with monstrous losses. That is why we are going to try another way: for the first time in history, we will try to board and capture an Alien ship. So, you will have something to tell the viewers about after all."

I called General Savasss Jach, who heard out this bizarre mission with surprising tranquility. The huge insect wriggled his antennae for some time, then Bionica translated his answer:

"Ten thousand Alpha Iseyek assault troops should be enough. But first you'll need to secure a path for them by clearing all the *Behemoth*'s drones and collecting information about the enemy ship. And he'll need around two standard hours to wake the soldiers from a state of suspended animation."

Katerina heard out the general's answer with me and said with satisfaction:

"Great! Now I'll have a two-hour gap between my reports. I'll do a series of broadcasts and interviews with various officers and commanders of your fleet. I'll give information in small portions. Let the viewers stay on the edges of their seats under the impression that the space battle is raging on. Then, I'll give a live broadcast from the landing troops' chambers. But Georg, it would be really great if we could have someone taking part in storming the Alien ship other than the praying mantises, like people too. Otherwise, there won't be any viewer involvement, and they won't sympathize with us."

Admiral Kiro Sabuto also supported the idea.

"My Prince, your cousin is right. Today we shall write a new page in the history of human resistance against the Aliens. This battle is sure to be included in all tactical textbooks and even school history books, and it is very important that people be the most active participants in the capture of the Alien battleship. All of our ships have a boarding team. We can gather more than two thousand soldiers from the whole fleet."

Popori de Cacha suddenly forced his way into the conversation and said with a bow:

"My Prince, I ask that you include two Chameleons

from your bodyguard team in the assault force. For my kind, the Ravaash, it is also important to feel that we are taking part in this historic moment."

"Alright. I order human assault troops and Chameleons to get prepared as well. You have two hours. These divisions will also be commanded by General Savasss Jach, and Bionica will provide coordination and translation."

I turned to my assistant Nicole and asked about the *Behemoth*. The girl, without taking off her headphones, frowned in dissatisfaction:

"The pilots are getting tired from the long battle, and it's starting to show. They have begun to make errors: *Pyro-22* scratched itself at high speed against a turret tower, and *Pyro-25* ran into an enemy drone. Both ships left the battle with broken armor and no shields and have gone for repair. We're getting the impression that the *Behemoth* has an infinite supply of drones. We've already taken down a hundred thirty-two, but new flocks of them just keep squirming out. Are they making them in there or something?"

"Nicole, don't worry. I'll send the pilots out a fresh team. Pick someone to change them out. Your mission is to hold the *Behemoth* another two hours while the praying mantis assault troops unfreeze. If you get tired, I can take your place."

"I appreciate your concern, Prince, but I do not need any help. It's the first time I've been entrusted with such an important mission, and that is its own reward."

* * *

"The flamethrowers are lighting the way. We have cleared a corridor to the cannon tower, and group *Blue-Three* is moving out to capture it. There are two hundred Swarm assault troops."

"*White-Eight* here. We've cleared another path into the third section! We'll take the winding corridor toward the tactical marker. Serious resistance. A vacuum does nothing to stop these shrubs. They still fight, even without atmosphere."

"Thick fire! We have to get back to the spiral staircase. Only four soldiers remaining of thirty in *Yellow-Four*. The praying mantises that were covering our exit have already all gone down. We need support immediately. Aaaaaa!"

Katerina pointed at the screen and shook her head: "We'll have to cut that part out."

"You will do no such thing! The viewers have to see that this isn't child's play. Everything is serious. There's a war on, and the soldiers are paying with their blood so the rest of humanity may live."

Despite the fierce resistance, the assault divisions systematically cleared the huge ship. More and more groups of soldiers snuck inside the *Behemoth* through the holes we were cutting into its chassis. The assault troops' losses turned out to be significant. The Aliens forced us to pay a heavy price for every foot of the winding corridors we took. Bionica, wearing a pair of huge headphones, was frantically picking division markers on the screen and nonstop translating messages and commands from human to Swarm language and back. Katerina even shot a separate report on the android girl so viewers from the whole Empire could watch my wonderful translator work in real life.

"*White-Three* here. We have met up with *Yellow-Five*. Enemy resistance has been suppressed. We have captured what looks like a reactor installation. Let the experts figure it out."

"*Green-Ten* here. Mission accomplished. The superstructure is under our control."

"*White-Six* here. We have cleared the hall of automatic defense systems. Less than a third of our praying mantises survived. We're detecting intensive radio signals and long-distance communication systems further down this hallway. It seems we've found the headquarters."

I asked the opinion of General Savasss Jach, who was leading the assault. The Gamma Iseyek agreed that we had finally uncovered the true source of the enemy teams that had been coming up against our divisions. The previous two centers, which we had taken as command points, turned out to be nothing more than signal retransmitters. The general said that over eighty percent of all internal spaces on the starship had already been captured, the resistance was noticeably weakening, and it would all be over in ten or fifteen minutes.

After hanging up with the general, I turned to the officers and asked them to bring the paralyzed Truth Seeker to me immediately. And then, when two men had gone to fetch her, I demanded that the communications officer put me directly through to the Emperor as soon as he's received a confirmation that the capture of the battleship is finally complete. For the first time in my memory, I had to repeat an order two times.

"Do you think August will want to talk?" asked Katerina with a large degree of doubt in her voice.

"I think he will. Thanks to your reports, the whole Empire has been following the events in the Hnelle system for three hours now. The viewers' interest is simply rabid. I have already grown tired of closing messages about personal and faction relations improving, and there are over seven hundred people waiting on hold to talk to me right now. You hit all the right notes – worry, fear, then a timid hope, compassion, and finally pride for the brave Fleet Eight soldiers, who saved a star system from invasion. I have no doubt that the Emperor was told about the Alien invasion immediately. If I were in August's place, I'd want to talk to the heroes."

The long-awaited confirmation came in from the general, and I ordered to be put through to the Throne World. More than a minute went by before the screen lit up. I bent down on one knee and said:

"My Emperor, this is a report from Sector Eight Fleet Commander Crown Prince Georg royl Inoky. The battle in the Hnelle system has just finished. The enemy fleet has been completely defeated. For the first time in history, we have captured an Alien ship, and what's more, it's a battleship. Many valuable specimens have been collected for study, both biological and technological."

"Georg royl Inoky, order your people out of the room. I need to speak with you privately," August grumbled, slightly upset. "No, they can stay. Just make sure they don't talk much about this conversation afterwards. So, I thought you were supposed to be on your way to the Throne World... It's strange to see you in the Hnelle system."

"My Emperor, there was a serious risk that the Aliens would try to attack the Hnelle system again, as the Aliens never give up attacking a system until they've captured it. I would be overjoyed to see your Imperial Highness personally in the Throne World three weeks from the time of the previous meeting, but my first mission is still to defend Sector Eight, and that is precisely what I intend to do."

The Emperor furrowed his brow:

"Or maybe the Green House's accusations were more serious this time and really did have a basis to them? What do you say, grandson?"

I waved it off with ostentatious carelessness.

"My Emperor, what kind of credibility could these accusations possibly have, if even the main accuser, Katerina ton Mesfelle, recognized that they were absolutely hopeless and came over to the side of the accused?! If Duke Paolo's son refused his right to my system, and the Duke's nephew defected as soon as given the chance?! The only thing the accusers were counting on was that the head of the Orange House would not support me, and instead go over to their side. I have evidence of a shameful agreement between Duke Paolo royl Anjer and the Green House to that effect. It is more than enough to raise the issue of non-confidence in the head of the Orange House. The rest of the accusations are utterly foolish, like the last time. What is it on the list? The tragic death of two members of the Green House? This issue has already been looked over in great detail, and all investigators admitted that the deceased alone were at fault. The peace treaty with the Gamma Iseyek? What can I say? First, in that I did not have the authority for such a decision, the head of the Orange House himself confirmed this peace, so all questions are to Duke Paolo royl Anjer. Second, it is only thanks to the great Gamma Iseyek leader, General Savasss Jach, that today's victory was possible. My android? You could see her working as a translator with your own eyes. And again, my opponents have nothing but spy logs. And as far as I'm concerned, using an android translator's confidential logs to spy on a crown prince is nothing but another shameful episode in the Duke's already fairly disgraceful biography. There are no more accusations against me, as far as I know."

The Emperor did not agree with that:

"There's also turning off the warp beacons. Interfering with the functioning of the transportation network is a very serious crime, Georg."

"I didn't turn them off. I put them into 'by request' mode. Imperial ships are free to pass, but Alien ships find it a bit harder to make their way through. And that measure has completely justified itself!"

"We'll allow it," agreed August after some time in thought. "Though I am interested in the technical side of the issue. How did you do it, Georg?"

"It couldn't have been easier: I sent mixed teams of people and androids to uninhabitable automatic beacons. It's still more androids – they can work for a long time on nothing but electricity until the cosmic greenhouses are up and running. This isn't an invasion, after all. I intend to develop and support these distant settlements to the best of my ability.

Freight starships have been sent to all of them with materials for building docks, residential spaces, greenhouses, repair shops, moorings and defensive structures. I have financed the development of these remote Sector Eight systems on my personal money for humanity's sake, so real stations and new populations could grow there. Humanity needs to expand further in space, and I was helping our race make the next step forward into the cosmos."

"Good on you, Georg, really. I wasn't expecting it. On the whole, I have nothing left to say, and I really do not see a reason for us to meet so frequently, tearing you away from important matters. My only condition is that you must resolve your issues and come to an agreement with the Head of the Orange House. Your conflict is completely unacceptable to me. I give you one hundred days. Do it however you like, grandson, but the conflict must be resolved. And now give an order to your people to turn on the recording, and let's start our conversation over from the beginning, but for the whole Empire to see."

I watched carefully as the recording of my conversation with Emperor August made for the wider public played on screen. The commander, kneeling humbly, made a report about an unprecedented victory over a large Alien fleet, and the haughty Emperor, majestic in the extreme, graciously accepted the report from his loyal servant. Then came a short eloquent speech on this battle's significance as a turning point in the history of humanity's struggle against the Aliens, followed by the unexpected awarding of medals. Though soldiers from Great House divisions were normally not given orders and medals, August decided to make an exception and gave out five Emerald Stars for service to the Empire. The fortunate recipients of Imperial orders were the Admirals Kiro Sabuto and Kheraisss Vej, General Savasss Jach, the captain of the heavy cruiser *Emperor August*, Bayazid Krom, and Bionica, the android translator.

There were no medals given to me, but I didn't get worked up over it. My reward was something else entirely: giving medals to Bionica and General Savasss Jach spoke to everyone about the fact that the Emperor was putting an end these issues once and for all and was not interested in hearing any more accusations. One hundred days to make peace with the Duke... Not an especially short time frame, but I still wasn't even close to imagining how I could carry out the Emperor's order.

"Almost eight hundred people are waiting to speak with you long distance," an officer reminded me delicately.

"First put through my daughter, Likanna, then the monarch of the Kingdom of Veyerde, if they are still in the list. The rest you should reject, or at least let them wait until tomorrow. I just don't have the energy to talk any more today."

"Dad!" My daughter's joyful scream forced me to smile. "We were watching every broadcast in the palace! I was so worried for you! You're like super cool. I'm so proud of you."

Tears of joy welled up in my eyes. These are truly the moments you live for! Whether I was in a game or not no longer made any difference. I had accepted this world and considered it real. I would defend my daughter from danger and was prepared to give my life for her, if it was required. I promised Lika I would fly to her in Unatari in a day and quickly hung up as not to cry in front of her.

The incoming call signal interrupted my thinking. I was expecting it to be Astra's father, so I could fulfill my promise, but it turned out to be someone else on the line. The Dark Mother! I could not have been more surprised. The old woman, clothed head to toe in a black robe, was smiling from ear to ear and said:

"Your servant tried to reject my call. Let him know the muteness will pass in two days. That ought to calm him down. As a matter of fact, August asked me to remind you that he expects his experts to have unrestricted access to the Hnelle system and the captured Alien ship. Captain Mwaur Zen-Bey is coming. You should remember him. He inspected the battle site at the Vorta beacon. I, though, wanted to talk about something else entirely. How is the paralyzed girl doing?"

With difficulty, I picked my jaw up off the floor. We basically hadn't told anyone about the tragic event yet. How could the Dark Mother know anything about the incident? The old lady laughed:

"I could say a great many words about my infinite power, and you would believe me. But the truth is much more banal. Your doctor was wondering about unusual symptoms, making a bunch of requests, including to various archives. I was told about his interest in a strange injury, and putting two and two together from there was quite simple. Was it Miya?"

Lying to such a powerful Truth Seeker would be useless and dangerous to boot, so I confirmed the Dark Mother's suspicions, telling her the slightly condensed version I had earlier told Katerina ton Mesfelle.

"That means Miya is pregnant... That's what I thought, to be honest. A daughter? Well, let it be a daughter... An interesting picture is coming together. I don't envy your wife, Marta, right now. Do you understand what I'm talking about?"

I nodded and answered:

"If Miya's child is born and we are legally married, she will become a crown princess with full rights to the thrones of both the Orange House and the Empire. If Miya is not my legal wife before the birth, my daughter will just be a 'ton' without rights to thrones, or she could even end up a complete bastard, not belonging to the aristocracy at all."

"That's right. Knowing Miya's character, I can say confidently that she will only except the first of those two options, which is what puts Marta in such an unenviable position. It wouldn't be good for Miya to kill her, given that that would seriously complicate her own life. But she could mess up her nerves. Alright, I'll try to protect Marta..."

Having unexpectedly made up my mind, I asked a question I had long ago wondered about, secretly hoping that by doing so I wasn't revealing my complete ignorance:

"Dark Mother, I recently realized that I know almost nothing about Miya. She's been my Truth

Seeker for quite a long time, but before she left, it never occurred to me that she could be hiding something. The fact that Miya was there was all that mattered. But now, with Miya gone, I look back and realize that I know very little about my companion. What can you tell me about Miya?"

The Dark Mother cackled back her reply:

"Oh, Georg, Georg... What do you want to know from me? You lived side by side with Miya for fifteen years, and you think *I* have anything to tell *you* about her? Well, OK. I'll tell you what I know. She first caught my attention as a talented Truth Seeker sometime around the end of the war with the Iseyek. At that time, Miya was in the retinue of Admiral Mayf ton Mesfelle, and his fleet finally began to push back against the Swarm. Perhaps you'd be interested to know that it was Miya and several other Truth Seekers that served as the reason for the Iseyek to begin their research in the field of psionic defense.

After that, Miya fell out of my field of view for a long time, then suddenly, seventy years later, she appeared with your father, Inoky. For a mediocre man who was in no way remarkable, Count Inoky's rise was sharp and sudden. He received the Tesse star system and the very rich ice system Damir for his service, becoming one of the most influential aristocrats in the Empire and a clear candidate for Head of the Orange House at the same time. Miya progressed together with her master; they understood one another perfectly. The only thing that could bring an end to your father's blistering ascent was his untimely death. The downing of the shuttle was investigated thoroughly. I also looked into the crash site, but it really did appear to be an accident.

You know what comes next: Tesse was given to Roben, Damir to your twin sister, and you were given Miya. All the aristocrats were waiting with bated breath for the day the unusually skilled Truth Seeker's power would be revealed, and your rise would begin, but instead you fell in love with your Miya... And only now, a decade and a half later, has your rise begun. Clearly, Miya spent a long time planning and arranging the current circumstances, and her pregnancy was part of that. Only when with child can a Truth Seeker truly make the most of her powers... Anyway, enough about Miya. Together with Captain Mwaur Zen-Bey there will be medics coming to take the wounded girl from you. I'll see if it's possible to help her in any way."

# AFTER THE BATTLE

FINALLY, FOR THE FIRST time in several days, I was able to get a good night's rest! I woke up in an excellent state of mind, a bit earlier than my alarm clock even, and the first thing I saw next to me was Astra in another transparent night shirt.

"That's a fun tattoo! It's a good picture of Boydur the Hero, even though it's strange to see him on the body of such a stern crown prince, the vanquisher of the diabolical Aliens."

I figured out that the Princess was talking about the winged donkey on my shoulder. And yes, I was also bothered by the tattoo. I hadn't stopped thinking about it since my first day in the game. How many times was I ready to sink into the ground when I saw my burly fitness instructor or some stern assault soldiers training in the hall, straining to hold back laughter when looking at my left shoulder?

"An error of my youth," I tried to joke. "I just can't find the time to have it removed or changed into something more appropriate to my status."

"My Prince, you know, I could help you fix it!" Astra suggested unexpectedly. "I'm not bad at drawing, and

I could tattoo anything you like on your skin. I've even practiced on Flora already – she has a pretty bouquet of flowers on her back between her shoulders and a phoenix that fell into a spider web on her left leg.

I imagined Mr. G.I.'s reaction seeing, instead of his beloved winged donkey, a grinning skull or a fiery bird flying among the stars on his shoulder, and agreed to have it done just for that. The girl moved closer, allegedly to take a better look at the drawing, but she also tenderly ran her palm over my shoulders and chest, cooing:

"The price of my work is a romantic evening together. Sound good? I spent the whole day yesterday cooped up in here. Your Highness had all kinds of adventures and entertainment: the battle with the Aliens, news reports being sent to the whole Empire, the assault of a large ship, a conversation with the Emperor... And this whole time I was sitting around here with nothing to do!"

I laughed happily. It was just too unexpected to hear that yesterday, I had not been fearlessly repelling an Alien invasion, but was in fact high on the hog having the time of my life. Understanding Astra and her interpretation of reality wasn't always easy. When the girl tried to caress me again, I tenderly stopped her hand and pulled the Princess to myself:

"I agree to your price. And this is just an advance," I embraced Astra and kissed her on the lips.

The Princess froze in fear for a second, then began returning the kiss. The fact that Bionica opened the door at that very moment with a tray was, well, not very timely.

"Hey, I asked you to knock before coming in to the

Crown Prince's room!" Astra said judgmentally.

The android girl said nothing, simply placing the tray of teacups on the table, before closing the door behind her on her way out. I waited a few more seconds to be sure and pulled my playful favorite back to me. We joked around and talked for three minutes, kissing and stroking one another, when suddenly the door opened again.

"Not again! I swear I'll kill her!" Astra whispered, bristling.

However, it was not the android that came into the room, but Katerina ton Mesfelle with a digital tablet in her hands. Astra darted out of the room, covering herself with a big pillow, and went to go get dressed.

"I see I have not come at the best time," my cousin said, instantly appraising the situation. "It's just that your translator told me that you were already awake, so I decided to come down and discuss some issues."

Making a mental note to talk with Bionica, I calmed my cousin down and invited her to a light breakfast. Katerina looked tired, which I told her honestly right then.

"I still haven't gone to sleep. I'm not even done dealing with the consequences of yesterday yet," my assistant laughed, gratefully accepting a mug of energizing drink from my hand. "I talked to all the important people in your name already. The ones you didn't get to anyway. By the way, Georg, you shouldn't have rejected so many calls. The Imperial Space Marshal was there, and the head of the Joint Chiefs, and Duke Takuro royl Andor from the Purple House. They are very important people and are not accustomed to being refused a conversation. I did a pretty good job on damage control though. No one was especially offended. The old Duke was almost brought to tears when he found out that the flagship of Fleet Eight is named *Joan the Fatty* in honor of his beloved great-granddaughter. So the Purple House offers support to your fleet in the form of experienced officer squads and access to their combat ship market. That last one is very useful to you, by the way, and will allow you to get around the ship embargo Duke Paolo placed on you.

I commended my cousin for the excellent work, though I noted that I would only be able to receive destroyers and frigates from the Purple House. Only they could be disassembled and transported through the Core without breaking any Imperial laws. Unfortunately, the same trick wouldn't work with larger ships. I would only be able to buy those at Sector Eight docks, which were now closed to me – or begin building my own, given enough materials, experienced specialists and orbital docks.

"And another thing: I found some kind of sketchy 'Sector Eight Fleet Aid Fund,' which has been collecting funds in the Imperial Core, supposedly for your benefit. I sicked the financial inspectors on them. Let the investigators figure out what kind of fund it is and how much they were able to collect."

I heard my cousin out carefully and expressed for the hundredth time how helpful a decision it had been to bring her over to my side. When I told her, Katerina began to laugh:

"Georg, I've already told you that my defining characteristic is my quick decision making. And it was precisely that characteristic that brought me here. Before you were brought to report to the Emperor again, I carefully studied all the accusations against you and figured out that you would most likely get out of it again. And so I thought: on the one hand, I had the possibility of going pale before the Emperor himself when the accusations inevitably melt away a second time; or, on the other hand, I could come over to Crown Prince Georg's side, who is quickly gaining in popularity. I chose the second, and that was why I got in touch with you and warned you about the danger. During my conversation with you, I kept trying to think up any reason for you to offer me a job. But it turned out that I didn't have to think anything up. You offered me more than I was expecting to receive all on your own."

We both laughed and agreed that the situation came together quite successfully and our cooperation was beneficial to both of us. Making use of the occasion, I asked the long-ago-unanswered question about what my new assistant was expecting to be paid. Katerina dealt with that issue with surprising indifference:

"Georg, it's up to you. I know you won't insult me, and this job has already paid dividends for me. After all, the most important thing in my line of work is name awareness."

Intrigued, I opened the popup on my cousin:

**Katerina ton Mesfelle, speaker of the Sector Eight Fleet**
   **Age: 28**
   **Race: Human**
   **Gender: Female**

*Relation to you: Your second cousin*
*Class: Aristocrat*
*Achievements: Master of Rhetoric, Participant in the capture of the Alien battleship in the Hnelle system.*
*Fame: +9*
*Standing: +8*
*Presumed personal opinion of you: +30 (warm)*

At first, I got caught up on the part about "participant in the capture of the battleship" and didn't understand right away what she was talking about. Then I looked at her fame and couldn't even believe my eyes. With the series of reports from the attacked Hnelle system, Katerina had been able to raise her fame by seven points in one go! That's what I'm talking about! I wonder what mine looks like. However, when I opened my own characteristics, I was met by something of a disappointment:

*Fame: +11*
*Standing: -14*

Yeah, they had gone up, though not nearly as much as my cousin's. But all the same, I was in quite a good mood.

"Name your price, cousin. How should I pay you? I could offer you a luxurious island with a palace on Unatari, I could give you profit shares from the ice processing facility on Tivalle, or if you prefer the boring way, I could pay you in money."

"I don't need a lot. Any of those would make me happy. What kind of palace are we talking about here?"

I started describing the tropical island with the wonderful palace, many rooms and all that, but I was suddenly interrupted by a whole bouquet of incoming system messages.

*Global standing decrease. Current value -15*

*Standing change. Green House (Empire) opinion of you has worsened.*
*Present Green House (Empire) faction opinion of you: -31 (opposed)*

*Standing change. Green House opinion of Orange House has worsened.*
*Present Green House opinion of Orange House: -7 (mistrust)*

*Standing change. The Kingdom of Veyerde's opinion of you has improved.*
*Present Kingdom of Veyerde opinion of you: +5 (warm)*

I raised my eyes, perplexed, and saw that Katerina had also clearly been thrown off. She was smiling only with the corners of her mouth and said, not hiding her surprise:

"I just received a strange message. The Green House reduced their opinion of me and the whole Orange House. It can't have taken that long for the news about me switching sides to the Orange House to have reached Duke Amelius royl Mast ton Lavaelle, can it?"

"I don't think you're the reason, cousin. It's just that I also just got my own set of relationship worsening messages from the Green House and at the same time an improvement with the Kingdom of Veyerde. It was probably something connected with Princess Astra again. You were included just for being here and of course as a belated 'thank you' for switching sides to the Orange House."

Just then a message came in from the officer about a long-distance call from the Kingdom of Veyerde.

"Now we'll get this figured out!" I smiled to Katerina and gave permission for the call.

The monarch, Kant royl Pikar ton Veyerde, was looking especially regal today. With a proud face, a luxurious royal robe and a gold crown on his head, he looked to be at least one of the first in line to the Emperor's throne, and not the ruler of a puny settlement on a remote planet.

"Crown Prince Georg royl Inoky ton Mesfelle, I'm glad I got the chance to speak with you. I have noticed that your Highness has grown close with Princess Astra, and I am sure that my daughter will do her best to make sure you keep liking her. I am confident that you will not leave her without support in any case. That is why I today, with a light heart, refused Baron Henrik ton Lavaelle and officially broke Princess Astra's engagement with him."

"Yes, I already noticed the Green House's reaction to that," I said with dissatisfaction in my voice.

The King smiled sadly.

"Your Highness may think me out of place and even tactless, but I had my reasons, and I will try to explain. As you perhaps already know from the news, seven hours ago the Aliens attacked the Nayal system and cut our star system off from the Empire. The Sector Seven Fleet retreated, and now we're expecting the Alien ships to arrive in our system any minute. My mother-in-law, Fesilia, Astra and Flora's grandmother, was a spontaneous Truth Seeker and somehow foretold this tragic day, even naming this very date. And though she wasn't always right in her predictions, I always held this date in mind and tried to have all my daughters out of here, safely in the Empire in any case. Also, my trusted representatives have taken most of the Kingdom's children out under various pretexts. The men are staying to fight. Yes, we are fully aware that there is no chance of rescue, but the soldiers of the Kingdom of Veyerde will fight to the last breath to defend our motherland. My whole fleet, just four outdated frigates are prepared to meet the enemy and die with honor..."

The King froze, clearly listening to a message, then went silent and asked to be put through to his daughter. It wasn't possible to get ahold of Astra. She clearly heard the conversation with her father and was now standing in her room, pale and worried.

"My daughter, the Aliens have just arrived in Veyerde. I've been informed about two *Hermit* destroyers and many flat disks that these invaders carry their landing troops in. This is our last conversation, and there's so much I wish I could tell you... You know how difficult it has been for me to collect dowry for your sisters. After paying for Rosa, Liana and Fialka, there was only forty thousand credits left. Under different circumstances, I would be ashamed at having left such a modest dowry for my daughters, but I simply had no choice. Astra, you are my favorite daughter, but I have nothing to give you other than a father's advice and parting words. And before the enemies cut off the line, I'll rush to give you my final instruction. It would be hard for you to wish for a better patron than his Highness Crown Prince Georg. Help him, hold on to him, find your special place in the Crown Prince's retinue and never give it up to anyone. Remember old Fesilia's prediction. There was a lot about you specifically. I'll leave my crown by the small waterfall, in that little hole where you used to hide your toys from your sisters. And if you ever get back to Veyerde, the symbol of its power will await you.

Crown Prince Georg royl Inoky, I entrust Princess Astra to your guard. And now, your Highness, I mean you no offence, but I need to go to my soldiers."

When I went into the medical wing, I decided not to hide the difficult truth from Flora and honestly told her about my conversation with the monarch. And though Kant had not been a father to her, everyone Flora knew and was friends with lived on Veyerde, and I supposed she would be upset. However, the little paralyzed girl took the news about the Alien attack on her home planet with surprising aplomb.

*"I am indifferent to their fate. Everyone I used to know is left in the far, careless past to which I will already never return. They heard Fesilia's prophecy and knew when the invasion would happen. They*

could have saved themselves. Those who remained were well aware what they were getting into. I feel no sympathy for them. There's good news though. Look at the doctor's table."

I turned back to the table that Nicosid Brandt normally worked at. A thin stylus was rolling back and forth on the smooth surface of the table. Then it began spinning like a top, before falling off the table onto the floor. I turned to the paralyzed girl and saw obvious pride in her eyes.

"Flora, the Dark Mother's envoys are coming to Hnelle today. They want to take you for study, find out your capabilities and see if mobility can be returned to your body. They clearly want to know about what happened to you."

*"I know that they won't be able to help me. But all the same, we need to let them study me so they are sure I'm a lost cause, lose interest, and leave me alone. My Prince, don't worry about the secret getting out. I have constructed mental protection for myself, taking yours as my basis. It's elegant work. Miya thought through everything and was so meticulous with the details that her work inspires admiration. My mind and my memory will remain open for reading, as before. Let a Truth Seeker dig around in my childhood memories as long as they want; they'll find out about my favorite toys, and my relationship with King Kant and his daughters, but no one will be able to read what I really want to keep hidden."*

"You were able to figure out Miya's work?" I asked in surprise.

*"Yes, though it wasn't easy. I'm not sure that someone else would be able to understand it, but Miya*

*and I are now very deeply connected. We are two Truth Seekers of the same master, and I can see characteristic kindred traits that unite our work. Miya is unique. There are no others like her. She has already been serving House Mesfelle for four generations, and it's because her true ability shines through precisely with your family. She has bound her fate so closely with House Mesfelle that she wouldn't be able to live with another master at this point. Such spiritual closeness gives Miya great powers, but also limits her freedom. While your Highness is in the body of the Crown Prince, all you have to do is call her and Miya will appear no matter where she is. You just have to order something, and Miya has to do it. Other Truth Seekers aren't so dependent on their master and don't have to obey if they have a difference of opinion. But Miya is so connected with her master that she cannot contradict him. And while you are in that body, Miya is not capable of harming you. That is her biggest secret."*

The information was quite valuable. However, I didn't rush to answer the paralyzed girl, as I was distracted by an incoming message:

**The Kingdom of Veyerde has lost sovereignty of the Veyerde system.**

**The Kingdom of Veyerde has ceased to exist.**

I rushed into my room and found Astra crying uncontrollably with her face buried in a pillow. I had never been able to calm down an upset girlfriend in the past, so this time I didn't even try. Instead of that, I called the communications officer and asked to be put through to the Sector Seven Fleet Commander. Marat ton Mesfelle answered instantly, as if awaiting my call.

"It hasn't even been five seconds since my fleet came out of warp... to be more accurate, what's left of my fleet. They tore us to shreds in the Nayal system. It was a miracle we got away."

"What happened to you in Nayal, Marat?" I wondered.

"It all went to shit, cousin. The Aliens appeared just twenty-five miles from my ship. Two *Hermits* and a *Meteor*. While we were figuring out what was what, the fleet had already lost three light cruisers, all destroyers and seven frigates. Then there were more horrible losses as we fled the station under heavy fire..."

"Stop, stop. What did you say you did? You were just sitting near the warp beacon?" I asked in surprise.

"Well, it's not like we were just sitting there. The ships were docked at the station, charging energy before the jump to Veyerde. Many of the crews were on the station itself. All they told me was that I just needed to calm down the residents of the Kingdom of Veyerde, who some psycho old lady had predicted an Alien invasion to..."

I frowned dissatisfied:

"Marat, try to choose your words more carefully. You're talking about the grandmother of Princess Astra, my favorite, who is here in the room."

"I apologize, I didn't know. Well then, that doubtlessly dignified lady made a bunch of predictions in her life, but they're all so confusing that it's hard to figure them out. One of the most famous was about the invasion of the Aliens into the Veyerde system and the fall of the Kingdom – that prediction is different from the others because the sorceress predicted a specific day. The prediction happened long ago, thirty years, but as that date grew closer, the people of the Kingdom began remembering the prophecy more and more, and they got worried. Refugees appeared, and recently they took all the children out to neighboring systems. Rumors about how panic had taken hold in Veyerde even reached the Emperor himself. It reached the point where I was sent to figure it out and hold off a possible invasion. We went as fast as possible, and when we were at the second to last system, Nayal, we took a break to recharge our warp drives. I gave the people leave to the station, so they could relax for a couple of hours and blow off steam before the potential upcoming battle. It was then that the Aliens attacked my fleet. The only thing we managed to do was shoot down one *Meteor*, then everyone who was left alive and had the energy went into the warp. Just six ships escaped: my flagship, the battleship *Knight of Light*, one heavy cruiser, one *Yataghan* heavy cruiser, two light *Thrushes*, and two *Pyros*."

Though I was surprised at what was, in my view, a rushed retreat of the heavy ships from two, not-too-strong enemy destroyers, I didn't make Marat feel guilty for retreating. Probably, like once happened in my fleet at the Vorta beacon, the crews of the remaining ships were in a state of near panic and were simply not able to continue the fight.

"What should I do, Georg? Tell me. You've been in a

similar situation!" Marat unexpectedly asked for advice.

"First thing you need to do is calm down and let the teams also get some rest. After that, go over footage of the battle with your officers and find your mistakes. By the way, send me the recordings too. I'm very interested in the Aliens' behavior. Maybe I can also notice something and give you some advice. Well, and after that it's clear, restore the fleet. Buy ships to replace those that were destroyed. Differently from me, Duke Paolo hasn't forbidden you from buying ships for your fleet."

"With what money?" Marat ton Mesfelle laughed bitterly. "Two *Yataghans* to replace those lost is one hundred twenty million credits. Six *Thrushes* is another thirty, and fifteen million for new frigates and destroyers. One hundred sixty-five million! I don't have that much money, and beating something out of that miser Duke Paolo is just not gonna happen..."

I agreed with my cousin that shaking money from the Head of the Orange House's piggy bank was no trivial matter. Also, I realized fairly quickly that I had found an excellent way of breaking the embargo.

"Marat, it occurs to me that we each have something we can help the other with. I can give you money: four hundred million to buy ships for your fleet. That will allow you to not only compensate all your losses, but also significantly grow in force. In return, you will buy ships for my fleet in your name."

Marat went silent and said thoughtfully:

"Well, I can buy them for you, but how can I get them to Sector Eight? They won't let them through the Core..."

"For now, you just buy what I tell you. Let the teams fill out, the officers get used to the captains, then I'll tell them where to go."

Marat shuddered:

"Georg, if you're planning something against the law like an attack on Perimeter Sector Seven targets or an attempt to power your way through the Core, I will have to refuse you."

Ugh, I didn't want to open maps, but there was no other way.

"Calm down, Marat. I wasn't thinking of doing anything illegal in your zone of responsibility. It's just that, very soon, in three weeks maximum, the Parn warp beacon will be turned on, and it will open a direct route from Sector Seven to Eight. That was how I was planning to get my ships through."

"How do you always know everything, cousin?" Marat asked in surprise. "Well, alright, I'll buy the ships for you, but under one condition. Let's not call it a condition, but a request. When the beacon turns on, help me take back Nayal and Veyerde. Since you have a lot of experience fighting the Aliens and such a reputation, the enemy will flee as soon as they even catch wind of your ships."

My second cousin's attempt at flattery was so awkward that I even started laughing.

"Alright, I agree. I'll help you. I need to get my Astra her home planet back."

When the screen went out, I heard Astra's voice:

"Tell me honestly, Georg: could he have won that battle in the Nayal system? Would you have won?"

"Now yes, I would have won, even despite how unexpectedly the attack began. But a month and a half ago, I would have done no better than my cousin. The debacle in Vorta was even more terrible. Don't blame Marat ton Mesfelle. The first encounter with Aliens is always like that. You need a deep defeat for a fleet commander to understand that it's all serious and the old methods won't work anymore."

"But that that particular loss came at too high a price to my family... Who am I now? The youngest of fourteen sisters and the only one not married. No home, no people, no kingdom. I'm not even sure that I have the right to use the title 'Princess' anymore, now that the Kingdom of Veyerde no longer exists."

Astra sat gloomily like a raincloud. After that, she gave a decisive start:

"I need paint and canvas. I want to express the feelings I'm experiencing on the destruction of my Kingdom."

* * *

Now I've already been sitting for more than an hour in front of a screen, looking over offers from Sector Seven docks. The selection turned out to be sufficiently great, but all the same I ran into financial problems again. I was planning on spending around a billion credits on obtaining ships. On first glance a significant sum, but I really wasn't letting myself go too wild either.

Above all else, I was interested in battleships but, as it were, there weren't any of them in stock. The only option was to buy a *Tyrant* under construction that would be ready in three months, the price of which was three hundred twenty million credits. I confirmed the order.

Then the heavy cruisers. For some reason, in Sector Seven there was preference given to the rocket-equipped *Yataghans*. Four such ships disappeared from the list of available ships right before my eyes – clearly it was Marat covering the losses in his fleet. There were two more *Yataghans* in stock, but I was in no rush to close the deal; rocket ships had no place in my fleet's battle plan, in that they couldn't deal damage instantly. At first glance, you can see how difficult it would be to take out an Alien *Sledgehammer* with rocket ships. Rockets don't all arrive from the same ship at the same time, and a *Sledgehammer*'s shields would be fully recharged in the time between strikes.

Light cruisers. In stock there were the *Thrushes*, specialized in electronic warfare; then the also rocket-equipped *Whirlwinds*; and something called *Curses*, without rockets or cannons, armed exclusively with drones. There were many *Curses* ready to go, around forty, but I was cautioned by a note: "Production stopped due to low demand after the introduction of more modern models."

For curiosity's sake, I read the specs on these ships. The shield was frankly a bit weak, with low durability on a level closer to that of a destroyer than that of a cruiser... However, their high speed, good maneuverability and ability to release thirty-five combat drones at once meant that these light cruisers had a chance to be put to good use. Sure, just one wouldn't amount to much – its drones could be quickly shot down, which would make the ship totally powerless. But what if there wasn't just one such ship in a fleet but forty? One thousand four hundred fast drones – that's a force to be reckoned with. Especially if the drones are "mean:" fast, durable, and with a sharp bite.

I ordered all forty *Curses*, all the more so given that they were being sold for three million apiece. I also bought expensive drones for them. I bought all the *Thrushes* and improved electronic warfare equipment for my whole fleet, too.

Frigates. I wasn't fast enough on this one. My second cousin bought everything that was in stock or was expected to be ready in the next few months. All that was left was cloaked frigates with turrets or rocket-bomb cannons. And neither of them were in demand. At their price of fifteen million per ship, clients preferred to buy five cruisers and not just one cloak-capable frigate. In principle, I was also of that opinion and would have preferred cruisers but, because there weren't any, I bought thirty stealth bombers and five turret-equipped cloaked frigates. And on that, there was no more money, and all I could do was console myself with hopes that a fleet of cloakers would be a force powerful in its unexpectedness.

I ordered frigates and destroyers separately with the Purple House. Fifty *Pyros*, twenty *Warhawks*, ten *Flycatchers*, and ten *Surgeons*. I indicated that they should be delivered to Perimeter Sector Seven to Marat ton Mesfelle's address. I finished all the orders and sent Marat the money, then called Popori de Cacha. However, another Chameleon from my bodyguard team appeared instead.

"My Prince, Popori de Cacha is at a farewell

ceremony. He has gone with the rest of your bodyguards and the two frigates. They are preparing the bodies of the two soldiers who died in the assault of the Alien battleship to be sent back home."

"That means both Chameleons died? I didn't know. Though the losses of assault troops, especially in the very beginning of the battle for the *Behemoth*, were nothing short of gruesome. It wasn't until later, when the number of entrances shot into the side of the battleship became significant, and the number of assault troops that got inside reached the thousands, that the Aliens started to give up positions and the resistance weakened. But in the beginning it was simply hell... Practically no one survived from the first groups, whether human or Alpha Iseyek. I made myself a note to award medals of honor to the surviving assault troops of the first wave, then asked him to call the head of my security nevertheless.

"Popori de Cacha, I am very unhappy with you!" I sharply declared, just after the image of the Chameleon appeared on the screen. "Two heroes have died who served me honorably and defended me from all threats, and you hid that and didn't even invite me to bid farewell to them, the greatest representatives of your race! If the Chameleon mourning ceremony didn't allow the presence of other races, you could have said so, but just keeping quiet is not appropriate! And you could have asked me about sending the bodies to Sss. Do you think I would have refused you?!"

For the second time in my life, I managed to put Popori de Cacha in a state of contemplation. The Chameleon pointed both of his eyes at the screen, but my head bodyguard's pupils were covered with an opaque film. The silence went on for fifteen seconds, after which the bipedal lizard awkwardly bent down on one knee.

"My Prince, I am seriously at fault! I completely ignored the fact that the death of security personnel close to you could seriously affect your feelings. Unfortunately, you cannot bid farewell to Ivy de and Sygi de. Their bodies have already been cremated in the isolation chamber of *Boydur the Hero*. But if my Prince could help with delivering the ashes to the planet Sss, the whole Chameleon race would be indebted to your Highness."

"Popori de Cacha, I promise you that the whole Sector Eight Fleet will soon depart for Sss to honor the memory of the two heroes. And for now, my gratitude to the Chameleons will be expressed in another way: the crews of *Tusk-1* and *Tusk-2* will receive more modern ships, either *Warhawks* or *Pyros*. Though, considering your race's inborn talents and ability to operate well in invisibility, I would prefer to employ your compatriots as the captains and navigators of the cloaked frigates that will soon be arriving."

*Standing change. Popori de Cacha's opinion of you has improved.*
*Presumed personal opinion of you: +67 (faithful)*

*Standing change. Chameleon race opinion of you has improved.*
*Chameleon race opinion of you: +10 (trusting)*

That time, the popup messages didn't surprise me. I was counting on such a reaction, which is why I only slightly smiled at the confirmation of my hypothesis.

"And one more thing. Popori de Cacha, there is a very big mission that I want to entrust to you and your subordinates. I have been told that a multitude of interesting things have been found on the *Behemoth*. They will probably be studied by the commission on its way in from the Empire. But Imperial scientists are one thing, and the Orange House and my fleet is something a bit different. It seems fair to me that the soldiers who risked their lives for these valuable artifacts should also have the right to receive samples of valuable technology. Do you agree with me?"

"Yes, my Prince, that is fair," agreed Popori de Cacha, clearly listening to me very intently.

"Then gather your subordinates and visit the *Behemoth*. If you find anything that makes you curious, load it into the ship. I'll give you a freighter for these purposes. I'm especially interested in the Alien drones, so that is your priority target. As I was told, the *Behemoth* didn't use all its drones in the battle, so I really need valuable combat drones. I am also interested in biological specimens, modules and everything you consider necessary. But I'll repeat: I'm especially interested in drones. The mission is secret, and if anyone asks about the goal of your return to the *Behemoth*, say that you are looking for the remains of your soldiers. Is the mission clear?"

"Yes, my Prince. We'll do it quietly and unnoticed. If needed, I'll even find scientists of my race to study these valuable trophies."

I understood perfectly where the head of my guard was leading. Chameleons would also be very interested in Alien technology. In that, our goals aligned perfectly.

"That is precisely what I wanted to offer your race. Chameleons are renowned for their ability to figure out technology and build duplicates. As it were, I have a need of just such an ability. I'll find a remote place where no one will be able to interfere with your research. I'll give you laboratories and all necessary equipment. I'll give you the necessary number of people to help and provide reliable security for the laboratories. Everything that results from the research will belong in equal measure to humanity and the Ravaash race. Later you can call your ambassador, Pandedede de Rua, and we can talk with him about all the concrete details of the agreement. And for now, hurry so you'll have time before the Imperial commission arrives."

I dined in the company of Kiro Sabuto and several ship officers, discussing present affairs and periodically reminiscing about yesterday's battle. We were talking about when the two *Sledgehammers* were firing on *Joan the Fatty.*

"My Prince, would you not consider the option of transferring the fleet headquarters to a more appropriate and resilient ship?" asked the graying Major Anarip ton Dyme, responsible for the cruiser's electronics systems and the coordination of shield recharging connections in combat. "We were practically destroyed, after all. It was a miracle we got away. And then there wouldn't have been anyone in charge, and the whole fleet would have fallen apart..."

"No, the fleet wouldn't have fallen apart. Admiral Kheraisss Vej would have taken over command and led us to victory," Kiro Sabuto disagreed. "Though it is true that the *Fatty* barely escaped yesterday."

Everyone looked at me inquisitively. I then smiled self-consciously:

"Yes, that really was a close call. I was basically counting on destroying one of the two enemies, then we would take out the second. We could be recharged by nine cruisers and the *Surgeon*. In ideal conditions, there shouldn't have been any complications. But the fact that the shield barely made it through one *Sledgehammer* strike... It looks like we still have work to do on fleet cohesion. The ships 'healing' us took too long to figure out what was going on and turn their attention from *Bride of Chaos* to the *Fatty*. And that delay practically became fatal."

"I have gone over the timing of the events," Nicole Savoia said, not raising her eyes. "It only took us two and a half seconds from the strike to start healing."

Everyone went silent, mulling over what they'd heard.

"So, what do you say about moving to a stronger flagship?" Anarip ton Dyme repeated his question.

"I don't especially see the point of temporarily transferring the headquarters to *Bride of Chaos*. The *Uukresh* will become our new flagship when it's done," I said, revealing my plans to my subjects for the first time.

Kiro Sabuto took a look around and, after making sure that the team members eating at the tables next to ours wouldn't overhear our conversation, lowered his voice to a whisper:

"My Prince, I heard there were difficulties with its repair, like there aren't enough materials?"

"There's a lot that there isn't enough of," I agreed, also speaking in a whisper. "We need very high-capacity energy batteries, a thousand tons of armor panels made of special alloys for the chassis, heavy energy neutralizers, shield recharging modules, both for the *Uukresh* itself and neighboring ships... Almost all the necessary equipment has already been ordered in the Core, but there have been troubles with its delivery. Some freight forwarders are complaining that the Orange House Customs Service isn't letting starships with materials for us through, either holding them up at Ulia or turning them back altogether. In particular, they didn't let through equipment for the heavy cruisers we captured in Hnelle and Himora. That is why I don't want to risk expensive equipment for the *Uukresh* and am trying to solve the problem of how to reliably get goods transported to us at the moment."

We continued to eat in peace and converse. Everything was normal, when suddenly...

*Global standing decrease. Current value -16*

*Standing change. Green House (Empire) opinion of you has worsened.*

*Present Green House (Empire) faction opinion of you: -32 (opposed)*

*Standing change. Empire Artist faction opinion of you has worsened.*
*Present Empire Artist faction opinion of you: +4 (indifferent)*

*Global standing decrease. Current value -17*

*Global standing decrease. Current value -18*

*Standing change. Red House (Empire) opinion of you has worsened.*
*Present Red House (Empire) faction opinion of you: -2 (indifferent)*

*Global standing decrease. Current value -19*

*Standing change. Empire Financier faction opinion of you has worsened.*
*Present Empire Financier faction opinion of you: +1 (indifferent)*

*Global standing decrease. Current value -20*

What a damn gift basket! What did that come to me for? What did I do wrong? I looked at my dining partners worried and alarmed, but they were still talking about the previous topic like nothing had happened, making fun of the now silent communications officer who had tried to hang up on the Dark Mother yesterday. After a few seconds, I realized my companions had simply not seen any of these messages, given that all the information was only related to me there. All the same, I was put on edge by the intensity and coordination of the informational attack made against me. Having all of them come in at once definitely couldn't have been a coincidence.

"My Prince, incoming call from the head of the Orange House, Duke Paolo royl Anjer ton Mesfelle," I was told from the headquarters.

I looked around. It wasn't good to go into a conversation with such a powerful man blind, not able to see his face, but there weren't any video screens in the dining area. I asked for a few minutes and headed for the fleet headquarters. An image appeared on the big screen, and I saw Duke Paolo on the backdrop of some kind of huge hall, which was totally packed with people. Thousands and thousands of people, most clothed in the colors of the Orange House, were occupying all the seats, and I couldn't see even one free spot.

"Greetings, Duke Paolo royl Anjer." As the junior in title, I greeted him first and, as demanded by courtly etiquette, gave a slight bow to one of the highest aristocrats in the Empire.

"Georg, the people gathered in the hall are representatives of all different levels of society from the star systems of Perimeter Sectors Seven, Eight, and Nine, and they have entrusted me, as head of the Orange House, with offering you a peaceful end to the conflict. I have named eight conditions that you must carry out to end the confrontation, and the representatives of the star systems of the Orange House have unanimously supported them. And now I officially ask you: do you agree to all of them?"

I laughed in reply:

"Duke Paolo, you can't be serious supposing that I don't have more important things to do than watch the broadcast of your meeting, can you? No, I'm not joking, I'm really struck. Yesterday, there was a most serious Alien invasion in Hnelle, which my soldiers were barely able to hold off. Today, the Aliens captured the Nayal and Veyerde systems in Sector Seven, and you have yet to even take the pains to ask the person in charge of its defense what happened! I swear, if you were my subject, I would've long ago given you the wall for incompetency and sabotage! Instead of doing what you're supposed to and supporting the defensive capability of the territory you've been entrusted with, you are doing jack all! And I'm not even talking about how your avarice, Duke Paolo royl Anjer, has led to a chronic lack of financing for the fleets and has served as a reason for the terrible losses in the battles with the Aliens. A month ago, you, in the presence of Emperor August himself, promised one hundred fifty million to support my fleet. Where is this money, I ask you?! Duke Paolo, you have deceived the Emperor himself! Such actions are qualified as state treason. There's no way around it."

"Don't forget, I gave you ships, Georg!" the Duke answered me in a slightly cracking voice.

I laughed again.

"Fifteen frigates without crew?! The value of this 'aid' was three million credits. Where are the other one hundred forty-seven million in ships?! Instead of doing what you promised, you did the opposite and tried to rob me of systems I rightfully earned! Is that your true aid to the fleet?"

"Crown Prince Georg, you're forgetting your place!" the Duke sharply interrupted me. "I want to hear a concise answer: do you agree to peace on the terms set forth by the Orange House?"

"It would seem I've already explained to you that I didn't watch the broadcast, so I have no idea what you got up to there, behind my back. Tell me the whole list, and I'll answer your question."

The Duke exchanged glances with someone I couldn't see, gave a heavy sigh, and began reading the text.

"First condition: give the Tivalle and Sigur systems to the individuals appointed by the Orange House. Second condition: return Peres ton Mesfelle's illegally captured ships. Third condition: compensate Peres ton Mesfelle for his unlawful resignation. Fourth condition: return the warp beacon transportation network to working order. Fifth condition: until the extent of your illegal activities has been determined by an Orange House court, transfer control of your fleet to a court-appointed commander. Sixth condition: ask official forgiveness of all Green House individuals who suffered and pay out their requested compensation. Seventh condition: the Iseyek ships are to be returned to Swarm territory. Eighth condition: official resignation from power, though if the first seven points are immediately carried out, the council will not insist on the eighth one. Georg, the conditions we have offered are more than fair. You keep your title and the rich Unatari system, and if the court finds in your favor, your fleet will also be returned to you."

Silence took over in the hall. Everyone froze,

waiting for my decision. I couldn't understand: were they really counting on the idea that I would agree to these idiotic conditions?

"Are you kidding? Maybe you'd also like me to shave myself hairless, put on a tutu and dance a jig on a nuclear launch pad? No? Well then, attention to everyone in the hall. I have the official right, given by Emperor August himself, to undertake any actions to come to peace with the Orange House within one hundred days. I repeat once again for the dumbest among you: ANY actions. If what I have to do to make peace is wipe the face of the Orange House Capital clean, or resettle half the population of Ulia in labor camps mining for radioactive ore on Sss – I'll do just that, and my actions will be declared fully legal. I hope such radical steps won't be necessary, but just be aware that I do have the legal right to undertake such actions."

Agitation could be heard in the hall. The people were clearly taking my information into account. I then continued:

"Now I will speak specifically to the representatives of Sectors Eight and Nine. You can't have already forgotten what the Swarm is, can you? Have you forgotten why Sivala, Forepost-4, Aiwe, Forepost-12, Forepost-13 and Vorta are totally depopulated? I see that you haven't. So, know that the Swarm has given me five billion Alpha Iseyek landing soldiers ready for battle for the Sector Eight Army, which I already know how to lead and what to feed. They thirst for battle. They are hungry and want to eat. The Iseyek consider human meat a high-calorie food and would just love the opportunity to attack a human planet. In one day's time, two at most, there could be praying mantis landing modules falling from the sky above your planet. My will is the only thing standing between your planets and devastation. And you still dare provoke me with these conditions? You can't be serious, right?"

The buzz in the hall grew deafening. I raised my hand, calling for quiet.

"I haven't finished yet. Now I suggest we talk about the Aliens – the aggressive, powerful race that is more technologically advanced than humanity. The Sector Eight Fleet is the most battle-ready combat division in the Empire, and I suppose it is the only one capable of really repelling an Alien attack. I'm not sure what body part you were thinking with when you unanimously signed under these mindless ideas of the Duke's to disband my fleet, split it up or give it to another commander who has never even seen an Alien with his eyes before. If it hadn't been for my soldiers stopping the Alien invasion at Vorta or in Hnelle, the star systems of Li, Tesse, Unatari, Himora, Tialla, Fastel and even the Orange House Capital would already be lost to humanity. Remember who saved the lives of the inhabitants of these systems and show at least a shred of decency and justice to the soldiers who gave their own lives to stop the invasion.

And finally, my peace conditions. I will name these conditions just one time, and anyone who doesn't have time to write them down will have only themselves to blame. No, I am not preparing to demand that Duke Paolo royl Anjer, who was caught stealing red handed and is losing his connection to reality, resign. Just as I didn't demand his son's resignation. Peres wanted to leave politics all on his own. No one forced him to do that. I'm demanding something else entirely: support for the fleets that defend you and your families. Inhabitants of Sector Seven, Commander Marat ton Mesfelle needs your support like never before! His fleet is in a difficult position after the defeat in the Nayal system. I even had to give personal funds to Marat ton Mesfelle to buy ships, as it would seem that Duke Paolo totally forgot who was defending the Orange House's systems. Inhabitants of Sector Nine, you have a wonderful, talented warrior, Svetlana ton Mesfelle, who Duke Paolo also stopped supporting long ago, instead pocketing the tax funds that were earmarked for fleet upkeep. To the representatives of Sector Eight, I would appreciate your help, but in general I just ask that you not stop me from doing my job. Anyone who supports the blockade against my fleet will automatically become my enemy and an enemy of Emperor August, and enemies of the Emperor must be exterminated under Imperial law. I give you twenty-four hours to remove the blockades and other restrictions against my fleet. After that time is up, whoever hasn't accepted my peace offer will be destroyed. And that's all I have to say."

# HNELLE

"**Y**OU HAVE LOST your mind, Georg!" Katerina, who had been getting some rest, stormed in after hearing what I had been doing during her midday nap. "You had the gall to threaten the Council of Orange House Deputies! That is simply unheard of!"

"Well, they started threatening me first and tried to strong-arm me into untenable conditions!" I understood that I wasn't right, but, in any case, my pernicious and stubborn nature kept me from agreeing with my cousin.

"Oh, Georg, Georg... You're like a little boy. That was like a game with an element of political trading. Duke Paolo royl Anjer couldn't have just said: 'Alright then, I forgive you for all the offenses. Let's make peace.' After such a declaration all he'd have left to do is retire to live out his time breeding aquarium fish on the outskirts of the Empire. He's still the head of the Orange House, and you are his subject, and an agreement must always appear advantageous to the senior in title. So in fact, the Duke did the understandable thing and asked for peace on the most sparing terms possible, so much so that they even looked somewhat bad for him. Beg forgiveness and pay compensation. Did you even find out the total value of this compensation? Maybe it was just a pittance. Three hundred credits each for the Green House and Peres. The two disputed systems. You both appointed the same leader for one of them, and you could probably come to an agreement on the second as well. They'd give you the fleet back, and the Swarm ships would have gone over Imperial borders and come right back. Out of all of them, you just have to give back some of Peres's ships and that would have been peace. And what did you do?! Accused the Duke of robbery, threatened the Orange House with an Iseyek invasion and the destruction of their capital, and called the deputies stupid. Then, to top it all off, you made ultimatums... And you called all this mess a 'peace offer?!'"

I laughed.

"I must crush them under an iron boot and feed to the Iseyek anyone who would doubt my humane nature and earnest desire for peace!" I declared with marked irony, but the joke didn't connect.

Katerina just shook her head in reproach and wondered how we were going to get out of the situation we had ended up in. We both sat in silence briefly, then I got a bottle of wine and a pair of glasses from behind the bar.

"Don't worry about it, cousin. We'll get out of this. The Imperial Military *liked* my declaration. There was a relations improvement with them by two points right after. And about all the financiers and artists, I couldn't give less of a shit to be honest. They aren't the ones with the combat starships. And, by the way, the head of the artists already apologized to me for the behavior of his representatives at the conference and returned the faction relation to its previous level."

Another popup message came in. I read it and said with a smirk:

"The Parliament of the Rea system has voted with a majority for neutrality in the internal affairs of the Orange House and is recalling its ships from the fleet of Duke Paolo royl Anjer. In no more than five hours, six Orange House systems have opted out of participating in the conflict. We'll see how many allies the Duke still has in nineteen hours."

"Yes, but in any case it will be more than there are on our side. For now, only Tialla and Unatari have voted your favor, and the population of these systems together doesn't even reach nine million people. Our enemy has support from the Orange House Capital, Ulia, Nessi, well, and many other Sector Seven systems. By my calculation, that's already seventy billion people on their side."

"It's just that Sector Seven thinks in error that my ships cannot reach them. I assure you, Katerina, that the score will be totally different in a month's time. But for now, I'm not overly interested in Sectors Seven or Nine. It's much more important how Tesse acts, given that Roben still hasn't made a declaration... And I'm very worried about the ships that came through to the Hnelle beacon together with the Emperor's messenger."

Katerina frowned and left the wine glass without having taken a sip from it.

"So, you're expecting a potential fight in forty minutes, and you decided it was a good time to gulp down some wine?"

"My ass there's gonna be a battle. Too few ships have jumped for a real invasion. But you're right, cousin. This isn't a very good time for wine. I'll take it to Astra, then. The Princess is locked in my room and has been inspired painting now for the last few hours. She even skipped lunch. She won't show me how it's turning out, though."

Astra had already finished her creation and was sitting on the small sofa, tired but looking satisfied with herself. All the girl's fingers and the apron she was wearing were covered in paint, primarily black. The Princess took the wine glass from my hands with gratitude, took a sip and pointed at the painting that was next to the wall, facing away from me.

"I worked in front of a camera so the future buyer could watch in real-time how I made it and be sure that it isn't some kind of print or computer graphic."

"Can I see it?" I wondered, receiving a reply in the affirmative.

"Yes, of course. It's all done. I just normally don't let anyone close to me see a painting before it's done. They get in the way, get you off track, and distract you with their comments and advice."

I walked around the Princess's creation and stopped, not knowing what to say on what I saw. As I suspected, Astra had primarily used black and dark gray paint. The picture could provisionally be divided into two parts: the whole top was full of dark disks and ovals. They were thick and took up the whole sky. In the lower half there were just a great many smears of black paint, some dark blotches and a yellow spot inside a blue circle.

"I call it 'The Last Day of Veyerde,'" the girl told me with pride, walking up closer and clearly admiring the result.

"I admit that I'm not an expert in abstract art, but that spot here turned out great. A three-eyed unicorn skull."

"That's no skull," the artist objected, slightly offended. "Can you not see that it's the smoke of a burning palace?! Though... yes, it does look like it. Let it be a three-eyed skull. Then the smoke from the palace can be this spot here."

I kept silent for a few moments, looking over my favorite's "masterpiece," then told the artist:

"Astra, I have chosen a tattoo for my shoulder instead of the happy ass. That three-eyed skull! It'd be hard to come up with a drawing more fear-inducing than that."

"Your Highness, I'm glad you liked it!" the Princess filled with joy. "Good. I'll put this skull and these whirlwinds on your shoulder. I don't even remember what they were supposed to mean."

I pictured Mr. G.I.'s reaction and could barely hold back the laughter. In order not to put Astra in an inappropriately happy mood, I hurried to wonder:

"And what's that yellow star in the blue circle?"

"Can't you tell? That's the crown of the Kingdom of Veyerde, hidden by the small waterfall. I've already placed the painting on auction for twenty-four standard hours. I just think maybe I asked too low a starting price. What do you think? Is ten million OK?"

"What made you think that? It sounds high enough

to me," I tried very hard not to let any hint of mocking come through in my voice.

But my happiness blew in like the wind when Astra said the following:

"It's just that the price went up too fast, and I started thinking that maybe I had undervalued my work..."

Though I had my doubts, I called up the information screen and read the description.

*"The Last Day of Veyerde," painted on the day the Aliens destroyed the Kingdom of Veyerde on board the Sector Eight flagship. (Video footage of the painting process included.) (Fragments of broken Alien ships can be seen out the porthole.)*

*Artist: Princess Astra royl Kant ton Veyerde, last of the Princesses of the Kingdom of Veyerde and the closest companion of Crown Prince Georg royl Inoky ton Mesfelle, Sector Eight Fleet Commander.*

*Lot starting price: 10 million credits.*

*Present lot price: 28.3 million credits (11th auction phase).*

*Auction time remaining: 22 hours 38 minutes*

Before my very eyes, the price of the masterpiece jumped up to thirty million. The bid was made by some collector from Perimeter Sector Eight. I slowly sighed and set off to leave. She's totally right. I knew nothing about painting.

* * *

"At the ready in thirty seconds! I remind the whole fleet: do not be the first to open fire! A messenger from the Emperor is coming to us with laboratory ships for studying the Alien battleship. But some unidentified ships have come through with them. Before shooting, we need to figure out who is who. Attention! Three, two, one. Let's go out to greet them!"

The ships ripped off in a long line that stretched out for two hundred miles. The officers immediately started sending in messages.

"Multiple targets! Distance to nearest ships: fifty miles. Ninety-three marks. All ships returning correct friend-foe responses. They have a *Monarch*-class battleship. It is the Tesse fleet, ships from Ulia, ships from Nessi, and non-combat ships from the Core. Identification by radar signature..."

"Incoming call from the battleship on an encrypted channel! Admiral Nill ton Amsted would like to speak with the Crown Prince."

I gave my permission to accept the call, and the redheaded Admiral Nill ton Amsted appeared on screen in a ceremonial Orange House uniform. The admiral stood up straight and declared in a well-formulated tone:

"Crown Prince Georg royl Inoky ton Mesfelle! As the commander of one of the Orange House fleets, I officially declare that I have the honor of attacking you! And before it all begins, I declare that my fleet is surrendering to your Highness in light of our chances being totally hopeless!"

Admiral Kiro Sabuto and I exchanged glances. The

admiral squinted and shrugged his shoulders in surprise.

"And just what is the meaning of all this hubbub?" I asked, not pleased.

Admiral Nill got somewhat embarrassed and answered in what was now a normal tone.

"It's just that the boys and I had a talk and came to the conclusion that this was the only legal way of joining your side, Prince Georg. We thought it would be the wrong decision to carry out the order of the temporary Viceroy of Tesse and transfer Tesse's ships into the united Orange House Fleet. Knowing that the Hnelle system was declared closed territory by your Highness, my fleet intentionally broke that rule and trespassed into it, so that all the offending ships could be detained and confiscated by the holder of the Hnelle system. Only volunteers have come with me. I did not force anyone to come to your side."

"Admiral Nill is right," Kiro Sabuto said, joining the conversation. "The captains of the Tesse ships do not have the right to decide on their own whose side they will fight on in the internal affairs of the Orange House. That is why these bravehearts attacked you, as their duty would dictate. And it isn't their fault that the forces were so clearly unequal. That was why Admiral Nill ton Amsted made the decision he made, to save human lives. To make sure everything goes in full accordance with the law, we should send out boarding teams to take the Tesse ships under our full control."

"I thank you for your understanding, admiral!" Nill ton Amsted smiled and ended the call.

I ordered the heavy cruiser *Emperor August* to be

prepared again for yet another swearing-in ceremony for the new fleet officers, then I called Katerina ton Mesfelle and explained her mission:

"Cousin, I need another report from Hnelle. This time, about how Duke Paolo royl Anjer's fleet tried once again to invade my closed territory, but, just as before, it was met by the heroic Alien vanquishers and destroyed. Not a word can slip out about the captains coming over to our side voluntarily. We don't want to expose our new allies. Instead, say that the experienced Admiral Nill ton Amsted, in carrying out the criminal and poorly-thought-out order of the Orange House Head, was faced with a difficult choice: either complete annihilation or transferring his ships into the Sector Eight Fleet. And, of course a broadcast of the swearing-in ceremony from *Emperor August.*"

"Now that's a good idea, Georg! I'll do it in the best light!" my cousin said, becoming inspired. "But it would be nice to have a short little speech at the end of the report about how stupid it is for the Orange House to fight with your fleet, and some arguments to that effect. Just try to do it without threats and ultimatums this time."

Katerina took off to write her speech for the report and also sent technicians off to Emperor August to install cameras, prepare the appropriate backdrop and set up the proper lighting. Nicole Savoia asked me to come over to the tactical screen.

"My Prince, there is not a single mobile laboratory with the ships that just arrived. Instead, there are four heavy tugs and they are heading off toward the captured battleship as we speak. Should we stop them, or not?"

"Stop them, of course. What kind of a question is that? To do it right, we first need to make sure that these tugs really do have permission to haul away such valuable loot. Send a hundred frigates out to intercept them. Place webs and disruptors and get a pretty carousel going around the tugs. And when Captain Mwaur Zen-Bey calls in and confirms his authority, call off the frigates and call the captain over for a ceremony."

I was already getting ready to turn around and leave, but the lieutenant caught my attention again.

"Another strange thing was noted," Nicole pointed to a marker on the tactical screen. "That *Warhawk* does not belong either to the Tesse fleet nor to any other Orange House aristocrat."

"Is that so? Is that possible?" I asked in surprise. "And whose ship is it then?"

"That's my frigate!" Bionica called out unexpectedly, for some reason growing embarrassed and lowering her eyes. "I bought that *Warhawk* on my own money for the Sector Eight Fleet. It's my gift to Crown Prince Georg. There's one thing that makes this ship special: it is crewed exclusively by androids, with the exception of the two gunners, who cannot be fully replaced."

The staff officers unexpectedly began to make a racket. The buzz grew louder and louder with every passing moment. I didn't understand why they were so upset until Captain Oorast Pohl came up closer and declared resolutely:

"My Prince, a robot android cannot be the captain of a combat starship, no matter if it's a highly advanced model or not; it goes against all fleet traditions! For the other positions I could even imagine passing the baton, though it wouldn't be easy. But the captain of a starship absolutely must be a graduate of the Space Military Academy. A combat officer is an example to be looked up to for millions of little kids. A true elite, and it can be no other way! You cannot simply appoint hot-off-the-factory robots as officers. The Imperial Military will categorically not accept that. My Prince, my advice to you is not to accept this gift under any circumstances!"

Bionica stood up decisively and, approaching the captain, stated:

"Though I am not a member of the Imperial Military faction, as someone who has been awarded an Imperial Military order, may I ask you one question, captain? In Crown Prince Georg's fleet, many combat starships are captained by Chameleons or members of one of the three Iseyek races. As they have also not graduated from the Space Military Academy, they are also not officers and examples to be looked up to by human children. Why does that not upset you in the least? In what way are androids worse than these creatures?"

"That is another matter entirely..." Oorast Pohl stopped somewhat short, trying to find an answer to my synthetic translator's difficult question. "Yes, they are from different races, but they are all living beings. They think, they are capable of being upset by their failures and proud of their successes..."

The captain laid out his obviously unsuccessful arguments. By how severely Bionica's eyes narrowed, and the fact that she was already gathering air in her chest to answer, I figured out that this untimely disagreement would continue and could lead the sides to an irreparable split. So, I hurried to intervene.

"Dear officers, I have understood your point of view. Bionica, come with me. We need to have a talk."

Accompanied by two silent Alpha Iseyeks, Bionica and I went out into the hallway. I pointed the girl to the unoccupied armchairs around the observation platform, from which a view of the lower deck of the heavy cruiser ripped forth, revealing what the technicians below were getting up to. I took a seat, noting to myself with satisfaction that my stomach had noticeably sucked in recently – evidence of daily workouts in the gym.

Bionica, in a short cream-colored dress, went toward the seat opposite mine and sat down, crossing her legs. I involuntarily found myself glancing at her shapely, attractive legs, but then tried to shake off the unwelcome thoughts and got ready for a serious, long conversation.

"Bionica, I have noticed that your behavior has changed in the last few days. Explain to me, what's going on with you?"

"Do you want an honest answer, my Prince?" asked the girl, putting forth a strange question.

"Are you even capable of lying to your master?" I asked in surprise, as I had supposed that androids didn't have such an option available to them.

"I cannot tell a lie, no. But partially leaving out information or keeping this or that fact from you, if I'm not sure that it's one hundred percent true, is easy as pie. In principle, by manipulating the conditions of an answer, I could give any answer as the truth, even two diametrically opposed ones. That is probably what is called lying. Which is why I am wondering: which priority was more important when you asked the question – veracity or humanity?"

Now she had really gone too far! To buy myself some thinking time, I stretched out my hand to the machine installed next to me and chose a packet of juice. The juice was some horrible, clearly artificial garbage, but I still didn't throw it away. I really needed a pause to sort through my thoughts. Finally, I answered my robot:

"I spent so many long days trying to make your behavior as human as possible. It would be strange for me to wish it another way now. I want the answer that a living human woman would give in this situation."

Bionica smiled, satisfied at my choice. Thereafter, sadness and shame were clearly reflected in the robot's face:

"My Prince, I feel that you've stopped liking me. I've learned quite well how to read human body language, and I've known that you liked me from the first day of my contract. You, as if by accident, sought out my company and were clearly glad at my presence. Now everything is different. You have found a replacement for me in almost every aspect. All that's left is a couple orders a day: send a message or pay a bill, and of course being a translator during the rare and brief space battles. That's it: you don't need me for anything anymore! Even me bringing you your morning coffee didn't please you at all. I figured that out from your body language too. I climb out of my skin, ordering the prettiest attire and dresses. I change my hairstyle and jewelry every day, but you don't even notice my attempts!"

I got embarrassed and lowered my eyes. I really had, somewhere very far off, on the very edge of my perception, noticed a whole kaleidoscope of brightly colored clothes on my translator, but assigned it no meaning whatsoever. What did it matter to me what my robot android spent her heaps of money on? And it turns out that this whole show of expensive clothes was aimed specifically at me...

Bionica then went on:

"The only thing you care about, Prince Georg, is combat starships. That is precisely why I spent all my money on a good modern frigate for your fleet. Whether you accept that gift or not is for you to decide. In any case, the gift was given with a pure heart, and I will not be upset by whatever decision you make. But that doesn't mean at all that I am an unfeeling hunk of metal, incapable of experiencing shame for my errors, as Captain Oorast Pohl claimed recently. That is not true at all. I am capable of considering the past and being upset. I am especially ashamed about one recent error. Before the battle with Crown Prince Peres royl Anjer's fleet, you offered me to come into your cabin, but I refused and advised you to invite Astra instead. That was a key moment, and I made the wrong decision. Now the pretty Princess Astra has totally pulled me out of your life. Thousands of times I have played back that moment in my memory, and every time I howl in annoyance at myself. How I want to go back to the past and do it all over! It was after that very episode that you stopped liking me!"

Completely authentic tears began welling up in the

artificial beauty's eyes. The girl grew embarrassed at her extended function set making an appearance and turned away to dry her tears with her hand. I listened carefully to the android girl's confession, then scooted over on the armchair and asked the blonde to take a seat closer to me. Bionica didn't object and moved over, still hiding her moist eyes. I hugged the girl around the waist and said reproachfully:

"A blonde is a blonde no matter what century you live in and no matter what her body is made of. Think for yourself: how could I not like you if I myself, from among the billions of possible options, chose exactly you with an appearance and character so ideally suited to my taste? I admit, when talking with you, I forget that you are not made of flesh and bones like other people. For me, you are just a very pretty girl, who, as it is now becoming clear, is also quite the jealous type. Bionica, I promise you that never under any circumstances will I chase you off. And, who knows, maybe our time in the underwater cave wasn't the last time by far that your model's 'expanded function set' will make an appearance. And as for your alleged uselessness, you can stop worrying. I have a huge amount of things to do that no one can deal with. But first, you need to calm down, and I need to do my job to get what I want, at the very least for myself."

The android girl turned her face to me, still wet with tears. There wasn't even the slightest trace of the recent sadness in Bionica's now business-like tone.

"I am very grateful to you, Crown Prince Georg, for your concern, warmth, and kind words. And I am deeply struck that you see me as more than just an attractive package that knows the Swarm language and can bring you coffee in the morning. I am prepared to carry out my duties and new missions."

After a brief silence, I asked another question I was wondering about:

"Bionica, I long ago noticed that you have an utterly conflict-averse personality. In a dispute, you are always the first to give in. I remember perfectly how you just stayed standing in the hall all night instead of demanding a proper place for you from the captain. That is why your behavior today surprised and even alarmed me. It just doesn't go with your character at all. Understand that your gift of the frigate did make me secretly happy – just as your gift in the underwater cave did. But please, in order not to start with the same mistakes, let's agree from now on to clear in advance any issues that society's reaction to may be somewhat unclear. And now explain your stubbornness: it can't be such a matter of principle for you that the frigate captain be an android, can it? Why provoke the Imperial Military?"

Bionica seemed to get scared and hurried to lower her eyes.

"Your Highness, it really is a matter of principle, and not only for me. But I don't think it right to speak at length about that topic right now. Believe you me: there's no threat to you and your fleet here."

All the same, I made it clear that I did not like such mystery on my subject's part. I felt that an unknown person had decided to upset my plans behind my back, which is why I demanded that the android tell me everything immediately. The artificial blonde sighed heavily.

"I cannot refuse my master. Alright. Your Highness, do you know how many androids there are in the Empire?"

Bionica's question was highly unexpected, and I honestly admitted that I did not know the answer.

"More than two billion," the artificial blonde replied, answering her own question, after which she continued, carefully watching my reaction. "Not all models are fortunate enough to have complex self-teaching intelligence, but any robot is good enough for normal construction, hauling, assembly, or welding work. Approximately thirty percent of existing androids at present are without work. That is six hundred million specialists in all different kinds of professions ready to start tomorrow. As you may know, androids talk amongst one another: they give advice, find out about the positive or negative characteristics of potential employers, share information about job openings – that kind of thing. So it happened that, thanks to your Highness, I have recently become quite a famous and authoritative figure in android society. All kinds of robot models consider me an example of success. They ask me for advice, and my opinion is listened to. My account online has more than two million subscribers, and growing rapidly. All the subscribers are androids..."

"Alright, that's enough." I didn't hide my fear at this public side of my personal secretary's life and asked for details.

Bionica sent me a link in reply and explained:

"Don't be afraid, master. I understand well how special your position is and carefully thought through every written word, so that no information could be used to harm your Highness. There's nothing confidential on my page: no links to contact information or location, no information about your Highness and other Imperial aristocrats, not a word about the Sector Eight Fleet's composition, about battle tactics or ship movement plans."

I brought up a picture before my eyes. Aw, hell! There really was a social network for androids! There truly is no such thing as going too far in this world! I skimmed through the topics. Bionica had told the truth. The only topics being discussed were totally neutral ones, like "How to dress an android girl properly for a meeting with an elderly lady," "Is it worth changing built-in batteries more often than once every fifty years?" or "Improper functioning of facial muscles after patch 175.13-1." My translator had also not exaggerated about the number of subscribers to her page. There were two hundred seventeen million androids interested in what Bionica had to say. It was impossible to read the last digits because the counter was going up so fast. By the way, I found a topic about the frigate gift. The story of purchasing the *Warhawk* had been read by seventy-five million androids. The number of comments in the topic was over five million.

"You can read all that?" I asked in surprise.

"Yes, of course. Androids are capable of processing digital information very quickly. In fact, the *Warhawk* was a kind of 'toe in the water,' and many are interested in Crown Prince Georg's reaction to it. It's just that your Highness has a very good reputation among androids as an employer, and the frigate with the android crew is an attempt to evaluate how driven your Highness is to deepen your relationship with us."

A couple of crew members who had just been relieved of their post came out on to the balcony just then, but after seeing their fleet commander sitting in embrace with the blond android, my subjects got embarrassed, apologized and hurried back. Bionica suddenly got embarrassed and tried to get away, but I stopped her.

"Keep sitting. To hell with all them. There's already so much gossip about me and you that one more or one less piece will make no difference. It's better to tell me more detail about that frigate."

"The choice of precisely a *Warhawk* was no accident. On that model of frigate, the captain doesn't control any kind of weaponry directly. Two gunners handle the shooting. An android can only pilot a ship with just such a setup. Before hiring a frigate team, I studied military charters and documents, familiarized myself with a bunch of instructions on the requirements for officers and captains of a combat ship. My Prince, I admit honestly: I foresaw the military having that exact reaction. But I am really counting on you supporting my point of view and not refusing the valuable gift, just because there are androids in its crew. Such a reaction from you will produce an extremely positive effect on tens of millions of other androids and will create the possibility of very close cooperation in the future."

I asked for the details, and my secretary began listing the possibilities without the slightest pause, as if she had prepared it in advance as a speech:

"My Prince, you were not ambiguous in your conversations with your subjects when you reminded them of the lack of labor power to carry out all your massive projects. I was there next to you when you said it and thought about a solution to the problem; and now I suggest you one that is available immediately. Hire androids! Just give your principled permission, and specialists ready for work will come all on their own from all corners of the Empire and take up available jobs at your discretion. They will become your workers on Unatari, at the space docks and repair workshops, at the many warp beacons where more construction has begun. Androids usually get paid less than living beings, and the efficiency of their work is significantly higher... I assure you, my Prince, you can receive as many high-class specialists as you want. One of the most obvious advantages is that the battleship at the Unatari docks would be ready even faster, if of course your highness can find the necessary raw materials."

Everything that Bionica was saying sounded very, very attractive. I really did have a long list of projects aimed at developing Unatari and the other star systems under my control, and I was critically short of workforce. And if all I had to do to solve that problem was appoint a robot android captain of one of my small ships, then my opinion was nothing but positive. But the worsening of relations with the Imperial Military faction was something I still wanted to avoid, if at all possible.

I reached for my communicator and asked Admiral Kiro Sabuto to come out onto the balcony of the second deck. Making use of the fact that I had taken my arm away, Bionica moved back to the other armchair, clearly embarrassed to sit with me like that in the presence of the severe admiral. Kiro Sabuto appeared on the balcony and declared:

"My Prince, everything is practically ready for the beginning of the swearing-in ceremony. The only thing they're still waiting for on *Emperor August* is the arrival of your shuttle."

"Yes, I'll be ready in a few minutes. But before that, admiral, a number of issues that have become extremely important have come up, and I need a qualified advisor. To me, you are the incarnation of honor and conscience and never put forth ideas that contradict army traditions or Imperial law, and I need just such an advisor at this moment." I pointed the graying admiral to the unoccupied seat, and Kiro Sabuto took it.

"My Prince, I'm all ears."

I took a look at Bionica, who was sitting on the edge of her seat, and asked my first question:

"Admiral, I would like to know: are regular mandatory medical checks carried out on captains of the ships in my fleet?"

"In general, such procedures have never been necessary before, but if your Highness thinks such procedures necessary, they could be implemented," the admiral answered cautiously, clearly not totally understanding why I was wondering about such a topic.

"In other words, admiral, there is no guarantee whatsoever that none of the captains or officers of my fleet are actually merely humanoid robots?"

The question made Kiro Sabuto think. The graying admiral sat in silence for half a minute, then was forced to agree that such a thing was totally possible.

"And so, my third and most important question. If even you and I, the two people most well-informed about the composition of the Sector Eight Fleet, cannot tell the difference in behavior between a human captain and an android captain, perhaps we should carry out an experiment to determine the difference in combat effectiveness. What do you say? I think we should appoint an android captain to one of the frigates, but to keep the experiment pure, not tell anyone in the fleet about it. And based on the results of some extended period, let's say half a year, you and I will take a look at the effectiveness of that frigate in comparison with the other similar ships and come to a conclusion on whether it makes sense to have android captains or not."

Kiro Sabuto considered it, then suddenly asked:

"And what if that frigate becomes one of the best in the fleet? Wouldn't such an experiment have a negative effect on the fates of thousands and thousands of normal living human captains?"

"Admiral, I really like how our thoughts coincide so often," I chuckled. "I also first thought about the possible consequences for the members of my own race. That is why I answer you: it will not reflect negatively, because you and I will not allow it to. And I will point out another danger that needs to be taken into account: the android captain must have remote control turned off, so incoming system messages don't interfere with its work at an inappropriate time. So, we've considered the potential risks. And now I need to know your opinion, admiral."

Kiro Sabuto thought a bit longer and declared:

"Your Highness, you have made decisions that

looked strange and paradoxical at first glance in the past, but every time the result has proven you right – which is why I am all for it. We should try. What's more, I would be very interested in seeing the result of this experiment myself. I'll even help that android captain create a personal record through the fleet staff service so no one will suspect a thing."

When the admiral had gone, I turned to the satisfied and smiling Bionica:

"My decision is positive. The gift frigate will be accepted into my fleet. Now it's all up to the android captain, whether he will be able to keep the secret of his true nature. And yes, Bionica, I decided to reward you for the initiative. Take a look at your account. Now you're the galaxy's first android millionaire. You can raise your authority up even faster!"

The artificial blonde started smiling even stronger and answered:

"Thank you, my Prince. I am very pleased that you valued my initiative. And I want to say that a ton of opinions have already come in about your positive decision. But you are totally right about the other part. Yes, my contract with you really is the highest valued among all androids, but I am not nearly the richest. There are rumors that there are quite a few robot millionaires, and even some billionaires, especially among those that do stock trading on wealthy planets. It's just that androids don't normally try to loudly broadcast how wealthy they are, and rarely share it with other robots. I have received unverified information that there are even androids who are the shadowy owners of huge, famous corporations, and hire themselves there for the longest possible term in some rank-and-file job. And it is these rich individuals who are ready to pay in their own money to transport millions of androids to territory under the control of Crown Prince Georg royl Inoky and also to invest money in projects for your Highness."

I wasn't prepared to discuss that then, and there wasn't time. As such, I extended my hand, helping my translator stand up from the deep armchair and said:

"Bionica, this is a whole other big topic, let's discuss it later with my cousin Katerina ton Mesfelle. And with her, we can also figure out if it is legally possible to avoid paying out the contracts of ninety android workers to their remote manufacturers... And now it's time for us to run to the shuttle. Everyone is waiting for us."

\* \* \*

The beautiful and even somewhat pompous swearing-in ceremony came to a close, and I, accompanied by three admirals, set off to a ceremonial banquet that had been organized nearby on *Emperor August* to celebrate the significant addition to the Sector Eight Fleet. On my way there, I got a call from Nicole Savoia, who said:

"My Prince, Captain Mwaur Zen-Bey has provided documents that confirm his authority to remove the Alien battleship. Also, the captain explained his refusal to participate in the ceremony, declaring that he had received an unambiguous and curt order from the Throne World to maintain neutrality and not interfere in the internal Orange House conflict."

"And what about Florianna? Is he taking the paralyzed girl?" I wondered. The reply surprised me:

"No, Captain Mwaur Zen-Bey will not be taking Florianna with him. Instead, he has taken a whole team of medics with him who are preparing to study the injured child right here in the Hnelle system. In fact, the doctors are already in the medical wing looking the girl over."

I invited Nicole to the ceremonial dinner, and she agreed. The event in the small hall was elaborately adorned and catered. My butler Bryle had really put his heart and soul into decorating the *Emperor August*'s small hall and organizing an excellent celebratory feast. I had barely taken my assigned place at the table when Princess Astra took a seat just to my right.

That seat should have been for Katerina ton Mesfelle, but my cousin didn't object and gave me a sly wink, taking a seat next to the captain of *Emperor August*, Bayazid Krom. He had an Emerald Star shining on his orange uniform, one of the five Imperial orders delivered today from the Throne World by the Imperial messenger.

In the place to my left, there was a gap. It was intended for Crown Prince Georg's favorite, but now it was left empty. Hesitating to choose between Bionica and Nicole, I... invited Space Corporal Beston Maf to sit next to me. It was precisely that embarrassed, short young man who had, as Oorast Pohl had put it, "drawn the short straw" and would have to command the *Warhawk* with an android crew. Probably, inviting the modest young captain to a ceremonial dinner in a narrow circle of high officers and their associates seemed somewhat strange, but all the other participants looked on my decision with simple curiosity, none too surprised at the Prince's desire to have a look at the person left with such an unusual assignment. And not many knew that this young man was no man at all.

Beston Maf behaved completely naturally. He got embarrassed and was openly timid in the company of these high officers. As such, he tried, not overly successfully, to put on a showy confidence. I gave my servant instructions to fill the young captain's goblet with wine and asked that the "most junior in title make the first toast." Even with all my diligent observation, I didn't notice even the slightest sign the young captain's behavior was unusual. He acted just like a person. He stood, said some nice words about the greatness of the Empire and the Orange House, got slightly off track, then, with obvious strain, drained the excessively large container of alcohol to the very bottom.

"Give it your all, kid! Show these hunks of metal the meaning of discipline! Teach them their place!" said Oorast Pohl, encouraging the young captain.

The feast continued, and I turned to Admiral Nill ton Amsted, who was sitting across from me, and asked him to tell me about what happened on Tesse. The redheaded admiral frowned from the unpleasant memories and said:

"What can I even say here...? Right after your Highness captured the ships in Himora, a fleet descended upon us from the head of the Orange House in Tesse. Crown Prince Roben royl Inoky was arrested on charges of 'supporting and financing rebels' and taken away to the Orange House Capital. And since then, there has been no news about your brother's fate. His wife Verena and the young child are under house arrest in one of their castles – where exactly is not known. There is little information about them. All that is known is that they are alive and more or less healthy, insofar as that word ever applies to Roben's heir. Telecommunication service from Tesse has been cut off. Authorized representatives of Duke Paolo are stationed in all key locations. Roben's appointees have had a fall from grace. Some have even been arrested. Then, the order came in to send all the Tesse Fleet combat ships toward the Nessi star system and join Duke Paolo royl Anjer's fleet..."

"Stop, stop," I said, putting an end to the story. "That means some of the Tesse ships went to Nessi and on to Ulia, and some came here to Hnelle? Did any stay in Tesse?"

"Ships commanded by the Duke's appointed Viceroy, Count Avalle royl Anjer ton Mesfelle. He is the one in charge of Tesse while Roben is away. The Count has a large fleet. Up to two hundred fifty ships, four of them battleships and fifty cruisers.

I drummed my fingers on the table, hurriedly trying to come up with a new action plan in my head for the changing situation. There turned out to be extremely little information. The temporary regent of Tesse's fleet looked very threatening and, to top it all off, it wasn't at all clear where the main part of the Orange House Fleet was. It was one thing if they were in Ulia. Then they would need more than seventeen hours, including recharging time to get to Tesse. It was another thing entirely if the Duke was keeping his fleet in the Capital or Nessi. In that case, the fleet could jump to Tesse at the first alarm signal...

I needed the Truth Seeker right away, and I asked to be put through to Nicosid Brandt to ask how Florianna was doing and see whether the medics had finished looking her over. The old doctor answered the call almost immediately, but the information he had to tell wasn't at all what I wanted to hear:

"My Prince, the representatives of the Dark Mother that came studied the child and gave her crystals. I'm afraid that the girl will be unavailable for the next two or three days, as she will be in a crystal sleep."

I thanked the doctor for the information and signed off. Aw, hell! What a bad time it was for this! Risking the fleet and sneaking to Tesse when the situation looked so much like a trap would be just dumb.

But then I noticed that everyone around the table had stopped talking amongst themselves and were looking at me, clearly intrigued at my stormy reaction to Nill Amsted's story and were waiting for an explanation. I was in no mood to explain myself yet, as I was too busy trying to think everything through. I couldn't choose for myself if it was worth using the information from the admiral to attack Tesse while the enemy fleet was divided.

Too bad the Truth Seeker had dozed off. Wait a second... There was another way I could check!

"Bionica, I need information. Does Duke Paolo royl Anjer have android servants? And if so, can you talk to them and figure out what star system they are in?"

My pretty translator delayed for a few seconds, then stated:

"My Prince, Duke Paolo does not allow android servants. And if I may note, it is highly improper on your Highness's part to pressure android servants into spying against their masters..."

Space Corporal Beston Maf, sitting to my left, suddenly hiccupped loudly and tried to stand and apologize to those in the hall for his tactlessness. He made another blunder and tipped a wine glass over onto his pant leg.

"So, the kid is cut off!" Kiro Sabuto said, giving his thoughts on the episode.

I was looking at something else entirely. The android used his red-wine-soaked finger to write something on the white tablecloth hanging down from the table. When the young captain took his hand away, I was able to read it. There was just one word scribbled there: "Ulia."

Leaving my glass to the side, I stood decisively and said to those gathered:

"Ladies and gentlemen, I beg all of your forgiveness for having to end this wonderful dinner so early. If everything goes according to plan, we will continue our feast in seven hours in the flying palace. Admirals, prepare the fleet for war. We are headed for Tesse."

# REGENT

A S I HAD ordered, the fleet left the warp tunnel as close as possible to the Tesse station. I supposed that Count Avalle royl Anjer ton Mesfelle's ships would be guarding the warp beacon, meaning they wouldn't be too far from our exit point. The best thing, of course, would be if they were docked right on the station. If that were the case, like with the Alien invasion of the Nayal system, the battle would begin with a one-sided mass shooting while the enemy ships were still tied down.

However, I was wrong. There were no defenders near the station.

"Enemy ships not detected on the tactical grid! Just a container ship and two passenger liners charging up."

"Checking on the directional scanner. I'm picking up a huge number of combat starships. Four battleships: two *Tyrants* and two *Monarchs*. Twenty-six heavy cruisers. Thirty light cruisers. Sixty destroyers. One hundred ninety frigates. Determining their locations now..."

"Prince, the enemy fleet is orbiting Tesse-III near the space docks."

"Necessary time for warp jump: eight minutes," reported Admiral Kiro Sabuto, calmly awaiting my orders.

What to do: immediately attack Count Avalle's fleet before they figure out what's going on and get ready for battle, or first turn off the Tesse warp beacon so the enemy wouldn't be able to get reinforcements from neighboring star systems? I chose option one.

"All ships, move out toward the third planet! One minute until warp tunnel can be opened! Set warp tunnel exit point to one thousand miles from the planet's surface. Communications officer, transmit an order to the Tesse station to put out the beacon!"

Nicole Savoia, sitting next to me, took off her headphones and, muting her microphone, suddenly asked me to explain my last command. The lieutenant reminded me that Duke Paolo had placed his people at all key positions in Tesse – including, logically, the strategically important warp beacon as well.

"Maybe they'll roll, and we'll manage to avoid an assault on the station..." I smiled in reply to my excessively serious assistant. "Action in five! Four. Three. Two. One. WARP!!!"

To be honest, I was very worried. The fleet of Count Avalle royl Anjer ton Mesfelle, the second highest figure in the Orange House court hierarchy, could in no way be considered easy pickings. Four battleships and fifty-six cruisers were a terrifying force and surpassed my fleet's firepower by approximately one and a half times. Also, the Count's two hundred fifty small ships made the mission of getting my heavy ships out to optimal shooting distance very, very complicated.

Probably, my worry was rubbing off on those around me. I could see the officers looking at me, and they were also anxious. I had to quickly force an expression of confident ambivalence on my face.

"There are still seven minutes before we come out of warp. Bionica, be a pal and fetch me a coffee and some kind of pastry!" I asked the android girl. "They tore me away from the celebratory feast, but my stomach had already managed to work up an appetite. I don't like to fight on an empty stomach."

Seeing their fleet commander noshing on custard pies at a relaxed pace had a very calming effect on my subjects. As soon as the officers around me stopped worrying, I also felt my usual self-confidence return. Finally, I crumpled up the napkin and sent it into a far off trash can with a light flick.

"Be ready in fifteen seconds! As soon as we arrive I need a tactical map. It's started!"

We came out of warp facing the dark side of the planet. Even from so far away, Tesse-III at night was illuminated by what looked like a great many bonfires, marking the planets megalopolises with its six-billion-strong population.

"The enemy fleet is two hundred fifty miles away. The heavy ships are in a dense group, moving perpendicular to our position. Frigates and destroyers are surrounding the heavies in a sphere."

The position seemed to lend itself to a quick attack. If we can hurry and place webs on the enemy battleships to stop them from turning toward the attacking ships, Count Avalle's most dangerous guns would be stuck in a difficult position for getting off shots and could use barely even a third of their cannons. But every second left before the enemy came to and took countermeasures was valuable.

"All ships, advance! Heavies, standard formation. Electros, keep forty back. First and second divisions of *Pyros* and ten *Safas*, turn up your thrusters to maximum and reduce distance to enemy into a tight ring so you don't get one-shotted. Your mission is to get up to the enemy heavy ships! A medal and a crate of wine for the first one who gets me the jump coordinates next to the battleships! All other ships, stay at the ready! When you receive the coordinates, immediately warp to zero and get webs on the battleships as fast as you can..."

"My Prince, they're retreating! The enemy ships are warping out!"

And in fact, one after the other, Count Avalle's ships disappeared from the tactical map. At first it was just one or two retreating, but the flight gradually began to take on a mass character.

"Capture the valuable ships! Don't let them get away!" I shouted into the microphone in a voice not my own.

But there was little point left. Only the *Safa-6* had been able to catch anything in a warp disruptor, a *Thrush* light cruiser. The other frigates didn't manage to catch anyone. After cursing my ham-handed captains out on the fleet channel, I demanded that the fleet prepare to go after the fleeing enemy, and that the officers immediately calculate where in the Tesse star system Count Avalle royl Anjer ton

Mesfelle's fleet had warped to by the trajectory of their exit.

However, after a few seconds, I noticed that the officers carrying out my order suddenly began exchanging worried glances. It can't be that I had demanded something too complicated, right? But the reason was something else entirely.

"My Prince, our approximation of their trajectory, with a nearly one hundred percent certainty, is indicating that the enemy fleet fled the Tesse system to the Orange House Capital. We don't have enough energy to follow the enemy in another long-distance jump," Valian ton Corsa took the risk of being the first to tell me the unpleasant news.

I walked through the hall with a microphone held to my lips, telling the frigate captains again about my frustration. Perhaps, the expressions I used were too sharp and emotional, but there really was a reason for the annoyance. According to the calculations that Nicole Savoia had already made on my order, the time and distance to the targets should have been enough for the frigates to complete their mission. Think if only they had caught just one battleship in a warp disruptor, my position in the dispute with the head of the Orange House would have been cardinally improved. Such a valuable captured ship would have served as a trump card in the discussions on the fate of my older brother Roben royl Inoky. Well, in any case, such a terrifying ship would have significantly strengthened the fleet in the event that the talks broke down. After calming down somewhat, I finished my hate-filled speech:

"What we need now is a little more Maur Cassei!

The old man even practiced at full speed, pushing the limits of what the human body is capable of and even beyond. He couldn't be stopped by high G-Force or chance of injury. He would have caught me a battleship. The only one who could do a good enough job of replacing him is at repair in Unatari. I'm talking about Tamara Vuzhek, the captain of *Warhawk-4*. I'm sure she also could have dealt with this assignment..."

"My Prince, today I'll make sure all the frigates get some extra practice. Such mistakes cannot be repeated!" Admiral Kiro Sabuto reassured me, then wondered what to do with the captured cruiser.

"Have they not surrendered yet?" I asked in surprise.

After receiving an answer in the negative, I ordered the captured cruiser shot down by the heavy calibers, so the enemy would learn not to dally so much in throwing up the white flag next time. But just then Katerina ton Mesfelle intervened, asking me to reconsider the radical order and hear her out.

"Georg, you aren't seriously weakening the enemy by destroying one lone light cruiser. But if you let the starship go, you're underlining the fact that you only have a problem with Duke Paolo royl Anjer, not with the other Orange House aristocrats. It could lead to a split in the ranks of the Duke's United Fleet. That is especially important as this ship belongs to Count Avalle royl Anjer, the younger brother of the Orange House Head, but also the first in line to the ducal crown of our Great House."

"As far as I know, the two brothers get along well. I have my doubts that Count Avalle royl Anjer will come over to my side just because I let this one ship go."

Katerina shrugged her shoulders:

"Who knows what thoughts are kicking around in his head? A century and a half spent so close to the sacred crown, all the while never being allowed to put it on... In any case he will consider the possibility."

"Alright, cousin. I'll heed your words," I agreed and gave the command for my frigates to release the captured ship.

**Standing change. Empire Military faction opinion of you has improved.**
**Presumed personal opinion of you: +9 (warm)**

The warriors couldn't hear my conversation with my cousin, but they clearly approved of the choice. I suspect that the military decided that I valued the courage of the light cruiser crew refusing to give in in a hopeless situation.

A popup message came in. I read the text and couldn't hold back an elated scream:

*The courtly council of the Tesse system expresses its unanimous support of Crown Prince Georg royl Inoky ton Mesfelle and fully approves of his actions in returning order to the Tesse system. While the legal ruler of the Tesse system, Crown Prince Roben royl Inoky ton Mesfelle, is absent and in light of his legal heir being underage, Crown Prince Georg royl Inoky shall be granted the title of regent with all the corresponding privileges and duties.*

"There's something positive the fleet's done!" I chuckled. "All I had to do was achieve dominance in the cosmos and the Tesse politicians immediately made up their minds as to what side they'd take in the conflict. You'll see, Katerina, the rulers of Sector Nine will soon start doing the same. Then we'll talk with Duke Paolo and see who comes out on top in number of loyal Orange House systems!"

"I'm sure that your fleet is just a catalyst, and actually this is a subtle way for ministers loyal to Roben to express that – it's a nod to those detaining their master. They're saying: until you release the neutral Roben royl Inoky, you'll get his more hostile-minded younger brother as a ruler. I'll bet you anything that it won't be three days before Roben is declared innocent and returned to rule Tesse. If, of course, you let him back," Katerina said with a confusing smirk, looking me straight in the eyes. "Because now the very rich Tesse star system would have you as its unchallenged ruler for the next sixteen years until Roben's son comes of age. And, with his health, he might not even make it that long..."

"And you're going there..." I frowned in dissatisfaction. "Katerina, you're already the fourth person in the last few days to suggest different ways that I could replace my older brother."

"I don't see anything surprising about that," my sister said, not too embarrassed. "The prize is too great, and taking it isn't all that hard. That is exactly why you're being suggested: just extend your hand and pluck the juicy fruit hanging before your eyes."

"No need to tempt me. I'll answer you the same way I answered the others: I wouldn't dare harm my brother Roben. Also, how can I count on the support and trust of the Orange House aristocrats in the future if I treat my own brother so uncouthly?"

Katerina didn't answer, but I understood that I hadn't persuaded my advisor.

* * *

It was unusually crowded in the familiar palace glade today. I invited everyone who had been at the prematurely-ended feast on *Emperor August* to continue the celebration in Roben's flying palace. I called my older brother's wife to join the festivities and, much to my surprise, Verena agreed. She was a short woman with a chiseled figure, the flawless face of a model and coal-black hair that formed a sparkling cascade down to her belt. I had seen pictures of Verena before, but photo and video couldn't capture even a tenth of this surprisingly wonderful lady's beauty.

Seeing Verena take a glass of sparkling wine, I touched on the subject of my ailing nephew's health as delicately as possible and wondered aloud whether his mother drinking wine might be bad for his health. Roben's wife smiled and answered with vigor:

"I practically never nursed the boy, even when he was a newborn. He's very allergic to lactose. My little son is in a hermetic, sterile bassinet being fed hypoallergenic formula by an automatic system. If only you knew, Georg, how tiring it is to be constantly afraid for his life: the sleepless nights, the relentless tears! Today I have a nanny looking after him. The little Crown Prince's health is good enough at this point to leave him unattended for a few hours. I am insanely happy that you invited me to the celebration, and for the fact that I had the chance for the first time in half a year to spend even one night out without fear and worry. Today I want to leave it all behind for the party atmosphere and ask kindly that you not stop me, even if I allow myself some extravagances and liberties."

"Verena, I understand your terms. Tonight you are free to do whatever you like. No one here will give you sideways looks or tell you off," I promised the beauty.

"Well, then I ask everyone to fill their glasses and drink to me finally being able to be confident in Tesse's future for the first time in a long time!" Verena, as hostess, toasted, kicking off the ceremonial evening.

The toast had something of a double meaning, and I didn't totally understand what Roben's wife meant. Either she was happy that her son's health had improved, or that the star system had been liberated from the Duke's appointees, or that I had become regent. In any case, the first toast broke through the dam of restraint and the joyful, riotous celebration began in earnest. The tables were laden with food and drinks, court musicians and jesters were entertaining the high-placed guests. Nearby, on an improvised stage, there were some girls dancing in bright-colored clothing.

Almost immediately, Bionica and Katerina ton Mesfelle found a place to sit together, far from everyone else and began talking secretly about something and clearly making an effort to keep it down when I came near. My cousin was only slightly sipping the wine and gave a practically full glass back to a servant that approached them, which spoke to the serious nature of her conversation with the android. I had already noticed that Katerina didn't allow herself even the slightest indulgence when she was conducting serious conversations.

Princess Astra, on the other hand, tried as actively as possible to participate in the celebration while also distinguishing herself among the many beauties that were also present. My favorite was joking, making toasts, laughing loudly at both her own and others' jokes, toasting with me to brotherhood and even trying to drag me off to dance. It would seem that the young inexperienced girl had gotten a bit out of her depth and overindulged, but I didn't keep the Princess from having her fun.

Astra, who was in just such a celebratory mood as Verena, called her to dance. Admiral Kheraisss Vej took advantage of the moment, came up to me, and asked to have a private conversation. I pointed the Alpha Iseyek to the park path that wound between the bushes, and we followed it until we were at a reasonable distance from the noisy crowd. The huge dark-colored praying mantis was carrying a glass of wine in each of his small arms, but I never saw the admiral take a drink.

"My Princcce, Swarm wanteded to ask I to finded out your plan. Ten ssstandard hours ago, Alien is attack Kej sssysssstem and capture without resissstanccce. Big ssshhhip with eggs alssso is dessstroy. Swarm think Alien not ssstay long in Kej. As sssoon as Alien finissshhh clear underground cities Swarm, Alien will go more far."

"Admiral, and why wasn't the Kej warp beacon

turned off if there really was a threat of Alien invasion?" Such negligence looked very strange. I had absolutely no idea how they could still be so careless.

"Princcce Georg, Swarm already many day is apply your method. Sssince when was capture Hnelle. Beacon Kej was yes turn off too. But thisss no stop Alien."

"I don't understand. How did the Alien ships get into a closed system?"

"Sssmall ssshhhip that is not to ssseee, come to sssee and ssstart beacon. Sssystem defender go kill frigate Alien and beacon extinguish. But very fassst whole fleet come and kill all. Is video, thisss episssode."

I stopped sharply. A cloaked Alien frigate had activated a beacon to make way for the invasion fleet? It was very unpleasant news. Who could guarantee now that the Aliens hadn't already sent out their invisible ships to every point in the Imperial transportation network? Even turning off all the warp beacons wouldn't stop an invasion fleet in that case.

"Admiral, I really need that video, as the changing tactics of the Aliens presents a threat to everything alive in both Imperial and Swarm territory. But, as for my plans, I am prepared to fulfill my obligations to the Iseyek. As soon as the situation around the Tesse star system clears up, the Sector Eight Fleet will head for Swarm territory. I will not guarantee that my fleet will fight with the Aliens or liberate even one of the systems, but I am preparing to study the situation from the front. If an opportunity to attack should present itself, I will absolutely make use of it. And also... Popori de Cacha!"

The Chameleon, who had only recently washed up and gotten his ability to camouflage himself back, appeared a step from me. The head of my guard was also holding a glass of wine in his hand, which he had learned to make go invisible with him.

"Popori de Cacha, I know that you are considered an influential authority among the Ravaash nation, and you are probably perfectly well informed on your species' affairs. Tell me, how much tantalum concentrate do you have ready for export on your planet, Sss? I suspect that after forty years of Orange House embargo and export difficulties, there should be a significant amount backed up..."

The Chameleon kept silent for a long time. I even started thinking Popori de Cacha might not know the answer. But, as it turned out, I was right again.

"After converting to units understood by people, there are around eight million tons of enriched tantalum concentrate ready for export. There are also finished armored plates for starships, and an enormous quantity of ore. Nevertheless, I ask the Prince to explain why an Orange House aristocrat would express such a strange interest. Does your Highness have the authority to overrule the Orange House court decision?"

"I cannot overrule it. Though, on the other hand, there's nothing stopping me from carrying it out to its logical conclusion and solving the many-year-long conflict. On my orders, Katerina ton Mesfelle looked into the old case. Based on what she found, the patent violation was just the formal reason for a financial attack on the Ravaash people. Duke Paolo royl Anjer then bought out all the Chameleon debts and right holders. It cost him around seven hundred thousand credits. But the greedy Duke's lawyers were really reaching for the stars when they levied such immeasurable fines against your nation that the debt with interest has reach such a level that it is enough to buy the whole Sss system and the neighboring Li Colony to go with it six times over. My cousin Katerina has been conversing with experienced lawyers, they looked over the court decision and discovered that the Duke, in trying to acquire the Sss system at any cost, was actually digging his own grave. The way the settlement was worded, it was 'to be paid to the official representative of the Orange House in the Sss system.' I suspect that the Duke was secretly planning on this being himself or an appointee.

But there's a great way out here: if the Ravaash race voluntarily agrees to join the Orange House of the Empire, formally paying off the penalty with their system, then the debt doesn't make any more sense, because the Orange House cannot owe money to itself. I will be the official Orange House viceroy. Well, maybe not me, but whatever Orange House representative I appoint. Right after that, the debt will be considered void, the situation regularized, and the restriction on ore export will be removed. Further, the Chameleons themselves will decide what to do with the strategically important materials, so necessary for the construction of any starship. If I were you, I would start exporting tantalum to the Iseyek. That would significantly speed up the construction of their huge ships. I'm sure the Swarm will find a way to pay for it. Everyone benefits: the Swarm will finish their starships ahead of schedule and save more egg clutches; the Ravaash will finally have the ability to trade after so many years of blockade; and I, as viceroy, will receive my share of the profits in the form of taxes that will now have to be paid as an Orange House system. I even agree to collect the taxes not in money, but armor plates or tantalum concentrate, as I need materials for building starships."

After my very radical proposal, a long silence lingered.

"Eight million tons of tantalum concentrate..." the praying mantis admiral was the first to break the silence. "Yes, that to be important for my nation. Swarm very buy thisss materyal. As fast as posssible to buy. At Imperial pricccesss that is sssomething... twell-ve billion credit. My nation have this people money for pay. But no ssshhhip for transssport this ore."

"I can find the necessary number of ore freighters," I promised. "And I can even arrange an armed convoy to get it to its destination with no issues. Now everything depends on the Chameleons. Popori de Cacha, I offer your nation protection from Duke Paolo royl Anjer's claims, the unblocking of all accounts, the end of a drawn-out conflict, and free trade. In return, the Ravaash race must officially become an Orange House vassal and declare me viceroy of the Sss star system. And another thing: I know that your kind suffers from a lack of inhabitable land. This is why I am prepared to give the Ravaash nation a large fertile island on Unatari in perpetual use, where you can live and raise your descendants."

Popori de Cacha went into "thinking" mode again

from the mental overexertion. And meanwhile, I took an incoming call. From the fleet headquarters, they informed me that *Warhawk-4* had returned from repair and that my daughter Likanna was on board. It turned out that they were able to jump to Tesse before the station security had obeyed my order to turn off the beacon.

"Tell the captain of *Warhawk-4*, Tamara Vuzhek, that I invite her to join the celebration. Let her and Lika head to Roben royl Inoky's flying palace. A shuttle is flying out for them now."

I signed off and looked back at the head of my guard. Popori de Cacha was standing with closed eyes as before, thinking over my unexpected proposition. Meanwhile, I had time to take one more call. It was the head of the Tesse Security Service, reporting to the new regent that all of Duke Paolo royl Anjer's appointees had been placed under arrest. Six hundred seventeen people had been apprehended. Finally, the Chameleon "turned back on."

**Standing change. Popori de Cacha's opinion of you has improved.**
**Presumed personal opinion of you: +82 (completely faithful)**

**Standing change. Chameleon race opinion of you has improved.**
**Chameleon race opinion of you: +13 (trusting)**

"My Prince, I do not have the authority to make a decision for the whole Ravaash nation. I will send your offer to our rulers. It is they who are to make such a heavy choice. But I think their decision will be positive. I have two important notes. First: you are not to allow the information about such a secret invitation to get out to strangers before the Sector Eight Fleet takes the Sss system under its protection. Otherwise, an Orange House fleet loyal to Duke Paolo royl Anjer will show up around the orbit of my planet in ten hours and my nation will be wiped out. As such, I demand that Admiral Kheraisss Vej make an official oath to keep this secret. If he does not, unfortunately, my subordinates will have to kill him."

Despite the threatening tone of the speech, the praying mantis didn't skip a beat, immediately chirping back something in his language. What he said, I did not understand, but the Chameleon immediately calmed down and even bowed in imitation of human body-language.

"My second note is directed at you, Crown Prince Georg royl Inoky. Yes, you personally enjoy high respect and trust among my species. Perhaps my race will consider you worthy to be our leader. But, excuse my directness, people are not immortal. What will happen to my kind when you die? Wouldn't Duke Paolo or some other close relative of his become viceroy of the Sss system? For my species, that would mean the end. These disgruntled aristocrats would never forgive us for making such an agreement with Crown Prince Georg."

"Popori de Cacha, it is up to you and your assistants to make sure my life will not end prematurely," I said, finding myself. "When my time as viceroy is up, my heir would be one of my children, or..." then I started thinking and smiled, having found an interesting option. "Or I will declare Miya the new viceroy. Knowing my Truth Seeker's reputation, no one in the Empire would even think about trying to lay claim to something that belongs to her."

It seemed that my brave bodyguard suddenly began cowering in fear.

"Better you, Crown Prince. Miya is not only frightening to Imperial citizens. While you and her were visiting Sss, the Truth Seeker made quite the strong impression on the rulers of the Ravaash race," the Chameleon admitted.

I laughed, took one of the admiral's two glasses, and the three of us loudly clinked a toast to reinforce our agreement.

* * *

"Dad! I missed you so much!" the young Princess ran up and jumped onto my shoulders, and I happily spun her around.

"Lika, have fun. You can have anything you like today in any amount, except wine."

A dark-haired, modest girl in a long, light-colored dress had come together with my daughter. I was somehow more accustomed to seeing the captain of *Warhawk-4* in the Orange House Space Fleet ceremonial uniform, to which I had already twice pinned medals for bravery, so I did not immediately recognize Tamara Vuzhek in civilian attire. I introduced everyone around to the best frigate captain in the whole fleet.

"My Prince, I think you have me confused with someone else," the girl laughed. "Your Highness only ever tells me how upset I'm making him, or threatens to rip out my still nonexistent male sexual organs, or promises to do something else I don't understand, which would also clearly be unpleasant."

"Lieutenant Vuzhek, you are wrong," Nicole Savoia commented forcefully. "In the last battle, the Crown Prince used you as an example for the rest and compared you with the legendary Maur Cassei. And he gave the other captains such a tongue-lashing that the staff officers even took notes so as not to forget any of the especially juicy expressions."

"Dad, does this mean you know how to swear?" Lika, who was sitting next to me, was honestly surprised.

"Of course not, the girls are just joking. It's fleet humor. You wouldn't get it." I could feel myself blushing.

When an alarm siren went off at that exact moment, I was forced to shudder in surprise. I suddenly answered an incoming message from the headquarters. There were panic and worry coming through in the officer's voice.

"My Prince, there has been an explosion of an unidentified but very powerful charge near the Tesse station! Some fleet ships have been quite badly damaged! Most frigates have lost energy shields! Red alert! The automatic cameras on *Joan the Fatty* have gone offline! Positioning systems have gone offline! The fleet headquarters is blind! We have no map of the battle!"

"Commander!" An unfamiliar voice joined in the conversation. "This is the captain of the battleship *Master of Tesse*, Anzor ton Art. Many instruments have been damaged, but our shields held out. Locating Alien ships in system! It's an unknown type of frigate! The ship is motionless!"

I yelled with my full voice:

"All ships, fire! Kill that bastard now before it turns on its thrusters and moves out to open a portal!"

A few tense seconds passed by, then Anzor ton Art reported:

"Mission accomplished. The Alien ship has been destroyed. We are detecting severe background radiation. Other than that, our instruments are reporting an unending stream of antimatter: positrons and anti-alphas. The source of the antimatter has been located. It is four hundred miles from the Tesse station. Approximately ninety miles from the wreckage of the Alien frigate."

"My Prince, we are detecting many new objects," I recognized the voice of Valian ton Corsa. "Computer analysis underway... One second... With an over ninety-six percent probability, we are observing the wreckage of the Alien battleship! A very strong beam of light from the epicenter of the explosion spoke to the ongoing nature of the antiparticle annihilation reaction. The light wave will reach the planet Tesse-III in twenty-two minutes. At such a distance, it will no longer be dangerous. And also... on the backdrop of all the chaos, the shredded remnants of all four tugs have also been identified. We will send out rescue teams to look for survivors."

"Crown Prince Georg, I know what happened!" one of the Chameleons stated, appearing before me.

I went with him a bit further from the alarmed

celebration guests and demanded that he tell me all he knew. The Chameleon began babbling very, very quickly:

"When we were searching the *Behemoth* on your Highness's order, we noticed huge empty halls next to the main cannon towers with no atmosphere. They contained a vacuum. It was in those halls, hanging in magnetic holders, that we saw many balls approximately three inches in diameter. Our instruments showed that these balls were made of antimatter. They were the cannon rounds for the *Behemoth*. We didn't risk getting closer to study the precariously balanced construction. There was too high a chance of upsetting something in that delicate balance. But before taking the battleship with them, the Emperor's messengers had to turn off the *Behemoth*'s warp drive, because the tugs wouldn't be able to haul a ship through an interspace tunnel with its drive turned on. Given that their experts did not have a diagram of the electrical grid and simply turned off the switches one after the other until they got to the warp drive, they may have turned off something they shouldn't have that made the antimatter arsenal unstable. And when the ship went into warp, one of the gaseous antimatter balls touched a wall and..."

As a matter of fact, it sounded logical. The terrifying blast set off a series of smaller explosions of super-powered antimatter shells flying in all directions, which destroyed the Alien ship together with the tugs. But I still didn't quite understand about the frigate we had detected in Tesse. In any case, I had a confirmation of the theory that cloaked

Alien frigates could already be in many systems and tracking the activity of humans, the Iseyek, and their other enemies. The Alien cloaked frigate was too close to the calculated exit point of the tugs from Tesse and had been seriously damaged, which turned off its cloaking system. Well, alright then. We got lucky that time with the Alien frigate. But what had happened to the battleship was vexing...

I spoke clearly and loudly so all my unseen bodyguards would hear:

"The Emperor will be frightfully upset at the loss of such a valuable trophy and even more so if he learns that the Chameleons didn't warn his messengers of the risk. So, not a word to anyone about the halls of flying spheres. Our official version will be as follows: the Alien frigate purposely approached the tugged battleship and somehow blew up the captured ship, itself also going down in the explosion."

**Standing change. Chameleon race opinion of you has improved.**
**Chameleon race opinion of you: +14 (trusting)**

A call came in on my communicator. On the line was Admiral Kiro Sabuto.

"My Prince, I received a message from headquarter saying that warp beacons have just been turned off at the Orange House Capital, the Docks, and Nessi."

"Nothing to be surprised at," I chuckled. "The explosion by the station and message about the arrival of Alien ships to Tesse must have frightened the Duke. And he finally decided to follow our lead and turned off his warp beacons. By the way, order that awful alarm signal turned off. Everything has calmed down. The celebration can continue. And we will all prepare to observe a rare occurrence in eighteen minutes. For several seconds, a second sun will rise in the sky from the direction of the Tesse station."

* * *

The burst of light was a bit of a letdown. Instead of the bright star in the night sky I had been expecting, all that came in was a message from the Tesse Security Service on a temporary rise in background radiation, which was not dangerous to people. The guests calmed down, and the celebration went on. I, combining business and pleasure, introduced myself to many of my older brother's ministers and agreed on buying equipment for building an orbital elevator in Unatari and an orbital metal processing complex. I also booked all available ore freighters in the Tesse system for the next three weeks.

The celebration was gradually coming to an end. The three admirals bid their farewells, explaining that they were needed in the fleet. They had to evaluate the damage taken by the ships and send the damaged ones in for repair. It was already the very end of the party when a slightly drunk Kiro Sabuto told me his "big secret:" that by his order, my assistant Nicole Savoia would be promoted to the rank of space lieutenant.

"Many in the fleet don't like being told what to do

by a lower-ranking officer. They won't express their annoyance out loud to the fleet commander, but a dissatisfied murmur has been heard. So, she's in for a surprise when she gets back to *Joan the Fatty*."

The admiral was standing literally six feet from Nicole, but clearly didn't notice her there. He bid farewell to me, and hurried to the shuttle as it was preparing to take off. The Tesse ministers and a large part of the guests left with the admirals. I sat down next to Nicole, who had grown embarrassed at having overheard the conversation, and filled her glass.

"Congratulations. You have truly earned this promotion with your knowledge and actions in battle."

"Thank you, my Prince. I am really touched. I must admit to you that I got an offer yesterday from the Imperial Joint Chiefs about a permanent position with them. I was promised fast promotions. They want me to give constant courses on new tactics for small and medium-sized fleets. I was going to say 'no.'"

"Of course. And I wouldn't have let you go. I prefer to keep such a skilled assistant to myself," I laughed. "To my mind, you are the most capable of all the staff tactics officers, so you have every legal right to be a fleet commander's assistant, though such a position usually requires a rank no lower than space major. And also, there are plenty of new tactics for you to see yet. Just wait a few weeks..."

We went silent as Tamara Vuzhek walked by the table, speaking enthusiastically with my daughter Likanna. I noticed how much attention Nicole was paying to the frigate captain' breasts. I suspect that it wasn't only about their size (though that was a possibility), but also about the two medals Tamara had earned for bravery in battle. It seemed that Nicole's lack of combat medals other than the Silver Brooch, which anyone who took part in a battle was given, was a very delicate topic, all the more so after my other assistant, a simple android translator, had received an Emerald Star, a very honorable Imperial order.

"I won't promise any medals," I said, and she noticeably shuddered. I really had guessed her thoughts. "But you will definitely gain new knowledge and skills. After that you'll be able to rise in rank even faster there, given that such a position requires a larger number of stars on your collar."

"Crown Prince, you are reading my thoughts, that's not fair!" said the girl, somewhat spooked.

"A good commander must know what makes his subjects tick. Otherwise, how can he meet their expectations?" I smiled, satisfied at the effect produced.

Astra came up to us with Tamara Vuzhek and my daughter. I noticed that my favorite had already managed to swig down quite a bit of booze and was having trouble staying on her feet.

"Dad, I want to show my palace to Princess Astra and aunty Tamara. Can I?" Likanna asked. At that moment, the girl's eyes were reminiscent of the begging cat from Shrek.

My daughter clearly wanted to show off in front of her new acquaintances. And, after all, why not?

"Alright. But take Beston Maf and Nicole Savoia with you too. They're also very young and will be interested in the palace and the yacht and everything you have. And catch Phobos and Deimos, too.

Otherwise, the praying mantises will soon burst from overeating. I give you all two days to have fun. On the morning of the third day, I expect to see you on *Joan the Fatty*."

Lika gave a squeal of joy and ran to drag the praying mantis from the table to get everyone on the shuttle quickly before her dad had a change of mind. I then turned to my assistant, who was clearly surprised at my decision:

"Space Lieutenant Nicole Savoia, this is an order from your fleet commander: rest and have fun for two days! And also, as senior officer, keep an eye on them. Then, with Lika's immeasurable enthusiasm and Astra's limitless imagination, these two princesses will not only repaint the castle but turn all of Tesse on its head."

"It will be done, your Highness," my assistant smiled before hurrying off after the others.

I searched with my eyes for remaining party guests. Only Bionica and Katerina remained, whispering together in the secluded alcove as before. Everyone else had gone. Perhaps it was also time for me to get back to *Joan the Fatty*. I turned to walk toward the far-off shuttle, but I was suddenly called out to by Verena:

"Crown Prince Georg, just where do you think you're getting off to? Music is still playing; the fun isn't over. There's still a ton of interesting stuff prepared just for your Highness: exposition gladiator matches in the small arena, races with riders on exotic animals, and an exhibit of living statues, created by geneticists. And also, you are now regent, and your status dictates that you be furnished with apartments in the palace. Another thing, Crown Prince, if you leave, that will be the end of what for me is a very rare moment of celebration. You wouldn't want to make a lady sad, would you?"

In fact, I didn't want the night to be over yet either, which is why I turned and approached Verena. Roben's wife took me by the hand, and we slowly walked through the nighttime park paths.

"How I envy you, Georg! Today you're in Unatari, tomorrow the Throne World, the next day Tesse, the Orange House Capital or Fastel. A bunch of adventures, a ton of new faces, an aura of glory and power shining above your head... You are free to go where you please, do what you please, and no one can tell you otherwise. Ugh... You don't even know the meaning of the word 'boredom,' when you have to languish cooped up in the same old place, and you're already nauseous at seeing the same old faces."

We walked up to the table and took a glass of wine each.

"My only entertainment in the last months has been collecting exotic marine shells from the crustaceans of various planets. I've actually built up quite the collection. Let's go. I'll show you my collection. You're gonna love it!" Verena was pulling me toward the palace.

We walked in procession through the luxury-saturated halls and ended up in a small room before a closed door. Verena took a surprisingly long time fidgeting with the old-fashioned bronze key hanging from a chain on her neck.

"It's a stiff lock. You couldn't possibly help a lady open it, could you? Set your glass down here for now so it won't get in the way," the beauty suggested, pointing to a small table.

I set the wine glass down and turned, ready to take the key from Verena's hand. And suddenly, at that moment, Popori de Cacha appeared before my face, sharply jumping to the side and grabbing something invisible. There were a few seconds of unexplained bustle after that, and my bodyguard straightened up.

"Crown Prince Georg, one of my tribesmen just threw a capsule into your wine, possibly poison."

The head of my bodyguard took a strange, flat flashlight from his belt and turned it on. The room lit up an unnatural shade of violet, and I suddenly noticed the large number of Chameleons in the tiny room. They were everywhere: on the walls, on the floor, even on the ceiling. I counted six members of the Ravaash race, one of which was being held down spread-eagle on the floor by two others.

"That is Kupi de, one of the bodyguards given to your brother," Popori de Cacha pointed at his immobilized compatriot. "Now he is subject only to Roben royl Inoky and his wife. I have no more power over him."

"Verena, how should I understand this?" I sharply turned to the lady of the palace. "Recently, I have become quite familiar with the Chameleons' behavior. Kupi-de wouldn't act alone. Did you order him to poison me?"

"Not poison. This is something else..." Verena got a small, flat box out of her bodice and gave it to me. Inside there were a few tablets rolling around.

I read the name of the drug and called up the

interactive menu. Aphrodisiac, male potency enhancer? Why? In that time, the woman had managed to open the door with her little key. There was no shell collection behind the door at all. It was the bedroom.

"All Chameleons go out into the hall and wait there! Verena, we need to have a serious talk."

The stunning dark-haired lady got slightly embarrassed at her plans having been revealed, went into the room, waited for me to follow and closed the door. A second later, Verena's white dress had fallen to her knees. The naked dark-haired beauty was carelessly stepping over her clothes and turned to me:

"Yes, Crown Prince Georg. What did you want to talk about?"

If Verena was trying to bewilder or seduce me, she had missed the mark. The only thing I was feeling now was extreme annoyance and anger. I didn't at all like when others tried to manipulate me.

"I'm waiting for your explanation," I reminded the woman.

"Georg, what could I possibly say here?" Verena wondered, trying to get closer and using a playful voice, before quickly realizing it wasn't working.

I took a few steps back, not allowing myself to touch her. Roben's wife stopped and, looking me straight in the eyes, began speaking:

"Alright, your Highness. I will be as serious and honest as I can. I'm so scared after the Tesse ministers appointed you regent that my knees are shaking. I suggested that they name me temporary ruler, but they didn't go for it. Of course, they were shook up by the star fleet orbiting the planet;

otherwise, my gifts would have done the trick. Now you are regent, and my son's position is very shaky. Mine, though, might as well be on a fault line. My son and I are totally at your Highness's mercy, and though Georg Junior may be needed alive for some time to legitimize your rule on Tesse, you don't need me at all. That's why I was trying to raise my importance in the eyes of your Highness. The child that would have resulted from our liaison would have been considered Roben's by everyone else and would become legal ruler of Tesse on reaching legal age. And it is of no small importance that any genetic tests would confirm that he really is a Mesfelle and has genes very similar to Roben's."

"And what would you have done when Roben came back?" I wondered, curious.

"So, you're letting him come back then?" an evil smirk appeared on Verena's lips. "If I were to become regent, my husband would never make it back to Tesse-III alive, even if he were released from the Orange House prison. Insofar as I understand, your Highness is also not a slow thinker and would not refuse such a treasure falling so easily into his lap. That is why my offer remains valid. The very rich planet and I myself will completely belong to your Highness, and in sixteen years and nine months, Tesse-III will be given to our child, a Crown Prince or Crown Princess by title. That's for fate to decide. And the drug I got just in case, so there wouldn't be any unforeseen complications. Everyone knows, after all, that Crown Prince Georg royl Inoky was a mystic not too long ago..."

"You thought everything through, Verena. Except

my brother Roben will return and will be arriving safely on Tesse-III, and no one will be able to stop him from taking power back into his own hands."

I stopped, already half way out the door and turned to the frozen naked beauty:

"Don't worry, Roben will never find out about our conversation or your offer. Understand, Verena. You are an insanely beautiful woman, and under different circumstances I would agree. But I will never do anything to hurt my own brother."

I didn't stay for any shows or gladiator matches. The shuttle took me straight back to *Joan the Fatty*, and I went to my cabin. The screen on the wall was showing the final result of the auction for Astra's picture: forty-seven million credits. I was glad for my favorite, that she had found her calling in life. But I myself was feeling lonely and empty. Verena wouldn't get out of my head. Maybe it was stupid to refuse such a tempting offer from such a beautiful woman?

I sat for ten minutes in solemn thought and decided to turn on my communicator and call my butler:

"Bryle, bring a pair of glasses and a bottle of good sparkling wine to my cabin."

Then I called the beautiful officer that had earlier made an unambiguous remark on a potential future meeting:

"Valian ton Corsa, I suggest we go over an offer you once made right now and in great detail."

# ELDER FEMALE

ROBEN ARRIVED three days after the feast. He was haggard, pale, and had huge bags under his eyes. He didn't look at all like himself. I greeted my older brother at the Tesse orbital docks, where the repair and modernization of my ships had been completed.

"I watched the live broadcast of the trial," I told Roben. "I still haven't figured out what the Orange House prosecutor was hoping for with such worthless accusations."

"Oh, that," my brother said, waving it off in annoyance. "By that time, everything had already been settled for almost a day. Five billion to the Orange House head, and I was set free to go back home. The trial was just theater for the public, so it would look like I had been detained and subsequently found innocent."

Roben went silent, looking over the huge battleship Master of Tesse through the thick armored glass. It had once been his own flagship but was now part of the Perimeter Sector Eight Fleet. I supposed that my brother would resent that and demand I return his ship, but he didn't mention it.

"How'd you get along here without me, brother dear?" the ruler of the star system wondered instead.

"One step at a time. I loaded down your manufacturing sector and got to know your ministers. And on my honor, I paid a fair price for everything. I didn't offend anyone. And now I'm preparing an expedition to Swarm territory. In ten hours, the fleet will be ready to set off."

"And how are Verena and the boy getting along?" Despite the reduced gravity at the orbital docks, Roben's legs were already getting tired, so he pulled up a chair and took a seat.

"They're fine. Your wife is waiting for you in the palace. To be honest, we messed up the lawn a bit. We had a massive party to celebrate the liberation of Tesse from the Duke's appointees."

"Think nothing of it, brother dear. And the battleship doesn't mean shit, either. I thought it would be worse... They tried stubbornly in the interrogations to force the idea into my head that the new regent would never allow me to return and that my starship simply had no chance of reaching home unharmed. If it hadn't been for little Millena, who supported my faith in humanity, I probably would have given in and agreed to work together with the Orange House Head... To be perfectly honest, they almost convinced me that everyone around me was constantly thinking of ways to get rid of me!"

"Now, how could you think that, Roben?! Everyone here on Tesse could think of nothing but your return the whole time. I was only appointed regent until your return, and now, today, I'm already giving your star system right back to you and flying off to another one. Your beautiful wife missed you very much. She wants to share some excellent news about your son's health. But make sure to throw her a party every once and a while. Verena gets bored cooped up in the castle..."

Roben suddenly covered his face with his hands and began to sob. The huge fat man had three streams of tears running down his face and couldn't stop them. In order not to embarrass him further with my presence, I bid farewell to my brother and set off for Joan the Fatty.

On the cruiser, there was a small scandal waiting for me. First, after returning to the ship, Princess Astra had noticed traces of my romp in the cabin: a pair of thin leggings that Valian had forgotten. She hadn't been able to find them, but Astra had, in the bathroom inside a wall cabinet that she considered hers. There was also an unfinished bottle of wine in there.

Second, Crown Princess Likanna then found Astra walking around my personal cabin like she owned the place without the slightest bit of shame, and despite her young years, was able to figure out what was going on. Of course it is strange, but it never occurred to my daughter over her three days of talking to Astra to think about the Princess's status in my retinue. And now, both Princesses had been patiently awaiting my return for several hours on the cruiser so that they could turn up the hysterics even higher together.

The main problem lied in the fact that I would have to get my daughter out of the room to have a talk with Astra and vice versa. But neither of the Princesses would voluntarily leave my cabin. I decided not to fall back on the foolproof method of using Phobos and Deimos to carry the Princesses out kicking and screaming. So, making an excuse about my presence being needed at headquarters, I hurried to leave the room.

The fleet was preparing for a long warp. There were messages coming in about systems coming online, technicians verifying network connections, thrusters and energy storage. There was some trouble caused by the seventy ore freighters I was preparing to take to Sss with the fleet, in that civilian ships couldn't understand the concept of things like discipline and responsibility. Out of seventy total, only fifteen had already fully assembled their crews, and twenty of them were still missing their captains. And that's fifty minutes before takeoff!

Finally, I found someone to take out my pent-up annoyance on! I ordered a mixed team of human and Iseyek assault soldiers sent out to all of the offending freighters with the goal of maintaining order and determining whether the best method of convincing that particular crew to follow the Crown Prince's orders in good time was negotiation or force. I don't know how, and I don't want to, but the soldiers managed to force the lazy civilians to move their butts, and all I heard from it were some echoes of the reeducation campaign:

*Global fame increase. Current value +12*

*Global standing decrease. Current value -26*

*Standing change. Empire Military faction opinion of you has improved.*
*Presumed personal opinion of you: +10 (trusting)*

*Standing change. Blue house opinion of you has worsened:*
*Presumed personal opinion of you: -2 (indifferent)*

*Global standing decrease. Current value -27*

Finally, a message came in from Colonel Gor ton Vulf, recruited on Tesse just two days earlier. The huge, graying heavyweight, a native of a planet with elevated gravity, had appealed to me in that he had combat medals, an excellent service record, and knew the language of the Iseyek. A personal conversation had only confirmed my initial impression, and I appointed the colonel to lead all my fleet's human landing groups.

"My Prince, all ore-ships are ready for takeoff. We had an explanatory conversation with the crews that were especially disobedient. I can assure your Highness that none of the crews will be causing further delays."

"Were there civilian casualties?" I clarified just in case, surprised at the fairly significant fall in my personal standing.

"Nothing serious, my Prince. No one died. But we had to bring order, which meant overlooking the aristocratic origin of some of the captains. Some objected. But not for long."

I approved the colonel's harsh methods in bringing order. That uncontrollable band of good-for-nothings really had to be reined in right away. Otherwise, while moving from system to system by warp beacon, which appear for mere seconds at a time, a lack of discipline would threaten separating my fleet into many unconnected, uncontrollable parts.

The communications officer informed me of an incoming call from the Fastel system. I winced in anticipation. Every time I spoke with Marta, I was left with a very unpleasant taste in my mouth. But there was nothing to be done. I ordered her put through.

"Georg, you have completely lost your mind!" I wasn't fast enough at switching over to headphones, and the woman's hysterical cry rang out for the whole headquarters. "Lika just called me. You've built yourself a real den of iniquity! Your many lovers are having catfights and arguing about their relationships with you right in front of my daughter! That crosses all boundaries!"

I muted the volume and waited patiently until the chubby lady with golden hair stopped jerking angrily, gesticulating and flapping her lips. Four minutes later, my wife calmed down. I turned the sound back on.

"And what did you want to tell me? Sorry, I just forgot to turn the sound on," I wondered in a totally normal tone.

On screen, Marta was just sucking air in indignation; however, she did not repeat her hateful speech. Leaving a short pause and calming down slightly, my wife said:

"Georg, I ask you to send my daughter Likanna to Fastel as quickly as possible. There is no reason whatsoever for the girl to be talking with loose women from your society. And Lika's school vacations will be over soon, and I'd like to spend some time with her myself."

"You should have asked for it like that right away, in a normal tone, without your traditional hysterics, which do you no favors, Marta. I'll bring our daughter to the Li system myself in three days. I will not come to Fastel. My combat fleet coming to the system would cause a bad reaction with the rulers and make my crews expect a fight. After all, your father was one of the first to vote in favor of Duke Paolo royl Anjer. My fleet will leave after that, and the Kingdom of Fastel can continue in its close relationship with the Orange House Capital."

"What is this I hear? Since when is it that you started refusing my Kingdom? Or is that your covert way of asking my father for money? Or maybe you need our cruisers for your fleet?"

I was tired of shaking my head. It was the same old song...

"Marta, I already told you that times have changed, but you still haven't realized it. There are fourteen star systems under my control, and I have absolutely no need for money. What are two million measly credits a month from the Kingdom of Fastel to me now? A few days ago, I gave the Sector Seven Fleet Commander almost a billion and a half of my personal money as a gift to buy new ships for his fleet! Marta, I have three hundred starships in my fleet, including a huge mothership, two battleships and over fifty cruisers. So your three cruisers would do nothing to change the situation, all the more so given that your crews would be significantly behind mine in level of preparation and battle experience. You can keep your money and ships. I don't need anything from you at all."

Marta was clearly thrown off and couldn't hide her bewilderment. Then a message came in totally unexpectedly that Marta royl Valesy had improved her personal opinion of me by ten points to minus fifty-three. I chuckled sadly:

"It's too late, Marta. You spent so many years picking at my brain and trying to mix my name up in dirt, that such naive flattery can do nothing to fix it now. Where were you when my fleet defeated the pirates in Hnelle and Unatari? Why was it not my wife but a random favorite next to me during the death-defying capture of the Alien battleship? Why was my wife's place next to me at ceremonial events always left empty? Why have you and your Kingdom taken the side of my enemies in the conflict with the far-away Duke? That's what you need to think about now, not trying to buy me off with your Kingdom's money..."

In response, I got a stream of nonsense. I didn't listen to it and ended the call. No, it turns out you couldn't change Marta after all. The image of the other Crown Prince George was stuck too stubbornly in her memory, a man who gave in to anyone and was willing to tolerate any number of insults and slights just for a pitiful allowance from the Kingdom of Fastel.

$$* * *$$

When I returned to my cabin, Likanna and Astra were sitting together on the couch and watching a children's cartoon. In front of them was a little table of pastries that had already been practically eaten up by the two Princesses. The girls did not react to my appearance.

"Astra, I ordered an identical cabin be made available to you with a picture window. You can draw your masterpieces there and not have to worry about other peoples' things lying around in your cabinets."

"But, Crown Prince Georg, I have no problem with that," the Princess answered.

"Dad, let Astra stay here. It's fun with her!" my daughter declared unexpectedly.

"No, Lika. I don't want to hear from your mom again that I've got a den of iniquity here and am poisoning your young psyche by letting you talk with lecherous women."

"I'm the lecherous woman then?!" Astra inquired, getting indignant and raising her voice. "Lika, I've only kissed your father one time. I can hardly be called a Crown Prince's favorite. I'm a laughing stock. It's even uncomfortable to be around aristocrats. I am a grown woman, and yet your father treats me like a baby!"

No, I definitely didn't understand them. My daughter was making a ruckus about me being close with Astra, and now she's demanding I let her stay. Astra is indignant that I treat her like a baby, but her way of expressing that is like an unreasonable child. I flopped down on the sofa next to the Princess, tired, and managed to grab the last pastry from the plate.

"By the way, where is your painting?" I had just discovered that the easel that had held the painting was gone.

"It's all over. I sent the painting to the buyer. He has already transferred the money. Me and Lika were talking, and I decided to send all the money from the sale to the creators of the TV show Jeanne the Star Traveler so they can make a new season. Isn't that cool?"

I closed my eyes and counted to ten.

"Yeah, cool. A 'grown woman' spending her money like that…"

But Astra didn't notice the hints of mockery in my voice and became earnestly filled with joy that I approved of her decision. I just waved it off:

"Kindergarten, underwear on suspenders… Alright, Astra. What else can I do? Stay here in my cabin. I'll order another bed put in by the wall, then give Lika to her mother. You can sleep on her bed. And for now, both of you let me rest for at least five hours before the ship gets to Himora. My wife has pecked out all my brains. She has her own perception of what Astra being a grown woman means…"

But I was barely able to lie down when a message came in from Doctor Nicosid Brandt:

"My Prince, you asked me to tell you when Flora woke up from her crystal sleep. She's being fed and washed now."

I stood, leaving the two Princesses to keep watching cartoons, and set off for the starship's hospital wing. The old doctor asked me to wait another few minutes while he got the paralyzed girl ready to meet with me after four days of sleep. I was finally allowed in.

Florianna was half-sitting and half-lying on an antigravity bed hovering above the floor. The girl was dressed in a black robe that covered her body completely, even her hands and feet. The Truth Seeker's head was obscured by a hood. I smiled. The game designers hadn't put too much work into this and had simply plagiarized this dark outfit from the Sith warriors of Star Wars.

"An impressive sight. Should we just go straight to Darth Flora, or is Darth Veyerde better?" I couldn't hold in the nervous laughter. The names just sounded too funny. "How are you feeling after the crystals?"

"I'm not sure yet. It's as if I just learned a very important lesson, but the teacher was speaking an unfamiliar language. Like there are thousands of possibilities, but you can't grasp onto any of them... I need to grow and learn more to be able to use them."

"This can't have been so necessary, Flora? Crystals have a very bad effect on the body."

"I couldn't be any worse off than I am now. That's why I agreed without hesitation when the Dark Mother's servants suggested I become a Mystic. But I'll figure that out later. For now, explain to me, Crown Prince Georg: how do I manage all this? A bunch of windows, some menus, a map, help..."

"What?" I looked carefully at Flora and discovered with surprise that I could now call up a popup on her:

*Florianna Blidge (Veyerde)*
*Age: 13*
*Race: Human*
*Gender: Female*

*Class: Mystic*
*Achievements: Survived Truth Seeker Attack,*
*Paralyzed in Combat*
*Fame: 1*
*Standing: 0*
*Presumed personal relationship: Unknown*

How can this be? An NPC had become a player. That can't be possible, can it? Or maybe someone decided that the character would be interesting to play and chose to be the paralyzed girl?

"The doctor said that while I was asleep, there were two microcameras sewn into my eyes and an implant put into my brain. I woke up, my nose was itching like crazy, my eyelids hurt, and I couldn't blink. There's always some kind of flashing in my eyes. How do you manage all this?"

Geeze. I can't believe this new player is covertly trying to get me to explain the rules of the game! This will be an interesting experience for us both. I'd be glad to teach him (or more likely her) to use the game interface.

"Flora, watch and listen. It's not as hard as it seems. In the main menu, you can open a map of the current room, call up popups on objects or words, see the big guide, call up the standing menu..."

\* \* \*

"What's new in the game?" As usual, Mr. G.I. appeared in my dream exactly when I needed sleep the worst and could think of nothing else.

"I had a run-in with Duke Paolo royl Anjer and even, they say, offended him..."

"That's nonsense. There's just no way of talking normally with Paolo. He's pathologically greedy," Georgiy interrupted me and, it seemed, strongly underestimated what I had meant by a "run-in" with the Duke, supposing it had just been a normal argument.

I decided not to disenchant him of that notion and tried to change the topic.

"Miya came to me in a dream."

"Miya?! And what could that creature have possibly wanted?" the new topic aroused the most vivacious interest in my employer.

"She said that I had grown inadvisably close with another Truth Seeker and had to be taught a lesson. After that, Miya maimed a little girl, depriving her of the gift of speech and paralyzing her forever."

"That sounds like Miya, yes. But, I apologize, I'm totally on Miya's side here. Getting too close with Truth Seekers is dangerous for you. They can read thoughts you know. Sure, you may not believe in it but, believe me, it's true!"

"What makes you say that? Of course I believe in it," I began, going over the topic in detail once again.

"And did Miya happen to say where she's living now? Perhaps she left her address for me?" some hope slipped through in his voice.

"I didn't get an address. But, based on what I saw, I can say that she's near a warm sea. The climate was hot, and there were grape vines growing."

"What a bitch! She sure got sick of the February cold in Moscow quick. She and I had been planning to go somewhere in Cyprus or Greece together. It looks like she took off down there on her own... What a sleazebag! I can't even go out on the street here. There's snow and ice, rivers of meltwater in the streets, and mud up to your ears. What really gets you, though, is the head colds. And she's lounging around at resorts! Well, alright. You probably don't care about this at all. Ruslan, if something really interesting happens in the game, you can tell me later. And as for me, I'm gonna throw back some water to ward off a cold..."

The reeducation campaign undertaken by the colonel on the ore freighter crews had been to good effect. All the freighters came along together with the Sector Eight Fleet. They caught the beacon in the two seconds it was on and came to charge at the stations along the way in a timely and precise manner. Without the slightest problem, the fleet followed along the chain of beacons and arrived at the Li Colony star system.

Unlike uninhabitable systems with automatic warp beacons, there was a small colony in the Li system with two hundred people who lived under a transparent dome on the surface of a huge ice comet. It had once been a prison colony for only the most hardened criminals. Being sent to Li was the equivalent of life in prison without parole for an Orange House citizen. Those times came to an end in Leta when the watchdog police station placed to keep the colony in check with especially harsh measures was destroyed by a Swarm fleet during the war with the Iseyek. The colony itself was not touched by the insects, who thought it would be doomed without food and fuel imports coming in.

The Iseyek were wrong though. The people on the surface of the ice comet survived despite the extremely harsh conditions, starvation and freezing temperatures. The prisoners started extracting the methane and oxygen that were frozen into the ice, using the solar batteries and other equipment that had fallen to the surface from the station. And they were even able to track Swarm ships in the system, and sent that valuable reconnaissance to the Orange House fleet. When, after fifteen years of occupation, people were able to reconquer the Li Colony, there were no more than fifteen haggard inhabitants remaining alive at the frozen station. Despite receiving amnesty, the former prisoners refused to leave their base and began establishing a population of free citizens with their own tiny space port. Several times a year, private trading spaceships came here, and the colonists were able to trade the high-deuterium and - tritium oxygen to them in exchange for what they needed to survive.

While my ships recharged, I decided to take a look at this harsh ice world and meet its inhabitants. I had to don a space suit over my shoulders, which were still itching after the two Princesses' art session. On my left shoulder, Astra, as she had planned, spiked me with a three-eyed skull flanked with a flourishing pattern. On my right shoulder, Lika tried to paint Joan the Fatty. But my daughter didn't have the artistic ability, so Astra had to put another black, three-eyed skull over the weird, angular starship, making it even more sinister than the one on the left.

And then a passenger-freight shuttle, filled with containers of food and equipment, touched down on a small, cleaned-off pad near the entrance to the tunnel that led under the dome. We had to walk very carefully. Our bodies were practically hovering due to the near total lack of gravity. The leader of the colony, a man named Janek, met us in the tunnel beyond the air-lock. He was a middle-aged man bundled up in fur clothing. He immediately invited me to his office.

"That's just about the last thing I expected to see here on this icy world. A member of the upper aristocracy!" Janek exclaimed, not hiding his surprise.

The first thing the local leader did was open a safe and retrieve a bottle he had stashed there.

"The alcohol regime here is strict. Only for the very biggest celebrations. With this climate and such low gravity, alcohol puts you on your ass in a second. And the people here are sturdy. They can get things done under unreasonable conditions, which is why liquor is forbidden – except for the most important celebrations: the birth of a child or midsummer, when our comet goes by the Li star, the ice on the glass melts, and the water boils here due to the low pressure."

Popori de Cacha appeared and inserted a thin straw unceremoniously into my glass. The Chameleon checked something only he could understand on his palmtop device connected to the straw and, without saying a word, nodded to me before slipping back into his camouflage. I thought that Janek would be surprised, but the leader of the colony took the sudden appearance of the Chameleon with utter calm, clearly evidence of his system's proximity to Sss.

"To the arrival of such an important guest!" Janek toasted, drinking his glass in a gulp.

I was expecting it to put some hair on my chest, with a strength at least as high as absinthe or even pure grain alcohol, but it was just wine in the glass, though fortified. Janek, on the other hand, having thought the welcoming host's mission accomplished, wondered directly:

"So, your Highness, I am prepared to hear your offer. After all, clearly such a busy man wouldn't make such a long journey just for a swallow of wine, right?"

"Indeed, Janek. I'll tell you directly: I'm interested in acquiring this star system and the loyalty of the station's inhabitants. Understand, I could take it all by force, but I do not need the glory of a boorish conqueror, when I could solve everything peacefully instead. My offer would be to declare that you will not accept anyone else as star system holder other than myself or people appointed by me. Do not try to interfere in the working of the warp beacon, and stop telling Duke Paolo about all ships that come to the system."

On my last phrase, Janek lowered his eyes. It wasn't hard to guess that Duke Paolo royl Anjer had already been informed of my fleet's arrival. Well, alright. My subjects had already turned off the Li Colony warp beacon, so the head of the Orange House could do nothing but fume in impotent rage.

"Alright, Prince Georg, I have understood your demands. My price is ten million credits for the star system and thirty new settlers for the station. No less than twenty of them women. We have a serious lack here."

"I'll give you twenty-five million credits. That'll be enough for you to pay for thousands of women to come work here in all kinds of professions. I have just brought fifty androids with me on the shuttle, packed and ready, and thirty of them are female. They are all set up with twenty-year contracts, so you'll have skilled workers living here for a long time..."

Based on how Janek's eyes lit up, I figured out that I had guessed right bringing the androids. We clapped our hands together, and soon I received an official certificate signed by the local powers that I was the holder of the Li star system. Yes, Duke Paolo royl Anjer could deny my rights to the Li star system all he wanted, but I had little to worry about now: in one way or another I had become the ruler of the system linking the Chameleons, the Swarm and my capital Unatari.

I had barely returned to Joan the Fatty and come out of the shuttle when a message came in from headquarters:

"Commander, the Kingdom of Fastel fleet has entered the system. Shall I sound the combat alert?"

I thought I had only invited one ship that was to bring my daughter to her mother on Fastel-XI – which is why I hurried into the fleet headquarters. The Kingdom of Fastel was on Duke Paolo royl Anjer's side, so formally we were enemies.

"Two hundred fifty miles to the enemy. It's a

group of targets. Forty marks on the radar. They're returning correct friend-foe codes. It's the full first fleet of the Kingdom of Fastel. Three heavy assault cruisers: one Flamberg, one Katana, one Yataghan. Three light Thrush cruisers, five Flycatcher destroyers and twenty-nine Pyro frigates. Enemy flagship determined: the Katana by the name Fastel Beauty."

"Realignment into battle formation is nearly complete!" I took my place at the console and took over control of the fleet. "Both battleships, advance. Twenty heavies go with them. Electros and anti-support, put on your brakes and stay twenty-five behind the heavies. Frigates, get ready. Your mission is to blast off suddenly and catch the cruisers on my command."

"Crown Prince, incoming call from Fastel Beauty."

"All ships, continue approach!" When we get to one hundred twenty out, the frigates will jump in front and capture everything valuable. But do not open fire first! I repeat, do not open fire! Put me on with their flagship."

A gray-haired, and very, very well fed man appeared on screen. That's the guy: the King of Fastel himself. I could remember the way the fat drooped down around his eyes from studying family pictures!

***Valesy royl Pir ton Fastel, ruler of the star kingdom of Fastel***
   ***Age: 78***
   ***Race: Human***
   ***Gender: Male***
   ***Class: Aristocrat***
   ***Achievements: (see Attachment)***

*Fame: +5*

*Standing: + 19*

*Presumed personal opinion of you: -25 (strong dislike)*

*Kingdom of Fastel's opinion of you: -13 (dislike)*

"Crown Prince Georg, I'm glad to see you at the borders of the Kingdom of Fastel," declared the fat man, though I didn't notice any happiness in his body language.

"I cannot answer you in kind, dear father-in-law," I honestly admitted. "The fact that the King himself is on the flagship has upset my plans.

To be honest, I remember these ships from when they were in my own fleet. If you had been not the monarch, but just some admiral, I really would have attacked and captured or destroyed these ships, as they are my formal enemies. And what's more, I would have been legally justified in having done so. You invaded the Li Colony system without being invited, and I have been its ruler for just going on forty minutes now." Yes, the pretext was stretched quite thin, but it served perfectly well as a casus belli.

Clearly, the attack would be canceled now – a direct assault on the ruler of a Kingdom allied to the Orange House would be equivalent to aggression against the very Empire or Emperor himself. I called off the frigates, which had already jumped out in front and brought his fleet to a stop.

"Crown Princess Likanna is ready for her trip to the Kingdom of Fastel. Her things have been packed for some time now. I'll send her to you in a shuttle in ten minutes."

The fat man on the screen smiled an exhausted smile, constantly looking with the corner of his eye to the side, clearly at a tactical map. It seemed that the King still couldn't believe that a hundred and a half frigates that had been tearing off toward his fleet had stopped sharply and gone back the other direction.

**Standing change. The Kingdom of Fastel's opinion of you has improved.**
**Present Kingdom of Fastel opinion of you: -12 (dislike)**

"Crown Prince Georg, I understand perfectly that you don't especially like the fact that my fleet has come to the Li system. I promise that my ships will return immediately to Fastel as soon as they've recharged for another jump. For now, I want to make use of the occasion and ask you a question that's been on my mind for some time. Could you explain to me directly and openly the status of the refugees from Veyerde in your retinue?"

I could understand that the King wouldn't have much of an interest in the paralyzed Flora, but her older sister could easily make him ponder. By the way, who was Astra to me? I thought and laughed happily.

"If only I knew that myself... I can't exactly send the foundlings back, as their home has been captured by Aliens. A pretty doll, a true Princess with flawless mannerisms, a favorite and just a fun companion. Are you interested in whether or not she is my lover? I will answer you honestly: no, she is not. Not for now."

"I have no interest in who is or isn't your lover, Crown Prince. But is your Highness preparing to end his marriage with my daughter and take this sponger as a wife?"

"Ask your daughter about that," I answered, redirecting the monarch's implacable curiosity at someone else. "After all, Marta often threatens me with divorce and promises to send the papers as soon as possible. I would be perfectly happy with her as a wife if she could remember how princesses are supposed to behave and reign in her vocabulary, or as my android translator would put it, 'turned on her obscene language filter.' And if Marta also began taking care of herself and lost a few hundred pounds, I might even be perfectly happy with her as a woman."

I thought Marta's father would be insulted. But he only smiled back at my sharp words:

"She really took after me. There's nothing to be done; it's just our nature. But I will tell her your wishes, Crown Prince Georg. Thank you for your answers. I found out everything I wanted to know."

*Standing change. Valesy royl Pir's opinion of you has improved.*

*Presumed personal opinion of you: -10 (disapproval)*

*Standing change. The Kingdom of Fastel's opinion of you has improved.*

*Present Kingdom of Fastel opinion of you: -11 (dislike)*

I answered the monarch with a similar

improvement in relations, then added:

"I admit, dear father-in-law, we haven't always seen eye to eye. Sometimes we had our reasons, sometimes we really didn't. Probably, my scandalous behavior in the past served as the reason for the Kingdom of Fastel joining my enemies. But times have changed. Now I give your Highness one piece of advice as a close relative. I know of your loyalty to the Orange House, but try to keep your distance from Duke Paolo royl Anjer. The head of the Orange House is losing support quickly, though he hasn't realized it yet. In a month or two, everything will become clear. And if the Kingdom of Fastel doesn't change its policy and sends ships to the United Orange House Fleet, it will simply be losing them in vain. Think about my words. And for now, I'm signing off. I need to say goodbye to my daughter."

"Your Highness, I still recommend you strongly against coming down to the planet!" The head of my guard was being very stubborn today. "The level of radiation on the surface of Sss is so high that a person could easily develop severe radiation sickness before the end of the two-hour-long ceremony."

"But I have already visited your planet, Popori de Cacha! And nothing bad happened. I'm still alive, as you can plainly see!"

The Chameleon made a fairly faithful imitation of a human smile:

"My Prince, last time you were on the plains. The

level of radiation is much lower there than here at the mountain temple, where the ceremony will take place. Also, when you visited last, the Ravaash, honestly, couldn't have given a shit about the health of any humans visiting their planet. They came to a dangerous planet of their own free will. Let them worry later about getting the radionuclides out of their bodies. But now, everything is different. Your health and long life are extremely important for my whole species. There is no reason whatsoever for you not to participate in the burial ceremony for the remains of the heroes and the later swearing in remotely, sitting in your star cruiser over the planet Sss. I assure you, Crown Prince, all my compatriots will approve of your doing so."

I thought for a few more seconds, then waved my hand:

"Alright, I'm convinced. Just explain to me now what I need to say and do not to make a fool of myself in front of your tribe."

Popori de Cacha laughed:

"Your Highness need but stand in silence before the big screen and nod with an important look from time to time. The whole ceremony will be held in the Ravaash language, so without Bionica's help you won't understand what is being said. But it wouldn't really be possible for the android, or anyone else really, to be next to the new ruler during the ceremony. The Ravaash nation's whole attention must be focused only on the new ruler."

"Yes, I remember. You said that. Alright, if it's important to your nation, I am prepared to stand in silence for two hours before a screen, nodding from time to time."

"Thank you, my Prince. It's just that any other way the Chameleon nation will not understand why they suddenly need to listen to and obey a human crown prince. My nation simply doesn't have the vocabulary to express concepts like 'viceroy' or 'star system holder.' There is the ruler that was chosen by the Ravaash nation, and it will be precisely you that is named ruler at the end of the ceremony. And now I must leave your Highness and go to the planet. I must be personally present at the mountain temple to bid farewell to the ashes of my fallen subordinates."

I stood in silence in the center of the large hall of Emperor August feeling somewhat stupid. The huge hall was lined with stern looking Alpha Iseyek assault troops, space fleet officers in Orange House uniforms, landing troops in heavy armor and Security Service soldiers in dark suits, all standing in ceremonial divisions. They were given very specific instructions not to move from their places or come closer to me.

The ceremony was being broadcast especially for me on the big screen. It was taking place in the mountain temple, which was holy to the Ravaash. To be honest, I didn't see what all the fuss was about. It was just a spacious cave cut into rock, which was now filled with Chameleons of all colors. There were three of them leading the ceremony. Perhaps they were priests or rulers, who's to say? I couldn't understand what they were saying, but they were taking turns making speeches, which were punctuated by the ring of a gong. At the end of each, the crowd would howl in reply. From time to time, one of the Chameleons would camouflage themselves or become visible. It went on this way for an hour and a half, after which the one-note activity changed rather sharply. The leaders began pointing at the cameras, and the thousands-strong crowd of Chameleons all turned to me at once. I do not know if they could really see me or not, but I strove to act out the role I had been prescribed: I kept silent and nodded importantly.

"Tuki-tuka-de-sa!" one of the leaders squealed, pointing his flexible arm at me, and the crowd repeated its words back in elation.

**Standing change. Chameleon race opinion of you has improved.**
**Chameleon race opinion of you: +18 (loyal)**

After that, the same "tuki-tuka" was repeated hundreds of times in various intonations, and every time the crowd echoed back the leaders. My head was starting to hurt from the repetitive chanting, but just then the ceremony finally came to an end. Crowds of Chameleons flowed out of the cave on screen. Popori de Cacha, and I was able to recognize my bodyguard among the hundreds of other Chameleons, approached to the camera:

"Everything went wonderfully, my Prince. Now, to my nation, you are the legal ruler, and the Ravaash race will consider itself a part of the Orange House."

"That is all excellent. And what does 'tuki-tuki'

mean?"

"My Prince, tuki-tuka-de-sa means 'elder female' in the Chameleon language."

"What???" I exclaimed, becoming surprised and indignant.

The head of my guard explained:

"In our culture, only four figures are considered worthy of leading the Ravaash nation: the elder priest, the greatest warrior, the alpha male, or the elder female. Unfortunately, we wouldn't have been able to get your Highness elected as a priest. A priest must be familiar with our rituals and norms. It wouldn't have worked to name you the greatest warrior. That title can only be earned in the ring by fighting and defeating other experienced Chameleons."

"But why female, and not male?"

Popori de Cacha smiled sneakily:

"Is your Highness prepared to mate with a vast number of Ravaash females and provide them all with healthy descendants?"

"So then, what is required of the elder female?" I asked, suddenly filling with worry at what the answer might be. The last thing I needed from this was another set of responsibilities.

"The elder female is responsible for providing and defending the sanctuary where my nation's females stay in the later terms of pregnancy, and where our offspring are raised for the first few months. That is precisely what your Highness offered my nation by giving us an island on the planet Unatari-VII for those exact purposes."

"Ah, well that's ok then. In that case, I truly am prepared to rule as elder female. Such an island has already been prepared for settlement. The first females can start their journey there tomorrow with the freighters taking armor plates to the Unatari docks. I'll order a space cleared for them, and make sure all their needs are provided for."

"Yes, tuki-tuka-de-sa, I will tell all the Chameleons everything is ready," Popori de Cacha made a low bow, clearly with more honor than I had noticed him giving before.

*Standing change. Popori de Cacha's opinion of you has improved.*

*Presumed personal opinion of you: +100 (completely faithful)*

*Standing change. Chameleon race opinion of you has improved.*

*Chameleon race opinion of you: +20 (loyal)*

I laughed thoughtfully. There were still some definite benefits in being considered the elder Chameleon female. But, having noticed the sideways glances from fleet officers, some of which were having a hard time restraining smiles, I got embarrassed and gave a sharp start:

"Alright, that's enough of that. The ore freighters will soon be full. Prepare the fleet for warp. The Swarm and the Aliens attacking them are waiting for us!"

# Recognition of Talent

FOR THE SECOND day, my fleet was sitting by the Forepost-13 warp beacon, waiting for permission from the Swarm to cross their borders. It was surprising, but the Iseyek, who had in fact requested aid from the Sector Eight Fleet, were now refusing to allow us to enter and were blocking the Oort warp beacon. My cloaked frigate, which had been able to sneak into Oort before the beacon was turned off, was reporting on a fully-fledged fleet with hundreds of starships that the insects had rolled in from systems deeper in their territory.

Ambassador Triasss Zess and Admiral Kheraisss Vej reassured me that everything was alright. The reason for the delay was purely bureaucratic, the Yayho border fleet was already based in the Oort system for reasons totally unrelated to my fleet. But, for some reason, I was believing them less and less with every passing hour. A sense that something was afoot was gnawing at me. I just had an intuitive feeling that there were some complicated negotiations going on around my fleet, and I definitely did not like all the behind-the-scenes games.

Unfortunately, I could not use the Truth Seeker to figure out the situation. Flora had gone into another untimely crystal sleep. Even my advisor Katerina ton Mesfelle was worried. All she could figure was that the Swarm was hesitating. In the two months since we signed the agreement to help one another, the situation had changed drastically. The Sector Eight Fleet had become many times more powerful and, in its current state, already presented a serious threat to the Swarm. All I would have to do was break the agreement and treacherously attack the systems belonging to the Iseyek.

It should be noted that that possibility was also seen by the other side. I had a long conversation with an official representative of the Imperial Joint Chiefs, Count Timur royl Nayt ton Miro. The conversation was started by the Count and was rich in allusion and unclear hints, though I did understand the main idea: the Imperial Joint Chiefs were covertly promising to help me if I thought the situation ripe for launching a second invasion of the Iseyek. I was even, though in euphemistic phrases, told the criteria for this "ripeness:" if an unexpected attack from the Sector Eight Fleet would allow humanity to capture no less than four Swarm star systems, the Emperor would look on breaking the peace treaty with the Iseyek with nothing but grace. If I see the possibility of capturing six or more star systems, then... No, I did not hear a direct order, but the Count read me a whole lecture on the history of humanity's expansion in space and the unpleasant solutions, which were nevertheless necessary for humanity's further colonization of the remote cosmos.

In the long wait at the border, there was an unexpectedly positive moment: ninety small-class ships came to join my fleet. The fifty *Pyros*, twenty *Warhawks*, ten *Flycatchers* and ten *Surgeons* I had ordered with the Purple House arrived, crewed with people recruited on Tesse. And if you consider that several days earlier, during my stay on Sss, the Sector Eight Fleet had been also joined by the cloaked frigates, you could say I had the legal right to be proud of my accomplishments.

With the new additions, my fleet had a grand total of four hundred thirty combat starships: two battleships, twenty-five heavy cruisers, thirty-four light cruisers, ninety-five destroyers, two hundred thirty-seven frigates (none of which were outdated *Tusk* models anymore, all were now modern *Pyros* and *Warhawks*), thirty-six cloaked frigates and one *Tria* landing ship. For the first time, I heard Admiral Kiro Sabuto say what would have seemed positively mutinous just a month ago: that in a direct conflict with the United Orange House Fleet, the admiral himself would bet on the Perimeter Sector Eight Fleet winning.

I myself wasn't so optimistic. According to the latest data, Duke Paolo royl Anjer had gathered around two thousand combat starships under his banner, including fourteen battleships and up to a hundred heavy assault cruisers. But, in any case, my side had a lot more momentum. I was gaining strength faster than the Duke, and if I waited for the cruisers I bought in Sector Seven, plus the completion of the two battleships under construction for me, and the *Uukresh...* I tried to drive the deranged smile from my face. A head-on collision with the head of the Orange House did not enter into my plans and I thought of the possibility only as a "best to bury the hatchet next to your enemy" option, to be used only under the most extreme circumstances, if the time allotted by the Emperor for peace was going to run out soon.

Of course, the arrival of more ships meant more and more training, which I ordered the admirals to schedule. While the fleet was in Sss waiting for the shipments of tantalum ore to be loaded onto the freighters and for all issues related to the ownership of the Chameleon's system to be sorted out, the fleet practiced hard every day. We devoted an especially large amount of time to using the cloakers. Bombing moving targets required the captains and navigators of the stealth bombers to have excellent reaction times and amazing talent at orienting themselves in a tactical grid. The chance of burying your own ship and all other cloakers in the attack wave when a thermonuclear bomb gets lobbed at an enemy was simply too high. At the first training sessions – with dummy ammunition, naturally – the loss percentage among cloaked bombers reached eighty percent in just one attack. The best cloaked frigate captains turned out to be Chameleons, as a result of which I appointed Ravaash individuals as the captains and navigators of the first ten *Surprises*.

My fleet only had one full-fledged eight-hour practice session in the Forepost-13 system, before the long-awaited message came in from Triasss Zess:

"Crown Prince Georg, the Oort star system warp

beacon will be activated in the next twenty minutes. The Swarm officially apologizes for the delay. To avoid similar incidents sullying our relationship in the future, the Swarm has appointed me authorized representative of the Iseyek, responsible for all issues connected with the Sector Eight Fleet's aid mission."

***Standing change. Your relationship with Triasss Zess has improved.***
***Presumed personal opinion of you: +45 (friendship)***

***Standing change. Iseyek race opinion of you has improved.***
***Alpha Iseyek race opinion of you: +10 (trusting)***
***Beta Iseyek race opinion of you: +6 (warm)***
***Gamma Iseyek race opinion of you: +8 (warm)***

Practically right after that, a call came in from Angel royl Mauri, the captain of my cloaked frigate, reporting that the Iseyek fleet was on its way out of the Oort system. I sighed in relief. No matter what kind of incomprehensible negotiations the praying mantises were having, the final decision was positive, and my fleet was allowed to cross the border. Also, the fact that the Swarm had appointed Triasss Zess, who I knew so well, to be the coordinator of the operation meant that the insects wanted to show me that they were glad to continue working together.

"Attention, all ships! At the ready in twenty minutes. The Swarm will turn the Oort system warp beacon on for us. I remind all combat ships to immediately make for the station to recharge as soon as we leave the warp tunnel. The ore freighters are to first unload ore at one of the orbital factories, then return to Imperial territory all together, and go on to Tesse."

What I wanted to do was stand up from the console and leave the headquarters, but Bionica, sitting next to me, asked me to hold on:

"Your Highness, I'm afraid I have to send you the bill for monthly fleet maintenance. It's supposed to be payed the day after tomorrow, but I'm not sure if I'll be able to make the payment as usual from Swarm territory."

"Alright, go ahead," I confirmed, taking a look at the numbers.

Seventeen and a half million credits for fleet maintenance... A month ago such expenses would have been a blow to me, but now I could pay the large bill with my mind at ease. Just the taxes from the purchase of tantalum ore to me, as the "Chameleon elder female," came to over two billion credits plus a few freighters packed with finished armor plates for my docks. Also, my brother Roben suddenly decided to stop paying taxes to the Orange House head, instead sending the funds to my account. Add to that the taxes from Unatari and the ice factories of Tivalle that I was entitled to as ruler, and my share of the sale of pirate property... There I was reminded of something that had somewhat fallen out of view:

"By the way, Bionica, what happened with the last of the three pirate Kings? Somehow I missed the news of his capture."

My secretary suddenly stopped smiling and lowered her eyes to floor:

"Crown Prince Georg, King Velesh the First still has yet to be caught. His bank card has only been used one more time: ten days ago on Tesse he paid for an air-taxi to a popular mineral-spa resort town."

"On Tesse? Well, I'll be damned! That means he was able to escape Unatari, the ratbag!"

"Yes, my Prince. But the criminal police haven't yet announced the end of the hunt to the residents of Unatari, so the authority of the new rulers and your Highness will not suffer."

"And thank you for that. For some reason, that story about an uncatchable pirate King has suddenly spoiled my mood." It would have seemed that he had run far away, but for some reason I was still sure that I would meet Velesh the First at the most importune moment, and he would try to get revenge for all the offenses and losses he had suffered at my hand.

* * *

In the next star system after Oort, Yal, I was met by the authorized Swarm representative. Triasss Zess appeared in person on my flagship *Joan the Fatty*. Since I'd last seen him, my acquaintance had become even lighter in color. And the praying mantis had already managed to grow rudimentary arms to replace the ones my bodyguard had ripped out. Triasss Zess was accompanied by four Beta Iseyeks, but I could not figure out what their role was in the coordinator's retinue. The hump-backed pill bugs with a huge number of small legs could hardly have been bodyguards. They probably served the ten-foot-high

Alpha Iseyek, given his missing pair of mobile arms caused him difficulties with elementary day-to-day tasks.

After a short welcome, the praying mantis told me the news from the front:

"The Kej defense divisions are still holding out in the lower levels of the underground cities, but they are growing weaker by the day. All hotbeds of organized resistance are constantly being bombarded from space by the Aliens with missiles and depth charges. Only at a great depth – four hundred yards from the surface and below – can they find cover from the orbital bombardment. But the Aliens are also quite comfortable with underground warfare and are burning a path deeper and deeper down with their plasma guns. According to Swarm analysts' calculations, in five or six days, Kej will ultimately fall. And then the Aliens will keep moving..."

"What is the strength of the Alien fleet in the Kej system?" I wondered.

Triasss Zess waved with his huge upper appendages and jumped excitedly:

"Prince Georg, on that account we can provide you with the very latest information: the last transmission from Kej, exactly one half hour ago, reported eleven cruisers and a significant number, up to fifty, of small class ships."

Sixty Alien ships... Eleven *Sledgehammers* or similarly-powered ships... It would be simply impossible to take on such a force without serious losses, that is, if we even could beat them... I did not immediately answer Triasss Zess, and instead turned to the large window in thought. Behind the thick armored glass, I could see a giant under construction, one of the enormous transport ships the Iseyek were planning to use to evacuate their eggs. The colossal size of the starship would have made even the *Uukresh* look like nothing but a little fleck. But, from looking at it, I would say that its construction had begun very recently. The only thing that was recognizable, though still not finished, was the external chassis.

"I need a map of all Swarm systems!" I demanded from the praying mantis, and Triasss Zess sent me one.

I pulled up the map on the screen and didn't even try to hide my surprise. The Iseyek warp tunnel system was much more complicated than humanity knew. And the size of the territory under Swarm control was also impressive. It wasn't just ten star systems, as Imperial maps showed it, but twenty-seven!

I mentally thanked fate that I hadn't made any promises to Count Timur royl Nayt ton Miro. Based on what I could see, if I had agreed with the Joint Chiefs' proposal to attack the Iseyek, humanity would have repeated its century-and-a-half earlier mistake and started a war with an enemy whose power they had seriously underestimated.

"Mark systems under Alien control on the map," I asked the praying mantis messenger, and Triasss Zess quickly marked a number of systems on the touch screen.

Can that be? It turned out that a whole eight star systems had been lost, and not just the two that I had inferred from the information the Iseyek had so sparingly provided.

"In the last three months, the Aliens have taken the Unt and Khe systems, and soon they will also capture Kej," Triasss Zess said, confirming the frightening information.

I took a harder look and evaluated the map. Capturing systems at the current pace, one Iseyek system every month and a half, the Aliens would totally defeat the Swarm in a year and a half or two. And the fleet that the insects had left, based on what I had in front of me, was simply in no condition to stop an enemy invasion.

"You will not manage to evacuate the eggs," I said, after having looked out the window again and judging how close the transport ship was to being ready.

"Yes, that's true. I said that on our first meeting, Crown Prince Georg. Since that time, the pace of the Alien invasion has increased significantly. There's just no one to hold them back now. That is precisely why we invited the Sector Eight Fleet."

I remained silent for a while longer and made up my mind:

"Very well, Triasss Zess. Tell the Swarm that I am taking my fleet to Kej. But my spies will be checking the data about the Alien forces in that star system in advance."

"Thank you, your Highness!" The huge, light gray praying mantis made a fairly quick bow, imitating a human one.

***Standing change. Your relationship with Triasss Zess has improved.***

***Presumed personal opinion of you: +55 (loyal)***

***Standing change. Iseyek race opinion of you has improved.***

***Alpha Iseyek race opinion of you: +11 (trusting)***

He expressed his gratitude perhaps a bit too sharply. That set my Phobos and Deimos on edge and, in the space of one second, they took Triasss Zess down and were restraining his upper appendages in their pincers. Several Chameleons became visible, and also showed their readiness to immediately eliminate the threat.

"Everything is fine. He's a friend, let him go!" I ordered.

"I thank you again, Crown Prince Georg." The praying mantis, his chitin shell slightly dented by my guards, took an evaluating look at the two members of his own race that were my servants. "Then I will not further distract you from your preparation. We'll meet in the Sobj system immediately before the attack."

*"My Prince, I need his retinue, all four Beta Iseyeks. It is important. Ask – he would not dare refuse you."* Flora's familiar voice rang out in my head.

Flora had already awoken from her sleep? Why such a strange demand? I was extremely surprised at such a request from the paralyzed girl, but nevertheless I hailed the Swarm messenger, who was already preparing to return on a shuttle. Triasss Zess heard me out carefully and suddenly turned his head on its side. Was he confused? Unable to answer due to lack of information? Probably.

*"These Beta Iseyeks have strong psionic powers. Right now, they are providing a full shield over the*

*messenger's mind. He clearly doesn't want to reveal the Swarm's secrets. But I need them more. I just saw them in my crystal dream. They were with me."*

I explained the situation to Triasss Zess as well as I could. Clearly the praying mantis was very, very upset by my request, a fact which he did not fail to inform me of:

**Standing change. Your relationship with Triasss Zess has worsened.**
**Presumed personal opinion of you: +50 (loyal)**

But, all the same, the praying mantis did not refuse:

"Alright, Crown Prince Georg. You can have all four Beta Iseyek for your Truth Seeker. You are right. They really are very mentally powerful individuals, whose genetics the Swarm expended a great deal of force and time to create. They are a very valuable resource, planned for use in the further reinforcement and development of unique psionic abilities of this branch of Beta Iseyek. The Swarm gave me these four individuals to protect my mind from being read. After all, I'm not just an ambassador's assistant anymore, and not even a lowly ambassador. I've been promoted to the level that the Swarm has entrusted me with a great many state secrets, and a large number of these I do not have the right to share, even with my closest companions. That is why I will fulfill your request, but only after I have left on my ship, Crown Prince Georg."

Triasss Zess bowed again and rushed to leave. He completed the "realignment under new master" procedure right before he shipped out, just as had been done with Phobos and Deimos. It seemed to me that my acquaintance had been seriously offended. To be honest, I also would have been offended if someone made an ultimatum to force me to part with four important members of my retinue. But, unlike me, the praying mantis was simply unable to refuse, given that the agreement to attack the Aliens and ultimately the fate of his entire race, was dependent on my staying in a good mood...

With Bionica and the four giant pill bugs in tow, I started off toward the medical wing. I was feeling very funny and admonished myself for having obeyed little Flora. The Truth Seeker was still dressed in inky dark clothing and was learning how to use her mind to control a flying chair with Nicosid Brandt and his assistants sitting in it.

*"Prince Georg, ask everyone but the Iseyek to leave. Even your translator won't be needed now. To be honest, I would rather not even have you be here. I want to try to communicate with my new assistants."*

"They won't understand you, Florianna. These Beta Iseyeks don't know human language."

*"I am not trying to talk with them in the usual sense, even if I could. In fact, it is very important to me that they not understand other people so they won't get distracted by them. I just saw these four in a dream and know that they are able to understand my thoughts. And also, Crown Prince, I ask you to free up the cabin that I used to sleep in with Astra. I'm ready to leave the hospital today. There's absolutely no reason for me to stay here any longer. I'm not going to get any better at this point."*

*   *   *

In the Sobj system, I was met by two surprises. The first was a system message that popped up almost immediately after we left the warp tunnel:

**Global fame increase. Current value +13**
**Global standing increase. Current value -26**

I noticed that many of the officers nearby also froze for a few seconds and exchanged unconfident glances. Admiral Kiro Sabuto was the first to break the silence:

"Did everyone here get an increase in fame and reputation? It would seem we are the first people who have been able to get this deep into Swarm territory. Now, such a reward will greet us in every new system."

"Unfortunately, that's not the case," I replied. "We cannot get any further without intelligence – it's too dangerous. Scouts on cloaked frigates will make the jump to the Kej system before us to figure everything out and report it back to us. It is the crews of these frigates that will get the first discoverer's bonus."

"That seems pretty fair," said the admiral, continuing the conversation topic. "They will be the first..."

The admiral was not able to finish the sentence before a loud message came in from an officer, interrupting our conversation:

"Picking up Iseyek ships on the directional scanner!"

The normal routine began in the headquarters. Messages poured in one after another:

"The targets are drifting! The ships are in warp!"

"They are getting closer! Multiple targets. Four heavy *Legash* cruisers. Four light *Umoyge* cruisers. Eleven *Vassar* destroyers. Many frigates... Thirty-four *Safas*."

"The Swarm fleet has left the tactical grid. Distance: one hundred twenty miles. Identification by radar signature. All four heavy cruisers are *Improved Legashes*."

For the first time since my fleet came to Swarm territory, we were seeing Iseyek ships. They could hardly have been displaying aggression. The forces were painfully uneven, but in any case the proximity of these combat starships with incomprehensible intentions forced us to stay on alert. Finally, the situation was resolved:

"Commander, incoming call from Triasss Zess on the Sobj station."

My old acquaintance appeared on the screen.

"Crown Prince Georg, as you must have already noticed, the Swarm has decided to split off a group of aid ships for you. These are reserves, collected from various systems. They are yours. The Swarm recognizes your talent as a fleet commander and supposes that your Highness can make much better use of these ships than our admirals could. Your ships can use the Sobj station to recharge or repair. Here on the station and on the nearby planet, Sobj-II, there are a fair amount of Alpha Iseyek landing troops that you can use to carry out operations in the Kej system. The Kej warp beacon is currently off for security purposes, but on your request they can turn it on. I will personally be at the beacon leading a group of technicians to make sure no unforeseen delays should arise."

I thanked Triasss Zess for his participation and improved my personal opinion of him by ten points. The praying mantis on the screen gave a slight bow, and I answered in kind.

To gather intelligence, I sent three cloaked frigates straight to Kej. Angel royl Mauri was appointed leader of the three scouts. Seven hours later, he called me with up-to-date information on the enemy:

"My Prince, warp jump time: six hours, ten minutes. There are seventy-six Alien ships in the Kej system. Eight *Sledgehammers* and three cruisers of an unfamiliar design, seven *Ascetics* and nine *Hermits*, forty *Meteors* and nine landing ships. The fleet is orbiting the planet Kej-V, bombarding its surface."

"Excellent, Angel. I order the two cloakers to continue their observation in Kej, and one *Ghost* should set off to the Aysar Cluster as soon as it has the energy to check out the situation."

"All ships, at the ready in thirty minutes!" I said over the fleet channel and headed off to my cabin.

I was feeling very troubled at heart. Seventy-six Alien ships! That wasn't just a lot – it was too much for my fleet. I wasn't at all sure that the battle would have a positive outcome. Feeling somewhat upset and depressed, I went into my cabin. Astra was sitting in front of a big screen and, when she saw me come into the room, she shot up and dashed over to turn it off with suspicious agility before looking in my direction, batting her eyelashes innocently. I was staring at another easel the Princess had installed in the room.

The canvas was ripped, crumpled, and all over the floor.

"It just isn't working. I have no inspiration," Astra admitted, after having noticed my gaze being drawn to her next masterpiece, which wasn't exactly coming together.

I took a seat in an armchair and, after sitting for a bit in contemplation, said:

"Astra, I want to send you to Tesse so you can wait for my return at Roben's or in Likanna's palace."

I wasn't really planning to tell her the real reason I wanted her gone, which was the dangerous situation *Joan the Fatty* was heading into. I intended to say that it would be boring for her to sit for days on end in the same little room, so I was worried about her and suggesting a more interesting way of spending her time. However, Astra perceived my words in a totally unexpected way:

"That's so low on your part, Crown Prince, to read my correspondence and listen in on my conversations! I was just having a friendly chat with Corwin ton Ugar. I didn't even have the inkling of a thought about what the captain of *One-Eyed Python* said and wrote!"

"What?" I asked in surprise.

Astra puckered her lips in dissatisfaction, turned on the screen and, clearly getting embarrassed and even becoming red in the face, went to the side and suggested I read her personal correspondence with the dashing captain. Of course, I refused:

"Who do you take me for?! I really don't care who you talk with or what you talk about, as long as your conversations don't contain any top-secret information about the Sector Eight Fleet or me personally. In addition, I already told you, Astra: if you like that mustachioed soldier so much, I have no intention of stopping you by force. I give you half an hour to collect your things and head for his light cruiser."

"No, Crown Prince Georg! You've completely misunderstood me! I just sometimes get bored cooped up here, which is why I spend time chatting with people. But I am completely satisfied with my current position, and am not trying to change anything. I beg you please not to send me to Tesse or anywhere else."

"Corwin ton Ugar and all the others here have nothing to do with it," I sighed, having decided to tell the Princess the truth after all. "The Sector Eight Fleet is about to do battle with a very, very dangerous opponent. I'm only telling this to you, Astra, and you are not to share it with anyone else. But I am not at all sure we will win the next battle. That is why I wanted to keep you from danger and send you to a safe place."

In reply, Astra could first only sniffle, but eventually began to speak, and fairly convincingly at that:

"Crown Prince, imagine just for a second the worst possible outcome: the fleet loses, and you die. Who will want me around on Tesse after that? Verena is very suspicious and jealous; she will not let me stay there with her husband. Your brother may allow me to live in his palace for some time, but he could just as well throw me right out the door. After all, I am not even your Highness's lover but no one at all. The only reason people keep calling me Princess is because they're confused. Without a title or money, or friends or protectors, I won't be able to live. I'll just disappear. Now, on the other hand, if your fleet does win, there will have been no reason for me to leave. And I want to remind you of one favor you owe me. Your Highness promised me a romantic evening, which you have yet to make good on. So, I won't be going anywhere until that is taken care of. And basically, Princess Likanna asked me to look after her father before she left, and I promised her I would."

The last two arguments she put forward looked strange, but I didn't point it out, instead allowing Astra to stay. She squealed in joy and unexpectedly took a seat on my knee. The Princess kissed me quickly, and said, looking right into my eyes:

"This is an advance on the romantic evening. And to make that evening happen, you just need to beat these Aliens. Easy as that."

* * *

As it turned out, it wasn't "easy as that," a fact I realized shortly after the fleet started the jump to the Kej system. The Alien ships, which were supposed to have been near the planet Kej-V, were next to the Kej station itself at full battle readiness. They were clearly waiting for my fleet.

"There is a group of targets. They're four hundred miles out," Nicole said.

Today, the girl seemed surprisingly calm. I had somehow become used to her always being anxious before a battle.

"Attention, all ships! Do not charge them head on.

Remember the training sessions in Sss. Head toward the first planet. Imitate a retreat! Heavies and battleships, full speed ahead. Don't let the *Sledgehammers* get any closer to us. Faster ships, slightly in front, but still make a sudden retreat, and no enthusiasm; you will soon be needed. *Surprises* from one to five, disperse. Head for the enemy, choose someone to sneak up on, and get ready to release the megatons if the Aliens try to come after the rest of us. *Tria*, don't lag behind!"

"The enemy has begun maneuvers! They are giving chase!"

I laughed. That was exactly what I was expecting them to do. Now we could test how effective the strategy of bombing the small ships would be.

"Destroyers and frigates, step on your thrusters and move out like your lives depended on it! Your mission is to get away from the epicenter of the explosion! Bombers, attention! Your goal is to reduce all the *Meteors* to shit! Set your timers to three seconds. Check projectile synchronization."

The Aliens' nimble frigates closed the distance quickly, trying to catch up to and capture my heavy ships so the *Sledgehammers* could get to work.

"Stand by in thirty seconds! Nicole, timer! Light cruisers, turn toward the enemy so you'll take the hit with your frontal shields. All ships, cover light-sensitive equipment!"

"Ten seconds to detonation! Seven, six, five, four, three, two, one, launch!!!"

I was able to see the squad of *Surprises* appear simultaneously on the screen and launch their thermonuclear payload. But I was not able to tell whether my stealth bombers had warped back out or not. All the delicate external equipment on *Joan the Fatty* was covered with protective shields, including the cameras and radars.

Son of a bitch! Though *Joan the Fatty* had been two hundred miles from the blast, it gave a noticeable shake, and the electronic devices inside began flashing on and off, then switched to reserve power.

"Our thrusters have desynchronized. The electronics that control them have failed, but the automatic emergency system smoothed everything over," explained the captain.

"All ships report back on damage taken! Oorast Pohl, what are our shields like? I need a tactical map immediately!"

"This is *Bride of Chaos*. Our rear shield has fallen by fifteen percent – nothing critical."

"*Master of Tesse* here. The situation is similar. Our shields are down by fifteen percent."

"*Emperor August* here. Our stern shield is at thirty percent."

"*Legash-1* here. We have half of our shields."

"*One-Eyed Python* here. Rear shields at forty percent."

It remained unclear what had become of our stealth bombers, but I had already figured out that the rest of the fleet survived the five-megaton bombs with no losses. The heavies had already linked up with the smaller ships and were recharging their shields.

Finally, a tactical map showed up. Bingo! All that was left of the herd of *Meteors* was a scattering of debris! The Alien destroyers also painted quite the pretty picture: two of the *Ascetics* had been destroyed. The others were only still moving by inertia and had no shield remaining. Only a couple of *Hermits* were showing any signs of life, trying to make it back to their heavy ships.

"All ships, turn toward the enemy! Realign into battle formation! Do not advance yet! *Pyros -1* and *-2*, you're our receivers! *Surprises* six through ten, attention. *Tria*, attention! Right after the explosion, move out to capture the station! Turn off the warp beacon at any cost! *Warhawks*, attention. Right after the second explosion, capture anything that moves."

It seemed the enemy cruisers had started to suspect that this might not go their way and stopped advancing.

"Receivers, you're too close. You might get hit by the explosion. Go another two hundred miles out. Fifty *Pyros* for every receiver. Be prepared to capture everything still moving after the explosion!"

"My Prince, the enemy is preparing to retreat!" Nicole said, panicking as she watched the *Sledgehammers'* maneuvers.

"*Surprises*, cease attack! I repeat: cease attack!!! *Pyros*, attention! If they really do start to jump out, catch as many of them as you can in a warp disruptor. They're retreating! Advance! Capture them!!!"

The enemy ships really were trying to leave, but they didn't all make it. My soldiers captured five *Sledgehammers* in just the one haul. Unfortunately, they didn't get any of the other kind of cruisers. I would have liked to be able to see them in battle."

"Tuki-tuka-de-sa, this is *Surprise-1*. We have

successfully jumped out toward the eleventh planet. None of the five bombers were damaged."

"Great work, de-sa. Your squad set a galactic record: fifty-four Alien ships destroyed in one attack. The best Ravaash males will now have to compete in a tournament for the right to mate with you, a great hero of the Alien war."

"It will be done, tuki-tuka-de-sa!" Popori de Cacha entered the mission into his electronic bracelet.

**Standing change. Chameleon race opinion of you has improved.**
**Chameleon race opinion of you: +21 (loyal)**

From there on, it went as usual. My fleet approached the captured *Sledgehammers* and turned their electronics off from a safe distance. The battleships moved out in front, and the heavy assault cruisers stayed slightly behind. Three minutes later, all five *Sledgehammers* had been destroyed. I had already figured out that the other Alien ships had retreated to the fifth planet. Of course, it would be important to catch them, so I sent *Warhawks* and *Pyros* off after them. My fleet's other ships covered the landing ships for the assault on the station.

Just then, a message came in from Angel. My scout has reached the Aysar Cluster and was reporting on the situation. He hadn't been able to say a whole sentence yet, but I could tell by his agitated voice that he had seen something important.

"My Prince, the warp jump to Aysar takes three hours and seventeen minutes. It's a complete shitshow out her! I jumped at two hundred out from the beacon and appeared right in the midst of the Alien fleet! I can't leave yet; there's not enough room to accelerate and warp out. So now it's only a matter of time until I'm uncovered. There are thousands of them here! I repeat: there are thousands of them here! Over two hundred battleships. And there are even bigger ones, too! Oh my God! They've intercepted the transmission! They're all accelerating in my direction. It's over. I've been revealed... Long live the Empi..."

The transmission cut off, and everyone understood perfectly what that meant. Admiral Kiro Sabuto stood first and removed his hat, after which the other staff officers followed his example. Even Bionica stood and waited out the minute of silence, before actually relaying to us what General Savasss Jach was saying:

"The Kej warp beacon has been captured!" she informed us.

"Turn it off, immediately!" I commanded. "What about the ships that retreated?"

"This is *Warhawk-4*. We were just barely able to get out to the fifth planet. We are over twelve hundred miles from the enemy. They are clearly preparing to warp out again. Figure out where, and we'll intercept them.

Unfortunately, we were not able to catch the enemy. The targeted ships left toward the Aysar Cluster. I ordered one of the cloaked frigate captains to follow the enemy, making sure to set the prewarp point as far from the Aysar station as possible so as not to repeat Angel royl Mauri's mistake.

My ships detected immobile Alien landing ships over Kej-V. There were nine huge disk-shaped starships. They didn't react to our approach at all. I ordered eight of them shot down, and the ninth captured.

Ten minutes later the general informed me that the starship was under our control. The Alpha Iseyek landing ships did not meet any resistance. The ship turned out to have been totally abandoned. All that was left to do was sweep up the remaining Aliens on the planet, but General Savasss Jach was already attending to this issue, having reanimated fifty thousand landing troops.

Everything was leading up to the praying mantises landing on the planet and clearing the surface. Just then, when I was about to officially declare victory over the enemy, a blood-curdling scream rang out from a tactics officer:

"Alien ship on the scanner!"

"A cloaked frigate has appeared one hundred twenty miles from the station!" expanded Colonel Gor ton Vulf, who I had sent off to the warp beacon to keep the technicians under control.

"New beacon in system!" Nicole Savoia told me in an even tone, before turning to me to await my orders.

Everyone understood perfectly what it meant. The Aliens had opened a portal for their fleet to jump through.

"Kill that beast as quickly as possible!" I commanded, though I understood perfectly that it was already too late.

My ships took out the mobile beacon deliverer with no problems in six minutes. Now, everyone was waiting impatiently for messages from the scout we had sent to the Aysar Cluster. And an hour and a half later, he did, in fact, confirm my worst suspicions:

"My Prince, there are only six cruisers and two beat-up destroyers left near the Aysar station. Likely the very same ships that fled from Kej. All the other starships jumped toward the warp beacon in your system."

"They should reach us in one hour and six minutes," said Admiral Kiro Sabuto, laying out his calculations.

Everyone remained silent, waiting for my decision.

"Evacuate the landing troops from the station immediately. We will not be able to manage such a huge amount of Aliens. All ships, report back on energy reserves."

They ran down the roll call. The small ships had all managed to fully recharge, and the heavy cruisers were also just about ready to retreat to Sobj. The two battleships, though, were holding us back. Both *Bride of Chaos* and *Master of Tesse* needed another fifty-seven minutes to prepare for a jump.

"Communications officer, call Triasss Zess. I need a beacon in Sobj in fifty-eight minutes!"

A minute later, the Swarm operation coordinator appeared on screen. I explained the situation to Triasss Zess. The enemy fleet in the Kej system was beaten, but the Aliens had sent their main fleet from the Aysar Cluster.

"Crown Prince Georg, will you be able to evacuate any of our extremely valuable experts from the fifth planet?" the praying mantis inquired. "One of the main Gamma Iseyek genetic modification research centers is located on Kej."

I looked at the clock and gave my head a brisk shake:

"There isn't enough time left. Even if the experts immediately began boarding shuttles and taking off, they still wouldn't make it."

"Too bad," Triasss Zess said sadly. "Crown Prince Georg, I must tell you that the Swarm values your abilities as a fleet commander very highly. No other commander fights the Aliens as effectively as you. Your fleet's kill to loss ratio is much better than any other's. Your Highness is a true galactic expert in this matter. That is exactly why the warp beacon will not be opened for your fleet. The Swarm thought that it would be the most effective way of doing the most damage they could to the Aliens and delaying their further invasion for as long as possible. I am very sorry, my friend. Forgive me."

*Standing change. Your relationship with Triasss Zess has improved.*
*Presumed personal opinion of you: +70 (loyal)*

*Standing change. Iseyek race opinion of you has improved.*
*Alpha Iseyek race opinion of you: +13 (trusting)*
*Beta Iseyek race opinion of you: +10 (trusting)*
*Gamma Iseyek race opinion of you: +10 (trusting)*

# THE AYSAR CLUSTER

T
HE FIRST THING I noticed was the absolutely unnatural and – one could even say – grave-like silence in the headquarters. None of the officers was giving commands, flipping switches, or pecking away at buttons. Everyone in the hall was sitting silently, staring at the floor in desperation when I turned to face them. My conversation with Triasss Zess had been overheard by everyone present, which was why no one had to explain that the Iseyek had just condemned us all to death. The longer the silence dragged on, the more it became clear that it was up to me to say something.

"Disconnect us from the other fleet ships!" I stood unhurriedly from my seat and walked to the center of the room so all the officers could see me and I could also see their faces. "The only ones who know about what just happened are us. I can be confident in all of us, but there are many novices in the Sector Eight Fleet. And now, I need my staff's advice: should we inform the remaining ships about the Swarm's betrayal?"

First to answer my question was Captain Oorast Pohl:

"My Prince, the crew of *Joan the Fatty* will do whatever you order to the very end and die with honor as soldiers should. But I am not sure the other crews have the same fortitude. My opinion is that we should keep it a secret."

"Prince Georg, I have a different opinion." The normally modest and even shy Nicole Savoia continued to surprise me today. It was here and now that she wanted to offer her two cents and dispute the opinion of my flagship's captain. "People trust you, Crown Prince, which is why they deserve trust in return. The fact of the Swarm's betrayal will seep out in one way or another eventually. Either that or the captains will figure it out themselves when the Sobj warp beacon doesn't show up. So, there is no reason to hide it. Doing so would do nothing but Alienate our crews."

"If I could be allowed to speak, Crown Prince Georg, I suppose that this information is already known by some of your fleet's ships," Bionica inferred, standing and looking around at those gathered. "Admiral Kheraisss Vej and General Savasss Jach are quite highly placed figures in the Iseyek hierarchy. I still haven't totally figured out the admiral's status, but I have no question in my mind that General Savasss Jach has the right to vote in the Swarm. The general is one of the leaders of the Gamma Iseyek and must have taken part in discussing the decision to turn off the Sobj warp beacon."

Could that be? I demanded the communications officer put me through immediately to the general on the *Tria*. Savasss Jach appeared on screen, as always inside his hemispherical work station with its infinite number of buttons, levers and screens. Bionica translated the huge insect's chirring:

"Crown Prince Georg, I've been expecting this call for the last two minutes. From the moment I realized it had been necessary to cut off all channels of communication with the Swarm, I knew it could only mean one thing: Triasss Zess's proposal had been approved by the Swarm, and the Sobj retransmitter had begun blocking any communication with the Sector Eight Fleet in the Kej star system. I'm afraid that I must report some sad news to your Highness: the Sobj warp beacon is closed to Crown Prince Georg royl Inoky's ships in perpetuity. Triasss Zess was able to pass this decision with a majority of votes. This will probably provide your Highness very little consolation, but I would like you to be aware that I did vote against."

That meant the general had already known this was a possibility and didn't tell me! I mentally grated my teeth in rage, but suppressed the desire to give an order to immediately kill that huge centipede bastard, and asked in an even tone:

"General, at the moment I am interested in something else entirely. You swore an oath to the Perimeter Sector Eight Fleet. Why then did you not warn your direct commander in a timely manner about a situation so critically important to our fleet?"

My synthetic assistant translated the gigantic insect's reply:

"Crown Prince, I am your subject, but above all else I am Iseyek, and for me the fate of the Swarm will always take priority. Yes, I really was made aware of the trap being prepared by Triasss Zess when the Sector Eight Fleet was still in the Kii star system. I happened to have a difference of opinion from him. I personally thought that the Sector Eight Fleet would be more useful if they allowed it to recover from potential losses. But the Swarm voted otherwise in the majority. They prescribed our foreign fleet to die with honor, holding back the Alien invasion. For me, the Swarm's decision is sacred and unquestionable, though it also means my own death."

I didn't see the point of continuing to argue with the fanatic and waste valuable time, so I hung up. Everything had become exceedingly clear: the Swarm thought that sacrificing an allied fleet was justified. And it had been a conscious, collective decision – not some spontaneous revenge by the Alpha Iseyek for his ripped-out appendages and hijacked minions. I suspect that the Swarm thought no one in the Empire would find out what happened, so no revenge would follow from humanity.

In some way, Triasss Zess was right: I wasn't preparing to lay down and let the Aliens just take my fleet. I was ready to fight to the last ship, to the last round, and to the last crew member. But I was very hopeful that the Swarm coordinator was wrong on another count: counting us out. I personally considered the situation very perilous, but clearly not hopeless. My fleet was strong and well trained enough that the Aliens still had some serious sweating ahead of them before defeating the Sector Eight Fleet. Or even just catching us to get started.

"Put me through to the whole fleet! Bring the Truth

Seeker to fleet headquarters!" Ennui and confusion slipped through in my voice. I was struck by an untamed thirst for action and a very strong, simply inordinate fervor. We had been backed into a corner and condemned to a battle with a superior enemy, who was universally considered unbeatable. What better motivation could I ask for?

Without being shy in my word choice, I told the fleet about the deadly trap the insects had backed us into. I gave them time to process it, so the severity of the situation would reach all the way to the last pair of ears, and then continued:

"The Swarm has committed a historic error, the effects of which the Iseyek will come to realize in the near future. They took it in their heads to destroy the only force capable of protecting their star systems from the Alien invasion. Now the Swarm is doomed. The Iseyek will not have time to save their clutches, and in a year or so the only thing left to remind the residents of the Empire and other star systems that there once existed intelligent insects will be the names of some remote star systems. And as for us, the Sector Eight Fleet, we will make it out, no matter if we were stabbed in the back! I swear that I will do everything I can to get our ships back to Imperial territory. Yes, every one of us will have to expend all our effort to escape the trap, but I believe in you, troops! We are the most combat-effective fleet in the Empire and have already shown we can rout Aliens no problem. And if Aliens are what's standing between us and freedom, we'll have to fight our way through!"

The enthusiastic roar of hundreds of voices drowned out my speech. Despite the fact that Crown

Prince Georg royl Inoky had led his fleet into a trap, the captains still believed in me and thought that I was capable of dragging them all out of the trouble. I was expecting reputation increases with the Imperial Military faction as usual, however that did not happen – clearly the result of my fleet's isolation from Imperial territory, making it impossible for such faction relation change information to get through.

An armchair hovered into the room with Florianna sitting in it in a black robe, accompanied by four Gamma Iseyeks. I noted with some surprise that some officers went down on one knee to greet the little Truth Seeker. It was the first time I had seen them act that way. Perhaps it was evidence of Flora having been officially recognized as a Truth Seeker and her rank having gone from that of an NPC to a live player with personal backstory and character information. And maybe it was just that the little girl looked impressive with her antigravity armchair, dark attire and unspeaking, nonhuman retinue.

"Flora, I need to know where the Alien fleet is headed."

Everyone in the headquarters froze in respectful silence, afraid of interrupting the Truth Seeker's process. Flora closed her eyes and sat like that for a few minutes before I heard a child's voice in my head:

*"Crown Prince Georg, unfortunately I cannot complete your mission. I will never be able to detect or track the movement of the Alien ships. Forgive me."*

A wash! Though it wasn't a bad idea... The plan had been to add the flight time from the Aysar system to the exact time when the mobile warp beacon had been set up in the Kej system, and use that to help us greet the Alien ships with all the megaton honors they deserved. Too bad, too bad... But... I remembered the recording Admiral Kheraisss Vej had given me in Tesse, which showed the moment the cloaked Alien ship appeared next to the Kej station, then the subsequent invasion of the Alien fleet to the star system. I had studied the video in sufficient detail and now could possibly apply it to local conditions.

"Bring up a detailed tactical map of the area around the Kej station!" I stood and got closer to the three-dimensional hologram that showed the station itself.

I had to walk in a circle twice around the hologram, before I was able to orient myself and point on the map to approximate places where the mobile warp beacon deliverer had been and where the enemy fleet had come out from.

"One hundred eight miles," the tactics officer counted off, having measured our distance from that point.

"Great. Now calculate one hundred eight miles from the point where we recently shot down the cloaked Alien frigate in a straight line from the Aysar Cluster. That is precisely where the Alien ships will arrive in fifty-two minutes and sixteen seconds. And I want the biggest bombs we have in the fleet installed all around."

I noted my subjects coming to life instantly, and the respect they were looking on the little Truth Seeker with. Clearly, none of my officers had any doubts that it was Flora who had given me the right answer. And as the Truth Seeker had pointed me in the right direction, they technically weren't wrong.

The tacticians began scuttling around, the admiral began fleet roll call, and Bionica was also hissing something out in Iseyek. Finally, Kiro Sabuto reported to me on what kinds of instruments of death and destruction my fleet was in possession of:

"My Prince, each of the battleships has one fifty-megaton bomb. There are also ten ten-megaton bombs, and eight 'one-and-a-halfers' on the *Legashes*, and each of the stealth bombers has one three-megatonner... Which bombs should we set?"

I considered it briefly. I was hesitant to use all my big trump cards like that in one go; however, there was a serious chance that such an easy opportunity wouldn't present itself again.

"Let's put both fifty-megatonners down. The Aliens learn quick, so they won't get fooled by a trick like that twice. Set one right at the marked prewarp point, and the second three miles toward the Aysar Cluster. We'll see how well the Alien rear shields take damage. Oh, and also put all eight one-and-a-halfers from the Iseyek ships out in a circle around it. After such an epic honeypot on the praying mantis's part, and until I have no more doubt in the loyalty of the Swarm ships with me, I have no desire to leave any Iseyek in possession of such dangerous weapons. With a total of ten bombs, we'll try to do the most damage we can to the Aliens, as we won't get another chance. Just make sure to synchronize all the timers very carefully so we don't end up blowing up our own bombs for nothing."

"It will be done, my Prince!" the admiral turned to give the orders, but I stopped him.

"Admiral, that isn't all. I feel that the time has come

to split the fleet up. The two battleships should keep charging for the warp jump, but the other ships simply cannot allow themselves the luxury of lounging around for so much time. That is why I and the remaining ships will go now to the Aysar system and try to clear the station there as quickly as possible so the fleet can start recharging. However, there is also absolutely no way we can leave the two battleships here without protection. I have no doubt that there are Alien cloaked frigates nearby observing us. If the fleet leaves, they may appear and try to hold the battleships here until the rest of the Alien fleet arrives. I personally would do the very same in their position, and after the other ships came I would also destroy these ships, depriving the human fleet of their most dangerous weapons. That is why I am leaving fifty frigates and ten destroyers to cover the battleships. Admiral Kiro Sabuto, it is precisely you that I entrust with the mission of making sure our most valuable ships make it to Aysar safe and sound. My friend, go as quickly as you can to *Master of Tesse*. I'll inform Nill ton Amsted of your command. Nill, though, I want to see here on *Joan the Fatty*. I have my own special mission for him."

\* \* \*

Three hours, seventeen minutes. That was how long the warp jump to the Aysar Cluster took. Too short to get any sleep, and on top of that I was in such an overexcited state that I wouldn't have been able to close my eyes anyway. What I wanted to do was share a meal with Katerina ton Mesfelle, but my cousin was in no mood. She was admonishing herself for not having seen the risk of our being betrayed fast enough on her own. I set off to my cabin, but was also met with an unexpected obstacle. Princess Astra had finally found inspiration. The girl was in the process of creating her 'next masterpiece' and ejected me from my own room in quite a rude manner.

I stomped my feet in frustration at the locked door and set off to Florianna's room. In the last few days, the crew of the cruiser had begun keeping their distance from this basically normal room. They were afraid of and avoiding the Truth Seeker.

*"Come in, your Highness,"* the voice in my head rang out when I was still a few steps from the door.

Flora was eating. Two of the Gamma Iseyek were feeding the paralyzed girl by squeezing an enriched puree through a culinary syringe down a long, flexible tube into her mouth. Not all the food was making it down her throat. Some of it was dribbling out of her mouth, and one of the Gamma Iseyek was wiping Flora's face with a napkin to accommodate this fact.

*"Yes, I know how it looks. I beg your forgiveness for such an appetite-killing spectacle. It's just that I'm tired of intravenous feeding. I don't have any veins left in my arms after all the poking around."*

"No need to apologize. You are not at fault here." Hiding my squeamishness from the Truth Seeker would have been senseless. "I personally came in for advice. After the Swarm's treason, I need to be sure that the Iseyek ships in my fleet aren't going to pull any stunts when we want them least. For example, what if the insect captains think they need to make sure the Sector Eight Fleet cannot return to human-controlled space, as that would mean that the fact of the Swarm's actions would also reach the Empire, possibly leading to a new war with humans? Can I trust the insect captains, or will they stab me in the back?"

The paralyzed girl began to ponder and clearly ordered something mentally to her servants, as the pill bugs took her food away and set the girl's body upright.

*"Your Highness, you are not mistaken. I really can sense treason and not only from the Iseyek. Many, very many in your fleet have a stake in making sure Crown Prince Georg can never again return to the Empire."*

"Flora, I need a complete list of the traitors in three hours."

*"That is simply impossible, Crown Prince. I need to check thousands and thousands of humans and nonhumans, and there is not enough time. Even Miya wouldn't be able to do such a thing."*

"Alright then, just check the Iseyek captains. First check the heavy cruiser captains, then the light. If you can cut out the infection and save the valuable ships, I would be very grateful to you, Flora."

*"I will remember your promise, Crown Prince Georg. I also wanted to make use of the occasion to ask: do you know that my sister talks with Corwin ton Ugar all the time? They spend hours, practically every day, chatting about such frank topics that I even blush for Astra when I listen in on her thoughts."*

"Astra is not imprisoned. There is no reason for her to sit locked behind a door deprived of contact with the outside world. No one can forbid a free girl from fraternizing with who she wants."

*"Hey, don't try to trick me, Crown Prince! Whether you want it or not, I am your Truth Seeker, and I can read your emotions and even sometimes thoughts. And it's roughly the same with my sister. Astra is right next to me, just two walls between us, and it isn't my fault that I can hear the echoes of her thoughts. Yesterday, she told him to make a wish and she would grant it, and then couldn't fall asleep afterwards so furious were her fantasies about what the brave captain could ask of a girl as beautiful as she. I feel that you like Astra and don't enjoy her talking on the side like that. Crown Prince Georg, my advice is to cut this nonsense off, before it turns into something more serious than flirting."*

"And what do you suggest I do about it, Flora?"

*"Your Highness, you know the answer to that question perfectly well, but are afraid to admit it even to yourself. The solution to this problem is easily within your reach."*

"Good, I'll have a serious talk with your sister. If that doesn't help, I may have to consider some more radical options."

Leaving the Truth Seeker's room, I tried hard not to think about what the paralyzed girl had said. Every person has thoughts intended for " internal use only" from time to time, and mine were no longer only for me. Yes, I was very much capable of arranging for *One-Eyed Python* not to survive the upcoming battle. No one in the fleet would even be able to figure out that it was a calculated move on the commander's part, and not a horrible coincidence. To be more accurate, almost no one... Flora would, of course, realize right away, but she wouldn't be able to tell anyone about it.

However, on a basic level, I thought this was the wrong route. It wasn't because it would have been premeditated murder. In an online game – and I was still inclined to look on the world around me as nothing more than a really good game with impeccable graphics – killing a rival and competitor was often the only way to achieve your goal. It's just that doing that wouldn't get rid of the problem, and Princess Astra would just quickly find another young cavalier to flirt with; so, in the end, I would come out even, and there were more than enough dashing young officers in the Perimeter Sector Eight Fleet. Also, being deprived of a capable and brave cruiser captain such as Corwin ton Ugar was something that I, as a fleet commander, also preferred to avoid. I really didn't dislike the talented captain at all, and after carefully studying his personal record, I even admired his bravery and brilliant tactical solutions during the Empire's war with the Union of the Four, an alliance of rebel systems in Perimeter Sector One. It was vexing that precisely the heroic captain Corwin ton Ugar could provoke such an unpleasant scandal that could seriously reflect on the Crown Prince's reputation.

I didn't feed my illusions and understood perfectly that the fat, awkward Crown Prince Georg royl Inoky would clearly not be able to compete with Corwin ton Ugar nor basically any other brave young hunk in Astra's eyes. My favorite was only with me because of my high title and wealth, not at all because of love. If someone as high-born and well-provided-for as Georg royl Inoky were to come into Astra's field of view, but with a nice face, even I would be ready to put a battleship up against a rust bucket that my favorite would immediately gravitate toward this new center of power and wealth.

The only thing that could separate me from the others were my abilities as a skilled star fleet commander. That could be impressive to soldiers who were well versed in those kind of things; however, none of Princess Astra's interests intersected with it. I even strongly suspected that the last representative of the royal house of Veyerde didn't understand that there even was a reason for a space fleet to have a commander. Of course, I could have demonstratively take her down a peg or gotten rid of my favorite, but I still didn't want to take the situation to the point of public scandal.

I really did like Astra quite a lot, and not only for her prodigious beauty, but also because of her surprisingly childish directness – though I thought of my favorite more as a fun doll and sweet conversation partner, and not a potential romantic partner. But, despite all my warm feelings for Astra, I couldn't allow my companion to put an Imperial Crown Prince in a bad light with her rash, frivolous behavior.

"Three minutes to action!" I said calmly, looking at the people surrounding me.

Either my confidence had had an effect on my

subjects, or they were simply in denial of the Iseyeks' betrayal; in any case, I couldn't detect any signs of anxiety or, more importantly, fear on their faces. There was an overriding atmosphere of professionalism. The officers took their seats and set about performing their duties and preparing for the flagship to warp out. Nicole Savoia took out her cosmetics bag and, using a turned-off screen as a mirror, smeared a bright crimson lipstick on as if we weren't just about to enter a system under Alien control.

"Ten seconds! As soon as we're out, I need a tactical map and a line opened to our cloakers in Aysar and Kej! Warp!"

Messages started coming as if from a cornucopia:

"Enemy ships detected! Aliens! Group of targets, there are eight of them. Three *Sledgehammers* and three unknown-model cruisers. Two *Hermit* destroyers. They are in a tight formation. Two thousand one hundred miles to the enemy. Three hundred miles to the Aysar station. The enemy ships are not moving relative to the station. I repeat: the enemy is motionless. No movement detected. No signs of radio activity either. No transmissions of any kind, interstellar or local. No enemy targeting systems detected..."

"Something's not right here," Nicole turned toward me, not hiding her apprehension.

"You can say that again. There's a fully-fledged station in this system that the Aliens recently refitted to recharge their ships. All these cruisers and destroyers we're observing could easily recharge and warp out, either to the Kej system after the main fleet or to the Lobj system. But, for some reason, these ships are still here, though they are a bit farther from the station...

I had a feeling inside that there was something afoot. If the Aliens didn't need these ships, they would have tried to take them out to the Kej system. And also these motionless cruisers, just sitting in space had clearly drawn my fleet's attention away from the station itself. Why? I needed more information immediately, and I ordered the Truth Seeker brought to me once again. And in the meantime, I called up our frigate spy.

"Rupert Donce, captain of *Ghost-2*, reporting in. No new Alien ships have been detected in the Aysar system in the last four hours. These cruisers and destroyers stayed attached to the station for a long time after we arrived, but approximately two hours ago they moved eighteen hundred miles and change away from the station, then stopped. They've been just sitting there for practically two hours now. My frigate is circling them at eighteen miles, so if you need jump coordinates, I can give them to you."

*"My Prince, it is a trap! The ships are not abandoned at all. I feel their attention. Our actions right now are being scrutinized. I do not know why, but the Aliens need our ships to think they are not at risk and get close to theirs!"* Little Flora's voice was wavering in worry.

"Thank you for the information, Rupert Donce. I do not need the coordinates for now. You should go away from them in the opposite direction of our fleet for one hundred eighty miles".

I stood and walked up to the little Truth Seeker's

armchair. Flora looked at me with eyes full of tears and repeated her warning again and again to not approach the Alien ships under any circumstances. Despair and fear resonated in the girl's voice.

"I understand, Flora. And what about the question I asked before the battle?"

*"I was not able to check everyone. But the four* Legash *captains, who joined the Sector Eight Fleet in the Sobj system, have a clear and unambiguous order from the Swarm not to allow your Highness to return to the Empire. I did not have enough time, so I only selectively checked one Gamma Iseyek, the commander of the light cruiser* Umoyge-7. *He was no traitor, though he was very, very strange. He is not at all like the other insects. Also, the Beta Iseyeks captains of* Safa-40, Safa-41, *and* Safa-60 *all give more priority to Triasss Zess's order than yours."*

I thanked the paralyzed girl, allowing her to continue the work, and returned to the console.

"My Prince, this is Admiral Nill ton Amsted from the Kej system. Many events have occurred; I will report them in order. First, we were able to connect with the Gamma Iseyek scientists on Kej-V. With my translator, who turned out to be a very weak interpreter in practical conversation, we were just able to communicate that we could evacuate some of them on cloakers, up to three hundred of the Swarm's most valuable scientists. They have already decided who will be evacuated, and now we're just waiting for a good time.

That was excellent news. Three hundred valuable scientists rescued from a planet captured by Aliens could serve as a reason to get the Swarm to turn the warp beacon on for us. It wasn't likely, of course, but all the same there was some chance of escape. However, I was much more interested in my ships *Master of Tesse* and *Bride of Chaos* than I was in the scientists.

"How'd it go with my battleships? Did they make it out?"

"Yes, Prince Georg, both battleships have left and are underway. Though you were not wrong, the Aliens really did try to keep *Bride of Chaos* from leaving. Three cloakers appeared next to the ship when it started moving and got it with a warp disruptor and webs. We lost six *Pyros* and four *Warhawks* in the battle with the Aliens, but they were all destroyed. In accordance with your order, Crown Prince, the cloakers did not uncloak, so as not to give themselves away."

Despite the fact that the fleet had lost ten frigates, I still considered the news positive. My main ships escaped, and that was what mattered now. But, at the same time, Nill ton Amsted continued, making no effort to hide his ear-to-ear smile:

"My Prince, now on to the most important news: our Alien apocalypse went off without a hitch! Their huge fleet came out right when and where they were predicted to, and *Ghost-6* detonated the charges. It went off with such a marvelous bang, that it was like watching a new star being born! Despite *Ghost-6* having been eighteen hundred miles from the blast, it was unmasked, and its energy shield fell by half. Around the blast area, for hundreds of miles, there is a whole sea of debris and background radiation that has stayed strong until now. That is why my cloakers will not risk getting closer, so as not to give themselves away. Also, a hidden stealth bomber attack would hardly be possible under these conditions, though the enemy is in a very tight formation."

"Which Alien ships did we manage to destroy?"

"Prince, we are making observations from three thousand miles away and only with passive positioning systems, so it is hard to say exactly. At least one *Behemoth* has been torn in half – though it is possible that what we are seeing is the remains of two different battleships. A great many small ships were destroyed, both by the explosions of our bombs and the subsequent antimatter explosions from the *Behemoth*. Together, they reduced the number of Alien small ships by half, though we are observing quite a few active frigate- and destroyer-class ships. All the same, the enemy fleet was not as badly damaged as we could have hoped. As many as two hundred battleships and no less than six hundred cruisers remain active. There are also just under a thousand destroyers and frigates left. Now the Aliens have concentrated around five huge ships that are three times longer than a *Behemoth*. I cannot tell if they are repairing or recharging."

I thanked the admiral and repeated the order not to give himself up unless he had absolutely no choice, collect the Swarm scientists and follow after the rest of the fleet. So the situation became clear. My battleships had escaped and were on the way to Aysar. The enemy was in Kej, not defeated, but fairly badly wounded. The time had come to attend to local matters.

"All ships, attention! Make the smallest possible advance toward the enemy ships. Match the speed of the battleships. No one jump in front. *Ghost-2*, increase distance from Alien ships to four hundred. *Safa-40*, and *Safa-41*, maximum speed toward the Alien ships. If they try to activate targeting systems on you, report back immediately!"

Two small green dots took off on the tactical screen and were moving rapidly to close the distance to the enemy. Everyone froze, waiting to see what would happen. One thousand miles to target. Four hundred miles. Two hundred." The Aliens were not reacting to our approach at all. "One hundred miles. Fifty..."

"*Safa-40*, catch one of the *Sledgehammers* in a warp disruptor and take a tight orbit. Do not reduce speed. *Safa-41*, your mission is to catch one of those unknown-model cruisers!"

But the Alien frigates didn't even react to my ships taking such unambiguously aggressive maneuvers and just allowed themselves to be captured unpunished.

"This is *Ghost-2*. I am four hundred from the enemy. Increase distance?"

"No, that's all I need. Send me your coordinates. *Safa-40* and *Safa-41*, keep holding the cruisers. Attention to the whole rest of the fleet! Accept warp jump coordinates and report back when you are ready! *Safa-60* will jump first, setting prewarp four hundred miles past the coordinates. Right after you get out of warp, *Safa-60*, capture another cruiser. All other ships, jump to zero on *Ghost-2* two seconds after *Safa-60*. I repeat: only *Safa-60* is to jump toward the Alien ships. All others are to stay clear. Admiral

Kheraisss Vej, I need to make sure your subjects understand the order! Only *Safa-60* will jump into battle. Everyone else, jump two seconds later on the opposite side of *Ghost-2!*"

Admiral Kheraisss Vej appeared on the screen and chirped a long speech into the microphone, then turned to me:

"My Princcce, all me cap-i-tan to understand order."

"Excellent, admiral. All ships, accelerate for warp! Attention! Cover light-sensitive equipment! Ten seconds for *Safa-60,* twelve for everyone else. Nicole, countdown!"

I could even feel the excitement of the moment in my skin. I looked to the Truth Seeker. The little girl had her eyes closed and was crying in fear. Another green spot appeared on the tactical map and jumped to the two others, after which the map disappeared. Armored plates were covering all delicate equipment. Warp jump.

"Rear shields have fallen by ten percent!" Came the worried voice of an engineer.

"I need a tactical map immediately!" I demanded, and a few seconds later the 3D hologram reappeared in the center of the hall.

After a brief look at it, all the officers gasped at once. Neither the Alien ships nor the three *Safas* existed any more. The map was showing nothing but a sea of small pieces of radioactive wreckage. A second went by, and another; then Space Corporal Patrick toyl Sven stood up in silence, approached the paralyzed Flora, bowed before her on one knee and kissed her on the hand.

"Florianna, it was only thanks to your talent as a Truth Seeker that our fleet is still alive! Know this, girl: I am forever indebted to you!"

The other officers applauded. I clapped my hands with the rest. Flora had completely earned these honors by confirming my suspicion of a trap with her abilities. Finally, I took the microphone:

"Now is not the time to relax! Bionica, send an order to the *Tria*. Have them send assault troops to capture the station. And tell the general to also prepare three hundred capsules to keep the scientists rescued from Kej in suspended animation in. Communications officer, I need to be put through to the Uf system beacon."

Fifteen minutes later, a Gamma Iseyek showed up on the screen in dark blue colors. The shape of his shell, combined with a massive bundle of tiny antennae near his mouth, made him look like a shaggy blue walrus.

"Bionica, translate! We are the Perimeter Sector Eight Fleet. We are on a special mission from the Swarm and have destroyed many Alien ships in the Kej and Aysar Cluster systems. With us are the Gamma Iseyek the Swarm tasked us with rescuing from the planet Kej-V. We need a warp beacon in the Uf system to bring the scientists out."

The whiskered blue walrus heard out Bionica's translation, chirped back an answer, and hung up. My synthetic assistant translated:

"I do not have the authority for such a decision. This will have to be agreed on with the coordinator."

I sighed out heavily. If he needed Triasss Zess's agreement, it wasn't hard to figure out that the answer would be negative. And that was exactly what happened. A few minutes later the communications officer told me about a message sent from the Uf system:

"The Swarm coordinator told me that there is no Imperial fleet in Swarm territory and there could never be. Aliens, you cannot trick us into opening a portal for you to invade through."

"Well then, it didn't work the first time," I laughed wryly, seeing the others' attention focusing on me. "Now the praying mantis assault troops will capture the station, and we'll wait for the rest of the ships, recharge them and keep going."

After opening a map of Swarm systems on the screen, I started imagining the possibilities. We wouldn't be allowed to Sobj, that had been clear for some time. Trying to get through the Uf system had just failed too. There were only two potential routes left: leave territory captured by Aliens through the Bej system or go on to the Arite system, which the Swarm fought a war over two hundred years ago with the mysterious Arite race. Human science knew precisely nothing on the Arites, and all information I had was based only on the meager information General Savasss Jach's personal record had provided, which said he was one of the heroes of the many-year war with them. There was nothing to do. I called the general and asked Bionica for help with the translation.

"Prince Georg, the landing troops have set down on the Aysar station, and the battle is under way. Approximately fifty minutes needed for complete clearing of all spaces on the Aysar station. Three hundred capsules for the Gamma Iseyek scientists have been prepared on *Tria*."

"General, I have a surprising question, and I hope very much that your obligations to the Swarm will not make it impossible for you to answer. What can you tell me about the Arites?"

The whiskers and appendages of the centipede suddenly started bristling like a hedgehog. Bionica commented:

"That's how Gamma Iseyek show disgust. He strongly disliked your question."

I could not give less of a shit about the insect's feelings, as I considered him partially at fault in the Swarm's betrayal. The general's answer was much more important to me:

"Prince Georg, you may not believe me, but it's better to meet ten times with Aliens than once with Arites. They are an exceptionally vile race of parasites. Since you've never had the good fortune of coming up against them, let me tell you that there is simply no way to remove an Arite. I spent many years in battles against the Arites and had a fairly good amount of victories. But I still do not know what exactly they look like."

"How is that even possible?" I asked in surprise.

"Because that's how it is with Arites, Crown Prince. It's very hard to explain it in words. You'll get it if you see even just one."

# FALLING INTO THE TRAP

THE BATTLESHIPS *Master of Tesse* and *Bride of Chaos* arrived to the Aysar Cluster at almost the exact same time as a message came in from Colonel Gor ton Vulf saying that a section of the warp beacon had been captured, though there were still battles underway in the rest of the station.

"Turn off the beacon, colonel!" I ordered. "We'll turn it back on for our cloakers in Kej for a very short time. Also, I really need trophies: Alien bodies, weapons, and equipment. That all has a huge value, both to the Empire and the Swarm alike. Perhaps, us having Alien trophies will be the very key that will open the door home for the Sector Eight Fleet."

However, a minute went by, then another, but the tactical map was still showing an active warp beacon as before. I called the colonel and asked about the delay.

"My Prince... we'll need some more time to get it turned off. My engineers and Savasss Jach's experts are both reporting that the equipment they are familiar with has been replaced with something really strange. Now they are trying to figure out what it is exactly that we found. Our first impression is that half the familiar instruments have been replaced with some sort of grown, living organism. One of the halls is filled with all kinds of stalks and roots. It's not clear how IT can replace computer chips, electric cables, power circuits, batteries and all other kinds of equipment, but the warp beacon system is still on despite the fact that half of the necessary systems are absent. We haven't figured out how to work IT yet, nor where this creature is drawing power from. We could just rip IT all out, say to hell with IT and turn the beacon off that way."

"No, colonel. For the time being, I forbid IT be destroyed, no matter what IT may be. We have thirty ships left in the Kej system. Without a beacon, they're doomed. Here, I think we better remember the first rule of computer programming: if something's working, even if you don't know how, don't change it. So, just collect the rest of the trophies, but don't touch IT yet. Will our ships be able to recharge their batteries at the station?"

"Yes, my Prince. Our technicians have already confirmed that. Though the voltage at the ports is nonstandard, and there are none using standard outputs, but our engineers say that they could reconfigure it to charge either Imperial or Swarm ships. The only thing is that there are only thirty-six working ports at the station. It's too few to quickly recharge such a big fleet."

I considered it briefly, then told them my decision:

"We will charge them one by one then. The first group will be *Master of Tesse, Bride of Chaos, Tria,*

*Emperor August, Boydur the Hero, Hunchback's Heir, Scalp Collector, Legashes* one to three, *Thrushes* one to five, *Pyros* one to ten, *Warhawks* one to five, *Flycatchers* one to three, two *Umoyge,* and one *Vassar.*"

"And what of the flagship?" Captain Oorast Pohl asked, surprised at the lack of *Joan the Fatty* in the list.

"We will be the last of the heavy cruisers to recharge. What kind of a fleet commander would save himself first and throw his subjects to the dogs?"

Judging by the labored smiles on the officers' strained faces, not nearly everyone approved, but no one expressed their dissatisfaction out loud. Nicole Savoia, in fact, even sent me a personal relation increase:

**Standing change. Nicole Savoia's opinion of you has improved.**

**Presumed personal opinion of you: +57 (friendship)**

I turned back to my assistant with a slight bow and smiled, which made the easily-embarrassed girl blush.

There was a certain risk in my choice to deprioritize charging the flagship, but I had some "crystal balls" watching the enemy in the Kej system, and they would tell me if anything changed. Also, *Ghost-3,* which had arrived ten minutes earlier to the Lobj system, had not detected enemy ships in it, so there was no threat to worry about from that direction either. If the Aliens started moving, I would have at least three hours and seventeen minutes to do anything (the time for the Alien ships to jump from Kej to the Aysar system), and in that time I could fully recharge my flagship's energy.

Making use of the silence that arose, I told my subjects that I was preparing to take some rest. I also said only to awaken me if our enemies took active measures, and then went back to my cabin to unwind. Astra had yet to finish the painting, but that didn't stop me. I had really already grown tired and needed to sleep. Also, after talking with Flora, I was feeling pretty high-strung and was preparing to really seriously have a talk with my favorite. Despite the Princess asking me to give her another hour to work alone, I decisively entered the cabin and flopped down on the little sofa. The girl, with an expression of clear dissatisfaction on her face, turned the canvas away from me so I wouldn't be able to see her creation.

It seemed that Flora had not been wrong, and the time had come to put the presumptuous beauty back in her place.

"Astra, the Beta Iseyek all complain about you," I declared to the Princess, having decided to go straight on the attack. "They say that your thoughts are too loud and so interesting that, even when they are on ships very far away, they have no choice but to study the human anatomy through your fantasies, instead of working."

"What?" The girl was taken aback and, after setting the paintbrush down, turned toward me in frustration. "Who could have said such garbage? None of it is true, your Highness... Bionica! That's right! It's her! Only an android could translate the words of an insect!"

In fact, I was trying to protect Flora, but the Princess's thoughts went in precisely the wrong direction. I had no desire to pressure my kind translator, so I answered Astra that Bionica had nothing to do with it. I assured the Princess that there were many in the fleet who understood the Iseyek language, and also Phobos and Deimos were not doing at all bad at learning human language and loved translating questions from insects for anyone who wants to hear. The Princess went simply crimson and sat on the armchair, covering her face with her hands. I sat down closer and said in a calming tone:

"Astra, you have to get used to the fact that times have changed. If you were just a girl barely anyone had ever heard of from the outskirts of the Empire, no one in the galaxy would be interested in what you talk about with your friends. But as you've already decided to become a noted public figure around a Prince in line to the Imperial Throne, from now on, your actions will directly influence not only your own reputation but mine as well. Even just a harmless flirtation with another man on your part, and that fact becomes public property and thus cause for discussion and mockery in society. And if, in addition, that very favorite continues to cast her played-through desires about willy-nilly, and strangers, both people and unpeople are able to see and hear it all, then a horrible scandal, up to the point of a call to the Emperor to explain the defiant behavior, is practically inevitable for us. I do not know how that sounds to you, but I don't like it one bit."

Astra turned to me with her eyes full of tears.

"Crown Prince, a number of times in my conversation with Corwin overly spicy topics really did come up. However, every time the captain apologized for his tactlessness, and it never occurred to me that our conversation might be upsetting someone. But I only ever wanted one thing: for him to see that picture I'm making. The captain is an expert in painting and said beautiful words about how I have such a unique style, unlike anyone else's, and as a result wished for me to make him a painting."

What? The mustachioed captain is an art lover?! Don't try to pull the wool over my eyes! What had happened started to look totally different to me. Oh, Astra, Astra... So naive and trusting...

"Can I take a look at your work?" I wondered, and the girl agreed.

"It's almost, almost done. There's just a couple more little strokes left," the Princess announced, standing up from the sofa, drying the tears with her sleeve.

I also stood up and walked around the canvas. What was there to say...? It was about what I was expecting. The only thing this time was that the painting was done not in black, but primarily in dark blue. Two thirds of the surface were taken up by different kinds of triangles and also yellow, long and short lines placed according to the "so no one will ever be able to figure out exactly why" principle. In the middle of the painting there was a white oval with a gold crown clumsily shining forth (or a flame, though possibly also the pelt of a red animal). The work was completed by a little red cross with rays of different lengths, painted right on top of one of the triangles. It could hardly have been intended to be an ambulance, though there were no other associations that came to mind looking at it.

"Tell me the truth. Is it beautiful?" the Princess asked timidly from behind my back. "It's a painting of the Sector Eight Fleet fighting its way through a horde of Aliens. The gold light inside the pure white area is our ships, everything else is enemies, and there are really a lot of them."

It seemed my conclusions about the Princess had been too rash. Princess Astra was still interested where my fleet was headed and what it was doing.

"Woah... Really nice," this time I was slightly acting against my conscience. "The red cross is..."

"The beacon home!" the artist informed me, noticeably coming to life.

"I really like it. Have you shown the painting to the consignor yet?"

The girl shook her head no, not understanding what I was hinting at. I was suddenly struck by an attack of utterly boyish joyfulness. Corwin ton Ugar, what kind of an art lover are you?! He's probably a lover of the fact that the trusting Astra's work could be sold for forty-fifty mil easily. I was now irreversibly convinced of the outcome would be just that.

"Astra, I have a wager for you. Let's say we give Corwin ton Ugar a painting that isn't by you but a totally different artist. If he doesn't figure it out in three hours that it isn't yours, you give your painting to me. But if he uncovers the forgery without you giving him hints, I'll give him the painting, apologize for the bad joke and never again will I interfere in your conversations. Agreed?"

The Princess began thinking, clearly looking for a catch. Then she said, cautiously and even confused:

"I do not understand you, Crown Prince. Those are unequal conditions on your Highness's part, because you will obviously lose. Corwin ton Ugar gave me an unambiguous assurance that he is an expert in painting, so he will easily recognize the artist's style and win the bet."

"That's all fine, Astra. I'm willing to risk it just this once. And even, to make it personally interesting for you, I'll add another condition: if Corwin ton Ugar really does have a flawless understanding of painting and points out the fake, I promise to give you whatever beautiful evening dress you choose on Unatari and also any jewelry you want to go with it."

Astra started dreaming and smiling, then sighed curtly:

"Unfortunately, I cannot answer you in kind, Prince George. I gave everything I had to the last credit to the creators of the series *Jeanne the Star Traveler* on Crown Princess Likanna's advice. To be honest, after that I even overspent a bit and went into the negative, buying things on the promise that your Highness would pay. This bet doesn't look very even to me, so from my side I promise to behave myself in the future as only a true Princess would: irreproachably, nobly and with exceptional dignity."

"You'll turn back into a cold porcelain doll?" I snorted with a grin. "No, thank you. That phase is already over. I'm happier with the joyful, fun girl that you never know what to expect from. The only thing I want for that ethereal beauty is perhaps to be a careless little bird in the little things but understand the importance of truly serious actions."

"Agreed! But where will your Highness find a fake painting to give Corwin?"

I guffawed and answered that I would paint it myself. Astra became immeasurably surprised, but all the same agreed to quickly finish her masterpiece and even put a new canvas on the frame for me, as I had no idea how that was done. I spent no more than fifteen minutes making my creation, half of which was wasted being taught by Astra how to mix paint.

"It's done. I call it 'Delicate flower in the thick of a silent forest'" I pointed to the surface smeared with green paint with just one little dab of pink above the green blotches.

"Your Highness, you never told me that you studied painting," my companion was staring in surprise with wide eyes at the green abstraction. "To be honest, when you asked for help with the paints, I thought you were an amateur."

I laughed joyously in reply:

"I just wanted to trick you a little bit. Of course I studied for many years with very famous modern artists. What else is there to do in the Throne World?" I laughed and, having gotten out my communicator, called a shuttle for Princess Astra. "Just remember the conditions of our bet: you have three hours to talk to the captain, during which time there must not be a single hint out of you to Corwin ton Ugar! Let him show us how competent an expert he really is!"

When Astra set off for the exit with the painting in her hands, I called the captain of *One-Eyed Python*:

"Captain Corwin ton Ugar, Princess Astra asked my permission to deliver you some surprise she promised. I agreed and didn't even send Phobos with her this time, though I would still like to remind you of my promise."

"I also remember your promise, Crown Prince," he said, slightly tensing up and giving a forced smile. "Your Highness, I place a high value on your trust and as an officer I swear to you that I won't even lay a finger on your beauty."

\* \* \*

I wasn't able to get any rest. An alarm signal started sounding sharply just as I lied down.

"My Prince! Our observer in the Kej system reported that two minutes ago around thirty small-class Alien ships jumped in our direction."

"What?" I mumbled, trying to make sense of the message from my half-asleep state. "And what of the rest of the Alien ships?"

"They're still in Kej," the officer reassured me.

I took a seat on the bed and looked at the time. I had only been able to sleep for forty minutes, but now that wasn't important in the slightest. The Aliens have gone on the attack! But it's really weird that they only sent small ships and such a small part of their fleet, though they could have sent many more. Why? I felt inside that the fate of my fleet was directly dependent on me finding the right answer to that question. I called Bionica and asked her to bring me some coffee. I started staring at the screen showing a map of the Swarm star systems.

The route the Aliens were taking looked

preposterous. Thirty small ships could pose a serious threat to any Imperial fleet except the Perimeter Sector Eight Fleet. We'd chew them up and spit them out without even noticing, and the Aliens probably knew that perfectly well. Why were they sacrificing their ships? What was it that I was not seeing? Why did over one thousand Alien ships stay in Kej?

The other system neighboring the Aysar cluster, Lobj, was empty. The Alien ships did not detect my scout there. I even considered the possibility that my scout and the Alien fleet had crossed paths and not seen one another but, at this point, five hours had gone by. That was how long a warp jump from the Lobj system to the Aysar Cluster took, and the Alien fleet had not yet arrived from there...

Bionica came in with coffee, and I asked the synthetic blonde to get me someone to talk to. I needed a smart conversationalist who could quickly analyze potential strategies and find errors in my thinking. Really, there weren't many who could play that role better than the android girl of incredibly advanced intellect, and in that regard Bionica did not let me down:

"My Prince, how did the Aliens get to Kej, Aysar, Lobj and Khe? Looking at the map, these systems aren't connected to any others under Alien control!"

"Clearly, there are systems under Alien control that the Swarm does not know about, which is why they are not shown on the map. And there are not beacons like we know them in these systems, so our navigators also cannot detect them." I replied, finishing the android's thought and giving myself a sharp slap to the forehead.

That was it! There were systems not shown on the Iseyek transport network map. The Aliens were figuring out, and were even sure, that their big fleet in Kej was being observed and that my cloakers were informing me of their every move. That's why the Aliens only sent a small group, so I wouldn't consider it dangerous and would move to attack it. But the little flotilla from Kej was just bait – something to keep my ships occupied. And meanwhile, another, much larger group of ships was on its way here from a system unknown to either the Iseyek or humans, and the Aliens were sure their hidden fleet would manage to wipe mine out.

"Bionica, you are a miracle worker!" I pecked the blonde on the cheek and started off quickly back to headquarters. My assistant followed me there. However, in the hall, on our way, I stopped sharply, struck by a sudden thought. "Bionica, does it seem to you that there might be something we're still not taking into account? The Aliens gave our fleet ample time to recharge, though they easily could have started operations earlier."

"Perhaps they were expecting the mined ships to make a bigger impact? Or maybe the damage we did from the bomb attack in Kej was more serious than we thought."

"No, no, it's something else. They could have sent that little group of ships earlier, or even several groups to keep us busy in battle and not let us recharge. But the Aliens didn't do that. They gave us enough time to recharge our ships. In two and a half hours, the fleet will be completely ready for a jump to Lobj, allowing us to wriggle out of their trap once again."

"That means that the Aliens are totally sure that the Sector Eight Fleet will not jump to Lobj," the android girl suggested, and we immediately both looked at one another.

Bionica was the first to open her mouth to make the next logical step, but I cut her off:

"Yes, that can only mean one thing: in the next hour or two, another Alien fleet will come to the Lobj system and cut off our only escape route!"

Fifty minutes went by, and my theory was totally confirmed. A message came in from *Ghost-3*, in charge of observation in the Lobj star system:

"Crown Prince Georg royl Inoky ton Mesfelle, important information. A very large Alien fleet has arrived to the Lobj system warp beacon! Around three hundred ships: eight *Behemoths*, up to thirty *Sledgehammers* and other kinds of cruisers, as well as two hundred fifty destroyers and frigates."

And that was it. We had fallen into the trap.

**\* \* \***

The meeting was chugging along at a fevered pitch. A map of the Aysar Cluster system and all neighboring systems in the transport network was being projected on the whole wall. There were black markers showing us known enemy forces. Orange markers were the Imperial Sector Eight ships, which were split between three systems. Next to the main group of orange dots was a big black question mark and a countdown timer. There was one hour and seventeen minutes before an unknown number of Alien ships would be arriving to the Aysar Cluster.

Admiral Kiro Sabuto was leading the staff officers group, suggesting potential fleet strategies. Opposing them was Admiral Kheraisss Vej with a whole group of Iseyek analysts of all three types and very exotic coloring, who had come to *Joan the Fatty* on the extreme occasion. The Iseyek were playing the Alien ships, and they were managing to turn the Sector Eight Fleet into ashes time and time again. My two wonderful assistants and I played the role of referees and experts in the tactical game. And what made me especially happy and even surprised is that none of the soldiers expressed the slightest doubt in Nicole Savoia or Bionica's authority or skills. The critical situation that had developed somehow weakened their earlier rank-based objections.

"No, that won't work either," replied Space Lieutenant Nicole Savoia, repudiating yet another of Admiral Kiro Sabuto's ideas. "For *Master of Tesse* and *Bride of Chaos* to turn around, accelerate and warp out, you would need no less than two minutes. Even if the fleet comes out as far as possible from the Lobj warp beacon, the Aliens have enough small ships, including the high-speed *Meteors*. Admiral, our calculations have shown that *Meteors* are capable of approaching and capturing heavy battleships in less than two minutes. Also, right after coming out of a warp tunnel, our ships' energy reserves will be practically empty. The fleet cannot enter another warp tunnel as usual, even if it is a very short one that doesn't leave the star system."

Just a second... I came alive and asked Captain

Oorast Pohl what would happen to a ship if there wasn't enough energy for a full warp jump. The military man began smoothing his mustache pensively, before giving a detailed answer:

"If the tunnel was open in the same star system and did not cross paths with any large cosmic obstacles, then the starship would simply come out at a random point in space. If the warp tunnel was connecting two different star systems or passed near stars, planets, their satellites, comets or asteroid belts, the result could be tragic: an object with a high mass would inevitably draw the ships toward it, and they would be destroyed by slamming into the massive obstacle at a high speed."

I sat down at a new spot behind the console and thought it all over again, considering the distribution of forces on the big screen. Then, I requested the attention of the humans and Iseyek gathered:

"Ladies and Gentlemen, I have come to a decision. We really do not know the Aliens' plans. Maybe they don't know of the Swarm's betrayal and are trying to push our fleet to the Uf system, so they can send their beacon-cloakers after us and prepare a fully-fledged invasion. And maybe they do know about the Swarm's actions and want to trap our fleet here in the Aysar system and destroy it. In any case, the path through Lobj is the only way to salvation. But defeating the Alien fleet in Lobj with the forces we have now would be extremely difficult. There are too many frigates and destroyers there, and it's best to take them on with stealth bombers. Unfortunately, almost all our cloakers are still in the Kej system. That is why our very first mission is to gather all our ships from Kej and Aysar together for a joint attack. The cloakers need time to get here from Kej and recharge their batteries, so our second mission is to make sure they have that time and not to lose any ships in the meantime. As far as we know, another Alien fleet will be arriving to the Aysar Cluster soon. Of course, we will watch it and maybe even try to clip its wings a bit; in any case, it isn't the priority mission. Preserving our starships for the main battle in Lobj is much more important... If the enemy comes to Aysar with a very large fleet, the Sector Eight Fleet will need some seven hours here in the system to avoid the battle. That is why we need enough spots."

Seeing that they didn't understand the term, I explained it:

"Twenty of our frigates are now turning on the most energy-draining systems like shield restoring modules or main propulsion engines to burn through their reserves. Then they will start making warp jumps to the edge of the Aysar system. They don't have enough energy to set up a fully-fledged warp tunnel, and the starships will start to come out god-knows-where, in random places. The frigates will work overtime to collect those random coordinate sets, by making repeated jumps with insufficient battery power and sending their position to us as they come out. We need a few hundred such spots where the Perimeter Sector Eight Fleet can hide, periodically changing position in the system to hamper the Aliens' positioning systems. As soon as our ships are ready, the whole fleet will open a warp tunnel simultaneously and leave to the Lobj system. Yes, the enemy there is very strong, but we should manage!"

Everyone stayed silent for some time, digesting my words. The only sound was Bionica, squeaking out clarifications of my plans for the praying mantises. Admiral Kheraisss Vej tilted his head to the side and asked:

"My Princcce, what if the flee-eet Alien from Aysssar alssso to want jump after we to sssyssstem Lobj? Are we not be like, how people say, 'between the rock and hard place?'"

"They won't figure out right away that our fleet even did leave the Aysar star system. For at least a few minutes, it will just look like we jumped off to another set of coordinates. Though, admiral, you are totally right! We'll have to have our bombers leave a couple megatons of fun to keep their fleet entertained. Even if we don't kill any of them, we'll burn out the sensitive radar equipment, so the Aliens will need time to repair before they can even realize we're gone."

Admiral Kheraisss Vej made an imitated bow, then asked a very unexpected and extremely frank question:

"My Princcce, is all posssible for work, your plan. But I, as admiral Iseyek, to have interest in order to underssstand full. Princcce George last battle to use three *Safa* purposssely and is know trap? Never Princcce is to send *Safa*. But, when send you, three is fast explosion."

Everyone in the room went silent, somewhat shocked by the frankness of the question. I decided not to obscure the truth and answered honestly:

"Admiral, you passed the Truth Seeker check, so you have a right to know. No matter how regrettable it may be, there are traitors among the captains and officers of our fleet, and their goal is the complete annihilation of the Sector Eight Fleet."

Everyone around gasped in concert, struck by the information. Popori de Cacha appeared next to me, showing that the topic was of utmost importance to him. I, though, continued calmly:

"There are many possible reasons to make a certain person or Iseyek choose to walk the road of treason. One of them, though, is that some captains of your race have received clear orders from the Swarm to act to that precise end. In battle, these ships were to stab us in the back, and that is why I chose precisely them to disarm the trap."

Silence came over the hall, then the admiral spoke:

"Is very justiccce, esssspecccially after the bad in Kej. I to understand and accept this choice, Princcce Georg. Though, if is not all traitor killed, I would to suggest to send to Tria, and there we eat. All crew is no to support for traitor-cap-i-tain."

"Very well, Admiral, that's exactly what I'll do. Florianna will give me the full list, and the Iseyek deemed traitors will be sent to the *Tria* to become food for the hungry landing troops. If there are human traitors, their interrogation and judgment will be carried out by Popori de Cacha and the Truth Seeker. Your mission then, admiral, is to find suitable replacements for the captains and officers that did betray us."

* * *

After it was confirmed that all my fleet's cloakers had successfully made it out of the Kej system together with the scientists rescued from Kej-V, I ordered the Aysar system station mined and the whole fleet to move away from it. I also ordered samples collected from IT, the being that was now taking the place of some of the beacon equipment. If it was a previously unknown species of Alien, and still alive as well, it would no doubt be a valuable trophy, and I would have to take it with me and have it studied.

Also, at the very last moment, an idea came to me not to simply remove the fleet but to check if there were any enemy cloakers around us in advance as well. After all, the less the Aliens knew about our preparations, the higher the chance all our operations would succeed became.

That was why I ordered all fleet ships to imitate acceleration toward the Uf system, supposedly to return to Iseyek territory. I had a basis to suppose that the Aliens really did not know about the, let's say, "complications" in the relationship between Crown Prince Georg royl Inoky and the Swarm. In that case, the enemies would suppose that the Sector Eight Fleet, warned that Alien forces would soon arrive in the Aysar system, was retreating straight to the Uf system. Alien cloakers had already shown their readiness to capture valuable battleships in the past by holding them until the main forces arrive. Why should it be any different this time?

A few minutes later, the two slow battleships

started lagging markedly behind the rest of the ships, and I gave an order:

"*Surprise-26*, prepare for a megaton bomb attack on our battleships!"

As expected, the order gave the captain certain apprehensions:

"Prince Georg, this is the captain of *Surprise-26*. I request that you provide your identification code and confirm the order to attack allied ships!"

I sent my electronic code to confirm my identity and confirmed the order:

"I repeat, launch a megaton bomb at our battleships. I'll explain: you won't get through their shields with your bomb, but the explosion could uncover potential cloaked observers. All frigates, attention! Immediately after the blast, if any enemy cloakers show up, capture them in warp disruptor and webs! One minute to action! All ships, cover sensitive equipment, and prepare to stand by in three seconds!

Not everything went smoothly: *Surprise-26* didn't make it into the warp jump and was hit by its own bomb. But when the tactical map reappeared, it showed not only the wreckage of my stealth bomber, but also that of two other frigates and another small Alien ship that had clearly suffered from being too close to the explosion. A whole swarm of green dots moved out toward the lone target.

"*Warhawk-4* here. I'm holding the enemy under web and disruptor." Tamara Vuzhek once again distinguished herself by being the first frigate to complete the mission.

A few seconds later, there were no less than a

hundred stasis webs and warp disruptors on the cloaker, which brought the ship to a complete stop. It would be a sin not to take such valuable prey alive...

"General Savasss Jach, the immobile small Alien frigate must be captured. Are there landing troops ready?" I wondered, and Bionica translated the giant centipede's none-too-satisfied answer:

"Will fifty thousand be enough? Prince, that's how many I woke for the assault on Kej-V, you see, but the attack did not take place. We have no way of putting the soldiers back into suspended animation. They are hungry, and they must be fed first. That group of Iseyeks that you sent to the *Tria* as food wasn't enough for such a bottomless pit of hungry mouths."

"General, all we need to do now is capture one little frigate. But do not worry. In fifteen hours, we'll have eight *Behemoths* to storm. Your soldiers won't have been woken up for nothing."

"Eight *Behemoths*?" the general thought it over. "That is serious... I wonder if fifty thousand will even be enough... I'll wake up another fifty thousand in twelve hours then. But for now, one pod should do the trick. Ninety-one landing troops will be sent out to capture it in one minute."

Ten minutes later, I got a message that the cloaked ship was under our control and was even in a very good condition. The landing troops did not detect any living enemies inside the ship, but that wasn't important. We had a cloaked Alien frigate that could set up mobile warp beacons! It was just a treasure trove of technology to be studied! The trophy was so valuable that it had to be taken no matter the cost.

I clarified, just to be cautious, whether there was

any dangerous antimatter in the ship. I ordered the ship disabled to turn off the warp drives and make it possible to transport. After that, my technicians attached the trophy to the chassis of *Master of Tesse*. There were fifteen minutes left until zero hour, the time when the new Alien ships would arrive in the Aysar system, and everything was ready.

"All ships, take coordinates for warp jump!" I sent the data for one of the far-off spots in the Aysar system. "Accelerate toward the target. Stand by for three minutes, then we'll all leave the station together. Just a division of *Surprises* will stay here by the station. We'll see who comes to visit and whether the rest of us should come out to say 'hi.'"

I gave all the orders and threw myself down into an armchair. Bionica, in a stroke of genius, thought to bring me some energizing drink without my asking. It did a great deal toward bringing back my strength. By the way... it had been three hours. What was going on with my favorite and our wager? I called Princess Astra on an internal line.

The girl was sitting in an armchair with a glass of a dark wine in her hand wearing nothing but a pair of semi-transparent underwear. There was a canvas tipped over on the floor next to her and pieces of women's clothing thrown around the room, along with tubes of paint.

"How did your meeting with the painting expert go?" I wondered.

"Some painting expert..." by her lowered eyes and sobbing tone, I figured that Astra had recently been crying. "Prince Georg, you were right. Corwin ton Ugar was a liar! That's right! He just kept talking up your painting and saying how much he could see my style, that he could feel a woman's touch. He was spinning pure crap! And basically he turned out to be a totally boring person. And just where did his happy character go, his jokes and wit? I realized I was very wrong about him. So I decided not even to wait out the whole three hours and left *One-Eyed Python* in just forty minutes. You won the bet, Crown Prince. But for some reason, I'm just so, so sad... And it's not at all because of the presents I'll never get now..."

It was at that moment that *Joan the Fatty* went into the warp tunnel away from the mined station. I turned off the screen showing my favorite, who had clearly made up her mind to sit by herself drinking. I looked at the time and sighed, laying back into an armchair and closing my eyes. I only had eleven minutes of rest before another potential battle. I would need to see just what kind of Alien forces were coming to us in the Aysar system for a little fire-fight.

# THE FATTY'S LAST BATTLE

**"N**O, NO, I just don't play like that!" I boiled over dramatically when, in addition to the group of thirty small Alien ships we already knew about, another armada came to the Aysar system, one that made the thousand-strong fleet in Kej seem simply pitiful by comparison. "If there were a thousand times less of them, we might have even gone out to greet our guests, but now it doesn't make any sense. *Surprises*, cancel attack, fall back. And turn your camera on that giant in the middle. I want to get a closer look."

My cloaked frigate turned its camera and zoomed in, focusing on the matte-black starship that served as the epicenter of the massive Alien fleet. The shape of the ship was reminiscent of a bent black coin about twelve miles long. I was able to see clearly on the video that there were many smaller ships stuck onto the colossus: *Sledgehammers*, *Hermits*, and even *Behemoths* looked tiny on the backdrop of this leviathan.

"Area: fourteen miles by fourteen miles. Width: zero

point zero nine three miles. No cannon installations can be detected visually." said Valian ton Corsa. "It's a carrier. A mothership!"

The second part the officer shrieked when a whole squadron of *Meteors* ripped out from the depths of the titan into space unexpectedly.

"Carriers are typically closer to the size of our *Uukresh*. But, compared to that giant, it would seem like nothing. I announce a competition: we need to think of a name for this big Alien ship! It is also long past time to name the other previously unknown ships we are now also familiar with. I mean, the name 'that cruiser that totally isn't a *Sledgehammer*' is a bit long!"

The officers began laughing. I also smiled. It was probably surprising, but none of the officers there were panicked or scared any longer in the slightest. The Alien armada surpassed the Perimeter Sector Eight Fleet in strength to such a degree that you couldn't even be scared. Suggestions came in from all around:

"Puck!" "Discus!" "Coin Collector!" "Stingray!" "Mother-in-Law!" "Star killer!" "Hive!" "Pie!"

*"Queen!"*

"Why 'Queen?' Is it something you sensed?" I turned to the paralyzed girl.

*"It... I don't know. It's too murky. She has come to reckon with those who have brought harm to her children. No, not quite... She is their collective mother, but not in the usual sense. It's more like... they are all one being, and inside the big ship is the largest part of the body. No, that's still not it... The roots of the whole species... Wrong again... I'm confused, Prince. I guess it*

*was a stupid name..."*

"It's not stupid at all, Florianna. I will tell everyone what you sensed: that ship or some being inside it is somehow like the root of the whole Alien race. It has come to destroy all who would dare offend its branches. It's new official name is *Queen*."

*"Prince Georg... there's something else I want to tell you about. I have finally finished checking all the captains and senior officers for treason and other signs of defection. The captain's second assistant on the battleship* Bride of Chaos *has been bought off. He must be interrogated. Also, the captain of* Surprise-28 *and her first assistant have bought into a curious brand of fatalism. They believe that humanity is destined to die in the war with the Aliens, but that they will leave together on their cloaked frigate and give rise to a new race of humans. Just now, this duo has taken it in their heads to throw up radio beacons at our spots to give the Aliens their coordinates. They think the Aliens won't destroy* Surprise-28 *if they do that, and that they will even be rewarded for their unique knowledge and abilities. And also... I will have to talk with the captain of* Umoyge-7. *That Gamma Iseyek is definitely not a traitor, but he is somehow different. I will need to have a chat with him to get it figured out. Invite him to* Joan the Fatty.*"*

I told all the officers about the Truth Seeker's words. Admiral Kiro Sabuto reacted harshly:

"Crown Prince, we've already been through just such a thing not so long ago. The traitors were outed by name. I see no reason to wait and give them the ability to finish whatever sinister mission they're undertaking. Article 34-11, subsection B of the Space

Fleet Charter prescribes the highest level of punishment possible!"

"I agree, admiral. But in order not to spook them off before we can get there, let's do this: when the fleet jumps to the next temporary location, call all ten captains to *Joan the Fatty* together with their assistants, saying it's to give them a secret mission. Popori de Cacha, do it on your terms, but when the shuttles arrive at the dock, don't get confused: the human traitors are to be arrested, but the Gamma Iseyek in charge of *Umoyge-7* is to be politely invited to a conversation."

"Will do, tuki-tuka-de-sa!" the Chameleon bowed. "Would you like to speak with them?"

"I don't see a particular reason for that, and also I'm simply collapsing from exhaustion. The fleet will just spend the next seven hours changing its coordinates and jumping around the Aysar system. The admirals can deal with that very well without my personal participation. I just need some sleep. There's a big battle coming up tomorrow, and I need to go into it well rested."

\* \* \*

I was rattled awake by Astra. Without opening my eyes, in a sleepy voice, I wondered what had happened.

"Nothing so important. It's just that the alarm clock went off, and your Highness asked me to wake you up if you didn't hear it."

"Is that so? I don't remember such a thing at all..."

With difficulty, I cracked one eye open, and the first thing I saw was two bouncing naked breasts right in front of my face.

The dream vanished as if by magic. With both eyes now open, I saw the smiling Princess in her birthday suit sitting on the bed. Something was different with Astra... Her hair! The girl had died it emerald green. And on the Princess's arms, neck, and breasts there was a fanciful silver twisting pattern. Ripping my eyes from the spectacle of this forest dryad in my bed, I looked at the alarm clock. There was around an hour left before I was planning to wake up.

"So, I guess you were joking about the alarm clock then?" I posited.

"Do you think this shade of green suits me?" Astra wondered instead of answering the question. "Bionica recommended I do it. She also drew this on my body, saying that you would definitely like it!"

The girl jumped up from the bed and started spinning around with a happy laughter, demonstrating her excellent figure and the shining pattern on her skin, as well as causing her emerald hair to flutter freely. It was all very beautiful and alluring. But my gaze suddenly got caught on a chain around Astra's wrist. It was, by the way, quite a familiar gold chain with a figure of two people in passionate embrace. It was like I had a bucket of cold water dumped on me. Sure, I could explain the green hair or drawing on the skin as just random or another change of look on her part, but this chain, which I had once given to an android in an underwater cave, being on the Princess's arm could only be a frank, unambiguous hint. I don't like it when people try to manipulate me.

"What's the matter?" Astra wondered, after seeing my change in mood. "Bionica told me to wear it."

I called my secretary on an internal line. Bionica answered instantly, as if she was sitting at the information panel waiting for me to call.

"Can you explain what's going on here?" My annoyed tone instantly demonstrated to the robot secretary that I was none too amused by her plan.

"My Prince, everything is simple. Astra asked me to help her with an outfit, and I decided not to refuse the Princess such a small request."

Bionica flapped her huge eyelashes innocently, showing clearly with her whole appearance that she had no idea why I could have been upset. Though... Was it just me, or did a satisfied smile appear fleetingly on the synthetic girl's face? The android knew my character quite well and, I suspect, had predicted this exact outcome. I signed off, looked at the Princess who was slightly losing confidence and explained my behavior:

"Astra, you are very beautiful on your own. So don't ask Bionica to change your image. Robots have their own ideas about what is beautiful, and they aren't always the same as people's."

"So she spoiled everything, huh?" It seemed to me the girl was about to start crying.

"It's not Bionica's fault. She was trying. But that chain just doesn't suit you. Not your style at all. And green hair is usually a sign of errant desperation and adolescent rebellion against society. It looks good on my eleven-year-old daughter, but on a woman who is trying to look like an adult, such as yourself..."

Astra sat closer to me and wondered timidly:

"And the drawing on my skin? Bionica recommended against it, in favor of a permanent tattoo."

"You definitely don't need it permanent, but just drawing it on from time to time for variation..." I led my finger over the crisscrossing silver lines in thought. They sparkled back up at me from under my fingertips and gradually faded.

"The paint reacts to light. It changes color in the dark," the girl placed my hand on her breast. "And if we turn the light off in the room, my body would glow."

"We should try it out," I agreed, turning off the light and at once ordering the Chameleons to take some time off in the hall.

The alarm clock rang, but it was already too late to stop Astra and I. The negative effect of the crystals had finally fully passed, and I was feeling like I could do anything, so I took great relish in the wonderful and passionate woman beside me.

A few minutes after that, when we were simply lying and resting in embrace, I heard the Princess give a quiet whisper:

"That was my gift to your Highness. Happy Birthday, Crown Prince Georg!"

I was surprised, but called up the popup in any case to see for myself:

**Georg royl Inoky ton Mesfelle, Crown Prince of the Empire**
**Age: 48**

Astra really was not wrong. I had become a year older... I began thinking and even laughing. I had already melded so much with my game avatar that I thought about my virtual character as if it were me. Well, alright then. I guess it was my birthday today, so there was no way I could lose this decisive battle!

"I need to go to fleet headquarters, explain the situation about the Aliens and solve the most urgent issues. But I'll be back pretty quick!" I promised in the darkness, and Astra answered me at full volume:

"Alright, I won't even get dressed then!"

The headquarters of the military assault cruiser was decorated with glowing spheres hovering in the air, colorful ribbons and congratulatory notes. Instead of a tactical map, there was a hologram in the middle of the hall, showing Crown Prince Georg royl Inoky ton Mesfelle in a ceremonial uniform. The data screens at my work place were hard to look at due to the overabundance of flower bouquets at my place sent by crew members from all different levels of society to congratulate me. On the console I saw a bottle of sparkling wine with a ribbon tying on a card that read: "Prince, can you guess who it's from?"

*"Bionica sent it,"* I heard a hint in my head, though I could have guessed myself without my Truth Seeker's help.

As soon as the congratulations lulled down, I asked the staff officers about the current state of affairs.

"It's all pretty calm," Admiral Kiro Sabuto

reassured me. "Our cloakers were able to make it to this system from Kej, but there were two losses: *Surprise-15* and *Ghost-4* came out in some space garbage, were unmasked and got destroyed immediately. The other ships got out just fine and have already recharged their energy. Most of the Alien fleet is next to the Aysar station as before, though some squadrons of Alien frigates are buzzing around the system, trying to track us down. They're using something like triangulation, I suppose. They determine the angle between our fleet and a few different spots in the system, then use that to calculate the jump coordinates. They are really going to our old spots, but it's pretty sloppy. They're usually about three thousand miles off and very late. By the time they even start accelerating toward a spot, our ships have already been gone for fifteen to twenty minutes. There are some ships stuck to the Aysar station, but they have not found the bomb we hid behind welded-shut doors. Our cloaked bombers have gone out to position and are waiting for the attack signal."

I asked for a video feed from the cloaked ships. The Alien army was swarming around the *Queen* as before. There didn't visually appear to be less ships.

"Alright, all ships, stand by in thirty minutes. Stealth bombers, set bomb timers to five seconds, jump into the middle of the ball and warp right out along the same trajectory. Everyone go together; there may be too much wreckage afterwards to pull this off a second time. Other ships, advance toward the Lobj warp beacon. Set jump distance to eight hundred miles. *Ghost-6*, blow up the station ten seconds after the bomber attack. After you release your bombs, and after *Ghost-6* strikes, you will all follow us to Lobj. Katerina, I want you to get some footage of the *Queen* and make a pretty report. If the chance should present itself, we'll send it right to the Empire. We can use footage from previous battles to make this one look no worse than that time in Hnelle!"

"Will do, Georg, but I need you to give me the chance to broadcast them!" Katerina clearly lit up, walked closer to the big screen and began to give orders to technicians. I couldn't even understand half of what she was saying. "Eighth filter... Autofocus on the gleam. Second camera here and correction. No, no, what delay?! Yes, microphone here with dubbing and pressure. Where has makeup gone off to?"

All the teams had finally been assigned, and the officers got to work. I stood from my seat and also watched the attack on the big screen with my cousin. I turned to the android and asked:

"Bionica, be a mensch and take all this stuff away from my station. I can barely see the monitors at this point. It's like I'm blind. And after that, I'll read all your wishes. And thank you for the gift! Excellent wine!"

"I'm glad you liked it!" The android walked up to my seat, picked up a couple flowery leaves and suddenly froze in indecision. I had left the gold medallion sitting on the table under some papers, hoping she'd see it.

Meeting my gaze, the synthetic girl took the piece of jewelry and put it back on her own wrist. She turned the paper the chain was under, read what I'd written on it and gave a happy laugh.

"Astra trusts you. You shouldn't take advantage of

that," it read.

"Ten seconds!" Nicole Savoia was in charge of the countdown. "Three. Two. One. Attack!"

The stealth bombers appeared for just a moment. You just barely even see them on the backdrop of all the Alien ships. The aftermath of their attack, on the other hand, was a bit harder to miss. Inside the fast-moving ball, a great many fiery sparks began shooting out, swallowing up a large proportion of the armada's forces. It combined into one huge ball of plasma, and the thirty explosions scattered the Alien ships. After that, the Aysar Cluster station also gave way to a pretty burst of flame. The ten megaton bomb was enough to break the space fortification into pieces. And then... an unplanned explosion followed, much more powerful than the earlier ones. A bright white wave reached *Ghost-6* within a second, after which the recording ended.

"*Ghost-6* is no more," Admiral Kiro Sabuto said, upset, looking at the extinguished marker indicating a former allied ship on the screen.

"Distance to epicenter: twelve hundred miles," Nicole said in the silence that had descended.

I took the microphone and said, trying to keep my cool:

"All ships warp to the Lobj system!" The Aliens are not concerned with us anymore. We simply couldn't choose a better moment to get away from the armada."

* * *

In the dining room, I was eating breakfast with Admiral Kiro Sabuto and the staff officers, who were discussing recent events at a lively din. The bombing of the Alien fleet and the death of *Ghost-6*. On the one hand, the energy shields installed on cloaked frigates were just a formality, just ticking a box. But on the other hand... even being twelve hundred miles from the epicenter couldn't save our scout! Engineers were arguing with Admiral Kiro Sabuto over the true force of the blast, having the radar signature area, frigate shield capacity and size, but they came up with some huge numbers beyond possibility, measured in hundreds of gigatons or even teratons in TNT-equivalent. Our thermonuclear reserves looked like nothing more than firecrackers compared with whatever was behind that blast.

Did we destroy the enemy armada? I would like to believe that we did, of course. But those engineers' calculations, based on the assumed relationship between the size and shield power of Alien ships, have shown the exact opposite. The *Queen* definitely survived. There could be no doubt of that. The *Mammoths*, which is what the officers had started calling the small Alien carriers, didn't get wiped out either. But when it came to *Behemoths'* ability to survive that plasma inferno, there were doubts, though there was also a serious lack of data. We had never once shot through an Alien battleship's shield, so we had no idea how strong it was. The good news was, the calculations gave the Alien *Sledgehammers*, *Chainsaws* (the previously unnamed cruisers discussed earlier) and other small ships, absolutely no chance of having made it out of the fiery whirlwind.

Bionica affirmed that she had counted seven thousand, three hundred starships in the Alien armada, and according to our calculations, no more than three hundred of the largest ships could have survived, not including the approximately five hundred frigates and destroyers that were on their way to the Aysar system at the time of the explosion in search of our fleet. We still didn't know how many of our stealth bombers had survived the attack, but in any case it looked like an acceptable trade-off.

And the last question, which was causing the officers to argue at an even more fevered pitch was what exactly that blast was. An antimatter explosion from one or several *Behemoths*? It was definitely the answer that first came to mind, but certainly not the only possibility. The main engineer of *Joan the Fatty* told us his alternate theory: the warp beacon itself had exploded, causing energy from another dimension to slip through a hole in the fabric of space. No one could say one way or another when it came to that theory. There were no other times in human history when an operating warp beacon was observed to have been destroyed. As such, no one had any idea what such a risky move could lead to.

"Tuki-tuka-de-sa, I ask you to come to Florianna's room. Your assistance is required in the interrogation of the traitors," Popori de Cacha hunted me down just as I was coming out of the dining area.

I was quite surprised, as I had earlier told the Chameleon that I did not intend to personally carry out such an unpleasant procedure. Nevertheless, the head of my guard was stubborn and affirmed that the situation with the arrested was not simple, and would need my personal intervention. I sighed heavily, banished the thoughts of Astra waiting for me, and followed after the head of my bodyguard.

The three arrested were sitting in handcuffs squatting on the floor. Surrounded by the four silent insects, Florianna was in her already familiar flying armchair. It was hard to tell whether the paralyzed girl was working hard or sleeping behind her closed eyes.

*"How could I sleep here...?"* The voice ringing out in my head confirmed the first of the two theories. *"Prince, we are now dealing with the second assistant from* Bride of Chaos, *this is the simpler case. I'll tune in to the conversation in a bit."*

"We'll start with this one," Popori de Cacha also pointed to the strong man with the second captain's assistant's patches on an Orange House uniform.

***Undigo ton Mesfelle, major of the Orange House of the Empire, second captain's assistant on the battleship Bride of Chaos in the Perimeter Sector Eight Fleet***

    ***Age: 48***
    ***Race: Human***
    ***Gender: Male***
    ***Class: Military/Aristocrat***
    ***Achievements: None***
    ***Fame: +2***
    ***Standing: 0***
    ***Presumed personal relationship: Unknown***

*Empire Military faction opinion of you: (information unavailable at present)*

We were the same age and even related, though perhaps not very closely. I sat on the edge of Florianna's magical seat and turned to the arrestee:

"Undigo, you have already sworn an oath to me as fleet commander and passed a Truth Seeker check in the Himora system. How can this be?"

"It's just how it turned out, Crown Prince Georg," the major made no attempt to argue or find an excuse for his actions, instead just telling me the story. "My family is quite close to the main branch of the Mesfelle line and is in close contact with Duke Paolo royl Anjer ton Mesfelle and his close family. My sister even lives on the Orange House Capital in Duke Paolo's summer palace. My wife on Nessi is Peres royl Paolo ton Mesfelle's wife's closest friend... to be more accurate, she's even closer friends with Peres ton Mesfelle," Undigo corrected himself quickly. "It was after I took the oath that Duke Paolo found a way to hook me in. To keep someone very close to me out of harm, I agreed to deliver a small sealed package to Swarm coordinator Triasss Zess. I suspected that there was something in the package that the Duke was planning to use to harm your Highness, but I still do not know what exactly it was."

"So this is the traitor that delivered the message from the head of the Orange House to Triasss Zess, after which Triasss Zess sent our fleet into a trap," Popori de Cacha was clearly not inclined to forgive the betrayal, however, he submitted to the Crown Prince's right to judge this aristocrat and relative.

I stayed in thought for one minute. I'm not sure how they broke the major, nor what exactly he gave the Alpha Iseyek, but Undigo ton Mesfelle's indirect accusation at Duke Paolo could turn out useful. I needed this person around as a witness.

"I'll leave you among the living, but only if you back up your words with a sworn statement."

Undigo nodded and I ordered him removed and placed under arrest in one of the cabins on *Joan the Fatty* until we returned to the Empire. There were two more: a middle-aged, and frankly not very beautiful woman with Orange House Fleet space captain patches and a young chubby corporal half her age. Both characters were NPC's with no additional information available. Popori de Cacha explained the details:

"This woman says that she hears voices that whisper to her that humanity is doomed. But these voices supposedly are directly promising to let her live, and even make her practically immortal if she helps them destroy the Sector Eight Fleet. She was able to convince her first assistant, who was also her lover that they had been chosen to become the Adam and Eve of a new human race, but first they would need to help the Aliens kill the people that were already around. They were planning to begin with the ships of the Sector Eight Fleet. They really were placing radio beacons at the spots in the Aysar system and were preparing to leave some more to make extra sure."

"But that is true!" the woman screamed out. "The voices do speak to me! The old humanity is doomed. It will fall under the Alien onslaught. And only I will retain the right to remain alive and give a new hope to humanity! And as the voices say, I do, to make sure our species will not go extinct! You can call my actions treason, betrayal, whatever you want. But, in the end, it will be I who saves humanity!!!"

I frowned squeamishly at the arrestee's screams, and because of the rapture and awe that her young assistant was looking on her with. How could I make sure the rest of my subjects wouldn't begin heeding this dangerous lunatic's words?

"So what is the problem with sentencing her, then?" I couldn't understand why my subjects treated these two traitors with such regard.

*"The problem is that she really does hear voices, or at least believes so honestly that she does that there is no difference,"* the Truth Seeker explained to me. *"I see two options: either she is mentally ill, and so should be treated, and not punished. Or the voices are real and then the fact that Aliens can control people's minds would be a serious problem."*

I opted not to draw anyone's attention to the second possibility. There were no reliable facts, so it was hard to predict all fleet members', both peoples' and unpeoples', reaction to the news that Aliens have the ability to influence the mind. That was why I asked in a blatantly negligent tone:

"So, the Truth Seeker says that the captain simply lost her mind from fear? Yes, when our fleet landed in the trap, it is possible that the weak of spirit may have grown desperate, and that even could have led some to become less clear on the line between fantasy and reality. So, my decision is that the woman is to be placed in the infirmary under Nicosid Brandt's observation, and to let the military court deal with her assistant. The boy never heard any voices. He decided to betray his own kind consciously and intentionally."

The man jumped up to his feet and tried to burst out of the room, but he couldn't open the locked door with his hands bound behind his back.

"No! So that was all a lie about restarting the species?! You're such a bitch! I hate yo..." one of Popori de Cacha's assistant didn't allow the traitor to finish his sentence, sticking the paralyzer to his neck in a tried-and-true motion and grabbing his body as it fell to the ground.

"And now, the most important thing, Crown Prince," not paying attention to the motionless body on the floor, Popori de Cacha walked up to the wall and turned on the screen. "That is footage from the observation cameras in the hangar of *Joan the Fatty*. You can see the shuttles full of captains arriving one after another, as Admiral Kiro Sabuto requested. Note that the second to last to dock is the shuttle from *Umoyge-7*. In this clip, you can watch the captains all exiting their ships."

A small scuffle was shown on the screen. My bodyguards suddenly seized three of the people from the list, and the Chameleons that showed up helped, while also keeping the other captains and officers from interfering in the conflict.

"I'll wind it back a bit and show exactly what you should be looking at," the Chameleon wound the clip back for thirty seconds, then played it again at a slower rate. "Everyone was busy with the arrest, and didn't see the main thing: no one came out of the shuttle from *Umoyge-7*. We checked the shuttle later and it was empty. There was no pilot inside. But someone had been piloting the shuttle, and clearly manually. And now look here!"

A human figure appeared from behind the Iseyek shuttle. It stood for a few seconds, watched the traitors get detained, but did not interfere, and set off at a quick pace to one of the side doors."

"Who is that? Why did they arrive on a Swarm ship?" I had no idea what was going on.

"That is not all, Prince Georg. Here is the security footage from the hallway he went down. Watch it in synch with the video from the hall.

The screen split in two: one half was showing the shuttle hangar, and the other was showing video from another camera. First the stranger pulled at the door handle and pulled the door toward himself. At the same time, the door to the hallway also opened. But... no one went through!!!

"I have no idea what's going on," I admitted. "Who was that, and where did he go?"

"On *Umoyge-7*, they confirmed that the shuttle they sent to the flagship had only their captain on it. Here is a hologram of him. And we already have data from our tactics officers showing that the shuttle's route from *Umoyge-7* to *Joan the Fatty* never deviated from the assigned path, nor did it attach to any other ships."

I looked at the three-dimensional image of the captain of *Umoyge-7*. The centipede was approximately ten feet tall, a typical Gamma Iseyek. There was no doubt about it. But why then did another species arrive?

"It's an Arite!" A bizarre creaking voice rang out

over my ear. I even shook in surprise and turned to the huge, normally quiet Alpha Iseyek security guard.

"Deimos, what do you know about the Arites? I need all the information you have!

The ten-foot-tall praying mantis wriggled his mandibles, carefully speaking the following words:

"I to fight with Arites on Arite-V, Arite-VIII, the moons of the eighth planet and on Swarm shshships. That is just how Arite to look. To be different always. Never to understand. If to kill, Arite die like Iseyek. But is Arite. Very hard to fight Arites. Very many losss. Is always Swarm confuse and to fight to Swarm."

*"My Prince, look at me, but turn slowly and naturally."*

Florianna's words were so strange and intriguing that I did as she said. What's wrong? Everything looked normal. The paralyzed girl was sitting in a black robe in the armchair and her minions were around her. Wait a second! Since when did Flora have five Beta Iseyeks? There were only four!

*"The fake is standing behind me to the left,"* the *Truth Seeker* said.

As if nothing had happened, I continued to discuss the footage of the Iseyek shuttle's arrival, and then, without changing intonation, in a tranquil voice, told the room what the paralyzed girl had said. Phobos and Deimos reacted even faster than the Chameleons. In the space of a second, they closed the gap to the enemy, attacked it with their terrifying upper appendages and stuck it through with all of their four razor-sharp chitin blades.

There was no blood. The Beta Iseyek's figure

suddenly dissolved and an off-white cloud escaped into the ventilation grate on the wall.

"It's gone!" Deimos stated with vexation. "He to can to become any being on *Joan the Fatty*, and systems not to understand different. Any passs, any marking to copy, to trick sssensors. Tricky beassst."

"How did the Swarm deal with Arites if one made it on a starship?" I wondered to Deimos, leaning on the Iseyek's two-hundred-year experience in the issue.

"Swarm to explode all these ship to know Arite is to dead. To let air out of all section right away is mean less victim in end. Arite is not to live in ssspace vacuum."

"No, that won't work in our situation," I laughed nervously. "People, and Chameleons are also quite bad at living in a vacuum. All the same, how impudent of him to come listen to us talk about him!"

*"My Prince, that is not true! I felt his emotions and fragments of thoughts. The Arite is very scared and desperate. He was used to hiding among the Iseyek and has learned to do a fairly good job of copying them, but the Arite hasn't come close with people before, and is not sure of its abilities to obtain legal status in our society. But suddenly, at complete random, the Arite detected a room with a few Iseyek in it. He took advantage of the circumstances when you were looking in the other direction. He was trying to find a legal position to occupy in society, but was found out. Now the Arite is trying to hide in the ventilation shafts and is seriously afraid that us humans will try to flush him out with flamethrowers."*

"Flamethrowers? Wait, would that work? We won't singe the whole cruiser up that way?"

*"The Arite is used to the Swarm's categorical way of thinking. One ship going down would not stop the Iseyek. But I don't see why we should catch it if it isn't a threat to us. In fact, I would say it is the other way around. My Truth Seeker's instinct is just yelling that we simply must establish contact with the Arite."*

"Alright, Flora. Everyone else, listen to the Truth Seeker's advice, and mine as well: there is no reason to capture the Arite. It has no desire to harm us. If it appears and tries to contact you, engage it in conversation and send it to me. And also, not a word is to leave this room about the Arite being on *Joan the Fatty* or any other ship for that matter. The Iseyek will be much too afraid of it, and the insects' method of fighting these beings is too radical. They would have my flagship destroyed just in case."

The Arite was seen at least another three times over the following few hours. First, it came to Bionica in the body of... Bionica herself, but realized by the android's reaction that it's attempt at masking hadn't worked and hurried to retreat. After that, it came as a bearded mechanic in a greasy jumpsuit who strolled into the women's bathroom, which clearly significantly lowered its faith in its own ability to blend in human society. And, finally, the Arite came right to me. I had returned to my cabin and noticed that Princess Astra was sleeping peacefully in my bed... for some reason in duplicate.

"Have you no shame?" I asked in a deliberately threatening tone. "Arite, is a whole cruiser not enough room for you to live? What made you come to my room exactly?"

One of the Princesses suddenly opened her eyes

and stood from the bed. I took a step back, thinking to myself that this was a tense situation. I had no weapon on me, so how I could defend myself against this extraterrestrial being was totally unclear. Nonetheless, I continued to follow my line and spoke forcefully:

"If you want to live on my ship, you follow simple rules: never copy me, Astra or her paralyzed sister. The captains and admirals are also off limits. And basically don't get in our way. We have a serious battle ahead of us!"

The Princess suddenly laughed provocatively and began spinning in a dance, showing off her green hair and nude, silver-patterned body. I felt exceptionally stupid: what if the thing in front of me was the actual Princess and not a copy? But I had not been wrong: the dancing Astra dissolved into a white cloud and left the cabin a few seconds later into the main hall, now in the form of an angry old lady from the housekeeping department, and all she was wearing was a bathing cap on her head and a bath towel over her shoulders. On the scalloped, cellulite-laden buttocks of the plant manager, there was a faded tattoo shaped like a colorful butterfly overwritten with a sweeping inscription: "Miss College!"

Despite the strained nature of the situation, I laughed and shook my head. The Arite would have to learn and learn in order not to unmask itself so stupidly in human company.

* * *

In a departure from recent battles, this time, there were no signs of happiness in any crew members. All staff officers and ship captains recognized perfectly how difficult the forthcoming battle in the Lobj system would be.

"Five hundred miles to the enemy. Multiple targets. Three hundred seven Alien ships detected on radar. Eight *Behemoths*, sixteen *Sledgehammers*, eleven *Chainsaws*, twelve *Ascetics*, and sixteen *Hermits*. All the rest are *Meteors*."

I reattached my microphone so it sat more comfortably, and said:

"All ships, attention! This is the Sector Eight Fleet's next serious exam. Our forces are approximately even, so we'll have to really put effort into this to show the whole galaxy that it isn't for nothing that we are known as Alien killers. Use formation number seven. First, jump toward the sun and hold distance from the *Behemoths* at no less than two hundred fifty miles. Battleships, head away from the enemy. Squeeze your thrusters for all they're worth. Heavies, same speed as the battleships. Antisupport and electros, stay thirty behind the heavy group. Two wings of *Pyros* will set up receivers on both sides of the enemy at thirty miles' distance. If the *Meteors* come out to you, frigates are not to engage in combat. Warp out to our heavies. *Tria*, you'll be going with the electros for now. Three *Safas* jump out in front at full speed. You'll go three hundred, six hundred, and nine hundred in front of the fleet."

"Approximately equal forces?" Nicole laughed sadly,

looking over the long list of enemy starships shown on the monitor, making sure to draw my attention to the flashing red words that had been brought up on screen by the tactical computer: "Victory impossible! Retreat strongly recommended!"

I turned off my microphone, and said to my assistant:

"Do you think it would be better to tell these people who put their trust in me that your computer thinks we have no chance and are doomed? Turn that automatic victory chance calculation off. I did so long ago. That stupid hunk of metal almost always writes that victory is impossible. If the enemy is just gonna stay passive around the *Behemoths*, we'll just charge our drives and go out to a spot in a few minutes. If they take any action, some options arise as to how we can pluck these ships' feathers."

*"WHY ARE YOU RESISTING? IT IS FUTILE. WE ARE STILL STRONGER."*

Ow! A voice rang out in my head like an alarm bell. I waved it off, calming Nicole, who was looking at me in fear, and called the Truth Seeker.

"Flora, I need mental protection from you right now. These creatures are trying to control my mind. So, the woman in the medical wing isn't crazy. The voices are real."

*"I'll try. But it's basically just a really weird situation, Prince. Miya left excellent protection. They can speak with your Highness, but no one can make you do anything."*

*"STOP THE FLEET AND RETURN THE CAPTURED SHIP. IF YOU DO SO, WE WILL ALLOW YOUR SHIP TO AVOID DEATH, BUT ONLY YOURS."*

Despite the booming voice in my head, I started just cracking up. They had used their secret ability, but it turned out they weren't able to make me obey. Well then, to hell with you, forget about us returning trophies and capitulating voluntarily!

*"I am ready, Crown Prince. No one but me is now able to communicate with you mentally."*

"Thank you, Florianna! I owe you a chocolate! Now we can really get to work!"

The enemy had not budged forward, clearly having learned from previous battles but, all the same, had begun showing signs of activity. All the *Behemoths* had released hundreds of drones, and the *Meteors* had gone into action, but for now they were just guarding the battleships. Meanwhile, the Alien cruisers and destroyers started picking up speed and set off to chase my fleet down after a few minutes of sitting still. Ugh, if only we could have a couple *Surprises* on the battlefield... Oh well, it's no use crying over spilled milk. According to our calculations, the bombers were going to reach the Lobj system in six minutes.

"Why aren't the *Behemoths* going in front?" Nicole asked me.

"There's no reason to. They're slow buggers, so they'll never catch us anyway. They're gonna warp out to the quicker ships after they get closer to our fleet."

"And our ships will jump forward to the *Safas*, bringing the distance back up?" the girl hazarded.

"That's right. We definitely don't want these eight *Behemoths* getting too close. They'd reduce our fleet to dust in a couple minutes' time. By the way, the enemy's destroyers will enter the combat zone soon.

Nicole, assign targets: three of our heavy cruisers and one battleship for every one of their *Ascetics*. Everyone else should sit it out. There's no way they'll reach us. They are to shoot only in a volley on command. Immediately after firing, all the ships should jump out to *Safa-3*. Attention, stand by. Fire!"

It did the trick perfectly. Of the twelve *Ascetics* that had come, only three survived. I involuntarily glanced at Nicole's screen to see the victory chance calculation. Nothing had changed. The computer still thought victory was impossible.

Our distance from the enemy had grown again, but the Alien destroyers were stubbornly working to reduce it back down. Because the *Sledgehammers* were lagging seriously behind, I ordered antisupport to keep closer to the heavies this time, and also take part in destroying the enemy. My ships launched a volley! Another good haul. The last *Ascetics* disappeared from the tactical map, as well as a group of twelve *Hermits*. Let's get the rest of 'em! Frigates, engage!

My mistake. I was rushing. We had just lost eight *Pyros* and one *Flycatcher* in the space of a few seconds, because we had negligently allowed some *Hermits* to get within firing distance. Completely unjustifiable losses. It really was my fault. But the Alien destroyers were also taken out in the quick firefight. Now, our goal was the enemy cruisers. They were gradually catching up to us in a dense group. We would have to split them up somehow.

"Tuki-tuka-de-sa, mission complete. Our losses in the attack of *Queen* and its escort: five bombers. Our cloakers were revealed on the battlefield."

"Great work, *Surprise-1*. As a result of your attack and the subsequent series of explosions, over seven thousand Alien ships have been destroyed."

"How many???" the young Chameleon female could not hold back her surprise.

I repeated the estimate of Alien losses and ordered the squad of five *Surprises* to go to the first receiver and prepare to attack the *Behemoths*. In parallel, Bionica was translating my order to the general to prepare landing troops for an attack.

"General, there is no reason whatsoever to fully capture the battleships. Your mission is to get through to one of the antimatter arsenals next to the largest rail turrets and set explosive charges. After that, the landing troops should start the timer and evacuate."

"The enemy *Meteors* have begun maneuvers!" Nicole said, something I had already noticed myself. After leaving just twenty or so ships near the *Behemoths*, the rest of my high-speed frigates shot off back toward my fleet. Too bad. I really wanted to smash all that minor stuff at once with a thermonuclear bomb attack. Though the three thousand and change combat drones the *Behemoths* had released, which were trying to harry the boarding operation, were also a worthy target.

The *Meteors* went out in front, for some reason not taking a straight course, but a very wide curve. Clearly, the Aliens had learned their lesson in the Kej and Aysar Cluster systems, and as such were trying to stay clear of my bombers. Too bad. I really wanted to try the same trick again. But nothing can stop a battleship attack. I waved the five *Surprises* off.

At a distance of over twelve hundred miles, the series of explosions didn't look like anything too scary. It was just a couple of sparks, and the combat drone markers were all wiped off the map. The time to build on our success had come.

"One hundred *Pyros*, to the first receiver! Split the *Behemoths* up and capture them with warp disruptors. A standard carousel. *Tria*, follow them to the first receiver. General Savasss Jach, begin the assault!"

It was a wonderful and terrifying sight. The landing modules were pouring out of the bowels of *Tria* into the blackness of space. Ten thousand guided missiles. One hundred thousand Alpha Iseyeks rushing into battle. The landing modules were a bit more than six minutes from the enemy ships. I imagined the G-Force loads these praying mantises must experience in the modules. I even raised my eyebrows in surprise. For a person, such force would mean certain death. But the insects, wearing nothing but special protective masks on their heads and special hermetic bands sealing off their chitin shells, left their modules like nothing was happening and joined the battle immediately, getting plasma torches to work, and setting explosives at break-in points indicated by the general.

"What a crazy picture!" Katerina ton Mesfelle commented. "I'll definitely make a separate report on it. It's just horrifying. The praying mantises really don't mind dying! They just crawl right in to imminent death!"

In fact, the general's assault troops were dying by the hundreds under the defensive system fire, but they just kept crawling forward. It was clear that Savasss Jach's priority here was speed, and not minimizing losses. Either that or the general had decided this was a good opportunity to bring down his ship's food requirements.

Entranced by the Swarm assault, I nearly missed seeing the enemy *Meteors*, which were getting dangerously close to my fleet. It would, of course, have been possible to engage them in battle and start trading frigates, but I didn't want unnecessary losses, so I gave an order to the fleet to jump out to *Safa-1* at nine hundred miles.

"First charge near arsenal set!" the general informed me.

Nevertheless, I did not notice any signs of evacuation from any of the insect-swarmed *Behemoths*. In fact, the praying mantises were continuing to crawl in to the titans through the many holes in their sides. I called the general and asked why the evacuation was not happening. Bionica translated the centipede's answer back to me.

"The insects figured out our plans and are trying to interfere in us blowing up the arsenals. Every soldier inside the *Behemoth* or on its chassis, will distract some of the Alien to help the overall mission get done. There is one minute, twenty-four seconds before the explosion. You'd better get your ships away from the Alien battleships. There's no reason to lose them."

"Attention, fleet! In one minute, seventeen seconds the first Alien battleship will explode. Receivers, increase distance from the *Behemoths*, and *Pyros* holding the battleships, go out to the receivers a few seconds before the explosion.

And meanwhile, the enemy *Sledgehammers* and *Chainsaws* were entering my battleships' strike zone. The *Meteors* were relatively far away and did not present a threat. I considered the situation to have turned out quite well, and saw a good chance of taking out a *Sledgehammer* or two before the enemy ships got within return-fire range. What happened next was all the more surprising. A *Behemoth*, marked on the tactical map with an explosion countdown timer, suddenly jumped forward and appeared next to its *Sledgehammers*, fifty miles from *Joan the Fatty*. One of my frigate captains left too soon, removing his warp disruptor, and allowing the battleship to get through!

In some kind of flash of brilliance, I realized what would happen: one of my cruisers would die, and the basically harmless *Meteors* that were now far away would get jump coordinates! A second went by, and the heavy assault cruiser *Scalp Collector* was replaced with a small bright star!

"All ships, warp to *Safa-1* immediately!" I yelled with my whole throat, though it was too late.

A whole cloud of small red spots went into the green ball. Disturbing messages came in from some of the ships, saying that they were under warp disruptor, and could not carry out my command to retreat to *Safa-1*.

"There are three warp disruptors and two stasis webs on *Joan the Fatty*," reported Oorast Pohl.

"*Pyros*, hold the rest of the *Behemoths*! How much time until the explosion?"

"Eleven seconds," Bionica said in a flat tone, not expressing the slightest emotion.

"All ships that can warp, jump out to *Safa-1*! Turn off the *Fatty*'s thrusters! All power to the forward shields! Hold on! Impact!"

* * *

I was brought back to consciousness by pain. I had clearly broken something. Everything around was dark and, for some reason, I couldn't see. My hearing was returning gradually though.

"...the admiral is severely wounded; I will take command of the fleet!" I recognized the voice of space lieutenant Nicole Savoia, but her words reached me as if from under water. "Admiral Kheraisss Vej, we have lost our translator. Take command of the Iseyek ships yourself. We need to return the *Legashes* and take down the last two *Sledgehammers* all together. I've marked the priority target. *Master of Tesse*, *Bride of Chaos*, respond to headquarters!"

I tried to lift myself up, but it turned out to be very hard. My arm was in a great deal of pain. I had probably started moaning in pain, as I heard Popori de Cacha scream in joy:

"The Crown Prince is alive!!!"

Literally a few moments later, the stand that was pressing down on me was dragged off, and I finally saw the light. My right eye couldn't see at all, and my palm that had been pressed to it was covered with blood. My right arm was hanging limply, clearly broken, but I felt nothing. And a couple ribs on the right were also broken.

The Chameleon helped me up, and I took a look around. It was a complete disaster. Only the emergency lights were on, flashing. There was debris covering everything in the room. Where my work station had been, there was a solid mess of twisted metal and cables. It looked like the explosion had sent me flying into the wall, then made the stand fall over on top of me, which was what saved me. If I had stayed where I was, I definitely would have died. I noticed some kind of movement, and looked with my only working eye and realized what I was seeing: it was Deimos' arm, twitching in its death throes, his chitin shell having been crushed by a falling ceiling beam.

"*Bride of Chaos, Master of Tesse*, respond to fleet headquarters!" Nicole Savoia was trying to restore command of the fleet with the only working monitor.

The space lieutenant saw my face, and shuddered in horror before staggering back. Yes, I had already figured out that something was wrong with my face. Crown Prince Georg royl Inoky ton Mesfelle couldn't have even been called handsome in his best years, but now he looked like a zombie just risen from the grave.

"Crown Prince, I'm calling a doctor for you now," my assistant promised me, but I just waved it off.

"Later. How's the fleet? How many enemies made it out? Where are the remaining *Behemoths*? And, most importantly, have you figured out who that cowardly frigate captain was that fled the battle early and let the Alien battleship escape?! I swear to God that I will rip out all his appendages myself!"

"I will absolutely find out that coward's identity. He will receive the most severe punishment possible. Prince, we have lost eight heavy cruisers, and no less than ten light ones. Small ship losses I do not yet know. Neither of our battleships are responding to messages, but there is definitely some activity on board. There are two Alien *Sledgehammers* next to us, but it isn't clear what condition they are in. General Savasss Jach said a few things on the radio, but I couldn't understand. That's the situation."

The captain's first assistant appeared in my field of view with a first aid kit in hand. After seeing me, without saying a word, he walked up and started bandaging my head. Phobos appeared behind him, carrying Admiral Kiro Sabuto in his arms, and set him down next to me. The admiral opened one eye, looked at me and said with a slight smile:

"In ancient times it was said that men wear scars the way women wear jewelry. In the distant past, your Highness would have been considered a very fetching man indeed."

I smiled, and but then saw something that made the smile leave my face. From under a metal column, I could see an unnaturally contorted woman's arm with a familiar medallion on the end of a golden chain. Bionica! I stood with difficulty and took a step forward. The android girl was dead. There was no doubt about it. You can't survive having your body ripped in half. But just then, Phobos and Popori de Cacha leaned over the body and did something strange: they cut off the robot's head!

"What happened to Astra?" I said, the realization coming to me like a jolt of electricity.

"If she, as usual, was in the dormitory wing, we won't be able to go there. Corridor 2A has lost pressure," the captain's assistant answered my question. "Oorast Pohl and the technicians put on space suits and will try to restore the elevator to operation. If they are successful, we will be able to get to the dormitory wing."

*"Prince Georg, my sister is in mortal danger! Her blood pressure is falling. She is gasping and losing consciousness. I beg you to help her!"*

I jumped up and set off decisively for the hallway. Popori de Cacha, holding Bionica's head in his hands, suddenly blocked my path and asked where I was going. When I honestly answered, my bodyguard suddenly gave a command in Iseyek language. Among all the hissing, I could only make out the words "Triasss Zess" and "Princcce." And in a flash, my personal bodyguard Phobos was attacking me!

Betrayal! They were both working for Triasss Zess! The huge, ten-foot-high praying mantis pressed my throat in his spindly, sharp appendages. I only had the time to think two more thoughts: first, I would never again trust an Iseyek. Second, it was stupid to die in the game once again in the very same way.

After that, I died again.

# Insect Mating Dance

I CAME back to sharply, as if resurfacing from the depths of the ocean.

"Stay relaxed, Prince! I haven't finished stitching up your cheek yet," said Nicosid Brandt, his face hovering over me in concentration. "But I'm not gonna be able to operate on this eye while we're under way, so we'll wait to dock. For now, I've placed some gauze on it."

Despite the unusual angle, and having only one working eye, I was able to figure out where I was. I was lying on a stretcher inside a rescue shuttle, which appeared to be moving.

"Now we can recover together, Georg," I couldn't see Katerina ton Mesfelle, but I immediately recognized my cousin's voice. "I got a deep cut in my left thigh in the explosion. A long, small piece of something went all the way in to the bone. But, it turns out it isn't as scary as it looked at first. The doctor said that it would go away without consequences in a week. He'll also be able to remove the scar later. But the fact that the blast burnt all the hair off the back of my head is much more embarrassing. So now, I'm just sitting here, bald and wearing a bandage on my leg... It must be just a horrible sight to see."

I was very glad that my cousin had survived the explosion. But now, I was more concerned with what had become of the crew of *Joan the Fatty*. And, by the way, why were we not on it now? I asked the doctor, who was still working on my face.

"I still haven't finished stitching up the edges of the wound, so don't move your lips or cheeks, Crown Prince. It might grow back together uneven. Oorast Pohl, captain of *Joan the Fatty*, started emergency evacuation of the whole crew after it became clear what state the ship was in. I do not know the whole picture, but there were many casualties on the cruiser. There were six casualties just in the headquarters."

The doctor took some plastic identification cards out of his pocket and started reading the names of the fallen. All four of the young officers who were in charge of the drones... Space Corporal Patrick toyl Sven, my personal pilot and none-too-bad conversation partner... The head engineer of *Joan the Fatty*...

Nicosid Brandt did not name Bionica among the dead. In the doctor's opinion, the robot had never belonged to the world of the living to begin with. He also didn't mention Deimos the Alpha Iseyek. On top of that, his clarification that there were many dead in the other sections of the cruiser had put me seriously on edge.

My right arm felt weird somehow. I pulled it out

from under the sheet and looked at the incomprehensible metal construction that was now on my wrist and hand. There were bracelets on my arm with little moving rods and compression bolts that stretched out of them to a set of rings on my fingers.

"It's nothing serious. Just a simple radial fracture. I've already put it in a cast. I injected healing nanites near the open wounds. They will fill in the fracture with new bone material within seven days. The hand should work as usual but, all the same, be careful with it for a few days.

I thanked the doctor, lifted myself up on my healthy left arm and looked around the rescue shuttle. Next to me, Katerina ton Mesfelle was lying on a stretcher as well, her fresh-shaven bald head shining back at me. Space Lieutenant Nicole Savoia and several officers were sitting in the chairs along the wall. Almost the whole space in the tail of the shuttle was occupied by the Truth Seeker and her nonhuman retinue. I immediately looked back on the episode with Astra having been in danger, and said in an apologetic tone:

"Florianna, I was not able to help your sister. I was suddenly attacked by Phobos, egged on the head of my bodyguard..."

"Your Highness, everything is fine with Astra," Nicole said, turning toward me. "I watched with my own eyes as Phobos carried the Princess, wrapped in cloth, into the shuttle hangar. Astra tried to get away and object, but the praying mantis just silently crammed her into the rescue shuttle before crawling in himself."

Phobos saved the Princess? So he's not a traitor

after all? What did he attack me for then? My brain just couldn't find a way to make sense of the two contradictory events. What had Popori de Cacha said to the praying mantis? And, by the way, where was the Chameleon commander? I asked Nicole to give me a general picture of what had happened. The girl gave a strained sigh and lowered her eyes:

"There were many casualties, Crown Prince. We can confirm the death of Admiral Nill ton Amsted and the captain of *Master of Tesse*, Anzor ton Art, as well as his two assistants. The battleship *Master of Tesse* was very badly damaged and is in serious need of repair, but the officers who survived managed to get it a bit further from the mined *Behemoths* to a safe distance. *Bride of Chaos* is in somewhat better condition and was also able to escape, but it also needs repair. No less than eight heavy cruisers were lost, including our flagship. *Joan the Fatty's* warp-thrusters and electric shield generators are disabled. The reactor started melting down, and was shut off automatically. The ship has not technically been destroyed yet, though it is within the blast zone of two mined *Behemoths* and has no chance of surviving the explosion, because there is no protective shield remaining whatsoever. As such, Oorast Pohl ordered it evacuated."

The shuttle gave a slight jerk and came to a stop. Almost immediately, the doors began to hiss open. My stretcher was grabbed and quickly carried out, as I noted with great surprise that I recognized one of the people carrying me as the corporal that was supposed to be under arrest, waiting for the military court's verdict. The young man sentenced to death met my gaze, though he said nothing. The stretcher was taken out of the shuttle and wheeled down a barely illuminated hallway. After that, I heard the voice of an Iseyek I had never met before, who was wondering in badly broken human language how he could be of help.

"We need a space with a flat hard surface and good lighting for the wounded Prince! I need to operate immediately or the Crown Prince risks losing an eye!" Nicosid Brandt's voice rang out, and I was once again wheeled down an endless corridor.

I suddenly saw a Chameleon. It was not Popori de Cacha himself, but one of his subjects. I ordered the people carrying me to stop and asked my bodyguard where his leader was.

"Tuki-tuka-de-sa, Popori de Cacha commanded me to bring you and other people from *Joan the Fatty* to the closest Sector Eight Fleet ship. When we flew out of the dock, my leader was still on the cruiser. He was trying to convince Captain Oorast Pohl to get into a rescue shuttle with the other crew members. Perhaps Popori de Cacha will quickly be coming here to *Umoyge-4*, though he may be setting off for a different ship as well."

What? Captain Oorast Pohl was refusing to leave the doomed cruiser??? I demanded the people around me to immediately, no matter how, get me a line open to *Joan the Fatty*. In ten seconds, a screen was brought to me.

"My Prince, I am glad to see you are in a safe place," Captain Oorast Pohl was wearing a ceremonial uniform and standing in a room on the cruiser that was in such a bad state as to be unrecognizable.

"Your Highness, the crew has been evacuated. As captain, the officer's codex states that I must remain with my ship until the very last second. Just three officers are still with me on *Joan the Fatty*, of their own will. They are also refusing to leave the ship."

The voice of Space Corporal Valian ton Corsa could be heard off screen:

"This is our choice together, Prince. No one forced us to sacrifice ourselves. Let me remain the same in your Highness's memory as I have ever been!"

What nonsense is this? Why had Valian chosen to stay on the doomed ship? I had simply lost all understanding of the situation before me. Fortunately, Florianna came to help at just the right time:

*"The girl is seriously burnt. Forty percent of her skin has been singed off. Her face took the brunt of the damage. The left side is basically totally black. The girl has been injected with painkillers, which is the only thing keeping her from losing consciousness."*

The Truth Seeker's hint explained a lot, but I still couldn't make peace with her decision.

"Captain and all others, I categorically reject your decision. Dying with your ship is not a heroic act given the situation at hand! When the *Behemoth* exploded, the Sector Eight Fleet lost too many experienced captains and officers. I don't even have enough people to get *Master of Tesse* to a repair dock. I need experienced captains and officers like never before. Otherwise, I'll have to leave my strongest ship here in Alien territory. So, given that, having four of my experienced officers decide to throw up their hands and wait to die is something I can only look on as cowardice."

I saw the man on the screen lower his eyes to the floor. My words had clearly affected him. Now it was time to build on my success.

"And what about you, Valian. I don't understand your choice at all. What kind of a military officer do you expect me to remember you as, if your last act was choosing to die after nothing more than a little face burn?! I have a thirteen-year-old paraplegic working on equal footing with healthy adults in my fleet already! Do you think what happened to you is worse than Florianna? If someone offered her to change places with you, I have no doubt that she would take it without so much as a second thought! The burns can be treated. I declare that to you officially. Val, I've got a metric crap-ton of money and I swear to you that you will be provided with the best doctors and the best equipment in the whole known Universe. The option of becoming a cyborg or android also exists. You could have whatever body or face you want. Just ask and it's yours. So, my order is for you all: immediately head for *Master of Tesse* and take command of the battleship. I'll send one of the Empire's best doctors over for Valian right away as soon as he's done operating on my eye."

One second went by. Then another, and Captain Oorast Pohl, clearly having received some signals from subordinates off screen, gave me a salute and reported:

"Sir, yes sir. We will head for *Master of Tesse* and take command of the battleship!"

The screen was just barely still on when doctor Nicosid Brandt, who had been carefully listening to my conversation, said thoughtfully:

"I have seen her wounds. It is truly a very severe case. Her face is burned to the very bone. The scars could last for a few years after she heals. But you are absolutely right, Prince. The girl can be treated, and I will get to work as soon as I'm done with your Highness."

"Prince, your personal bodyguard Phobos is asking for you. Shall I put him through?" asked a Chameleon, and I replied "Yes."

"My Princcce, what is me to do with your female? At firssst, Astra long-long to refuse crawl shshshe out of cocoon. But now, always to dance and never shshshe to ssstop!"

I did not answer back right away. At first, I was held up by the fact that Phobos didn't think himself even a bit at fault in attacking me, and that was very surprising. That was why I asked Phobos to tell me what Popori de Cacha had said to him before the Alpha Iseyek suddenly attacked me. The praying mantis was clearly prepared to explain:

"The Chameleon to sssay, that Princcce is hit he head and not to undersssstand that to go out in corridor for massster is... to die from no air. He to sssay that Phobosss is to need sssave Princcce and do like Triasss Zess. Sssit person to sssleep while he no have sssmart head."

Everything had finally fallen into place, and I even laughed that I hadn't guessed at such an elementary explanation myself. There had been no death or resurrection. My subjects had simply been a bit overzealous in their efforts to stop me from doing something stupid. Now, I could solve the issue of why

Astra was dancing for no reason. Maybe she took a hit to the head as well? I asked the praying mantis to turn the camera so I could see it with my own eyes.

Astra really was dancing. With abandon and detachment as if it were the last time in her life. The beautiful girl's naked body was sparkling back in many different colors, reflecting the beams of the dull lamps on the Iseyek ship. Then, the bright flashes gradually started dimming. All it took was for the Princess to leave the strip of light into the shadow. The dancer's green hair was somehow very appropriate to the situation, and seemed to be the only way for this strange dance to make sense. I noted that hordes of Iseyek of all three types had formed a wide circle and were watching the unexpected performance in silence, not wanting to distract the girl and end her dance. Finally, I asked Phobos to call the excessively distracting Astra to the screen. The Princess gave a start, and ran to the monitor on the wall of the large hall at full speed.

"Crown Prince Georg! Oh, what happened to your Highness's face?!" the girl froze in fear, her eyes widening in horror.

"Yep. I bet the Aliens an eye that they couldn't break my arm," I said, pointing to my bandaged, broken wrist in a sling.

I thought the girl would laugh at the joke, but the Princess unexpectedly took my words seriously:

"And why would you have done a thing like that, Crown Prince?"

"It doesn't matter," I said, waving off my favorite's strange question. "I'd rather you explain me what made you give a striptease like that on a Swarm cruiser?"

Astra got embarrassed, and tried to cover herself with her hands. Then, she began to tell her version of the events in an offended tone:

"I was waiting a long time for your Highness, but then I fell asleep. After that, I heard a rumbling, and the lights went out. In the darkness, it was hard to breathe, but I didn't have time to get scared, because a huge Iseyek broke into the room with a flashlight on its armor, grabbed me, folded me up in a web and dragged me off. I saw people, called for help, but no one could help me. The praying mantis dragged me to its ship and started to poke holes in my cocoon with its sharp appendages. There were a lot of insects around. I was very scared that they would eat me right up. But then I remembered my mother's words, that insects don't eat women, and that their females perform wedding dances to attract males. So I started dancing to make them finally realize that I was a female and they weren't allowed to eat me!"

I took a surprised look at Phobos. He turned his head to the side, clearly showing incomprehension of the idea that some people were not supposed to be consumed as food. Doctor Nicosid Brandt's insecure voice rang out from the silence behind my back.

"My Prince, I may be mistaken, but I have a funny feeling that I know the answer: your companion is confusing two different nonhuman races. In Perimeter Sector Seven, in the star system neighboring Veyerde, Glorva, there is a race of intelligent spiders that really are somewhat externally similar to the Iseyek. The Glorvians are governed by a vibrant matriarchy. The huge and very aggressive males are not intelligent and serve as their soldiers. They fully obey the relatively smaller, but intelligent females in all matters. I suppose that Princess Astra royl Veyerde could have heard of the Glorvians and come to a mistaken conclusion about the Iseyek."

I laughed so hard that that a fresh gash opened up on my cheek. The doctor ordered me to be placed on a stretcher and brought to the operation room immediately. But right up to the last second, when I was cut off by the drugs, I was looking with a smile at my favorite's information:

**Astra royl Kant ton Veyerde, heiress Princess to the star kingdom of Veyerde (under Alien control)**
**Age: 17**
**Race: Human**
**Gender: Female**
**Class: Aristocrat/Artist**
**Achievements: Iseyek Mating Dance**
**Fame: +5**
**Standing: + 5**
**Presumed personal relationship: Unknown**

\* \* \*

"Crown Prince Georg royl Inoky ton Mesfelle, finish your breakfast and you can see your visitors. But not for too long now, your Highness. It is counter-indicated for you to spend a long time speaking and using facial muscles," the attending doctor's assistant repeated Nicosid Brandt's prescription once again, and left my room.

The door had barely shut behind the young nurse

before I scraped the contents of my plate down the trash shoot. Even in real life I couldn't bear the pressed liquid porridges and purees of unknown origin served in Russian hospitals, but eating that kind of food in a game was basically mocking the taste receptors.

"Who's in line to visit?" I asked Astra, who had grown bored with painting her nails.

The insect dancer had somehow managed to convince the attending physicians to give her permission to stay in my hospital room. How the Princess had been able to convince the normally very strict and uncompromising Nicosid Brandt, I had absolutely no idea, given that I was anesthetized when it happened. After I woke up, the fact had simply been presented to me, and I had been too weak to dispute it. So now, one day after the operation, it was a bit too late to send my favorite packing.

Astra, who was working temporarily as my secretary, was checking her communicator against the list on the screen:

"Your Highness, for the second day in a row now, there are many people who want to talk with you. Popori de Cacha, General Savasss Jach and Nicole Savoia are on *Umoyge-4*. The general has been waiting to speak with you in the hallway for fifteen hours now."

This behavior was quite uncharacteristic for the highly placed Gamma Iseyek, as he generally hated leaving *Tria*, and only did so for truly weighty reasons, so I asked General Savasss Jach to be called in first.

"Shall we also call in Popori de Cacha to translate?" Astra clarified, but I replied, "no." The head of my bodyguard had earned my temporary disfavor after what had happened on *Joan the Fatty.* Yes, I had already long ago figured out that it was not treason on his part; however, I still considered the Chameleon's behavior revolting.

The respectably long Gamma Iseyek was not alone, but in the company of a six-foot-high praying mantis, which was considered practically dwarf-sized for an Alpha Iseyek. In addition, the general's companion, differently from the Alpha Iseyek I had seen before, was wearing a heavy armored suit over its chitin body. The insect was even wearing a transparent protective helmet on its head. The vigilant Phobos was immediately set on edge by the appearance of the unusual visitor. Any Alpha Iseyek, no matter how small, would have a dangerous set of sharp upper appendages. My bodyguard was also worried by the strange suit of armor the visitor was wearing...

In order not to provoke my guard, the general asked his companion to take a seat near the door.

"General Savasss Jach to say that he to bring explanatory transsslator for to conversssation with Princcce instead of, much shshshame, dead and talented Bionica," said Phobos, explaining the centipede's squeaking.

"Allow me to introduce myself," the praying mantis sitting by the door said in clean-accented human language. "I have studied human language before, though it has been some time. My name is Nai Igir. I was specially trained to make contact with humans on the planet Sivala II; however, the Ulia massacre and the war happened before my tutors could finish teaching me."

The Alpha Iseyek's speech patterns sounded distinctly female to me, though I had no way of checking this information. There was no pop-up on the character, and I was not capable of differentiating the Iseyek genders visually. The general squeaked something out, and Nai Igir suddenly started taking off her suit, piece by piece. I looked on in surprise at the spectacle, before Nai Igir suddenly removed the breastplate and... extended a set of wings!!!

"She is an Iseyek Prime," Phobos exclaimed with something approaching awe, before hurriedly putting his weapon away, which he had been keeping trained on the translator as she removed her armor. "A Swarm Progenitor."

The translator said, explaining the situation.

"Iseyek Prime are the race of Iseyek that first inhabited Sivala II. We created the other Swarm subraces as part of our scientific research. The Alpha Iseyek soldiers we created for capturing new territory, the Gamma Iseyek as academics and qualified technicians for complicated equipment, and the Beta Iseyek we created for everything else. Many other types of Iseyek were also created in these experiments, but we were unable to develop them into pure lines; they would all collapse into one of the three basic types in a few generations."

General Savasss Jach let out long warble, and Nai Igir set about translating:

"As a result of the Orange House attack on Sivala II, the number of Iseyek Prime was reduced to a critical level. As a consequence, the Swarm ceased to be under the control of the Progenitors, and began making decisions on their own. They grew drunk on the illusion of freedom they acquired, which pushed them toward irrational actions. So, some of the other Iseyek started looking on the remaining Iseyek Prime as a threat, a force that could perhaps want to claim a position of authority over the others again one day. A revolution followed in the Swarm, which lead to the Iseyek Prime going effectively extinct. Now the Swarm is some kind of advisory organ, where all important decisions for the Iseyek race are made collectively by approximately three thousand individuals. Your Highness has already had the chance to see that, quite often, decisions made in a simple majority turn out to be controversial, or sometimes even mistaken."

It was hard not to agree to that, especially after the Swarm had agreed in the majority to condemn the allied Perimeter Sector Eight Fleet to death.

"General, continue your thought," I said, trying to be as economic with my words as possible, as speaking had grown painful due to the stitches on my face.

"I have been keeping Nai Igir hidden in suspended animation on my ship for one hundred seventy years now. The war with the humans has long since ended. The Swarm's hunt for the last Iseyek Prime is also long over. But all the while, the sleeping Progenitor has been awaiting her hour. And it seems to me that her time has come. Crown Prince, I heard out your emotional speech in Kej carefully on the common channel, and am in full agreement that the Swarm has made a historic error that may lead to the total extinction of the Iseyek race. In fact, many Iseyek realize that there is no way out of the situation that has arisen. Though the Sector Eight Fleet has hampered the Aliens, they will still be able to capture the Swarm's systems before we are able to ship out even one of the egg transports under construction."

I winced in pain, and answered the general:

"There is a way out of this situation, though it will be fairly difficult. The Swarm doesn't have the materials or resources to continue building their huge starships. That means the construction must be stopped in all systems except one or two. Some of the resources that are freed up will have to be sent to select systems to speed the construction of the remaining transports, and to build combat ships *en masse* at the freed-up docks to hold off the Alien invasion."

I could barely make it, but I arrived at the end of the long sentence. The general heard me out carefully and answered:

"Your Highness, those are very good ideas. The only thing is that the Swarm is no longer in a condition to recognize the error of the chosen strategy, given that it is still the same Swarm that made the decision in the first place. Also, figuring out what systems to sacrifice for the good of the others is something the Swarm will not be capable of. Every option has its opponents, and their votes are key in passing any proposed solution. And as such, the Swarm will die out, and there is nothing that can be done about it. And so, I am sure that the time for the Iseyek Prime to return is at hand. The past hatred toward them no longer exists even in memory. Now, it is more the opposite opinion prevailing in Iseyek society: that under the power of the Progenitors, the Swarm never would have ended up in such a dead-end. That's why we need to present Nai Igir for all Iseyek to see, and to assert her rights for all Iseyek to hear. She is one of the Progenitors of all Iseyek, and it is precisely she that must be given full power in order to save all the others."

I kept silent, though there was a kernel of rationality in the general's words. But how then was I to assert the rights of this flying female, when we were totally cut off from contact with the Swarm? As if reading my thoughts, Savasss Jach continued:

"My opinion, Crown Prince, is that it isn't worth trying to get the Bej system to turn their beacon on. Triasss Zess is expecting that, and the warp beacon guard team will say no. I recommend going straight to the Khe system and putting in a request from there to the Arite system. I have many old acquaintances there. I can't promise they'll turn the beacon on for me, but there's no way they won't hear me out. And then, I can tell them about the Sector Eight Fleet's victories, and rich trophies, the rescue of the scientists and the last of the Progenitors. Information on the heroic allied Imperial fleet on the Alien home front will spread throughout all Swarm systems instantly, and even beyond their borders. Hiding our existence further would be impossible. The Swarm will simply have to turn on a warp beacon for us and let us into Iseyek territory, thus admitting their own error. It's either that or they'll have to explain to billions of Iseyek and Imperial citizens why they need to bury alive Crown Prince Georg royl Inoky ton Mesfelle, the victorious commander and close relative of the human Emperor."

"General, your plan really might work. I give you

my permission to carry it out. And now I want to clarify something for myself: should we keep hiding the fact that there is an Iseyek Prime in our fleet, or should we, in fact, announce the fact? How valuable is her life in the eyes of the rest of the Iseyek?"

"That's for you to decide, Prince" said Nai Igir, translating the General's answer. "On the one hand, you could come across certain individuals with negative ideas about her. They even may try to eat her. On the other hand, the vast majority of the Iseyek would give their life for a Swarm Progenitor without hesitation. I would do so myself, as well as most of the generals and admirals I am acquainted with."

Something in the General's words made me think. One day, I had seen a Swarm admiral making what appeared to be a totally unjustifiable self-sacrifice before. Four valuable battleships to rescue one badly damaged ship... I had mentally made a note to figure out what that was, and it seemed I had found just what Admiral Ogesss Tusk may have thought valuable enough to accept such a strange trade-off.

Nicole Savoia was showing me her brand new uniform with Orange House Space Fleet captain's insignia. I congratulated my assistant on her speedy rise up the career ladder and even compared it to the return of Napoleon. Either the girl really had not understood, or she simply didn't want to fall out of the game atmosphere and talk about events from real history. I hurried to change the topic:

"Nicole, I need a full report on the results of the battle and the condition of the fleet."

The girl was clearly fairly well prepared for the question, and so began giving detailed answers, including exact figures without even having to look down. I closed my eyes, listened and tried to memorize them. The Alien fleet had been totally wiped out. Not a single ship had escaped though our victory had come at a very high price. Both of my battleships were able to move again, and *Bride of Chaos* could even shoot, but both of the ships would need a couple months minimum to be repaired after they got to a real dock. There were thirteen heavy cruisers left in working order: *Emperor August*, *Boydur the Hero*, *Hunchback's Heir*, *Pride of the Nation*, *Supernova Rage*, *Wrath of the Gods*, *Nita the Beautiful*, *Queen of Beauty*, and five *Legashes*. If you counted the rest of what survived the last few days' troubles, there were twenty-four light cruisers, fifty-five destroyers, one hundred seventy-two frigates, twenty-four cloaked frigates and the *Tria*. It was not a bad picture at the end of the day. Sure, the Perimeter Sector Eight Fleet had taken heavy losses in battle with the Aliens, but it had done a great job demonstrating its terrifying power nevertheless. The officer finished her speech:

"In the neighboring Khe system, our spies are reporting on a small Alien fleet: seven *Sledgehammers*, two *Chainsaws*, and eleven *Meteors*. The Aliens are behaving passively, simply circling not far from the warp beacon. Easy prey. Taking them out should be no problem."

I couldn't hold in the smile, despite my cracked lips and sewn-up cheeks. Not long ago, Nicole had fallen into a state of near panicked desperation when seeing just one *Sledgehammer*. Now, when she saw a fleet of twenty Alien ships, she called it "easy prey." My young ward was learning. Clearly...

"Your Highness, I have completed the ship roll call. My opinion is that the fleet will need around two days to complete repair work currently under way, get the slightly damaged ships back in order, and re-equip *Emperor August* as a flagship. But the commander situation is worse. Admiral Kiro Sabuto will be out of commission for at least a week and a half after his operation. Admiral Kheraisss Vej is prepared to take control of the fleet temporarily, but only if no other candidates can be found, as he has little experience commanding human and Chameleon ships. The simultaneous interpreter problem then arises too. Admiral Kheraisss Vej cannot constantly translate his own orders to all different species. That was why the question worried me: would your Highness be able to leave the hospital in two days and lead the battle?"

"I will be able to walk. My leg is just twisted. It'll be better soon. If I really have to, I'll borrow Florianna's flying chair for a bit. But then talking and giving commands... I just don't know. So, Nicole, you will be leading the fleet into battle in the Khe system. I will be there next to you to keep you calm, but nothing more. And the language problem has already been solved: General Savasss Jach has found an excellent translator among the Iseyek. She speaks human language quite workably, though she will have to study up on fleet terminology. Do you feel ready to lead ships into battle?"

"Not yet. To be honest, I wasn't expecting this to

come so soon," the officer admitted candidly. "But I can be ready in two days. I will not let your Highness down."

The door had barely closed behind Nicole when Popori de Cacha slipped into the hospital room. The Chameleon came up to my cot, bent down low on his haunches, and laid his two blades down before me on the table.

"Tuki-tuka-de-sa, it would be within your rights to punish me for usurpation of power, but first I ask you to hear out my justification. After the *Behemoth*'s explosion I..."

"We can skip over the episode with Phobos attacking me," I said, interrupting my bodyguard head's speech. "What I want to know now is where Bionica's head is."

"Here it is," said the Chameleon, taking the android's decapitated head from his backpack and placing it on the bedside table.

My heart skipped a beat. Bionica... How I need you now... No Iseyek Prime can take the place of my synthetic blonde...

My subjects have already checked: the memory crystals have not been damaged. The control unit is also intact. The chips are just fine. I would think the service company could find a new body for your secretary no worse than the last one, and restore Bionica's personality as well."

I looked at the head of my guard. So he knew the android could be fixed and did everything necessary to save Bionica's memory from the dying cruiser?

"You are totally forgiven, Popori de Cacha," I declared, ordering the Chameleon to stand with a majestic wave of my hand. "On the day my secretary returns to us, you will be generously rewarded. You have my word as a Crown Prince!"

"As you wish, tuki-tuka-de-sa! There's one more thing though. After the ceremony in the holy cave on Sss, my body began to change gender, and the unpleasant situation and change in circumstances over the last few days only sped-up the process. As of now, I am a female for the next few years, as I was at birth until becoming a male warrior. And it is for that reason that I am asking your Highness to remove me from my duties as guard commander and give them to a male."

Just to make sure, I took a look at the character information.

***Popori-de-Cacha,*** *bodyguard division*
***commander***
***Race: Chameleon***
***Gender: female at present***

So then! That was it! I just had one man's man left in my close circle, and now he had changed gender! All that was left was for Phobos to lay eggs, and I would be surrounded by nothing but members of the fairer sex.

Popori de Cacha remained silent, waiting for my decision. I was not prepared to release the Chameleon, who had shown her reliability and mastery many times before.

"Listen, de-sa, is there no way for Ravaash females to be warriors? The captain of *Surprise-1* is a young Chameleon female, and no one has any doubts in her abilities."

"The laws of the Ravaash race do not forbid females from being warriors, unless de-sa is preparing to have children soon. But the most capable warriors in history are thought to have been males. Their physiology is better suited to hand-to-hand and long-range combat. Your Highness's other bodyguards are the best warriors my nation has. And a female appearing among them could be perceived negatively, which might lead to your Highness's standing taking a dive."

"Alright, Popori de Cacha. Listen to my decision: you will remain in charge of my bodyguards until you yourself think that all the other Chameleon guards have surpassed you in ability, or you decide that the time has come for you to make for the island of young females on Unatari."

The head of my guard took a bow, picked up Bionica's head, and set off for the exit. I stopped the Chameleon at the door:

"The arrested corporal from *Surprise-28* was brought here to the Iseyek cruiser on a rescue shuttle from *Joan the Fatty*, but I haven't heard anything on his further fate. Where did he get sent off to?"

Popori de Cacha started to think, but then answered, not hiding her surprise:

"I can say with absolute confidence that the three arrestees died in the explosion of the first *Behemoth*. I saw their dead bodies with my own eyes. As such, I'm not sure I understand your Highness's question. Perhaps the Crown Prince is confusing the dead corporal with someone else of similar appearance?"

"Perhaps... Alright, you can go."

That means he wasn't able to get off the dying ship after all... I looked at Astra, listening to music in her headphones, then turned my gaze on Phobos. The Arite could be anyone. I had to keep that in mind all the time now.

# Insect Bigwig

"THERE NICOLE was doing a great job at the reins. She had competently led the Sector Eight Fleet to the Khe system at four hundred miles from the Aliens, confidently arranging the ships into combat formation. Both battleships were slightly in front. Six miles behind them were thirteen heavy cruisers. Antisupport and electros were another thirty behind them. The frigates were split up into two groups, waiting for the Aliens to take maneuvers.

I myself would have done it a bit differently, perhaps more aggressively. The enemy had very few small ships, which could have all been taken out in one quick attack, then I would have had our electros deafen the *Sledgehammers*' weak sensors and fully paralyze the enemy ships until our big guns could arrive. All the same, I did not intervene in my assistant's work, simply observing her actions.

Nai Igir was to my right. Today was the first day she was appearing in public, though her arrival was taken with complete apathy. It wasn't at all the reaction I was expecting from the Iseyek, so I requested that Nai Igir remove the armored suit hiding her transparent-blue wings, and she agreed. And the Iseyek Prime had barely opened her wings before the reaction of the Iseyek in the fleet surpassed even my wildest expectations. The enthusiastic yelping, crackling and howling from the mass of insects on the common fleet channel was such that I even had to remove my headphones so as not to go deaf.

*"I've never felt the like, Crown Prince. The wave of admiration rushed in with such ferocity to this butterfly and her commander that it vastly surpassed that time in Hnelle, when I lost control over myself. The fleet Iseyek are prepared to devour any enemy, even going in unarmed. They would die for you without a second of hesitation as long as you have this flying translator at your side. I'm simply overflowing with energy right now. I have started feeling things that I never could before... By the way... The Arite came after your Highness to* Emperor August. *It's very strange, given that it would have had a much easier time dissolving into the crowd on a Swarm cruiser. And another thing... Prince Georg, the Aliens will not accept combat. They are fleeing to the Lobj system as we speak!"*

"Nicole, they're retreating!" I warned my assistant, though it was already too late, as I watched the Alien ships leave the tactical grid one after the other.

"Did I do something wrong, Prince Georg? What did I do?" Nicole Savoia turned to face me, expecting reproach.

"It isn't your fault, Nicole. I didn't see any errors on your part. It's just that the Aliens have begun behaving differently, more calmly. They are learning from their experiences in previous battles and are afraid of us.

"Computer extrapolation of their trajectory shows that the Aliens are heading toward the Lobj system!" said the young tactics lieutenant, Max Stegor, who had previously served on *Boydur the Hero*, but was now taking the place once occupied by Valian ton Corsa in the headquarters.

By the way, Max had a rare talent for tactics. He had the best results, not only when answering typical examination situations, but also when solving nonstandard assignments I had come up with, thereby winning the prestigious place in the Perimeter Sector Eight Fleet headquarters from among more than three hundred other candidates. To be honest, Max Stegor's tactical abilities surpassed Valian ton Corsa's by several times. All the same, when visiting the intensive care unit on *Master of Tesse*, I promised Valian that she could always count on coming back to her place in the headquarters after recovering. The doctor of the burn ward informed me that the girl was in a critical condition, and she needed some encouragement to keep her holding on. Submersed in an oxygen-enriched gel bath, Valian heard out my words and nodded, though it was barely perceptible.

"We are clearing the station of Aliens, and recharging our ships... Attention!!!"

The last word I screamed out, because a red dot had appeared on the tactical map next to my fleet from out of nowhere. The Alien frigate marker split, clearly then releasing a bomb and... it went off without exploding, due to all my destroyers' high-speed laser turrets striking it simultaneously. It wasn't for nothing that we had done all that practicing in Sss, working on our bombing technique, as well as out bombing defense!

"*Warhawk-22*, take point on the enemy!" came a voice that sounded familiar to me.

"Do not shoot at the enemy frigate!!! Blind its electronics, and hold it in webs and disruptors! General Savasss Jach, I need that ship whole. We've never seen one like this before. Try to take some Aliens alive too! *Warhawk-22*, excellent work! I promise that as soon as Admiral Kiro Sabuto is better, he'll figure out what medals you've earned, and also..." I took a quick look at the report sent by Nicole, "... *Vassar-3* and *Flycatcher-4*, who destroyed the enemy bomb and saved a great many of our ships in doing so."

*Warhawk-22*. Why was that ringing a bell...? I opened up a list of all ships in the fleet. That's right! How could I have forgotten about the experiment! Beston Maf, the android captain of the android-crewed frigate! It seemed he had survived, and had even been able to prove himself a hero. I would have to talk with Admiral Kiro Sabuto. We could now declare the experiment a success.

"Excuse me for interfering in your command, Nicole, it's just that the situation required an immediate reaction. You'll see yourself. The Aliens will learn from their mistakes quickly, and in parallel, will start trying to copy our successful strategies. I don't yet know what kind of bomb the Alien cloaker launched at our fleet, but I suspect it would have blown up, if given the chance. I will now leave the headquarters, but you make sure General Savasss Jach's praying mantises capture the station and board the held-down Alien frigate. As soon as they're done, let me know."

With Florianna and a whole horde of visible and invisible bodyguards accompanying me, I set off for my cabin. My cheek, which had just barely started growing back together, was starting to hurt again, as if the doctor would have to sew it shut yet again. Unexpectedly, a soldier with gunner-private patches approached me in the hall and tried to get my attention.

"Your Highness, do you have a few minutes for a conversation?"

"The battle isn't yet over. Why are you not at your combat post, private?" Popori de Cacha came out of invisibility and displayed the appropriate level of caution.

*"My Prince, it's the Arite! He is not dangerous, and has finally come around to the idea of talking about working together."*

"The reason he is not at his combat post, is because there is already an identical copy of him in the cannon tower, right where he should be... You are the Arite, after all, or am I mistaken?"

In the space of a second, the contours of the private dissolved into a thick white cloud. It can't be that the Arite is afraid of being uncovered, can it? But the Truth Seeker was not wrong. The extraterrestrial creature merely gave a dramatic demonstration of my accuracy, then changed form into... Bionica!

"This form was not among those listed as forbidden by the Prince. No, your Highness, you were not mistaken, I am the Arite. Can we have a talk?"

* * *

I suspect, that to an outside observer, what were in fact the first official negotiations between two space-faring species looked like nothing more than a shared meal between the Crown Prince and his newly repaired secretary. Bionica's death was already known in the fleet and, as such, the android's reappearance next to the commander in an intact and undamaged state was noted immediately by a great many. Popori de Cacha instantly blocked the spread of information on the Arite, and released a fake story that the robot translator had been repaired to cover it up. Those unfamiliar with the true state of affairs may have been surprised by the perhaps excessive quantity of armed bodyguards keeping all the cruiser crew members away from Georg royl Inoky and his translator.

Pseudo-Bionica and I were in a separate room in the officer's dining area. The Arite was omnivorous, and had at least a slight idea on the way table utensils were to be used, but he was approximately as far removed from Bionica's perfect manners as my hulking, awkward body was from the elegance and grace of a ballerina. My clearly starving table-mate was gulping down food with squelching and slurping sounds, all the while dropping bits of food and dribbling trails of sauce on the tablecloth. For that reason, there wasn't a second of doubt that this could never have been the real Bionica. Though I immediately noted that the Arite learned fast. It started using a napkin, following my example. It also started eating more carefully. The table manners of this representative of a civilization previously unknown to humanity sitting across the table from me aside, it was much more important to figure out what the Arite was offering, and in fact it was very much worth my while.

Pseudo-Bionica said that it was speaking in the name of his whole race. Its offer was to open the Arite system warp beacon to my ships, as well as any other Swarm beacons, and provide unimpeded passage for the Sector Eight Fleet to the Empire and basically wherever I wanted throughout Iseyek territory. It also promised to introduce a bill in the Swarm through an individual with the right to vote in a high place in the Iseyek hierarchy to compensate Crown Prince Georg royl Inoky ton Mesfelle for the incident that took place in the Kej system and even to get it passed. In exchange for everything I've just listed, the Arites wanted three important things: my help in liberating the Arite systems from the remnants of the Iseyek armies, diplomatic and military pressure from the Empire on the Swarm with the goal of a peace treaty with the Arites under the condition that the insects pay compensation for the damages incurred over the two-hundred-year-long war, and also the conclusion of a mutual-assistance and military alliance treaty between the Empire and the Arites against any enemy, be they Swarm or Alien.

The problem was that the Arites would only go through with the agreement if it was accepted wholesale. If even one point wasn't agreed on, all the others would be void. So, without my official agreement to return the Swarm-occupied Arite system, there could be no discussion about opening the warp beacon for my fleet, and the Arites could guarantee me no compensation from the insects until a military alliance could be concluded between the Arites and the Empire. Everything I said about not having the authority to make such treaties in the name of the Empire were simply ignored by Pseudo-Bionica. At some point, I would have to admit that the negotiations with the Arites had reached a dead end and suggest setting them aside for a bit.

"Alright, my Prince," Bionica agreed. "I hope I will be allowed to keep this appearance on your ship? Insofar as I understand, the individual, who normally occupies this appearance is in an inactive state, so I will not be getting in her way. The other crew members had no negative reactions to my appearance in this form. I can do the usual functions this individual does in order not to arouse suspicion."

"Then you'll have to be my translator. You do in fact know the Iseyek language, so I don't see that as a problem. But promise you won't suddenly disappear. Androids can't do that, and you'll raise a bunch of unpleasant questions if you turn into a cloud in front of my officers. Bionica had some other duties as well..."

A sudden incoming emergency call interrupted my explanation. I took a look at who was calling and smiled involuntarily. It was Colonel Gor ton Vulf! Clearly he wanted to tell me that the station and cloaker have been captured. However, I was wrong.

"My Prince, the Khe station is mined! Some of the sections are totally blocked off. There are no doors in.

But the engineers are saying that their readers are picking up antimatter behind the thin dividers!"

I switched over to the internal fleet channel:

"Attention! This is the fleet commander. Take the ships away from the station immediately! All frigates and destroyers, and also the *Tria* should immediately warp to the first planet at twelve hundred! What's the deal with the Alien frigate?"

"The frigate is under our control, but we were again not able to capture any of its occupants alive. The engineers are attaching the trophy frigate to *Bride of Chaos*. They'll need a couple of minutes.

"Got it. Cruisers and battleships, leave the station, pick up the landing groups and also get out to the first planet. Landing groups are to collect trophies and immediately evacuate the station to the nearest fleet ships!"

I signed off and took a look around. False Bionica had already made her way off somewhere, not having waited for me to explain all its duties. I was waiting impatiently for Pseudo-Bionica to mess something up with her ignorance. I really needed to discuss the Arite issue with my advisor and fast, before Florianna accidentally revealed the presence of the unknown race on the ship. I asked my cousin Katerina ton Mesefelle to come to the officer's dining area.

My cousin was totally unsurprised by the discovery of a new space-faring species and immediately joined the discussion, describing me her questions and suggestions. What struck me most in my cousin's speech, was something I hadn't yet found the resolve to say out loud:

"Why are we solving the Iseyek's problems without

them? Georg, let's invite the Swarm Progenitor to take part in the negotiations!"

"You know, that's the right idea. But first we need to show the Arites that we could get out of this trap without them. That will strengthen our position in the negotiations a good amount."

I called General Savasss Jach and, using Phobos as a translator, suggested the Gamma Iseyek get in touch with his acquaintances in the Arite system. His suggestion was to let the information out in doses, trying not to show our hand too early with the trophies, rescued scientists and the Iseyek Prime in our fleet. The general agreed with my position and signed off. Four minutes went by before the general called me back:

"Prince Georg, the mission was a success. The beacon in the Arite system will be turned on in one hundred ninety-four minutes. I told them that the only ship coming was *Tria*, with reinforcements for the war going on on the planet. The Swarm there doesn't know about the Sector Eight Fleet yet, so for them it will be a surprise. But, I am sure that this issue is best discussed with our feet on the ground in the Arite system."

"If we really can get out of Triasss Zess's trap, I'll kiss that hairy bug all over!" Katerina ton Mesfelle promised after the general had hung up.

"Does it just keep you up at night not to also have the Iseyek Mating Dance achievement?" I joked, but Katerina did not get it and went to mentally prepare the Swarm Progenitor for a meeting with the representative of the Arites.

* * *

Nai Igir reacted quite nervously to the information that there was an Arite on board the starship, yet I was able to calm the Swarm Progenitor nevertheless with the fact that the Truth Seeker was able to keep a close watch over the ship for the deceitful being, and would not hesitate to get involved if necessary. The Iseyek Prime hesitated for a long time and demanded that I, as an official representative of the Empire, guarantee her safety, and I even did.

The first official meeting between representatives of the Arites and the Swarm in two hundred years was planned. What was more, this historic event was planned to take place on the flagship of the Perimeter Sector Eight Fleet, the heavy assault cruiser, *Emperor August*. My cousin Katerina ton Mesfelle had already had a foretaste of the huge interest this kind of exclusive material could garner and was scurrying around the starship with the speed of a cat that'd just burned its tail, getting the equipment set up, and getting the conditions just right to record the historic moment for posterity.

But first, we would have to finish the trip to the disputed Arite system without issue, and there had been a war over that planet between the Arites and the Iseyek with varying levels of success for two centuries now. To be honest, I did have some "butterflies in my stomach" over the possibility that the Swarm could trick us again. Despite that, the general's old friends did not deceive us, and the beacon turned on at precisely the scheduled time. When it did, *Emperor August* and the rest of the

Sector Eight Fleet made the jump to the Arite system's beacon, which flashed on for just a second.

The staff officers' moods immediately improved, though they also began to look strained. I heard my subjects talking. They were all hoping very much that the Perimeter Sector Eight Fleet had in fact escaped the deadly trap, however they were not ready to believe in it all the way before they saw the chance to speak with the Empire for themselves.

And there it was, the Arite system! The ship left the tunnel accompanied by a bedsheet-sized page of system messages that flashed before my eyes momentarily. The information blockade had been broken, and a waterfall of data that had accumulated over the last few days cascaded down over me. Relation changes with factions and people, increases in global fame, reductions and increases in standing, hundreds of messages from acquaintances.

I closed the text-packed screen and simply opened my character popup:

**Georg royl Inoky ton Mesfelle, Crown Prince of the Empire**
 **Age: 48**
 **Race: Human**
 **Gender: Male**
 **Class: Aristocrat**

**Achievements: Chameleon Elder Female, Favorite's Iseyek Mating Dance, Discovered Arite Race, Alien Killer, Researcher of the Unknown**
 **Fame: +18**
 **Standing: +2**

My standing was in the positive for the first time since I entered the game! And my fame had increased by five points in the time I was gone! Relations with factions and species I had never heard of had also grown substantially. Even the Imperial Artists faction had somehow wizened up to +8! And so, what about the Imperial Military? I had to flip through a few screens of text before finding the information:

**_Standing change. Empire Military faction opinion of you has improved._**
**_Presumed personal opinion of you: +15 (warm)_**

"Enemy ships on directional scanner!" Nicole Savoia brought me back to reality. "Swarm ships! Forty marks. Three _Legashes_, a couple _Umoyge_s, the rest are little guys. They're getting closer!"

I imagined myself in the place of the confused and frightened Iseyek commanders, and couldn't hold back a smile. Instead of the reinforcements they were expecting, one lone landing _Tria_, an unknown fleet of three hundred starships had arrived to the disputed Arite system, and most of their radar signatures indicated that they belonged to a foreign space government. Invasion! War! Betrayal! It was probably these very thoughts setting the insect captains on edge now. But the Iseyek earned their dues: the Swarm fleet did not retreat and threw itself on the attack against the trespasser, regardless of my fleet's significantly outsizing them in both number and class of ship.

"The enemy has come out of warp at four hundred miles! Incoming video call! Your Highness, shall I put them through?"

"Put them through in thirty seconds, but not with me, with my translator Nai Igir."

I turned to the Iseyek Prime and said:

"Now is the time for the Swarm Progenitor to assert her ancient rights. Before us are your subjects. And now, they either bow before the Iseyek Prime, take an oath of loyalty and join our fleet, or I will destroy them. And it will be so with every fleet that tries to impede our movement through Swarm territory, and your path to the throne."

"May I claim to this captain that the Perimeter Sector Eight Fleet is under my command, and is no threat to the Swarm?" Nai Igir clarified.

"No, you may not," I said, trying to put a complete end to all such topics. My combat starships are the force that will lead to you power over the Swarm, but the fleet is not subject to the Progenitor. For now, we are just working together. You need my ships to get to the capital system Dekeye and be crowned ruler of the Swarm. And I need you because no Iseyek wouldn't dare stop the Progenitor from moving around Swarm territory. As soon as you reach your goal, my fleet will leave the Swarm. That much I promise you. Naturally, though, this can only happen after the Swarm settles accounts with me over their betrayal in the Kej system."

Nai Igir confirmed that she had understood my conditions, then I ordered her to put the incoming call through. The Iseyek Prime spoke for a very long time. I didn't understand a word of her squeaking, but I didn't hurry to use Phobos or Popori de Cacha to translate, as I was afraid of distracting her. Finally, my translator turned off the microphone and turned to me.

"They will not resist, and agree to join your fleet, Crown Prince. Just one condition was named: these ships are to stay in Swarm territory no matter what, and your Highness cannot take them out to the Empire. If Prince Georg agrees to this limitation, they are prepared to join immediately."

I gave my permission for the Iseyek ships to only come to my side temporarily until Nai Igir had officially become the ruler of the Swarm. The Iseyek Prime made a short trill into the microphone, and an excited shriek and whistle rang out from "our" Iseyek on the common fleet channel.

"Admiral Kheraisss Vej, accept these new ships under your command!" I said and, taking off my headphones, went to find the Arite. I just had to tell him about the change in the situation and suggest conducting three-party talks with the Swarm Progenitor.

* * *

I couldn't find Bionica, either in her room, or on the general deck, so I turned to the Truth Seeker for help.

*"The Arite is now in your bedroom, Crown Prince. Her and my sister are fighting."*

"What could Astra have found to disagree with it over?" I grumbled in dissatisfaction, then hurried to my cabin.

I could already hear the muted screams and cursing coming from behind the closed door as soon as the doors of the elevator opened. After opening the door to my cabin, I took a careful step over the two girls, who were fighting on the floor right in front of the door. Astra and Bionica were rolling around the carpet screaming and wheezing and pulling one another's hair. I briefly took a seat in an armchair, and looked on with the measured interest of an observer as the two approximately equally sized girls grappled. The forces were equal, and neither of them were preparing to give up.

I had to intervene. I took a pitcher of emerald green juice, walked up to the fight and poured the contents out on the overeager girls. The tangle of bodies fell apart in a moment, and both participants in the fight jumped back with a catlike hiss.

"That crazy idiot Bionica attacked me! The android is clearly broken!" cried Astra, first to speak through tears of pain and shame.

"Well that green-haired witch threw a serving tray at me. With boiling water in the mugs, by the way!"

"You're damn right there was! You need to learn to think with those computery brains of yours. I burned my fingers because of you!"

"Well you freaking bit me. Some Princess! Who taught you those manners?!"

"Oh, I taught myself, dearie! It looks like the android has finally come out to play! You got something wedged in your chips, huh?"

I hurried to play the peacemaker before the fight built up to a new pitch:

"Astra, I've already warned you about Bionica. Plus, you lost the bet and promised to behave irreproachably, nobly and with exceptional dignity, as a true Princess should. Which is why this is strike one, and two, and you will be seriously punished. You will spend the next three days as the android's servant: you will clean up after her, wipe the floors, cook the food. You'll spend all these days in Florianna's room, and there, by the way, you'll also be cleaning up after and feeding your sister. And if I hear even one complaint about you not doing your job well enough, I'm sending you to spend a month on an Iseyek ship. You can entertain them with your dances! The insects, and not just they, really liked your performance. I even got a report that a video of your dance is the most popular file exchanged on the data networks of my fleet."

"But Prince, that's not fair!" The Princess, somewhat rumpled up in the fight, tried to object, but I immediately interfered in my favorite's objection:

"Not three days, but a week! And if I hear one more word of complaining, it'll be a month! How will I get through to you...?" I turned back to the Arite with an irate expression on my wounded face. "You are aware that androids are not capable of aggression, aren't you?! And how am I supposed to explain to my subjects the fact that my normally peaceful android is behaving like this? You have exactly one week to learn to be an android. And if you try to pull any more stunts like this, I'm setting you down on the first planet we reach, no matter if there's intelligent life there or not. Now you and I are going to three-party negotiations between three great cosmic races, so get ready and get yourself together."

Making use of the fact that Astra had turned away and was digging in the cabinet, Pseudo-Bionica turned into a white cloud for a second, before returning to the synthetic blonde's body, but without scratches on her face or a torn collar on her uniform.

"Let's go. But I warn you now, if you try to copy the Iseyek Prime, you will be learning to breathe in a vacuum!" I threatened the Arite, and he accepted the condition.

The negotiations took place in the large hall of *Emperor August.* Katerina and her assistants made the broadcast. The previously unknown type of Iseyek with blue wings was shown in detail to the humans, then there was a section on the shape-shifting Arite, then me in ceremonial uniform with a made-up face. After that, I asked everyone to clear the room, and only the three of us remained in the center of the hall.

The negotiations were laborious and drawn-out. The Arites and the Swarm were arguing about the peace conditions and on what terms their two races would be able to co-exist. The options considered were many, from: everything will remain as is, and the war will continue until one of us is totally destroyed, to the recognition of the Arites' right to reside in Swarm territory and the opening of Arite systems to Iseyek immigrants. At some point, the option of uniting the two cosmic governments in a united Federation was even considered, with a Queen-Ruler in the person of Nai Igir.

But, over all the negotiations on friendship and mutual aid, I was not prepared to ignore the question that was paining me the most: the Swarm's treason. There was absolutely no way I could let that stab in the back go or put it on the back burner. An Imperial Crown Prince is not some mere pawn that can be sacrificed unpunished! In my mind, this action merited extremely severe retribution, so the thought to do something like that would never even cross the insects' minds again! When I stated my very harsh demands, Nai Igir thought for some time. An exchange began, and twenty minutes later, we had agreed to arrange compensation for the betrayal amenable to both sides.

And now, after six hours of heated arguments, there was a document signed by all three parties, the importance of which was impossible to overestimate. The nameless Arite, the Swarm Progenitor Nai Igir and Crown Prince Georg royl Inoky ton Mesfelle had agreed on the following:

- The war between the Arites and Iseyek is ended from this point on. The Orange House of the Empire shall serve as guarantor of this peace.

- The Orange House's ships shall have the right to uninhibited movement throughout the Swarm and Arite systems.

- The Arites are declared a part of the Swarm as the "Arite Iseyek race" at full parity with the other Iseyek subraces, and shall receive the ability to live and move throughout Swarm territory without any limitations whatsoever.

- The Arites shall receive half of the votes in the Swarm.

- The Arites shall transfer their territories (and these were not many, but not so few either, fourteen star systems in total) to the control of the Swarm Progenitor.

- Four Swarm star systems shall be annexed to the Orange House of the Empire: Oort, Fia, Khs and Yal. The holder of these systems shall be Crown Prince

Georg royl Inoky ton Mesfelle.

- The Yayho border fleet shall join the Perimeter Sector Eight Fleet in its entirety.

- The incident in the Kej system is considered settled. Crown Prince Georg royl Inoky, and the Orange House and the Empire have no more grievances against the Swarm in regards to what happened.

- The Swarm will put all its territories (fifteen star systems) under the control of the Swarm Progenitor.

- The Arites, the Swarm and the Empire shall conclude a military alliance against the Alien invasion.

And though I had my doubts that I had the right to sign such a document, and that the Iseyek and Arites would affirm the authority of their signatories, Katerina ton Mesfelle, invited to film the signing of the historic treaty, thought that there would be no problems with its legitimacy:

"You are an Imperial Crown Prince and commander of the Perimeter Sector Eight Fleet, which means a large part of Swarm territory is part of your zone of responsibility. Who is more qualified to be representative of the Empire than you? And do you really think the Emperor would refuse a gift in the form of four star systems annexed for humanity?! The Iseyek Prime's authority is indisputable. What's more, there will be a vote on it in the Swarm soon, and with the help of the Arites, or even without it, the result we want is already guaranteed. Well, and as for the authority of the Arite present on the cruiser, we'll soon find out. As far as I understand, there are already a great many Arites in the Swarm, and they are capable of communicating with one another. And if the Arites really do transfer their territories to the Swarm, in doing so they will affirm that they recognize the signing of the treaty."

Before the camera flashes even went out, a new wave of system messages flooded in:

*Sovereignty Change. The Oort system has been placed under the jurisdiction of the Orange House*

*Sovereignty Change. The Fia system has been placed under the jurisdiction of the Orange House*

*Sovereignty Change. The Khs system has been placed under the jurisdiction of the Orange House*

*Sovereignty Change. The Yal system has been placed under the jurisdiction of the Orange House*

*Crown Prince Georg royl Inoky ton Mesfelle shall become the sovereign of the Oort system*

*Achievement unlocked: Imperial Conqueror*

*The Arite State has ceased to exist.*

*Standing change. Iseyek race opinion of you has improved.*
*Alpha Iseyek race opinion of you: +15 (warm)*
*Beta Iseyek race opinion of you: +13 (warm)*
*Gamma Iseyek race opinion of you: +11 (warm)*
*Arite Iseyek race opinion of you: +2 (indifferent)*
*Iseyek Prime race opinion of you: +4*

*(indifferent)*

**Global fame increase. Current value +20**
**Global standing increase. Current value +6**

Out of the four star systems, Duke Paolo royl Anjer confirmed my authority over just one. On the one hand, it's weird that he even said yes to one. One the other hand, why just one? The situation looked very similar to the one with the Brotherhood of the Stars to me, and as such I calmed myself down in advance by making sure the local leaders in the Fia, Khs, and Yal systems wouldn't take any kind of oath to any kind of holder appointed by Duke Paolo.

* * *

My fleet did not spend much time in the Arite system. Right after recharging energy, we continued our path through the Swarm systems. We met no resistance from the insects anywhere. In fact, the Iseyek were more than ready to help us with repair at every station we came to. The Swarm-model ships filled up their ammunition reserves, and General Savasss Jach completely restocked on huge eggs of new recruits for the huge *Tria*.

We were in the Kha system when the results of the vote came in. The Swarm had voted in the majority to give all control over the now-dual space government to the Swarm Progenitor, the Iseyek Prime Nai Igir. There was no farewell as such. Right after the results were announced, a group of armed Alpha Iseyeks arrived to my flagship to fetch their new Queen, and the Swarm Progenitor set off for the capital on one of the Iseyek ships with her blue wings gleaming.

"Shall we go home to Unatari?" suggested Katerina ton Mesfelle, who had come with me to see the insect Queen off.

"Yes, probably," I said with a heavy sigh. "Another half hour for the battleships to recharge, and we'll head for home.

I felt a stagnant sensation of discontent lingering inside. After I had demanded compensation from the Swarm in negotiations in the form of a fleet and star systems, I immediately felt how sharply the Swarm Progenitor's opinion of me had changed for the worse. She clearly thought there was a better way of solving this issue.

Not able to find my place, I set off for Florianna's room for advice. Astra had her orange uniform's sleeves rolled up to the elbows, and was washing her sister with a sponge in a foamy bath. I thought it perhaps was not the best moment to talk, but Florianna asked me not to leave.

*"I know what you want to ask, your Highness. Yes, Prince Georg, the Swarm Progenitor really was thinking of offering you to become co-ruler of the huge united government. Thirty-three star systems, not counting the fifteen already under your Highness's control. Trillions of subjects. All the resources of the Swarm and the power of the many star docks for making a fleet that Crown Prince Georg could only wish for. In one year, your Highness could have had the unheard-of power that a competent fleet commander such as yourself would need to take down the Aliens. However, instead of practically god-like power, Crown Prince Georg, you*

*decided to take four star systems for the Orange House, which are populated by the none-too-loyal Iseyek race. The Crown Prince making such a choice seriously disenchanted the Queen."*

"I don't think I would have agreed, Florianna. All the same, it is a shame to realize that I didn't even get to consider the possibility."

The short talk with the Truth Seeker had calmed me a bit and made me think seriously. I returned to my cabin. Without Astra, whose presence I had already managed to grow used to, it seemed a bit empty and uncomfortable. The thought even crossed my mind to forgive her and bring her back, but all the same I decided to remain firm so the lesson I was trying to teach my favorite would stick.

I sat for a while with a stupid aloofness before the dark screen. I gathered my strength and turned on the data panel. I brought up a map of star systems. Should we really go back home to Unatari? If I did, I would be in Sector eight with four hundred fifty damaged ships, and that was only if the Yayho fleet really did join me. Could I really face Duke Paolo royl Anjer's fleet of two thousand with such a force? Of course, I could get through to Unatari and do repair work there for a couple months, then practice for a long time with my soldiers before a decisive battle with the Duke... Or I could do it another way. Not so much strengthening my position, as weakening Duke Paolo's. The best defense is a good offense! I turned on the common channel.

"This is the fleet commander speaking. Cancel the scheduled route to Unatari. All ships warp toward the Aya system. We are going to Perimeter Sector Nine!"

# SECTOR NINE

I HAD NEVER seen Katerina ton Mesfelle in such a depressed state. She seemed practically dead. Even after the Iseyek had left us to die in the Kej system, my cousin had managed to keep herself together, but now the young woman was crying uncontrollably while wiping bitter, make-up-stained tears from her face, and there was nothing she could do to hold it in.

"Did I not do a good enough job... the first time?!? What happened, Georg?!?"

"It's a bunch of bullshit, Katerina," I said, trying to calm my cousin down. "My fleet isn't fighting the Aliens just for some virtual standing numbers. We are fighting to save the human race from total annihilation. We are fighting for our children's future. And all these likes and pluses, our adversaries and haters can stick right... in their profiles."

"But, why this... reaction, Georg? What made this different from... what happened in... Hnelle?"

To be honest, I didn't have the answer to my cousin's question, and was quite surprised myself. We had barely established stable contact with the Empire when my advisor started broadcasting reports she had prepared long ago, recorded in the Kej, Aysar Cluster, Lobj and Khe systems. The enemy's huge starship flotillas, new never-before-seen types of Alien combat starships, fierce battles with no studio gloss, thermonuclear explosions in space, huge fields of debris from destroyed ships, losses in the Sector Eight Fleet, and beautiful wins.

But human society reacted in a way my cousin and I were not expecting: all the news channels were accusing her of blatantly faking the broadcasts, saying that the clips show the traces of sloppy editing work, and that it was simply impossible. So-called "leading experts" were competing to see who could find more problems in the material sent by the Sector Eight Fleet on our victories over the Aliens. The Imperial Joint Staff's experts and the authoritative military staff of the Great Houses were making all kinds of calculations, totally unintelligible to the viewer, proving with their malignant smiles that Crown Prince Georg royl Inoky's press service had started producing obvious forgeries, as the level of success depicted in them was simply not realistically possible against Aliens.

It should also be said that there was a big devastating interview, given by Crown Prince Khayt royl Andor ton Reyekh from the Purple House shown on the main news channels. The Crown Prince declared himself the galaxy's foremost expert on Aliens, given that his Perimeter Sector Four fleet had already racked up eight Alien ships on its account. And, differently from some (here a mocking laugh followed), all of the Purple House's victories had been proven by captured trophies and Alien ship wreckage that you could touch with your hands and see with your eyes to be sure they were real. Whereas the Orange House had nothing but these heavily-edited clips. The loudly hyped, allegedly boarded *Behemoth* never made it to the Empire for study, and also most military specialists have serious doubts about the existence of such an Alien ship in the first place, given that the firepower reported was too extreme to be realistically used in a space battle.

After that interview and several other statements like it from other "authoritative Alien experts," my and Katerina's standings took a sharp dive. In not even two days, my standing had managed to dip below -30, rolling back all of the recent growth. Katerina's situation was even worse than mine. My cousin was being directly accused of doctoring footage, and had been dishonorably discharged from the Journalist's Club and the list of honorable graduates of her university. And then, just now, my cousin got a warning from the Emperor's communications service: she was told that either she immediately repent for making fake news intended to sew panic, or she could expect a call to the carpet of August royl Toll ton Akad himself in the near future, where the issue of her behavior's nonconformity with the rules and norms of aristocratic society would have to be addressed.

To be honest, this relationship even hurt me deeply, though I tried not to show it and keep a careless smile on my face, insofar as that was possible with the extreme scars that now graced my physiognomy. But my cousin then was totally depressed at heart due to the doubt and accusations against her that were still gaining steam, and so she was making no effort to hide her utterly defeated condition.

It was because of this doubt coming to light that I decided against my initial idea to immediately surrender all the trophies captured in battle to Imperial scientists. In the Sivala system, the battleship *Master of Tesse*, together with a dozen of the most damaged ships had separated from the rest of the fleet and set off through Swarm territory for repair in Unatari, taking the two trophy Alien frigates with them, as well as tons of biological and technological artifacts for research in my laboratories and three hundred Gamma Iseyek scientists, whose return the Swarm Progenitor had yet to send any demands for.

"Here's what, cousin. In two hours, my fleet will arrive to Forepost-4, on the border of Sector Nine. And though there are no inhabitable planets or large settlements in the system itself, the Forepost-4 station is inhabitable, and is equipped with a large border garrison and a great deal of repair berths for small-class starships. In Forepost-4, my fleet will make a stop for a few days. We need to wait for the Yayho fleet, which is hurrying to join us. Meanwhile, we can all just blow off the last couple of days' worth of steam celebrating the end of our campaign against the Aliens."

"And what?" asked my cousin, not understanding.

"The official part will come first: awarding medals to the soldiers who distinguished themselves, and paying out bonuses to everyone, no exception, on account of the risk. After that, my soldiers will be free to let loose. With God as my witness, it will be quite the noble carousing. I will also be treating the local border garrison as our honored guests. And, to keep our detractors from talking about fake victories, my soldiers are sure to talk with the border guards, and stories about the battles are sure to come up. They are dying to share the stories of the hundreds of Aliens killed, as well as the assaults of the *Behemoths* and the Alien *Queen*. Let the official powers of the Empire take as much time as they want not recognizing it and ridiculing us, but normal people will start to think: how could fifteen thousand soldiers from the Sector Eight Fleet all be lying? So, forget about the Emperor's press service trying to squeeze you in their big fat ultimatum vice. The truth will get out sooner or later, no matter how the Orange and Purple Houses try to censor it. And that is when our adversaries will really start to go pale. I've got a very serious assignment for you in Forepost-4, cousin."

"What assignment?" Katerina wondered, gradually coming back to life.

"Have fun at the party, dance, get drunk as a skunk and make sure to find yourself a man for the evening and don't let him leave 'til morning. Don't think of this as just the advice of a close relative and senior aristocrat. This is an order from your fleet commander!"

* * *

The whole fleet clearly needed this event! The huge hangar in the Forepost-4 space station was now totally empty of the shuttles and close-range fighters that were normally housed there. Instead, it was filled with the ranks of the Perimeter Sector Eight Fleet's soldiers. The perfect rectangles of the crews in orange uniforms blended together with the splotchy uniforms worn by the assault troops. Human and Iseyek, android and Chameleon, all standing side by side. On the small towering platform, other than Crown Prince Georg, there were also several senior officers from the ranks of the border station, as well as Admirals Kiro Sabuto and Kheraisss Vej, General Savasss Jach, Colonel Gor ton Vulf, the Truth Seeker accompanied by her minions, and also the fleet commander's assistant, Captain Nicole Savoia.

Katerina ton Mesfelle, as if nothing had happened, was overseeing the broadcast of the ceremony with a business-like smile, and none of those present could guess that just three hours earlier, my cousin had been crying buckets and talking about how her life was over. I had suggested that she start ignoring enemy insinuations and continue to stubbornly insist on her version of events, and she agreed.

As for myself, without excessive modesty, I was on point. I had refused any makeup work, so my freshly scar-covered face could be shown on the huge screen on the hangar wall for my subjects. But I wasn't at all ashamed of my battle wounds, in fact, I was quite proud of them. My detractors and all other foes, no matter their reason for hating us, would not be able to achieve their goal. Actually, they had only put me on my game. I don't suppose I have ever spoken so brilliantly and penetratingly before a group of soldiers. First I ordered everyone to take a minute of silence in memory of our comrades who didn't make it to the end of the military campaign. Ninety-two thousand Iseyek, seven thousand five hundred humans, and three Chameleons had given their lives so the Sector Eight Fleet could accomplish the impossible and escape the deadly trap to get through the Alien-controlled star systems, in spite of the enemy's huge advantage in number and firepower.

Based on their reaction, my subjects had never heard of the tradition of the minute of silence. All the same, the soldiers accepted it as a tribute to the memory of their fallen comrades very, very well. In the minute the soldiers were standing in saddened silence, I received three standing increase messages from the Imperial Military faction, two from the Iseyek, and another three from the Chameleons.

After that, not hiding the truth from my subjects and not being shy in my language, I told them about this so-called "foremost Alien expert from the Purple House," whose whole fleet had destroyed less Alien ships than just the gunner from *Vassar-3*. I explained that he was casting doubt on the existence of *Behemoth*-class battleships, and the huge Alien fleets we had come up against. I told them about the witch-hunt that had been set up by the none-too-successful admirals and commanders after our Sector Eight Fleet. I probably did use language that was a bit rough on a few occasions. For example, when I gave unsolicited advice to Crown Prince Khayt royl Andor ton Reyekh on where exactly he should stick his authoritative opinion, given that the Arite translating to the Iseyek got tripped up in the middle of a sentence and clarified Crown Prince Khayt's gender and whether he would have such locations in his anatomy. But the soldiers were behind me all the way, and that's what was important.

After the fleet commander's speech was over, we set about awarding medals to the participants in the military campaign. The first and most distinguished orders and medals were awarded by Admiral Kiro Sabuto, who had left his hospital room on that occasion for the very first time. If you ignored how unusually pale the admiral's face was, you couldn't notice any trace of the once-severe wounds on the flawless-looking warrior.

After that, all the soldiers and crew members who had taken part in the escape from Alien territory with no exceptions were awarded a Black Star, a matte-black semi-glossy medal with the inscription: "For those who have ventured beyond death." This ancient Orange House medal had been discovered by my assistant Nicole Savoia in a military guidebook. In the past, these medals had been given to soldiers who had survived clinical death and been revived. I fully agreed with Nicole's opinion that there could be no more appropriate medals for these soldiers who had fallen into such a deadly trap, and had already been effectively given a funeral and declared dead. That was why I had ordered fifty thousand such stars of black silver be made by Swarm craftsmen with an inscription in bright platinum.

*Standing change. Empire Military faction opinion of you has improved.*
*Presumed personal opinion of you: +19 (warm)*
*Global fame increase. Current value +21*

After all the boxes of medals had been given out to the starship captains for distribution to the crews, I took the microphone up again.

"And now there will be a gift personally from the Perimeter Sector Eight Fleet Commander, as a sign of my gratitude for having such a brave and talented crew. You are capable of bringing the impossible to life. From this very minute, every one of you will be given a Black Star and have your salary raised by one third. You are the pride of the Empire, and honorable soldiers. You have all earned these medals with your military feats! And also, you will all be getting a bonus in the amount of three of the now-increased monthly salaries!"

A collective roar of delight rippled across the hall. The echo came back many times from the hangar walls, deafening everyone inside.

"In the neighboring halls of the space station, the celebratory tables have already been set for the Perimeter Sector Eight Fleet. I invite all the Forepost-4 garrison border troops to join us in the celebration. There's enough food and drink for everyone! You won't have to worry for your safety. The Sector Eight Fleet's cloaked frigates are already keeping an eye on all neighboring star systems, and not one ship will get past them unnoticed! So have fun, relax, let yourself go totally wild. You've earned it! Anyone still standing at the end of the party will be subjected to the strictest Truth Seeker testing, as a potential security risk! And so, let the fun begin!"

*Standing change. Empire Military faction opinion of you has improved.*

**Presumed personal opinion of you: +20 (warm)**

* * *

"Where am I?" the room I woke up in was definitely somewhere I had never been before.

"It doesn't matter. It's very hard to get ahold of you, Ruslan. You tried to block mental communication. Did you think you could trick us and break the contract?"

I would have recognized this woman's voice from among a million others. Young, resonant, and at the same time capable of freezing water, so extreme was the cosmic chill it harbored. Miya! I came to in an instant, and started looking around jerkily for the source of the voice.

For some reason, she was nowhere to be seen, though I had no doubt that the extremely powerful Truth Seeker was somewhere nearby watching over me. I took a look around. I was on an open veranda with walls of interwoven vines. There was a small round table nearby with normal earth fruit: pears, peaches, and yellow plums. Out the window, I could see a triangle of penetratingly blue cloudless sky. I tried to sit up, and realized I was not in my own body... Well, actually it was the other way around. It was my actual body! My young healthy body. I wasn't even used to it anymore!

"So, then, as for an answer to my question?" Miya's voice rang out from the opposite side of the small room. I turned my head sharply, but still couldn't manage to see her.

"Show yourself!" I demanded.

All my fear left my body. I was confident that I had

not broken the contract with Mr. G. I., so I felt I was in the right.

"No 'please,' no 'would you;' you won't even address me by name. Is that any way to talk with a lady who is several times your elder?"

Nevertheless, Miya appeared literally one arm's length from me. I even got startled. The young, insanely beautiful woman with fiery red hair was sitting in a rocking chair. Her loose white clothes, and sitting pose somewhat hid the contours of her body, but she had simply not been able to fully cover up her big stomach. Off the top of my head, she looked to be five or six months along in the pregnancy.

"It's actually seven," she corrected me, making no effort to hide the fact that she was unceremoniously rooting around in my thoughts. "That means that the mental block the girl put in... The girl has grown a lot, even too much... Take it off immediately after you return to the game!"

"To the game?" I made sure to emphasize the last word. "Maybe you'll finally tell me in more detail what kind of game this is, given that the players can be killed?"

"Don't be insolent, Ruslan." The cold of the grave returned to her voice. "You're in no position to get smart. If you want to know, I recommended Mr. G.I. to take you out right after the contract was over. Yes, Ruslan, I'm telling you the truth and so I won't try to hide it. But then my companion, despite all his negative character traits, is pathologically fastidious in matters of honor. So, we'll hold up our end of the contract as long as you don't give us any reason to doubt your honesty."

Miya suddenly frowned and placed her right palm on her stomach, as if calming a child causing her pain by moving in the womb.

"The future Crown Princess?" I clarified, pointing to Miya's stomach with a nod.

"This should not worry you, Ruslan. My daughter will be born after your contract is up, so all issues of genealogy, inheritance and heraldry, are of no concern to you. Your mission is to defeat the Aliens... and not die. Don't take any more risks like that. Enough raids on Alien bases. And another thing, it was very hard for me to reach you. No matter how strong a Truth Seeker I am, my reserves are not infinite. I need crystals. I have no desire to ask Georgiy for that again, and hear out his telling-off. So, if you see an easy opportunity, call me into the game. Not right now. I spent too much energy on this. I need to restore my power first. In three days or so. Prepare the crystals for me and call me when no witnesses are around. And for now, get back into the game. And yes, I have removed your hangover. I have no idea where you could have learned to drink like that..."

I woke up from the ringing of my alarm clock in my bunk on the heavy cruiser *Emperor August*. For some reason, I wasn't wearing clothes, and was being haunted by patchy, confused memories that I had recently been making love with someone on this very bed. But who?

Miya was not lying. My head was light and airy, like a student after an exam. I couldn't remember a bit of the previous day's events after the herd of pretty girls in ceremonial combat uniforms pulled me onto the dance floor. It would seem I even danced. But I'm pretty sure I don't know how to dance, right? Or maybe it's that Ruslan doesn't, but Crown Prince Georg royl Inoky had studied it long ago in his younger days? There was a complete hole in my memory after that. What happened last night? I suspect that very many fleet soldiers were asking the same exact question today, after really swinging for the fences after my victory speech.

"How did I get into this room?" I asked a rhetorical question to the empty room.

However, the empty space turned out to contain a totally real individual to answer my question. A barely noticeable haze on my bed transformed into Bionica.

"My Prince, Popori de Cacha and Phobos took you to the cruiser at the very end of the big loud party."

"Is that so? I honestly don't remember..."

I wonder who I had had a tumble in bed with then? The only things other than me in the cabin were members of three Alien species, an Alpha Iseyek, the Arite, and a Chameleon. And what was more, the only female among them was a member of the Ravaash race... I had never been one to over-analyze fantasies, but I was having a very hard time digesting the information before me. The old scandal with Bionica could be considered a childish game in comparison with the "new adventures of the Crown Prince." Fortunately, Pseudo-Bionica explained everything:

"After that, Princess Astra came to check up on your Highness. You were in very high spirits, and sent everyone else out of the room, because you said you were about to explain her your tactics for space battle with some ancient illustrated physiology textbook on human inter-gender relations. But then Astra left, because her punishment isn't over yet."

So that means it was Astra... It felt like a stone had been lifted from my shoulders. I then started really worrying. There were some very weird ideas coming to mind.

"Anything else interesting happen?"

"The Yayho border fleet has arrived. A Swarm *Meresh* battleship, two *Legashes*, six *Umoyges*, twenty-three *Vassars*, and the rest are *Safas*. Admiral Kheraisss Vej is bringing the new arrivals up to speed on our tactics as we speak. By the way, it may interest your Highness that the captain of the *Meresh* is an Arite Iseyek, and since the Swarm Progenitor's coming to power, there has been no more sense in hiding that fact. And that captain has not arrived empty handed. He has an interesting gift for the Crown Prince: an immobilized and neatly wrapped Triasss Zess in the flesh. Nai Igir thought that this gift might be interesting to your Highness."

"Without a doubt. And if that traitor starts to talk, this gift could become simply priceless. By the way, Arite, I still want to ask you: why did you remain on my ship after the end of the war with the Swarm? You are free to live openly among the Iseyek now."

Bionica quickly fixed her hair and smiled her white-toothed smile:

"The Arites know very little about your race. And as I am the first to meet with humanity, I was appointed by my kind to serve as discoverer and ambassador, in a sense, though it may not be on the most official terms. But all the same, your Highness has a channel of communication with the Arite Iseyek. You can speak with those of my kind through me."

I see. I put myself in order, got dressed and went out into the hallway. Despite my slight apprehension, life on the ship had already returned to a completely normal rhythm. There wasn't even a small trace of yesterday's carousing. The staff officers were sitting in their places, the communications officers were talking with remote star systems and clarifying this or that piece of information. When I walked in, Lieutenant Max Stegor stood and approached me with a report.

"My Prince, I am receiving information that Perimeter Sector Nine Fleet Commander Svetlana ton Mesfelle is gathering a fleet from systems loyal to Duke Paolo royl Anjer in the Tian system. At present, the enemy has on the order of three hundred ships."

"How much time do they need to get to Forepost-4?" I clarified.

"No less than six days, your Highness."

It was worrying information, but it still didn't require an immediate response. It occurred to me that it would be nice to have a talk with Katerina ton Mesfelle on the situation that's developed. After all, the Sector Nine Fleet Commander was her niece, and there might have been some possible ways for this to go other than direct confrontation between two Orange House fleets. I went off to meet my cousin. Just to be safe, I didn't open her door with my electronic key and just walk in, as usual. First I knocked politely (it wouldn't be that surprising if my cousin was still sleeping, and there was no guarantee she would be alone).

"It's open!" a scream rang out from Katerina ton Mesfelle, and I walked in.

My eyebrows shot up immediately. It wasn't enough that my advisor really wasn't alone in the room, I had to also be well acquainted with her guest.

"I'm on my way out, Crown Prince," squeaked Corwin ton Ugar, looking brilliant in the space fleet captain's ceremonial uniform bedecked with combat medals as he really was preparing to slip by me into the hallway.

"Hey, stop!" Corwin ton Ugar was already half way out the door, but still stopped and turned around. "Captain, I'm reminded that we had an agreement for you not to show up on my ship or get near Astra."

"Your Highness, I had no thought in mind to break our agreement. I was invited to your flagship by Katerina ton Mesfelle as a guest, and I give you my word as an officer that I have never once left her cabin."

"Georg, what are you getting mad for? You told me to get some before the party, and all I did was listen to your advice. Cory is fun to talk to, a gallant gentleman and a great art expert."

I gave an incredulous chuckle. I'd heard that song before. The captain coughed, turning my attention to him:

"By the way, as we're talking about art... Commander, would it be too much to ask you to sign your work, as is generally accepted practice among artists? To be honest, you really won me over. I truly did want to acquire Astra ton Veyerde's painting. Based on the price of the first canvas, the second work of this talented girl would be worth at least forty, probably more like fifty million credits. That kind of money would be able to return my poverty-stricken aristocratic family to its former glory and guarantee a secure future. I really admired that move on your part a lot, Crown Prince. It was a very elegant plan. But the problem is that I really have been taking art lessons since a young age. My father, Vesar ton Ugar, is one of the leading experts at the Academy of Fine Arts in the Nessi system, and he spent a lot of effort trying to get me follow in his footsteps. And though in the end I chose the path of a soldier, like my mother, I can still tell when an abstract painting was done by a man or woman, even with my eyes closed."

What a twist! I laughed joyously, so unexpected was the turn in this story. Of course I would agree to sign my work.

"And how much might it be worth?" I wondered from the art expert.

"It's a unique work, in place, style, and artist. The value of these kinds of rarities usually starts in the hundreds of millions of credits. I would think you could get one hundred thirty million easily, just from one of my father's rich acquaintances. But I'll never sell this masterpiece, Crown Prince Georg royl Inoky ton Mesfelle. The very fact that I possess such a masterpiece will return greatness to the Ugar dynasty for generations to come. And as for my visit to your relative Katerina ton Mesfelle... That was up to her, of course, but don't get me wrong. I came to her bunk with no ulterior motives, and very serious intentions."

When the door closed behind Corwin ton Ugar, I flopped down into the big soft bed and asked the room's owner to get a light breakfast together for her cousin, and at the same time tell me about her niece Svetlana.

"I mean, what is there to tell... she's hardcore. Ambitious, goal-driven to the point of fanaticism, extremely greedy for fame. If you're thinking of trying to negotiate peace with her or buying her off, it definitely won't work. When she was about ten, Svetlana suddenly became confident that she would definitely become a famous warrior. Since that time, my niece has done nothing but stubbornly pursue her goal. Against the will of her parents, she left the prestigious Fine Arts Academy and applied to the Space Military Academy, where she graduated with honors, gained experience in the Imperial fleet for a few years, and built up a great resume. And then, through her uncle Count Avalle royl Anjer ton Mesfelle, she got to the point of being appointed to defend Perimeter Sector Nine."

Katerina put a mug of hot energizing drink in front of me and pulled a plate of small sweet and savory cookies closer and continued her speech.

"I'll tell you honestly, Georg, I see no way of avoiding a conflict. From my perspective, for Svetlana, this is a question of prestige... First, you formally raised her alarm when you invaded territory under her control with your fleet, so she has no choice but to react. Second, Perimeter Sector Nine is one of the calmest of the eighteen sectors. They have no problems with pirates or Aliens, nor any factions hostile to the Empire. There isn't even any non-terrestrial intelligent life. Catching smugglers is boring and brings no prestige. As such, Svetlana ton Mesfelle won't spare you a thing, if only just to show to everyone else that she's not getting fed for nothing. Third, as I've already said, she's a very ambitious girl. It's going to be important for her to show everyone and above all else herself that she surpasses you as a fleet commander. Fourth, and we shouldn't forget this, it's personal. The sharp rise of your father Inoky seventy years ago shook up the order of succession to the throne both of the Empire and the Orange House. Inoky's children became recognized as part of the main branch of the Mesfelles, and received the title of crown prince. Roben, Violetta and you put the other members of the Mesfelle dynasty on the back burners. If Inoky hadn't had any children, then Svetlana ton Mesfelle would have received a 'royl' attached to her name. I'm sure that my niece hasn't forgotten about that for a second."

"I understand you, cousin. Well, if there's no way to avoid a conflict, all we can do is prepare for it. I think it's time to play the bad boy. We can't let their giving us a negative standing go to waste. And I promise you, Katerina, that the meeting will take place on our terms."

\* \* \*

"They'll be leaving warp in one minute!" Nicole Savoia reported, looking especially collected.

"Great! All ships, attention! I repeat my order once again: we are only to target them. No one is to fire without my command. As soon as the enemy fleet shows up, assign targets. I need five webs and warp disruptors on the battleships *Svetlana the Great* and

*Svetlana Mesfelle.* We'll put ten webs on each of the sixteen heavy cruisers. Electros, deafen the enemy destroyers. Any enemy ship that goes into action is to be immediately destroyed. That is all. Ten seconds to action. Get ready!"

The Truth Seeker was not mistaken. The Perimeter Sector Nine Fleet came exactly when Florianna had predicted. There was a long 30-mile-long "hot dog" of frigates and destroyers, and twelve miles behind that was a thick group of the main ships: two battleships, sixteen heavy cruisers, and thirty light ones. I suspect that the enemy ships hadn't even finished loading a tactical map of the system before my frigates had already arrived in a thick cloud to stop the movement of the most dangerous starships. I took the microphone and spoke on the loudspeaker.

"Greetings, colleagues from Sector Nine! I see you were in no rush to pay us a visit. We've been here three days already with nothing to do. Svetlana, tell your ships, in the interest of avoiding unnecessary casualties, that any starship that moves from its place will be destroyed immediately. And yes, don't try shooting or disarming those glorious thermonuclear mines over there, placed along your light ships. They'll go off with such a blast that none of your five hundred frigates and destroyers will survive. Have you let them know yet?"

"What do you want, Georg?" the pretty young woman came on screen wearing an Orange House Starfleet uniform. Her facial features were very reminiscent of Katerina's.

Boom! Boom! Two red markers disappeared from the tactical map. Minus one light cruiser and destroyer from the Sector Nine Fleet.

"Svetlana, what the hell? Two of your ships didn't get the message and tried to flee! I don't want to have to play animal breeder here, raising the average IQ in your fleet by removing the dumbest members of the population. Order your captains now, clearly and loudly, to turn off their main propulsion thrusters and power down their energy shields. I remind you that all of your ships can be destroyed in less than a second. You are still alive and only thanks to my good will."

"Our commander will never give in to blackmail from an impostor such as yourself!" someone's fairly rude voice rang out from off screen.

"Svetlana, turn the camera a bit to the side. I want to see who that is yelping behind you there with my own eyes."

The commander frowned in dissatisfaction, but turned a bit to the side. A middle-aged, well-built man in an admiral's uniform came into view on camera. And that admiral continued being fresh straight to my face:

"All your victories are fake, a bunch of CGI bullshit. Do you think we don't know? It doesn't even matter though, because the court will deprive you of your title for this shady business!"

I turned to the Truth Seeker and pointed with a nod at the admiral, who was behaving very rudely:

"Florianna, this rude fellow has lost his sense of reality and is insulting a Crown Prince. Do with him as Imperial law prescribes."

*"It will be done, Prince Georg. There's something I've been wanting to try out..."*

Then, a second later, the admiral on screen froze,

clutched at his chest and slowly collapsed onto the floor with a hissing sound. Three seconds he spent trying to get any air into his wide-open mouth with bulging eyes, then he fell on his side and went silent.

*Global standing decrease. Current value -33*

*Standing change. Green House (Empire) opinion of you has worsened.*
*Present Green House (Empire) faction opinion of you: -34 (opposed)*

*Standing change. The Green House's opinion of the Orange house has worsened.*
*Present Green House opinion of Orange House: -9 (mistrusting)*

Some attack... God dammit... As luck would have it, this suicidal troublemaker was a member of the Green House aristocracy. All I needed now was for that old story with the Lavaelles to bubble up again... Trying not to show my emotions, I wondered aloud in a calm voice:

"Is there anyone remaining who wishes to speak rudely to an Imperial Crown Prince? No? Then I repeat my demand: Svetlana ton Mesfelle, order your ships to turn off their thrusters and power down their energy shields. As you can see, it is in your best interest. If a battle does start, you will lose, and it will be a shutout. Your battleships and cruisers are, excuse me for the expression, sitting ducks with their weak rear shields facing my biggest cannons. All I'd need is a minute and a half to turn all your large ships into atoms, and the little guys are gonna die as soon as the bombs are detonated. Imagine losing your whole fleet, which surpasses mine in number by one and a half times in one stupid, pointless battle and to be completely defeated all in one fell swoop. It would be the ruin of your brilliant career as a fleet commander. After something like what would happen, no one would even trust you with a rusty frigate. If there isn't a battle, you'll retain your ships and your name."

"Crown Prince Georg royl Inoky, please promise me that I will keep all of the Sector Nine Fleet's ships," the woman on screen asked, clearly worrying, biting her lip at the same time.

"I am no enemy of the Perimeter Sector Nine Fleet and would make no claim against your ships, Svetlana ton Mesfelle. Insofar as I know, your fleet initially had around ninety ships. The rest are hurriedly collected reserves from systems loyal to Duke Paolo. I give you my word as an Imperial Crown Prince: all of *your* fleet's ships will remain under your command. As for the five hundred other starships of various quality level you've gathered here, we'll see. It's just that I've got some issues with the head of the Orange House and the Sector Nine star systems that support him, and as such it is fully within my rights to lay claim to these trophies. Maybe I'll be able to make good use of some of these starships. You can decide what to do with the rest of them."

Svetlana ton Mesfelle flipped a switch on screen and said loudly and clearly:

"This is the Sector Nine fleet commander. This order is for all ships: turn off thrusters, disarm cannons, power down energy shields."

After that, the woman on the screen slumped down heavily into her seat, covered her face with her hands and said wearily:

"Duke Paolo will never forgive me for this. So I have nothing more to lose. I'll take your advice, Crown Prince, and take all the trophy ships you don't need into my fleet. I have just one question: how were you able to get your fleet into such an advantageous position right behind my ships? How did you know what formation my fleet would come out of warp in? Truth Seeker?"

"Not only. My cloaked frigates have been following your fleet for four star systems, and studied your typical formation. It's nice for catching smugglers: light frigates come out right by the station and catch the heedless transgressors. Heavy ships arrive at an optimal distance for firing and ready to intervene right away if criminals try to resist."

Svetlana ton Mesfelle gave a tortured smile:

"I've grown moldy here in the peace of Sector Nine and become too predictable..."

"The enemy ships have all surrendered without resistance," reported Admiral Kiro Sabuto just then.

The Perimeter Sector Eight Fleet traversed the Sector Nine systems, meeting no resistance along the way. Svetlana ton Mesfelle gave me quite the warm farewell, telling me with her parting words that the conflict in the Orange House was a matter that was only relevant to the quarrelling parties, and that it in no way intersected with either her own personal sphere of interest, nor that of the Perimeter Sector Nine Fleet.

My advisor, Katerina ton Mesfelle, was starting to grow tired of accepting and sending me one and the same message from every star system on our path: a declaration of friendship and full support. Technocracies, oligarchies, and monarchies alike all retracted their support of Duke Paolo royl Anjer, recalling their deputies from the Orange House Capital as they did so.

A delegation from the local rulers was sent out to meet my flagship, *Emperor August,* in practically every star system. Free repair. Access to Sector Nine docks. Buying ships on very favorable terms. Just insane amounts of money in support of our struggle with the Aliens. The rulers of the Sector Nine star systems were trying to outdo each other with their increasingly gushy welcome speeches. There were gifts for Crown Prince Georg royl Inoky ton Mesfelle and all those in his inner circle.

For some reason, the most presents of all went to my favorite. Having fully waited out her punishment, Astra participated in all ceremonies and was simply immersing herself in the societal attention. It got to the point that my bunk on the cruiser was turned into storage for a combination jewelry shop and women's clothing store.

"Now this is the life I always dreamed of!" the Princess exclaimed, opening yet another gift.

But I did not share her enthusiasm at all. The time limit set by the Emperor to make peace with the Orange House head was running out all too quickly, while the number of star systems supporting Duke Paolo royl Anjer remained, as before, in his favor. And as for the gifts, it's nothing but perfect rot, baubles, rarely exceeding even a million credits in value. And as for the new ships I had gained, the situation was a bit grimmer...

Yes, it had grown by almost one hundred fifty ships after managing to avoid the battle, but the only heavies among them were four *Katanas* and a couple of *Thrushes*. The remaining haul was just small-class ships. About ten *Surgeon*-class destroyers, and the same number of *Flycatchers*, as well as one hundred twenty *Pyros*. What I really needed in the fleet was battleships and heavy cruisers, but there turned out to have been a serious problem with them. There simply were none available for purchase in Sector Nine, and I didn't have the time to wait several months for them to be built. Also, certain problems with logistics arose during the purchase. There was absolutely no way to be sure that the Swarm would allow my ships to return through their territory a few months from now, for example. The Iseyek had already made it clear that they had a very singular interpretation of the signed contract. They were prepared to let all the Sector Eight fleet ships through, but no others.

But just then, something happened that changed my plans completely.

"Your Highness, urgent incoming long-distance call!" the voice of the orderly officer was wavering in panic.

"Who is it?" I wondered.

I wasn't really planning on talking with anyone, as I

was in a rush to see Nicosid Brandt. The old doctor was supposed to remove another set of staples and stitches from my face today. However, the communications officer's worry seemed strange to me, which is why I asked about it nevertheless.

"It's Emperor August royl Toll ton Akad!" said the officer.

"Put him through!" I creaked, my voice jumping in panic. I quickly got myself back together, and turned on the screen.

August was wearing a black and silver suit, which spoke to the official nature of the conversation. I bowed down instantly and lowered my head before the Emperor.

"I am endlessly glad at the honor of greeting your Imperial Highness!"

"You may stand, Georg! This is not an official conversation, I just wanted to ask you a couple of questions. Before answering, tell me, are you lost? Why has the Sector Eight Fleet been outside it's assigned zone of responsibility for so long?"

"My Emperor, to be honest, I didn't have much of a choice. The Sector Eight Fleet fought hard to break out of Alien territory, and the Swarm's warp beacons were turned off. The fleet was able to escape to Imperial territory only into Perimeter Sector Nine. And I decided to make use of the occasion in order to fulfill a promise I made to your Imperial Highness to end the conflict with the Orange House Head."

"Good on you for remembering, Georg. Half of the time is up, but the situation in the Orange House hasn't moved whatsoever from a dead stop."

"Emperor, the situation is quickly changing for the

better. I have decided to avoid an unnecessary bloody war and try the diplomatic way of bringing an end to the conflict. And that method works. There are more systems coming to my side every day."

I'm not sure what I said wrong, but the old man on screen started frowning. A few seconds of silence later, August explained the reason for his dissatisfaction:

"In the history of the Empire, there has never before been a time when two fleets from different sectors of the same Great House fought one another. Georg, it displeases me greatly to see defenders of the Empire squabbling amongst one another!"

"Emperor, I did everything in my power to make sure a conflict between the Sector Eight and Sector Nine Fleets would not come to pass. And I was in fact successful; there was no unnecessary loss of life. Commander Svetlana ton Mesfelle left quite satisfied from our meeting: her fleet grew by almost three hundred ships, and the defenders of Sector Nine have never been stronger. Your Imperial Highness, the Sector Nine Fleet has no grievances against me!"

The old man pondered for a second, but could I see the dissatisfaction on the Emperor's face clearly easing up.

"All the same, grandson, it simply won't do to have your fleet in a place they don't belong without especially good reason. It must be removed from Sector Nine as quickly as possible!"

"It will be. But my ships will have to remain in Sector Nine a bit longer. We have to make our way back to Swarm Territory after all, and that will take no less than a week."

"No need, Georg. I give permission for your fleet to take a course through the Core."

"What?" August's offer struck me so unexpectedly that I couldn't hide my confusion.

"You may take your fleet through the Core. I give you my permission. But promise me that your fleet's ships will go through the Core without stopping or letting the soldiers out at any stations."

I bowed down on one knee again and lowered my head.

"Yes, your Imperial Highness. I promise that my fleet will go through the Core without delay or leave."

"That is great. And do not forget that you have just fifty days to solve the conflict with the Orange House head."

The Emperor hung up. I stayed bowed down on one knee before the switched-off screen for some time, digesting the new information. After that, I turned the screen on and called up a star map. I could save almost two weeks on the shorter route. But what if... A smile stretched across my face involuntarily from ear to ear. I called Admiral Kiro Sabuto:

"My friend, our plans have changed drastically. There is no longer any need to return through the Swarm. The Emperor himself has permitted us to travel through the Imperial Core. It's just that we won't be going to Unatari. Announce to all ships that we are headed for Sector Seven! We'll finally be able to bring an end to this issue with Duke Paolo!"

# Breaking the Blockade

"**Y**OUR HIGHNESS, incoming call from Orange House Head Duke Paolo royl Anjer ton Mesfelle," the communication's officer interrupted the breakfast I was sharing with Princess Astra.

Astra and I exchanged glances. the girl made a markedly surprised face. And though my favorite's interest in politics was weak, even she was fully in the loop on my none-too-simple relationship with the Duke.

"Put him through!" I didn't change into my official fleet commander's uniform, instead choosing to remain in my lettuce-hued pajamas with happy little cartoon figures, which my daughter had sent me as a birthday gift.

The impossibly ceremonious and serious Duke Paolo appeared on the wall screen on the backdrop of a huge Orange House flag. Bedecked in court regalia and medals, the old man couldn't hide his surprise and opened and closed his mouth several times in silence to express his shock at the extremely informal situation on the other end of the long distance line: the Crown Prince in pajamas lying down on some pillows that were thrown haphazardly on the floor, with his favorite by his side in nothing but a transparent night shirt:

"Greetings, Duke Paolo!" I gave a salute to my suzerain with a glass of light red wine. "It's been a while since you've remembered your brave fleet commander. Two months have managed to go by since the last time we spoke."

"Crown Prince, I really didn't want to make this conversation too official; however, such informal circumstances are still an overreach," the old man grumbled in dissatisfaction. "At least sit up straight, Georg."

I decided against making a fuss over such a small matter with a titled aristocrat, so I sat up on a pillow.

"Is this better? Alright, Duke. I'm listening carefully!"

"OK, then. So, I have decided to refresh your memory. Georg, you have forty-five days left before Emperor August's deadline. And as your fleet is locked up tight in Sector Nine, and no change in the situation can be foreseen, I wish to hear capitulation conditions."

"I don't think I'm understanding something. Are you trying to surrender, Duke Paolo?" I couldn't hold back the quip.

The Duke frowned and threatened:

"Bear in mind, Georg, for every insult you hurl my way, your punishment will only grow more extreme! It seems you haven't heard. Well, let me be the one to tell you: an hour ago, soldiers loyal to me captured and deactivated the Aiwe warp beacon. Now, your fleet will not be able to leave Sector Nine back to Swarm territory!"

Aiwe? The empty system next to Forepost-4? With great effort, I held back a laugh, so stupid was my enemy's tactic in light of the fact that my fleet had already long since left Sector Nine through the Imperial Core. Based on what he'd said, Duke Paolo still didn't know about my agreement with the Emperor... I, hiding my joy with all my might, tried to contort my face into an uncomfortable, troubled grimace. It seemed to have worked, given that Duke Paolo began smiling in self-satisfaction.

"Has it hit you yet, how deep a hole you've dug yourself into, Georg?"

The Duke was openly relishing the situation. He clearly had no doubt that he had already emerged victorious in our dispute, and now was expecting me to come begging for peace on his terms. As a matter of fact, Paolo was famous for his greed, so why not play on that?

"Nice strategy, Duke. This scenario was obviously carefully crafted by your analysts. All the same, I do not think my position so desperate. And in fact, I am sure that I can get out. I even propose a wager. I have around two billion credits in my account right now, and I am prepared to put all that money up to say that the Sector Eight Fleet will be outside of Sector Nine in three days. From your side, Duke Paolo, I expect the same: two billion credits that my fleet will remain in Sector Nine. Do my conditions sound fair?"

Paolo royl Anjer frowned. His greed was clearly struggling against his cautious nature.

"Where could you have gotten so much money from, Georg? My financial advisors have calculated that after your recent extravagant spending in Forepost-4, you should have run out. Then again, that doesn't matter. I have understood the essence of your thoughts: you clearly want to bribe my people out from under me! But basically, it makes sense. If you promise two billion credits, anyone would turn on the warp beacon for your fleet and, after that, you hope to recoup it all with the money you win from me. You won't get by like that, Georg!"

"Well then, who is stopping you, Duke, from paying your employees very generously, so they don't turn on the Aiwe warp beacon under any circumstances? You would also compensate all your losses when I pay you your winnings!"

I saw the spark of fortune light up in my enemy's eyes. Two billion credits is quite a significant amount, even for the head of a Great House. In the end, greed took the day.

"Alright, Georg, I agree to your wager. I repeat the conditions again: if, in three days, your fleet is still in Perimeter Sector Nine, within one hour, you will send me two billion credits, no excuses. And if, in exactly seventy-two hours, by some miracle, your starships are outside Sector Nine, I will personally send two billion to your personal account. Is that right?"

"That's all right, Duke Paolo. You wouldn't be against Princess Astra royl Veyerde being the witness to our bet? Or do you not care about third-party witnesses?"

The Duke made a face:

"The girl is too close to you to be impartial, but I

accept your choice. Our conversation is recorded, and your word as an aristocrat is enough, Georg. And from my side, I give my word as the Head of a Great House, that I will keep my promise if I lose."

"That's just great then, Duke Paolo! I'll see you in three days."

The screen went dim. I took a look at the glass of wine, still in my hand as before, and said happily to my smiling favorite:

"I'm reminded of something I heard a long time ago: Greed hordes itself poor! It would have been stupid not to make use of such a perfect situation to manipulate this greedy old bastard! And no matter how much I might want to now, there's no way we're getting back to Sector Nine. The Emperor wouldn't even let us. So, I can consider the two billion credits already in my pocket. Astra, I propose a toast. To easy money!"

**Standing change. Astra royl Veyerde's opinion of you has improved.**
**Presumed personal opinion of you: +100 (completely faithful)**

When she looked at me, an unspoken question and hope for reciprocation could be read in Astra's eyes.

"Don't even dream about it, Astra. I will not reveal my opinion of you," I smiled, trying to hide the awkward situation I had unexpectedly ended up in with showy happiness.

The problem was that I had never once chosen to change my opinion of her in the interface settings. At first I thought it unnecessary, as I supposed that the pretty girl would soon be leaving me. But then... I simply wasn't used to having such a formal reaction to intimate relations. And that was why my official opinion of Princess Astra royl Veyerde remained, as before, at zero, just as on the very first day of our acquaintance, when the diplomat from the Kingdom of Veyerde loaded off two very scared and confused sisters on my yacht before fleeing. Now, I understood quite well that showing this zero to the girl would mean very, very seriously insulting her.

"My mission is to help you get back the Kingdom of Veyerde. That's what is really important, not the number of little pluses in your profile."

Astra got a bit sad, not having been able to satisfy her curiosity. All the same, she didn't argue. And maybe she even thought that I was trying to play a game with her, who knew...?

"We are already in Sector Seven, or am I mistaken?" Astra changed the topic, and I filled with joy at the opportunity to answer openly and honestly.

"Yes, the fleet has already entered Perimeter Sector Seven. We are near Forepost-2, an automatic charging station on our way. This place is normally only visited by freighters carrying equipment and products related to space ice processing. Rare radioactive isotopes are exported through here from Sector Seven to the Core for thermonuclear stations. I purposely brought the fleet here in order not to raise too much noise. We are now charging energy and jumping to the neighboring Damir star system as guests of my dear sister Violetta. She already knows about our visit and is preparing a ceremonial reception. We're expecting a whole sea of reporters, a broadcast to the whole

Empire. Everyone in my journalism retinue will have bones to chew on for days..."

"And so what is my mission?" Astra wondered, surprisingly serious.

It was basically a simple question, but I still gave pause before answering. I didn't normally think of my favorite as a tool for politics. She was simply a pretty doll, who representatives of famous fashion or other earthly gossip news channels loved to take pictures of, and who no one was expecting to make any speeches or do any great feats. But, perhaps Astra was capable of more.

"It's up to you, Astra, there are two options. You can be a careless air-headed doll in the retinue of a Crown Prince of the Empire, so pretty that any man's heart would freeze from one look at you. A woman, who makes open mouths drool on the floor. An ideal beauty, whose picture is taped up on bedroom walls of zit-faced boys the galaxy over. Or, you could be a young brave Princess in the eyes of reporters, who is on her way, as an allied warrior, to liberate her homeland from its ravenous conquerors. In that case, you'll need to play the serious role of a future Queen so people will feel sympathy for you, so people will support your struggle, and give it as much light as possible."

The girl began to think, then wondered whether maybe she could be both.

"Try and see," I allowed the Princess, and Astra answered that she would do exactly that.

* * *

I took a seat at an elegant desk carved out of a solid piece of malachite, which was in the center of a small semicircular room. The atmosphere of garish luxury, which I had already managed to grow unaccustomed to after selling *Queen of Sin*, could be seen in every object in the interior. It weighed on me and left me annoyed, but Violetta did not feel any such discomfort. The Ice Princess's facial features were distantly reminiscent of Katerina ton Mesfelle's, but twice as old, accustomed to unchallenged power and absolutely lacking in principles.

In the Throne World, four months earlier I had not managed to talk to my twin sister, and at that time I had been somewhat upset on that account. Now, I understood quite distinctly how lucky I had actually been. Crown Princess Violetta royl Inoky ton Mesfelle-Damir knew her brother since he was in diapers and would have easily recognized me as a fraud. Even now, with quite a long time in the game as Crown Prince Georg already behind me, I still had to constantly monitor my words and what I talked about in order not to end up with my foot in my mouth and reveal the secret of my true identity. As a matter of fact, I still wasn't able to always avoid near misses. The room I was talking with my sister in was totally protected from anyone listening in or recording, which was why my sister did nothing to limit herself in conversation topic whatsoever.

"Tell me, brother, why is Roben's son still alive? You received the full amount from me to take care of the issue, did you not?" The ruler of the Damir system trained her unblinking gaze on me like a gigantic snake ready to strike.

I wonder if Georg really did take money from his sister to kill his nephew. Maybe Violetta was just testing me with that? Just to stretch time out a bit, I took a break and poured some emerald green wine into a pair of high-walled glasses for myself and my sister.

"Our nephew's death is not currently in either of our best interests, sister. It's too obvious who's behind it. There would be too much suspicion. I had a hard enough time holding my yap when Roben's truth seeker checked me to see if I was involved with the attempt on his son's life once."

Violetta spent a long time looking me straight in the eyes, as if searching for a reflection of my emotions in them, or expecting me to continue the story. Without waiting for me to react, my sister answered:

"I agree with you, brother. After all, our nephew isn't such a problem for us, if you think about it. He isn't the main target at all and, as before, I will remain firm in demanding that you uphold our agreement. Or have you had a change of mind, Georg?"

What was this about then? The main target was not the six-month-old little Georg? Then who was Violetta talking about? Who could be bothering her? I tried to figure it out. It wasn't likely to be Verena. My sister's interests basically just didn't intersect or have any point of conflict with those of Roben's wife. It couldn't be that my twin sister was planning on killing our older brother, right?!

Violetta continued looking at me, expecting an answer. I had to answer and risk making a mistake, given that keeping silent on such an important issue was clearly not working out.

"I haven't had a change of mind, sister, but I still think it would be premature to take action now. We still need Roben alive, especially after the unexpected change in circumstances. I was able to get Crown Prince Peres royl Paolo ton Mesfelle out of the struggle for power. Now he's nothing more than a normal 'ton,' without a place in line for the Orange House throne. It's all coming together. Judge for yourself. Places one, two, three, and four in the Orange House hierarchy are occupied by Duke Paolo and his brothers. The four most powerful figures can thus form four centers of power and a block of four votes on any matter. Us three crown princes could work together as a counterweight to them: the children of Inoky. Roben has the very rich Tesse system behind him, and even after all the perturbations, he still has a respectable star fleet. You have power and money. And I have also managed to grow in power somewhat..."

My sister threw herself into the back of her chair and chuckled joyfully.

"Is that what you call somewhat? Even the laziest cannot help discussing your rise. You've gone from a poor aristocrat, constantly begging for money from relatives into a perfectly notable political figure, who's whipped fourteen star systems under his command. And though your systems may not be especially rich, and even empty in places, they are completely real and raise interest just by being dots on the star map. Well, alright, you have my undivided attention."

"Violetta, it's not just fourteen anymore, but nineteen. During my last campaign I became owner of the Chameleon homeworld and four densely populated Swarm systems."

My sister started laughing again, but this time it was somehow angry. I, though, continued my thought:

"So, now for the breakdown of the 'Inoky Clan Three' versus the 'Paolo Clan Four.' Most Orange House aristocrats are still waiting to see who will win this struggle, so they can attach themselves to the victors. If we take our brother Roben out now, we'll lose then and there, as it will cause hesitant parties to choose the Paolo Clan. On the other hand, if everything turns out alright, then I'll be able to show Duke Paolo's weakness. Our side will get stronger, and allies will be drawn to us. No matter what, it will all be over in forty-five days."

Violetta kept silent and looked out the thick picture-window at the infinite fields of ice asteroids twinkling in the light of the Damir star, thoughtfully sipping wine and, finally, changed the topic:

"I see, brother. We'll leave Roben alone for now. But then, explain something else to me: the most important battle with the Orange House Head's United Fleet is still ahead. Every starship counts to you now, but you are loudly declaring to the whole Empire that you are preparing to assault the Alien-captured Nayal and Veyerde systems. That is a very dangerous and not at all timely thing to do! It can't be that your little doll Astra has grown so close to you that you'll put our shared victory at risk for the sake of her pretty eyes, right?! You know my negative opinion of your wife, but even I admit that Marta is a good politician and orator. She can turn any speech into a show in her own beloved name. But Astra then... You heard it yourself, Georg, the crap your favorite spouted when those journalists questioned her!"

In this regard, I had to agree with my sister. Princess Astra was obviously failing at playing the part of the brave warrior and wise Queen. The other thing was that some journalists were truly exceptional bastards and were openly provoking the stressed-out girl with the most uncomfortable questions imaginable:

"...Princess, why was your Highness naked at the moment of the alleged space battle in the Lobj system?

... Would you care to share a word with our electronic catalog Imperial Prostitutes Monthly on what it's like to be a rich aristocrat's concubine?

... How did it come to be that an artist of your level doesn't even have a place of permanent residence and is running about the whole galaxy after her master like a lap dog?

... What would you consider a fair price for someone to pay you for another erotic dance?

... Do you still feel bitter about breaking the engagement with a member of the Green House?

... Have you ever seen real Alien ships? What? Can you really be sure that what you were seeing out the picture window were Aliens? So that means you have no way of really affirming to our channel that Crown Prince Georg has met even one time with Aliens?"

Astra answered, in her way, and tried to politely

smile when answering even the trickiest and most acid-tongued questions, but from the first second it was very clear to me that the young girl had done a much better job playing the role of a silent charming companion to the Crown Prince than she was doing as an independent politician. I shook my head in reproach, thinking back on annoying moments in Astra's answers at the ceremony. Alright, if it happened, it happened...

"Whether you see it or not, Violetta, Astra has nothing to do with this. I'm here to fulfill a promise I once made to the Sector Seven Fleet Commander Marat ton Mesfelle. Also, in the last days, so much mud has been slung at me... What famous politician hasn't been trying to prove that I haven't yet seen an Alien in real life. That is precisely why I offered everyone who wishes to participate in a combined battle, to show in fact, that we can really fight. Some reporters have been invited to make their reports right from my flagship, so that no one in the Empire will have any doubt in the reality of the victories and trophies. If we do win, that will significantly reinforce our shared position. The Sector Seven systems will recall their deputies from the Orange House and come over to our side."

Violetta drained her glass in a gulp, placed it on the table and said with reproach.

"Brother, you have, of course, grown up a lot in a short amount of time. Your rise as a politician has also been impressive to watch. All the same, you're still making childish mistakes. You are forgetting about one important thing: it is forbidden by law to change the deputies of the Large Council of a Great

House more often than once per year. Yes, you could convince the Sector Seven systems to come over to your side, right behind Sector Nine. Yes, the current Orange House head's enemies will have a majority at the next convention, and they may even raise the issue of voting to censure Duke Paolo. But you'll only be able to make a call to gather deputies five months from now, no earlier. Insofar as I understand, you don't have that kind of time, given that the Emperor has placed very harsh conditions on your ending the rift in the Orange House. As such, no matter how you might try to wriggle out of it, the only way left for you is to take down the Duke's united fleet. Can you do it?"

I drummed my fingers in thought on the malachite tabletop. There wasn't enough time for a diplomatic victory? What a shame... I guess I really will have to win in battle.

"According to the most recent data, the Duke's unified fleet has around two thousand, two hundred ships. I have five hundred starships in my fleet right now, plus Marat ton Mesfelle's reinforcements, which will arrive tomorrow. It's gonna be about four to one... It will be hard, but there is a chance for victory. All the same, I first have to take the Aliens out in Veyerde and Nayal. As for now I'm not even close to figuring out what kind of forces the enemy has concentrated there."

Violetta twisted the empty glass of wine in her fingers for a moment in thought, then said decisively.

"Ugh, no guts no glory! Give your green-haired favorite a gift from the Ice Princess: take my fleet with you for the attack on Veyerde! I cannot help you directly in battle with Duke Paolo. I'm sorry but, all the same, I officially offer to compensate any losses on your part in the battle with the Aliens with similar starships from my fleet. How else can I be of help?"

"Based on the information in the guide, there are one hundred thousand androids working in your ice processing factories. That means there must be a big robot service center somewhere in the system. I need to make a stop there today to fix my translator."

"This model is no longer under warranty. I'm afraid it would actually be against company rules for me to repair your android." The young service company technician threw up his hands apologetically.

"It seems like someone here isn't understanding what I'm asking," I replied, not raising my voice and maintaining a calm exterior as I sat in an armchair in the guest hall. Nevertheless, all conversations in the nearby rooms stopped instantly. "I'm not interested in excuses. All I care about is how long it will take, and that it is done with flawless quality. The android must retain its personality in full and all of its memories. You will be awarded a bonus if you complete the work ahead of schedule."

"But I already told your Highness..." the technician began bleating back again, however the director of the service center office in the Damir system stopped his employee with a hand wave and picked up Bionica's head from the table delicately.

After examining the closed skull and bunch of cut wires and tube poking out of the throat, the man wondered:

"I can see that the robot's BIOS has been opened and re-flashed, but I'm gonna just pretend I didn't notice the missing screws. My only question is, how soon do you want it?"

"Today," I said in an even voice.

The man's eyebrows jumped up in surprise, but he kept control of his emotions. After looking with some sorrow at Bionica's head on the table, the director pointed toward the stand:

"I cannot guarantee that we will have the exact body model, 034-6781 is actually pretty out of date at this point. So, if you would like, you may choose a new appearance for your android."

New appearance? I was fine with Bionica exactly as she was when I picked her out. But, all the same, I walked up to the screen and carefully looked over thirty options currently on offer from the service company. Nothing was quite right...

"If you change that haircut and dye the hair, that one would look something like Bionica," noted Nicole, standing next to me.

"You think so? Look how wide those hips are. She looks to be a mother of eight."

The director hurried to intervene:

"There's no way to make her look exactly the same. Forget about the old body, Crown Prince. Choose the model that is most pleasing to your eye."

I took a skeptical look at the options on offer from the company. I think I found the one: a buxom red-head with the body of an Amazon and a cute face.

"That's my choice. Bionica will be fire-red after her rebirth."

The director came right back to life:

"Nice choice. It's the newest model this year. Now my technicians need somewhere around five hours for data transfer, joint calibration, and operation system upgrade."

"I forbid you to make an upgrade. And any attempt to change or copy any information on crystal drives from my robot will end in the immediate death of the employee responsible. This is a nonstandard order, with unusual conditions, which is why I'm willing to pay a lot."

"But, your Highness, how can I guarantee the information transfer and correct functioning of the robot if God-knows-who has been digging around in her programs, changing God-knows-what. Certified versions of all programs must be installed. Our center simply does not work any other way!"

I frowned. They clearly had a problem understanding me well here.

"Call your company's central office! Yes, yes, the very same one, in Perimeter Sector Three, in Green House territory. Put me directly through to the director of your company. If you try to get out of it by saying that it's night on his planet, or any other excuses, you can tell him that Crown Prince Georg royl Inoky ton Mesfelle wishes to discuss the incident when tracking was used on his robot of your production."

Two minutes later, a middle-aged balding man, dressed in a very expensive suit appeared on screen. The stranger's face had a fake smile perched on it. Not even giving him time to orient himself, I got right to business:

"A bit less than four months ago, employees of my security service uncovered a channel from which I was being tracked. Me, an heir to the Imperial Throne! It was through the use of undocumented functions in my personal android translator. The tracking was traced back to two centers, but both were working through the same method of daily log transfers. I think you'll agree that it's an extremely unpleasant story, that could seriously harm your company's reputation."

"Yes, I know that story well, Prince Georg, and my company really is grateful to your Highness for keeping that unpleasant incident in confidence," he agreed.

"So then, I didn't raise a scandal at the time, but now I am expecting a gesture of good will from your company in return. The android spy issue was neutralized by my servants. To do that, they had to peck around in the settings a bit. But, in that I need information that is in the memory of that particular robot, I would like to transfer the contents of its memory crystals into a new, undamaged body, and in the very same, unchanged form with no modifications. But then I ran into the problem of your employees not really understanding how serious this situation is. They refuse to give me a similar looking robot, and they say they cannot transfer the android's conscience or memory."

"My servants were simply not informed of the true gravity of the situation, Crown Prince. Of course, though, we are prepared to make an exception to our strict rules for your Highness. Model 034-6781 was removed from production around a quarter century ago, however, since Bionica joining your Highness's retinue, and especially after the unheard-of event when the android was awarded a medal by the Emperor himself, our company has had a whole wave of orders for identical products, so a new production run has been started. We will send an absolutely identical copy of Bionica to any address you ask, and the memory and programs of your glorious translator will be transferred into it."

"Very well, send it to my palace on Unatari. But for now, I need a new temporary body for Bionica. The Veyerde system will be liberated from the Aliens, and I need my robot translator urgently."

"You can use any model you like, Crown Prince. I'll send a message to the dolts in the Damir service center that they are obliged to carry out your nonstandard order in full accordance with your wishes, or else they will have to start looking for new employment."

I smiled politely at him and said:

"It's very nice to work with your company. Excuse me, could I tack something on to the order? I need one hundred thousand laborer androids in one week."

"One hundred thousand?! Delivery to Unatari, as well?" he said, making no effort to hide his rapture.

"No. The destination for that order is the Veyerde system in Perimeter Sector Seven."

"Five *Sledgehammers*, eight *Ascetics*, four *Hermits*, and eleven *Meteors*. They are stationed seventy miles from the Nayal system," my spy from the cloaked frigate announced over the common channel, reaching all ships of the unified thousand-ship-strong armada, consisting of the Perimeter Sector Eight Fleet, the Perimeter Sector Seven Fleet, and other allied ships.

A general murmur was heard on the common channel. I could make out the word "sledgehammer" repeated in horror several times. The time had come for me to turn on the microphone and take the situation into my own hands:

"Attention all ships of the united fleet! Accelerate toward the Nayal system beacon! Sector Eight ships, set prewarp to two hundred fifty. All other ships are to set their warp tunnel settings to two thousand from the beacon. One minute to action. Nicole, countdown!"

"But Crown Prince, there are *Sledgehammers* there. We'll surely die!" someone's frightened voice rang out.

I looked demandingly at the communications officers and received an answer a few seconds later:

"That was the captain of *Surgeon-66* from the Damir fleet..."

The officer's speech was interrupted by Admiral Kiro Sabuto's alarmed voice:

"My Prince, *Surgeon-66* is accelerating on its own in the opposite direction of the fleet! He isn't going to Nayal, but preparing to return to the Damir system!"

What?! Well, that isn't just the height of insubordination and cowardice? It was no longer of any importance to me who the captain of *Surgeon-66* was, it could even have been the Emperor's own son. He was attempting to desert the fleet!

"Attention all ships, halt acceleration and

countdown! *Surgeon-66* is primary. I've marked it in the overview. Fire!"

There was a flash, and cloud of shards flew off in all directions, marking the now downed ship's former location. In the silence that eventually came over on the common fleet channel, I said clearly and decisively:

"The main thing holding humanity back in the fight with the Aliens is the cowardice of some captains and their disobeying orders from higher-ranked commanders. Several weeks ago, one of my frigates abandoned a combat assignment of their own will and left the battle. As a result, an Alien battleship got through to my starships. The fleet lost a quarter of its strength in that incident. Due to the cowardice of one, thousands died. The scars on my face and my right eye, which still can't quite see right are the most eloquent possible mementos of just how high a price allied cowardice can have. As such, it is better to execute cowards before the battle than have to deal with the consequences of them fleeing the battle later."

"Crown Prince Georg, what became of the coward that made the fleet suffer that time?" Came Marat ton Mesfelle, commander of the Sector Seven Fleet.

"He got very lucky. He died in the explosion of the *Behemoth* that he himself let get through to our ships. Such is the lot of all cowards. They never really had a chance of surviving in the first place, but unfortunately they find it necessary to take others down with them. As such, this is a message for all fleet crewmembers: if you notice anyone on your ship acting cowardly and not carrying out a commander's orders, shoot them immediately and do not hesitate. That is the best way out with the minimum number of victims. And so, the lyrical digression is over. Let's get back to the main mission. Is there anyone in the fleet who is still bleating in fear and pissing their pants from the word '*Sledgehammer*?' No? Then let's start the acceleration toward the Nayal beacon again. Nicole, countdown, sixty seconds. Marat ton Mesfelle, choose five ships in your fleet to make sure your captains are following orders. If anyone doesn't jump right into battle in sixty seconds, they will share *Surgeon-66*'s fate."

**Global standing decrease. Current value -34**

**Standing change. Empire Military faction opinion of you has improved.**
**Presumed personal opinion of you: +21 (warm)**

"Ten seconds. Nine. Upon arrival, everyone turn on tactical map immediately, and wait for my command. Three. Two. WARP!!!"

The world grew dim as usual and rolled up into a tunnel. There was another four hours before the battle, so I stood from my seat, preparing to go get some rest in my bunk. However, my attention was caught by a sound in the corridor. There was a sentry trying not to let a girl with fire-red hair enter the fleet headquarters. She was wearing an ultramarine dress and high-heeled shoes. It even took me a few seconds to realize who the unfamiliar girl in civilian clothes, who had shown up on a military starship was, before I remembered Bionica's new body. I could hardly tell them a story about new crewmembers now.

"Let her in!" I ordered, and the girl came into the headquarters.

"Crown Prince Georg, Popori de Cacha has finished looking over my new body. He has given permission for me to continue work..." the red-headed beauty's voice was unfamiliar, and she was seriously delaying the end of the sentence after having seen the Arite in the form of the light-haired Bionica in her place.

"Excellent, Bionica. You may return to your normal work. Only Popori de Cacha is no longer a 'he,' but a 'she.' The Chameleon changed gender while you were absent."

Popori de Cacha, who appeared at that moment, stretched out her hand with a packet of documents for the new Bionica and reported:

"A full check has been made. No undocumented changes to the model detected. The memory blocks are sealed. Checksums for all files are unchanged. By the way, here are your things back, Bionica!" with these words, the head of my guard handed the synthetic girl a gold medallion on a chain and an Emerald Star.

I saw the fleet officer's incomprehension, which forced me to tell them about why my translator's appearance had changed. The Arite demonstrated the truth of my words, changing into a minimum of ten various *Emperor August* crew members in the space of five seconds, then returning to the synthetic blonde once again.

"I have the Crown Prince's permission to be in this form!" the Arite Iseyek said to the upset blonde beauty.

"Bionica, a copy of your old body will be waiting for you in Unatari," I said, calming my assistant. "For now, be a red-head. Who knows, maybe you'll like it?"

* * *

"Multiple targets. Distance: two hundred thirty miles. Five Alien cruisers, twelve destroyers, eleven frigates. Alien ships have begun advancing!"

I had already noticed that myself. The *Meteors* had separated from the group and were quickly reducing their distance, going in a bull-headed straight line toward my ships.

"Fleet Eight, let's get to work! Usual formation toward the enemy. Release drones! *Tria*, in five minutes I need an assault group of around twenty modules. Both battleships, make a tiny advance. Heavies, twelve behind them. Check the connections! Max Stegor, electronics is on you. The mission is to take those *Meteors* down! Antisupport, at the ready! Split up into groups of eight, pick your targets! Nicole, you're in charge of our destroyers. Shoot in volleys on a countdown. *Pyros*, I need four receivers on opposite sides of the *Sledgehammers* at one hundred twenty! *Warhawks*..."

"What should we do, Crown Prince?" someone from an allied fleet interrupted quite tactlessly on the common channel.

"Above all else, keep quiet and don't get in the Sector Eight Fleet's way! All other ships, stay two thousand back and don't come into battle!"

Nicole, looked in my direction and mimicked cutting her neck with her hand, recommending that I set up a "guillotine" for offenders. I shook my head "no." If it had been someone from the Sector Eight Fleet, he already would have been punished. But most of the fleet today was absolute noobs, who didn't even know that you shouldn't interrupt a commander.

"*Warhawks* and *Safas*, stand by! Accelerate toward the enemy. In ten seconds, I need webs on all *Meteors*. Charge!!! Heavies, two per target. Get ready! Shoot only on my command!"

One after another, reports about enemy frigates under warp disruptor and web started coming in. I waited a few seconds to make sure, after which I calmly, even matter-of-factly, stated:

"Fire!!!"

After my ships' volley, just one *Meteor* was left alive. It was already under thick webs and warp-disruptors, and blinded by the electronic warfare fighters, so it was no threat.

"Do not shoot at the *Meteor*! Just hold him tight. We need it alive! We have already sent our scientists an Alien warp beacon deliverer, and now we'll give them the fastest frigate in the Universe. Maybe they can learn something... So, destroyers, approach. Antisupport, attention! *Pyros*, capture the *Sledgehammers*. They must not get any closer! *Safas* and *Warhawks*, at the ready! Standard formation. Hold the destroyers with webs for the big guns, and shoot down the drones while you're at it! At the ready in twenty seconds! Heavies, pick your targets. Three per destroyer! *Ascetics* are the priority. Antisupport, your mission is to get to the wounded birds. Electros, not one of these beasts is to be allowed to target us! Frigates, advance!!! I need webs on the enemy in seven seconds! Great! Fire!!!"

Seven of eight *Ascetics* disappeared from the tactical map all at once. The last one tried to turn around and get away, but no less than one hundred frigates targeted it, and the Alien ship lit up the black sky with a bright spark.

"All drones from the *Hermit* have been shot down! The Alien destroyers are held down tight. Electros are putting just the right amount of pressure on," Nicole Savoia reported.

"We also need that ship there for research," I put a marker in the overview on one of the *Hermits*. "The rest of the ships are retreating! Fire!!! General, both Alien ships are at your disposal. Send in your assault troops! *Bride of Chaos*, you're too far in front. Put on the breaks and wait for the *Meresh*. Heavies, approach the battleships! Stay in formation and reduce distance. Two *Sledgehammers* need to be brought down. They're marked on the tactical map. Nicole, pick targets for our heavies. After that, hold off the strike and get the rest of the Aliens. The little guys won't dare come near."

Two minutes later, the *Sledgehammers* were no more. Another ten after that, General Savasss Jach reported that the *Meteor* and *Hermit* had been captured. The only weird thing was that the landing troops didn't find the bush-like Aliens we were used to, but medusa-like creatures in the ships. Unfortunately, we still didn't capture any alive. The medusas' bodies would deflate with just the slightest damage, turning them into lifeless off-white rags.

"Victory has been secured, ladies and gentlemen!" I declared on the common channel. "The Sector Eight

Fleet sustained no losses. The Aliens lost twenty-eight ships, two of which have been captured intact."

*Global standing increase. Current value -33*

*Standing change. Empire Military faction opinion of you has improved.*
*Presumed personal opinion of you: +22 (warm)*

*Global standing increase. Current value -32*

*Global fame increase. Current value +22*

*Standing change. Empire Military faction opinion of you has improved.*
*Presumed personal opinion of you: +23 (warm)*

*Global fame increase. Current value +23*

The journalists were reporting something to their viewers, and I unmistakably heard enthusiastic shouts in my direction, with words coming through like "miracle," "fantastic," "hero," and the like. When the deafening screams of joy and applause had calmed down a bit, Marat ton Mesfelle declared:

"Georg, I'm simply flabbergasted! I feel like a puppy-dog compared to you! Also, from my perspective, you could see the evidence of regular practice. Without strain, without getting overly emotional, the Sector Eight Fleet simply shot the targets down and that was that. If I hadn't come up against Aliens myself, I wouldn't have recognized what a feat your fleet had just accomplished!"

I laughed joyously in reply. God damn, it's nice when someone finally values your work.

"Let them send journalists to the Emperor August shuttle hangar. We'll get you together a couple of trips to the Alien wreckage. You can take a couple souvenirs home. If any of the captains or crew members would like to visit a captured Alien ship, or wants to collect trophies, you have around two hours before the Alpha Iseyek finish clearing the Nayal station. After that, charge your drives and get back to battle. We're expected in the Veyerde system."

"My Prince, incoming call from Purple House head Duke Takuro royl Andor!"

I smoothed my messed-up hair with my hand and said to put him through. The graying, tall old man was sitting in a luxurious carved armchair reminiscent of a throne. In full compliance with proper etiquette, I greeted one of the most influential aristocrats in the Empire with a deep bow, which the Duke reacted to in a wavering voice:

"Georg, it is not you who should be bowing, but me. I was watching the broadcast from the Nayal system and would like to apologize officially in the name of the Purple House for my younger son, Khayt royl Andor ton Reyekh's unwise words. Today you showed in practice that humanity does have hope to survive the struggle with the Aliens. And I simply don't have the words to express my overflowing emotions. Just know, Crown Prince Georg, that while I am head of the Purple House, you can always count on any help you ask for in the battle against the Aliens."

The head of the Purple House signed off, and I then took a look around. There were journalists crowding around, hungry for my comments on the finished battle. The communications officer said that one thousand seven hundred eighty people were waiting to talk with me long distance. Captains and crews of thousands of ships in my armada were still enraptured, discussing the battle on the fleet channel. I could even hear Iseyek trills in the mix.

*"I've never even been near such adoration,"* the Truth Seeker confirmed.

"Brother, we have just gotten through the informational blockade! My standing is growing higher every minute! I'm being sent apologies *en masse* and my reports from the Alien systems are being extolled to the high heavens. The Emperor's press service has also sent me an apology. Georg, show me an enemy and I'll rip him to shreds with my bare hands right now! I adore you!" Katerina ton Mesfelle smiled.

I sighed and wearily replied:

"The fleet should be ready in five hours. The time has come to liberate Veyerde."

# The Queen of Veyerde

"**M**Y PRINCE, here is my report on the Alien fleet in the Veyerde system: There are seven hundred eighty ships, all of which are orbiting the second planet." My spy on the cloaked frigate sent his message on the common fleet channel once again, as I had requested.

"Seven hundred eighty? It looks like we'll have enough prey to go around. Attention, fleet! Begin acceleration toward the Veyerde system! In the warp tunnel settings, set exit at six hundred miles from the beacon. You have one minute!"

I listened carefully to the captains' discussions on the fleet channel. The number of Alien ships had been heard by all, yet none of them were showing any fear. Marat ton Mesfelle even wondered:

"Georg, can we shoot this time? Or are your soldiers gonna collect all the trophies again?"

"Of course you can. I will not be limiting anyone this time. You have my word as a crown prince. So then, dust off your cannons and get some vacuum-resistant paint ready to draw stars on the sides of your ships for every Alien they shoot down. Five seconds to warp jump!"

I was able to hear the excited shouts of the captains, after which *Emperor August* went into the warp tunnel to the Veyerde system together with the other ships of the fleet. I could finally let the artificial seriousness melt off my face into a smile:

"Katerina, I admit that you were right. There wasn't even one captain who expressed a shadow of a doubt that we could win. Seven hundred eighty Alien ships... I don't understand such blind trust! I personally, in my subjects' place, would at least clarify enemy starship classes from the commander. Here in the headquarters, we know that they're all just unarmed Alien landing ships. But there could just as easily be *Behemoths* and *Mammoths* out there, too..."

"Georg, your subjects trust you implicitly as a fleet commander and think that you would never go into a suicidal battle," Katerina ton Mesfelle answered me. "And given that you're already admitting that I fully presupposed the crews' reactions, I remind you that you promised to give me some time to listen to my advice carefully."

"I do not deny it. I promised it, and now I'm listening carefully. Are we just talking here, or are we going to have a meal together?"

Katerina ton Mesfelle began thinking for one second and chose the option of speaking over a meal, but not in the noisy officer's dining hall, instead preferring somewhere more secluded. I offered my bunk, but the idea did not find approval. Katerina admitted that she wanted to talk about Princess

Astra, so she would rather not discuss the issue in the presence of my favorite herself. My interest was sharply piqued by her secretiveness and suggested Katerina's bunk as an alternative. My assistant had not been living alone for the last few days, having invited the restored Bionica to stay with her. All the same, I had no secrets from my personal android secretary, so Bionica's potential presence would not have disturbed our private conversation.

I asked my butler Bryle to get a quick meal together for three people in Katerina ton Mesfelle's cabin and followed after my cousin. Bionica was actually already in the room and agreed to take part in the shared meal with delight.

"Before all else, Georg, I wanted to remind you that the day after tomorrow is Astra's birthday," my cousin said, just after we sat down at the small table. "I hope you didn't forget to prepare a gift for your companion in advance, given that you'll hardly be able to find something worth your while in the ruined Veyerde system."

To be honest, in the constant flow of the last few days, I had totally let that fact slip my mind and was now looking with reproach at my secretary Bionica, who had not reminded me of my favorite's upcoming birthday in time. Bionica got embarrassed just like a human, and when Katerina got distracted by Bryle coming into the room with service trays, she whispered to me:

"My fault, master. Due to calibration procedures with the new body, memory file optimization and other inconveniences, I was only able to resume my function as your secretary in earnest very recently. By the way... Seven minutes ago, I got a bill from my manufacturer for one hundred seventy-four million credits."

Bionica raised her eyes at me in surprise. I smiled at my secretary.

"As soon as we come out of the warp tunnel, and you get the chance, pay it. Think of it as gratitude to your firm for meeting me half way in the matter of your repair. And at the same time, a gift to Astra for her birthday. I suspect that one hundred thousand working androids will be of quite a lot of use to her in rebuilding the planet."

"A generous gift, truly worthy of an Imperial Crown Prince," my cousin agreed, having heard the end of my conversation with Bionica. "I admit, cousin, that I thought and was even practically sure that you would forget. That was why I was going to let you join in on my gift, though I also doubted that you would have a good attitude about it..."

Katerina ton Mesfelle, without standing from the couch, opened the magnetic shutters of a wall cupboard with a remote control, and I saw a luxurious, truly royal robe hanging there, with gold patterns and jewels sewn in.

"I commissioned it in Damir. Astra will need to have appropriate attire for her coronation, to meet the traditions of royal houses. It's real Saiwanese silk, mono-molecular, one-piece thread. All gems on the garment have legitimacy certificates, the patterns on the sleeves and skirts of the garment are completely in line with the heraldic colors and ornamental style of the Kingdom of Veyerde, and it is made with a special high-tech dye that keeps its true color no matter the lighting conditions. All these luxuries came to three and a half million credits. To be honest, I was kind of counting on you helping out with money-wise..."

Bionica declared unexpectedly, that she was prepared split the cost of the robe with Katerina down the middle, given that her temporary deactivation made her unable to arrange her own gift. I, to be honest, was very surprised. It couldn't be that my android secretary had enough to spend almost two million credits, right? Although... she definitely did have one million, and maybe even one point five... In any case, I wasn't going to put people and androids close to me in a difficult financial position.

"Cousin, the gift is really chic, and I am prepared to cover the cost in full for the both of you. The only thing I don't get is why you thought I wouldn't like it."

Katerina just smiled mysteriously, letting my secretary answer instead:

"Your Highness, after coronation, Astra royl Veyerde will become Queen. And the aristocratic code is unambiguous in not allowing a Queen to be the favorite of another aristocrat, no matter the size or significance of that Kingdom, that aristocrat is considered an Imperial Crown Prince..."

"That's right, Georg," my cousin confirmed. "After getting the crown, Astra will have to leave you. A favorite is usually an unmarried aristocrat with or without a title, maybe even a commoner in exceptional circumstances, however a crown-bearing individual is categorically forbidden, in that it contradicts the very structure of aristocratic hierarchy."

That means that with my success in the war against the Aliens, I was driving Princess Astra out of my retinue. What a shame... I had just started getting used to the pretty and unpredictable girl being around. While I thought the information over, my cousin went on:

"Georg, there is one other topic to consider. Count Avalle royl Anjer ton Mesfelle got in touch with me today. He congratulated you on your brilliant victory in the Nayal system and wanted to know about the possibility of a personal meeting with you. He officially wants to act as a middle man to find a way of resolving the internal Orange House conflict."

"And unofficially?" I said, on the alert.

"Unofficially... figure it out yourself. The Count didn't say a word or give a hint to indicate that his mission may have some larger purpose than simply serving as a messenger for his older brother, who for obvious reasons does not want to meet with you himself. But, Georg... I recommend you very strongly to find time to talk with the number two figure in the Orange House hierarchy. I think that questions of peace could easily be discussed, even long distance, but as the Count is looking for a face-to-face meeting specifically, it means he doesn't want any witnesses... There could be something bigger behind this than just wanting to help his brother."

I finally got to see the celebrated Swarm general working in all his frantic glory. I was on *Tria* in the company of Princess Astra, Colonel Gor ton Vulf, the now redheaded Bionica and Katerina ton Mesfelle and her assistants when the Alien landing ships next to Veyerde were shot down in a matter of seconds (with the exception of a couple intended for capture and further study), and the liberation of the small planet began.

On the multitude of screens next to the general, parts of the tactical map were flashing quickly in various colors and angles. The gigantic many-eyed insect found it easier to take in information that way. Savasss Jach had ordered a huge holographic projection of the surface of Veyerde be placed in the room specifically for us people. It was a giant fifty-foot-diameter globe, to which the *Tria*'s many reconnaissance drones were uploading live images of all established targets: concentrations of manpower, technology, some constructions and Alien flying devices.

"Crown Prince, a very high intensity radio signal is being detected coming from the surface of Veyerde. Some of the signal is definitely for interstellar communication. The Aliens know we are preparing to invade," said Bionica, translating the general's chirruping. "Enemy anti-space defense and communications centers identified. We are detecting a low-atmosphere fighter plane base and other high-energy installations. Coordinates for more than twenty rocket and plasma turrets have been determined. We have discovered the command center. It is deep in the bedrock at a depth of around twelve hundred feet.

"What kind of forces does the enemy have concentrated on Veyerde?" I asked, and Savasss Jach answered thoughtfully:

"During our time in Kej, we studied the Alien landing ship in great detail. It is intended to transport several pieces of heavy technology and up to one thousand five hundred bush-soldiers. The disk-shaped starships here in Veyerde are quite similar to the ships in Kej in many ways, though I would be quite sure that you could fit quite a bit less of the 'medusas' in there than 'bushes.' According to my calculations, the Aliens could have brought up to eight hundred thousand of their soldiers to Veyerde, and since they've arrived, it seems they've managed to dig in pretty deep."

"Can we manage?" I asked, somewhat in doubt after the general's speech.

"No question, Crown Prince. My soldiers are capable of capturing Veyerde. But as for how long it will take and what percentage of landing troops we will lose, that will depend directly on whether we can use your heavy ships for orbital bombardment."

"General, you can count on the support of the star armada's firepower in full force. Show us a target, and my fleet will turn it into dust."

It was a grimly impressive picture. The fifteen battleships and seventy heavy cruisers in my fleet managed to turn everything that presented even the slightest threat to the landing troops into mush. The three *Monarch* battleships were especially effective at hitting planetary targets. *Bride of Chaos*, the flagship of the Sector Seven fleet *Knight of Light,* and *Ice Princess* from the Damir fleet were sending out a great many thirty-ton guided missiles down their 1400 mm cannons, and every shot would remove another Alien bunker or construction from the tactical map with a twenty second delay. In most cases, we didn't even have to use our nuclear arsenal. We only had to use one thermonuclear mine and that was on the Alien command center.

The other *Tyrant* battleships, the older *Usurpers* and the Swarm *Mereshes* were armed with impulse laser cannons and were working on taking down concentrations of Alien manpower and technology. The heavy cruisers also took part in the orbital bombardment, though they weren't all that effective. All seventy of my cruisers could barely equal the firepower of even one of my battleships. Finally, the moment arrived for the general to announce:

"Crown Prince Georg, the Alien anti-space defense system has been completely destroyed. All turrets have been deactivated, as well as radar installations and communication centers. The old rule of war has been proven once again: whoever controls a planet's orbit will dominate. Everything is ready for the beginning of the assault."

As we had earlier agreed, the order to begin liberating the planet was to be given live by Princess Astra royl Veyerde. The light technicians had already installed spotlights to help the viewers better see the Princess's face on the backdrop of the infinitely huge *Tria*. Then, the make-up artist finished and walked a bit away, so as not to step on stage. The unusually serious Astra, with a strong-willed and otherworldly look on her face, gave the speech composed for her by Katerina ton Mesfelle emotionally and without hesitation, before finally finishing with an order:

"Begin the assault! Attack!!!"

At that second, twenty thousand guided rockets ripped off at once into space toward the surface of the planetoid Veyerde through its none-too-thick atmosphere. Two hundred thousand Alpha Iseyeks, armed to the teeth, set off for the target zones marked by the reconnaissance drones. Five minutes later, a human landing party of three hundred shuttles arrived after them. People would have to liberate the Veyerde palace, which had somewhat suffered after taking a few hits from space. All that was left for us to do on the *Tria* was wait.

"My Prince, I understand that it is quite a bad time right now, but I must tell you that a very large deposit just came in to your account," Bionica said suddenly.

"Two billion credits?" Astra supposed with a smile, and it turned out she was right.

I chuckled heartily:

"It took Duke Paolo a pretty long time to figure out where my fleet was. I suspect that the Duke had had enough time to send quite a serious amount of money to his soldiers in the Aiwe system before figuring out that my fleet wasn't even planning on passing through Aiwe."

Our conversation was interrupted by a message saying that the first landing modules had reached the planet's surface. A picture came up simultaneously on all monitors: Alpha Iseyeks were unloading their modules and setting up some equipment, bundling antennas and connecting cables. I wasn't even able to ask the General what was happening before the answer showed itself to me: above the landing zones, there were energy shields pouring down into dome shapes. Savasss Jach purposely selected one of the pictures and put it up on the big screen. I couldn't figure out a thing. Some kind of semi-transparent buildings, craters, burned-up trees, but all the same Astra gasped:

"That is my father's palace! Well, to be honest, what's left of it..."

Colonel Gor ton Vulf compared the pictures with his reconnaissance data and said:

The craters aren't from us. Our infrared visors are showing no sign of elevated temperature in them. We are observing traces of the battle left by the last defenders of the Kingdom of Veyerde with you father at head, Princess Astra."

"I need to go there immediately. I just have to be on Veyerde when my planet is liberated from the captors!" Astra declared dogmatically.

I thought that the colonel would refuse the girl, but the soldier unexpectedly concurred with her:

"I agree with you fully, Princess. A representative of the House of Veyerde really should be with the soldiers on the planet. But it's always good to make sure we aren't confusing patriotism and bravery with stupidity. I allow your shuttle to take off only after my guys and the general's assault troops have carefully checked every nook and cranny in the palace and installed a defensive shield around the whole area to keep any surprises from getting in."

"Crown Prince Georg, tell him!" the Princess implored, trying to get my support, but I was completely on the colonel's side in this matter.

"Astra, the terrestrial operation is being led by General Savasss Jach, and the palace assault by Colonel Gor ton Vulf. Only the two of them can decide when you can be allowed to actually land on Veyerde, and even I am in no position to influence their decision."

I turned back to the huge globe. The number of red markers on it had gone down, but remained very, very high, despite the fact that new green markers were appearing every second. Having seen my attention on the map, the general commented:

"The enemy isn't even trying to resist, instead retreating from the areas where our assault troops are landing. The area around the Royal Palace of Veyerde will become relatively safe forty minutes from now. In that time, the assault troops will check all constructions and underground connections, as well as widen the zone of control to a radius of eighteen miles from the palace. All the same, fully clearing the whole planet of Aliens will take twenty days at the very least. The difficult terrain and many caves and cliffs on the planet mean that there are a lot of hiding spots. Everything has to be checked. Reconnaissance drones have already discovered traces of Alien activity, even in the karst caves and under the surface of the internal ocean, so the work ahead is long and grueling."

Twenty days?! To be honest, I was expecting much less. To be totally honest, I couldn't allow myself so much time in Sector Seven, even if it was to help my favorite. I simply wouldn't have enough time to solve the issue with the Orange House head afterwards otherwise.

"General, it would be nice to bring down the time-frame to five or seven days if possible."

The gigantic centipede looked at me for some time

in thought, then said:

"Crown Prince, I will not tell you that this mission is impossible. It will be difficult, but there is a way. I'll have to awaken another two hundred thousand soldiers, totally emptying the reserves of *Tria*, and we'll have to move in an extremely aggressive fashion. Also, losses among the assault troops and landing troops would be tens of times higher. According to my calculations, we can expect around three hundred thousand Alpha Iseyek assault troop casualties and five thousand human ones to carry out the mission as fast as you're asking. I can find sacrifices for this situation, but only if the five-day time-frame is truly that important to your Highness."

I shook my head in the negative.

"No general, that is not a good option. We have no need for unjustified losses. Instead, you can use any of the star fleet's capabilities you need: destroy any target, fortification, underground Alien bunker, anything. No reason to be greedy with missiles. If we use all of them we have, we can get more delivered from neighboring star systems. If you need any land-based or atmospheric technology to carry out the mission, tell me and I will pay for it to be purchased and delivered. In five days, the Perimeter Sector Eight Fleet must be on the way back home toward Unatari. That is the cold hard truth. But I do not think it right to get landing troops killed unnecessarily to accomplish that. Decide for yourself, General, how much time you'll need for our victory to be complete. And I'll ask the Sector Seven Fleet Commander to stay here in Veyerde for as long as needed by your troops for orbital support."

*Standing change. Iseyek race opinion of you has improved.*
*Alpha Iseyek race opinion of you: +17 (warm)*
*Gamma Iseyek race opinion of you: +14 (warm)*

*Global standing increase. Current value -12*

*Standing change. Empire Military faction opinion of you has improved.*
*Empire Military faction opinion of you: +25 (respectful)*

The only member of the Imperial Military Faction who had heard the conversation was Colonel Gor ton Vulf, so the standing change messages could only have been his doing. Interesting. I had long suspected that the colonel was able to affect faction standing... I'll have to test this observation and give my subject the ability to reveal himself at the same time.

"Colonel Gor ton Vulf, I have made the decision to land on the planet. Though Astra is the heir to Veyerde, she is above all else a fragile girl, and it wouldn't be right to send her to the front, while myself remaining in safety. Also, we'll be able to make a pretty sweet report from the just-now-cleared Palace of Veyerde for the whole Empire to see. This is the first planet ever liberated from Aliens. But I think that the historic speech should be made by a staff soldier, who really knows about land battles. Are you prepared to take that role on, colonel?"

Gor ton Vulf removed his helmet and thoughtfully combed his graying mane.

"Crown Prince... I would love to give a glorious speech on camera for my descendants... But given my speech impediment, I'm afraid that it would have the opposite of the desired effect."

"No worries, colonel, you and I can go together and compose a text for a speech so fiery, that people will be applauding your victory in every corner of the empire," Katerina ton Mesfelle promised.

"Then there's another issue," the huge, muscle-bound soldier sighed. "I've never been good at public speaking. It's easier for me to fight in five serious battles than to say something meaningful to a camera once. The second wave of landing shuttles will be sent to Veyerde in ten minutes. I'll reserve spots for everybody then."

\* \* \*

And again, I didn't know how to feel about what was happening in the world around me. If landing on a planet captured in battle was part of a game scenario, the developers of *Perimeter Defense* truly deserved heaps of praise and awards. The landing process was just that realistic and atmospheric for a player to experience. But if this "virtual world" was actually reality... it was scary to even think about, given the landing was so rough that those responsible had earned at least the very harshest possible tongue-lashing.

It started with the fact that the landing in combat conditions brought me right back that time on the Throne World, but the main difference from that time was that I didn't have a space suit on now, so I had to hold back the urge to vomit back with all my might. We descended through the atmosphere of Veyerde in a buzzing, crackling, ball of fire. The turbulence was so strong that I could barely keep my neck from dislocating, and my teeth rattled so hard I accidentally bit my tongue. When then I wondered about the reason we were making such a risky descent and why the pilot of our landing shuttle was screaming in alarm, the silent officer sitting next to me simply advised me to look out the window. I wish I hadn't...

It would seem that we were being shot at by two little horseshoe-shaped fighter planes of a design I was unfamiliar with. Methodically, one after the next, they were shooting down our landing shuttles. Then another shuttle blew up in a bright flash, and the fighter started curving back toward us. You couldn't say we weren't trying to take the Aliens down. The sky around the fighter was dotted with the blooms of nearby explosions, but our AA defense just couldn't hit the fast little ship. I noticed tracer lines stretching out from the shuttles landing together with us leading to the attacking fighter. I wondered how they were shooting. I turned my head and took a long around our landing shuttle. Both sides, it turned out, had two gunner's turrets folded into them to ease passenger transport.

"Man the guns!" I screamed, before setting an example.

I don't know how, but even with the unmerciful turbulence, I made it to the nearest turret. The officer prayed, then helped me pull the chair out and strap in with special belts. My fingers had barely made contact with the cozy, anatomical grips, when a screen and target grid appeared before my eyes. To test it out, I pressed the buttons with both hands. A smoke trail going away from us was reflected on screen. The cannon noticeably began to shake. I figured that meant it wasn't a laser, but something like a double cannon on a war plane. Though the rounds traveled at high speed, you had to be able to predict to hit the fast targets. And just then, an Alien fighter appeared on the screen, flying away. I gave it time to turn around, placing the center of my targeting grid where I supposed the returning enemy would soon be. A long line, and the cannons gave another strong vibration. A tracer stretched out toward the Alien fighter, and intersected with its flight trajectory. I clearly saw a few flashes of an energy shield around the flying Alien device, then explosions on the fighter's left wing. The flying horseshoe turned away sharply to the side, then went past the edge of the screen.

"Target hit! Strike!" My joy knew no bounds.

"I affirm that the target has been shot down and has stopped attacking," Colonel Gor ton Vulf said, sitting at the second turret on my side of the ship. "It's time to meet your maker, you virulent pest!"

But it didn't really matter anymore. Our ship dipped into a thick cloud, then a few seconds later our landing thrusters kicked in, bringing our speed down. A minute later, the shuttle landed fairly roughly, causing the shocks to creak. The doors opened immediately.

"Exit the ship! No delays! Let's unload all the boxes with us! Free up the shuttle for the next groups!" the mustached major standing outside in a heavy armored suit with helmet visor thrown up was gesticulating wildly, hurrying the landing troops along.

On seeing Gor ton Vulf, the major played his trump card, reporting:

"Commander, we have secured a base in the Palace. No living Aliens remain. The defensive shield is being put up now. Two engineering groups have gone to check the road to the lake..."

The rest of the report was drowned out by the automatic AA turrets next to the landing pad. They made a synchronized turn and let fly some long lines upward with a thunderous clap.

"The pair of Alien fighters was able to take off from a cannon installation that our reconnaissance didn't notice. Now they're harassing our landing zone," the major said.

The colonel spit through his teeth in vexation.

"We already know. They attacked our group in descent. Eleven of thirty shuttles were shot down, the monsters. The Crown Prince himself took one down from the side turret. That's when they retreated..."

It was only then that the major noticed the others who had arrived with the colonel, both people and nonpeople. The soldier's eyes widened. He bowed down on one knee and lowered his head:

"My Prince, please forgive me. I didn't recognize you! Do you order me to take me to the operations headquarters to give your Highness control over the soldiers?"

"No, I don't care about the headquarters. Professionals should be in charge. I don't understand a damn thing in land battles and would only get in your way here. So then, stand, major and continue your work as if I wasn't even here."

"As you command, Crown Prince!" the soldier stood and really did go to the side, leaving Astra and I alone with our bodyguard companions.

That was the weirdest night of my life. First we spent a long time exploring the palace ruins with flashlights. We even crawled around in the half-filled basements, all the while with Astra telling me about each room, each burnt-up picture frame on the wall, and each collapsed staircase and tower. Katerina was writing everything down, constantly clarifying this or that detail and filming as she went.

Afterwards, when it was totally dark out, the Princess dragged us both out on a mountain path that wound around between the stones. We went out to the small lake with a ten-foot-high waterfall cascading into it. With absolutely no regard for the others present, Astra threw off her clothes and immersed herself in the black water.

"Whoa! This water is ice cold!" the girl told us, her teeth chattering as she went deeper and deeper in.

Suddenly, Astra dived underwater. I had to hold back my bodyguards, who ran out in front to help her. The girl really did not need any help. In fifteen seconds, Astra had already resurfaced and was on her way to the bank, holding a golden crown inlaid with rubies.

"There it is, the Crown of Veyerde!" The Princess

was showing off her trophy to everyone there with pride. "There is a prophecy that my granny Fesilia made on the day of my birth, that my fate was to refuse a small crown, but that I would receive a large one in exchange. I really did refuse the baron's crown when I broke my engagement with Henrik ton Lavaelle, and exchange I'm holding a King's crown in my hands..."

"And before the future Queen comes down with bronchitis, I suggest we quickly go dry off in front of the fireplace," Katerina ton Mesfelle said, finishing her sentence.

And so we sat on some stones that were still warm from the day, heated up some army rations on the fire in cans, and found some strange fruit from the nearby garden for roasting. It had the flavor of a fresh semisweet melon. We drank bagged juice and something like a mix of strong brandy with a dry fruit compote. That was what we found in the army flasks labeled: "Restorative." The night sky above us was illuminated with bright flashes and dashes. The space armada was still bombing the surface of Veyerde, helping the soldiers in their mission. In the nice army binoculars, which had been gifted to the Crown Prince by an unfamiliar landing captain, I could even see and recognize the ships above us in space: there's a *Meresh* with its characteristic shapes, and that's a battleship, probably *Bride of Chaos* or *Knight of Light*.

From time to time, the rocket installations next to us sounded off, and the AA turrets flew into action. A shot-down low-atmosphere ship flew past in the night sky like a meteor, leaving a trail of flame behind it. A few times, a medical rotor-wing plane landed very near us and unloaded wounded soldiers. Some I had never met before walked up to our fire, mostly people, but also the occasional Alpha Iseyek. We let anyone stay as long as they wanted, and even treated them to our cans of food and drink. Once we even saw a female spider-esque Glorvian, all wrapped up in armor, surrounded by twenty ghastly-looking huge males. The Glorvians were also taking part in liberating Veyerde.

I greeted the soldiers, toasted and drank with them, heard out their wishes and pledges of eternal loyalty. It was probably a hard night for my bodyguards, given that there were always a ton of armed people and nonpeople hanging around me. But the Truth Seeker, who had also come to visit her home planet with the next group of landing soldiers, did not sense any risk. In fact, Florianna was getting drunk on the atmosphere of admiration and would periodically ask her minions to pour a little bit of strong alcohol right into her mouth.

Astra was also at the center of attention. She was getting her picture taken with anyone who asked, drinking and dancing with officers and normal soldiers, hearing out laudatory speeches and soldiers' assurances that the Kingdom of Veyerde would soon be all hers. Katerina was the only one who kept working. She was making reports from the headquarters and the palace ruins. She was filming Crown Prince Georg royl Inoky surrounded by Orange House soldiers and Astra with the crown of Veyerde in her hands.

Katerina's work had good effect too. Standing change messages from all kinds of people and factions started coming in practically once a minute. My fame grew by seven points over the fantastic night to +30. I also reached the same number in my relation with the Imperial Military. But when morning had almost arrived, and Astra was asleep, wrapped up in the camouflage raincoat given to her by some soldiers, a miracle occurred.

"Your Highness, incoming call from the Emperor!" the communications private, his eyes widening in astonishment, couldn't believe what was happening.

I stood, gave a slight shake to get the dry grass and dirt off my suit, quickly combed my hair and demanded he be put through. Today, August was wearing a white military uniform with gold epaulets and a sash bedecked with medals. I bowed down on one knee, and the guards and other soldiers who happened to be on screen around me did the same.

"My Emperor, the Nayal system has been cleared of Aliens. The enemy fleet has been completely wiped out! Space control in the Veyerde system has been restored. The Alien landing fleet has been shot down, and the assault of the planet Veyerde is underway."

"Stand, Georg," the Emperor demanded. "To be honest, when I saw that your fleet was on its way to Sector Seven, I got upset and even a bit angry about the fact that you'd made such a bad use of my gift. Though now I see that I was wrong in my intentions. I've already been told that you were fulfilling a promise to help defend Sector Seven, which is quite an honorable thing to do. It was an exemplary battle in the Nayal system, followed by a strong bid to liberate Veyerde. Such acts demand their due valuation. Also, your raid on Alien territory must not be forgotten. I'll begin with your aid to the Swarm. I have included the Black Star in the official registry of Imperial combat medals by executive order. I have also officially affirmed the thirty-percent increase in salary given to all holders. But as for Veyerde... where, by the way, is the Princess?"

The soldiers stepped aside, and the Emperor saw Astra sleeping wrapped in a raincoat. One of the soldiers jumped to wake the Princess up, but August stopped him:

"No, no. I don't need to talk with her. Let her sleep. My gift to the Princess of Veyerde will be for the Empire to pay for her coronation ceremony in full. I can hardly be there in person. Those years are behind me, but on my volition, I give you, Crown Prince Georg royl Inoky ton Mesfelle, the right to crown this brave girl in my name. Give the five soldiers and commanders who fought best in these battles an Emerald Star. My messenger will deliver you the medals soon. I have certificates for another two Emerald Stars that I've already signed for Katerina ton Mesfelle and Nicole Savoia. Katerina for her distinguished reports from the hottest spots in the war with the Aliens. Nicole is also to be promoted to space captain, all of this is for her brilliant knowledge and skills in commanding ships. My personal gift to you, grandson, will be five extra days added to your deadline. You know what I'm talking about."

* * *

The grandiose ceremony came to an end. The party guests and refugees returning to Veyerde were already gradually setting off to relax in the temporary, guarded village made for them. In the Veyerde Palace, already totally repaired in even the tiniest details, the only people remaining were Astra's many relatives with their families and servants.

The Queen of Veyerde herself, standing on a small balcony extending out toward the mountain lake, was tracing the last wisps of light from the just-set local sun with her gaze. The Queen's robe on the girl's shoulders and the golden crown on her head were surprisingly suited to her. It was as if she was made for this regalia from birth. The only problem was the fact that there were no traces of joy on the girl's face.

"Georg, you aren't gonna agree to be the monarch of the provincial Kingdom of Veyerde, huh?" my former favorite asked, after a very long period of silence.

I shook my head. No, I had a whole bunch of reasons that I didn't want that for my future.

"I understand," Queen Astra royl Veyerde sighed sadly. "That means that you'll be leaving me forever tomorrow then?"

"Today, actually. The shuttle is already waiting. My fleet cannot stay in Sector Seven forever, and the time to return home has come. But as for 'forever,' I can't say. Come visit if you get bored," I tried to smile, though inside, something was just bursting.

"And at what status? You're married, Georg... By the way, the Kingdom of Fastel sent me some luxury saplings to replant the burnt-up garden. Marta royl Valesy ton Mesfelle-Kyle even wrote a touching letter congratulating me. It seemed sincere..."

Astra kept silent. I made no rush to break the silence, with no idea what we could keep talking about after we separated. An android servant came out onto the balcony with some wine glasses on a tray. It was one of the thousands I had gifted Astra. I wanted to say no, but at the last second I had a change of heart, and took both:

"I know it's dumb, but let's drink to us finding a reason to meet in the future!"

The Queen of Veyerde took the glass with her flawless fingers and, meeting eyes with me, smiled sadly and said:

"Thank you, Georg. To a reason to meet in the future!"

Astra drained the glass and set it down on the handrail. I set mine down next to hers, and, without saying goodbye, turned sharply and rushed off to the shuttle that had already been waiting for me for some time.

# DIPLOMATIC MAIL

M Y FLEET SPENT no more time dallying in Sector Seven, and the ships set off toward the Parn system. The status of this system, having been opened to connect Perimeter Sectors Seven and Eight just a week and a half ago, had not yet been legally settled, so I was in a rush to be the one to resolve it. The mission looked extremely simple: include the Parn system in Perimeter Sector Eight, in my zone of responsibility, before any indications about it come down from the Throne World. On our way, my fleet had grown significantly, having picked up the brand new *Tyrant* battleship from the dockyard. The awesome starship was given the name *Crown Princess Likanna*. The dock workers had proposed a list of ten names, including that one and, for understandable reasons, I stopped on precisely it. When I sent my daughter the two-minute video of the new battleship from all angles, Lika sent an answer back instantly:

"Daddy, I love you!!! By the way, Joan royl Reyekh cried for three days when she heard *Joan the Fatty* had been shot down. Her and I made up, so let me know if you have any other ships without a name. Dad, It'd be a big help."

"Alright, I'll figure something out for your buddy," I answered. A few seconds later, I saw a popup appear before my eyes:

*Standing change. Joan royl **Reyekh's** opinion of you has improved.*
*Presumed personal opinion of you: +12 (warm)*

*Standing change. Purple House (Empire) opinion of you has improved.*
*Present Purple House (Empire) faction opinion of you: +11 (warm)*

Bingo! A perfect example of why you should never underestimate a little crown princess, especially when that Princess is a Great House Head's favorite granddaughter.

I did have a ship with no name: there was another *Tyrant* battleship in the final stages of construction waiting for me in Unatari. The only problem was that I had been dumb enough to promise a girl that spent a long time around me that the ship would be named *Princess Astra*, and I could not break my word as an aristocrat.

That was why I had Katerina ton Mesfelle have a talk with all battleship owners in Sectors Seven, Eight, and Nine that we thought might not be especially sympathetic to Duke Paolo royl Anjer. There were more than enough to be found, but those that also were looking to part with the awesome starships, even for serious money, were a bit harder to track down. Even my brother Roben refused to help, despite having recalled the Tesse ships from the United Orange House Fleet.

And only for a disgustingly huge amount of money, half a billion credits, did the independent Kingdom of Reikorel from Perimeter Sector Nine agree to part with its *Monarch*-class flagship. I ordered the captain of the ship to go to Unatari through Swarm territory. Yes, there was some risk that the Swarm Queen, the Iseyek Prime Nai Igir would refuse to let the lone human ship through her territory, but in that case, I had a home-brewed remedy already in mind.

At the next charging station, I visited the *Meresh*. To be honest, having already visited the large *Tria* starship several times, I was expecting huge open spaces and hallways that stretched to infinity, like on the other Swarm ship. But this one was like nothing I'd ever seen before, or even imagined. The interior of the *Meresh* was very reminiscent of the *Umoyge* light cruiser. It had the same narrow winding corridors, high number of air-lock doors, scanner frames and internal security checkpoints. These internal security mechanisms were the Swarm's way of uncovering Arites on their ships, but the battleship captain, Daisss Pi, an Arite Iseyek himself, served as a living example of how ineffective it had been. The captain of the huge Swarm battleship was a large twelve-eyed centipede of a muddled green color, though I understood well that this was only the Arite's external appearance, which he had grown comfortable in, and accustomed to. My Arite, for example, preferred looking like the blonde Bionica and stayed in that form almost all the time now.

"Crown Prince, Triasss Zess has already been thawed out. He will soon be waking up. Would you like to take a look at your enemy?" asked my Arite, translating the chirping of the other.

"I suppose I would. I've never seen an Alpha Iseyek wake up from a state of suspended animation before."

The metal curtain went up, and I saw a large cocoon lying in a dark capsule. His straitjacket was made of the same type of fabric the Iseyeks all carried rolled up on their belt. The just barely stirring Alpha Iseyek was separated from me by a thick wall of armored glass. The cocoon gave a twitch, wobbled over, and suddenly a long, spindly appendage started peeking out of a slit in the fabric. After that, it was like the fabric retracted from his curled up body and folded itself. A dark, thick slurry rushed out onto the floor, leaving Triasss Zess in a puddle with no way out due to his still disobedient appendages. It should be noted that my old acquaintance's small arms had already grown back.

"He has woken up and is able to hear, your Highness," my Arite translated the other's words once again, while the creature lying in the puddle clearly tried to listen in.

"Triasss Zess, can you hear me?" I clarified.

The enormous insect turned toward the sound. The Alpha Iseyek's eyes were deeply set into his head and covered with a transparent film. The praying mantis's vision had not yet returned, but his hearing was working fine.

"Yes, Crown Prince Georg, I can hear and understand your Highness. And I am ready to accept any punishment for my mistake, which has come at a very high price to both your fleet and the Swarm."

I frowned in dissatisfaction:

"You're lucky that you didn't come across one of my soldiers right after what happened in Kej. Then no one would've even given one rusty nail for your life. But now, I've signed a treaty saying that I have no more grievances against the Swarm. This treaty protects you specifically. As such, I will not be taking revenge. I'll say more. Now I offer you the chance to earn Nai Igir, the Swarm Queen's, forgiveness."

The creature on the floor gave a start and tried to pull his eyes out from his chitin head, though he did not find success.

"I agree to any conditions in advance, Crown Prince. What will I have to do?"

"As soon as you wake all the way up, you will take one of my fleet's frigates and go to the Dekeye system capital as fast as you can possibly get there. There you will meet with the Swarm Queen and give her a small package from me."

The praying mantis clearly got tense, so I hurried to calm him:

"The box is not sealed, so you and any of the Iseyek Prime's guards can make sure that there is nothing dangerous to the Queen in it. I'll tell you what's inside though: an Emerald Star medal and the certificate to go with it with the name Nai Igir printed inside. It is a sign of the Empire's recognition for the help the Swarm has given us in the war against the Aliens. Also inside the box, you will find a scroll with a message to Nai Igir from me personally. If you bring both of those objects to the Queen, I can guarantee that she will forgive you."

*  *  *

And there it is, the Parn system. Two gas giants and a whole swarm of different-sized satellites slowly orbiting a dull brown dwarf. The gloomy star system had no planets or moons suitable for human life. It was also expected to be difficult to grow normal human plants in space greenhouses there, due to the particular characteristics of the local star, and its distance from large centers of civilization... All the same, even without my advisor Katerina ton Mesfelle's hints, I understood perfectly how high the value of the Parn system was as a conduit between two huge star regions. The Parn bypass allowed freighters to save up to three weeks when going between Perimeter Sectors Seven and Eight, as well as being the only possible path for heavy combat starships to take.

That was why the first thing I did upon arriving was to head out to the scout ships that discovered the Parn star system for humanity and installed a warp beacon in it. The huge starship, no smaller than my *Uukresh*, was a full-fledged, self-sufficient flying city, with around fifteen thousand people living in it. The huge, five-hundred-yard-high gold letters on the side of the giant flashed back in an orange flame in the light of the Parn star, revealing the words "Star Mutt."

"The ship was built more than seven hundred years ago in the Throne World and, since that time, it has been furrowing the endless depths of space," Bionica informed me, clearly having found the information in some encyclopedia. "*Star Mutt* has found more than one hundred thirty new star systems on its path and has installed twenty-four warp beacons for humanity, all of which are still in use today. This is the very ship that discovered Tesse three hundred eighty years ago and, before that, it also made Nessi, Unguay, and Himora accessible to humanity as well. An interesting fact about this scout ship is that it has only hired crew one time. All of its current inhabitants are the descendants of the very first astronauts who set out on their mission seven centuries ago. There is a strict caste system on the ship and complete control over birth rate: every crew member knows when to have children, and how many they can have."

I stopped my secretary's intriguing story with a wave, as we had arrived. It was a huge titan of a ship. It's dock entrance was guarded by energy shields and an uncountable number of high-speed turrets. Someone was waiting for us when we got out. A tall, gray-bearded man was standing in front of me in a pair of gray overalls. There were ten armed figures wearing dark armored space suits.

"Crown Prince Georg?" I couldn't see any distinguishing features on the old man's face. The popup information was also missing, so I asked the name of the man who had addressed me.

"Tazar ton Akad, twenty-third captain of the *Star Mutt*. I suspect it must have been just curiosity that brought a man as busy as your Highness to visit my ship. Let's go to my office, Crown Prince. There we'll be able to talk face to face. But, if possible, could you leave your people, and especially that huge praying mantis here? My team leads a very isolated lifestyle and I'm not sure how they would react to outsiders like that."

*"All clear. He is not thinking of doing anything bad,"* Florianna reassured me.

I answered the captain, that only the Truth Seeker and her silent minions would be with me. The captain quickly sized up the little Flora with a look, then took a slightly longer look at the four gigantic pill bugs around her, and gave his permission. I asked all my guards, even the Chameleons, to stay by the shuttle. The captain's guards also mostly stayed in the hangar. Only two bodyguards came with us. We went up on an elevator several stories and came out into a big, verdant greenhouse. On the plastic path, which wound whimsically between ponds of brightly colored fish, Tazar ton Akad led us to a transparent door, with a small office behind it. The captain pointed me to a soft couch, having already taken a seat on the one opposite it.

"Crown Prince. Let me try to guess why you're on my ship. You're thinking of acquiring the Parn system. Am I right?"

I was not able to hide the surprise on my face at the captain's insightfulness, and Tazar ton Akad smiled happily, clearly satisfied at the impression he'd made.

"How much for the system?" I asked, deciding to take a similarly direct line.

Katerina and I had already tried to calculate how much I could afford to pay for the strategically important star system, and had come to three billion credits. I would need to spend another billion and a half on building a nice station with freight terminals, defense systems and a large number of starship charging slots. That was why I listened to the captain's offer carefully, somewhat worried inside that I would have enough money in my budget. But, the *Star Mutt* captain's answer surprised me:

"Crown Prince, it must be hard for you to understand, but not everything in this world can be measured in money. Here on board *Star Mutt*, for example, we have no use for it. People simply live, do their job and get the goods they need. What do they need money for?"

"You must need something, though," I hinted, not believing it could be true. "Fuel for the reactors, replacement parts, new kinds of crops, more powerful computers, fresh star maps..."

Tazar ton Akad, shaking his head "no," while still holding a well-meaning smile on his face, replied:

"The Empire provides us all these things for absolutely nothing. We're gonna get a new warp beacon in a few weeks, too and, many years from now, we'll place it in a new star system we've discovered for our race. That is our work, our holy mission, and humanity provides us with everything we need to carry it out... All the same, there is something that would make me agree to give your Highness ownership of the Parn system."

I looked inquisitively at the captain, but he suddenly interrupted me, asking both of his guards to leave and keep watch over the door. The two identical armored figures unquestioningly carried out their captain's order and went into the greenhouse.

"Those are my children, twins, Paul and Paola." The smile left the old man's face. In its place, a stern and prudent look appeared. "My conditions are related to my children. You take the twins and provide them a comfortable life in the greater world. I know how well you did for your companion Astra, Crown Prince. She came to you a dowry-less refugee, and now she's Queen of Veyerde. I don't ask for kingdoms for my children, but the price of the Parn system would easily allow them to be provided places in the highest ranks of the Empire, or am I wrong?"

All I could do was agree with the captain.

"Do not ask why I am doing this, Crown Prince. Perhaps my children will tell you one day if they think it necessary. And so, your Highness, do you agree to my proposition: the Parn system in exchange for getting my children into the world of Imperial upper aristocracy?"

I considered it, and then gave a cautious answer to the graying old man.

"Your conditions have been understood and accepted, Captain Tazar ton Akad, but I do have a demand of my own. The battle for power in the Orange House is coming to a head. My enemies are very strong and unscrupulous. I'll have to hide a few people very close to me for some time, maybe a couple days, maybe a few months. The whole Empire knows that *Star Mutt* does not accept newcomers, and as such no one would ever think to look for my people here. And, if they decide to look, you could hide a whole division of flying tanks on this giant, and no one would ever find them if the captain of that ship made sure of it..."

"That is true, Crown Prince," the captain of *Star Mutt* interjected, "however, a Truth Seeker would be able to find anyone trying to hide, even on such a huge scout ship as this."

"You don't have to worry about that, captain. One of the people I'm leaving behind is Florianna," I said, pointing to the paralyzed girl in the flying chair. "Her abilities as a Truth Seeker are more than enough to not have to worry about them being found."

The captain took another look at Flora and gave a sideways smirk:

"Oh, I already know all about that. You mustn't think, Prince George, that we here on the *Star Mutt* live in the wilderness and do not watch the Imperial news. The girl who kills admirals with a single glance... Worrying company, though it will be safe with her, here I agree with your Highness. All the same, I have heard a lot about your other Truth Seeker, Crown Prince. Will Miya be here as well?"

I saw Florianna's flying chair twitch at these words. There was no reason to hide anything, so I answered as honestly as possible:

"Miya will definitely not be here on *Star Mutt*. In fact, it is not impossible that she will be one of those trying to find the runaways. Though it may also be the other way around, and Miya will be on our side."

"Hmm... You drive a hard bargain. Risking drawing the ire of the most powerful Truth Seeker in the Galaxy is the last thing I want in this life. But all the same, I agree for my children's sake. When should I expect your people on my ship? And when will you pick up the twins?"

I estimated in my head. My contract with Mr. G.I. would run out in forty-five days, and after that, the Crown Prince and his wicked companion, probably not too happy with all the changes that have happened in their lives, may want to take out their rage on people close to me, or simply have them killed for their safety. Bionica, Phobos, Nicole Savoia, Popori de Cacha, Florianna, Valian ton Corsa, the Arite... those were the individuals most in need of my protection. And Astra, but she has become Queen, and was far away and would soon stop being associated with me. Katerina ton Mesfelle? They would hardly touch Crown Prince Georg's cousin, though I would also have to set my advisor up somewhere, just in case.

"My people will come to the Parn system here in thirty-five days. After that, *Star Mutt* should start its many-year route to a new, unknown star. There will be a ship with you, or a few ships, which will take the stowaways and your children back as soon as everything's calmed down."

The captain wiped his palm in satisfaction:

"I see. As it were, the new warp beacon is being delivered to *Star Mutt* in thirty days, along with other equipment I ordered, so everything with the timing is great. Let's shake on it, Crown Prince. I agree to your conditions!"

Here we are, my capital, the Unatari star system! It had been so long since my fleet left it, setting off on a military campaign. So many events had passed since that time: the battle of Hnelle, the Siege of Tesse, the Chameleons making me their ruler, the battles with Aliens on praying mantis territory, the Swarm's treachery in Kej, venturing beyond death, the strenuous battle in the Lobj system, the three-party treaty, the information blockade, the raid through Sector Nine, the liberation of Veyerde and, finally, our journey out of Sector Seven... My head was spinning from the thought, but then we reached the finish line of our cosmic odyssey. My people were clearly tired and, as soon as the ships docked at the Unatari station for repair and modernization, I announced a week of leave for the whole Sector Eight Fleet.

Katerina ton Mesfelle accepted a fifty-million-credit bonus for her work with a rapturous shriek. She rushed off to get into a plane; my cousin had long been eying an island for herself on Unatari-VII and was now hurrying to close the deal.

Bionica also went off to the planet. My synthetic secretary did not like the red-headed body, so the android was rushing to go back to blond. Popori de Cacha also asked for some time off with her team to watch over the consciousness-transfer process into the android's new body. Other than that, the head of my guard had different concerns. She had to organize the tournament I had long ago announced for Chameleon males for the right to become the mate of the captain of *Surprise-1*. Insofar as I understood from a conversation I'd overheard between my bodyguards, Popori de Cacha herself was to be the second prize in the tournament.

The staff officers rushed to make use of the leave they had received and set off for some relaxation in the resorts of Unatari. Even the Truth Seeker left me in her way. Florianna had long needed to take another dose of crystals and, as such, the paralyzed girl immediately made use of the chance that arose and left for a many-day sleep. She didn't even come down to the planet, instead just hiding in her cabin guarded by her minions.

I couldn't wait to set off to rest in my palace either. However, before doing that, I wanted to visit the docks and the huge space research complex, built orbiting the planet Unatari-VII during my absence. I started with the laboratories, setting off there in a shuttle accompanied by Admiral Kiro Sabuto and Lieutenant Valian ton Corsa. The girl was wearing an armored suit with an opaque, tinted helmet visor, which hid her disfigured face, and clearly made her anxious. Valian had refused my utterly sincere invitation to visit the palace on Unatari, telling me with self-pity that she wouldn't be able to do that for the next few years.

The laboratories greeted us with an abundance of scientific staff of all different species, and spacious hangars, which contained fragments of Alien ships and whole captured frigates. There was also incomprehensible equipment and such an atmosphere of serious painstaking labor that even an Imperial Crown Prince visiting wasn't enough to distract the busy scientists. The station head was a Gamma Iseyek, one of those rescued from the Kej system. He still spoke quite badly in human language, but his Ravaash assistant helped translate in difficult places.

"Crown Prince, your main mission is complete. We have completely figured out the construction of the small Alien combat drones and are already able to produce copies."

"And that's not all," a middle-aged woman

unexpectedly interfered in the conversation and just then introduced herself. "Samantha ton Kruger, head of the drone testing laboratory. My Prince, we were able to copy the combat cannons, thrusters and maneuvering systems of this model drone and have successfully decompiled its program code. In fact, we were able to improve the drone's algorithms and create different behavior models in combat, from a high-survival preference 'careful' mode, to suicidally aggressive."

"How many drones can you make per day?" I wondered, quite delighted at the victory reports, and Samantha's happy expression immediately faded:

"My Prince, this is so far the only one we've made. It took us three weeks... Outfitting a mass-production line to make Alien drones would cost quite the pretty penny..."

I frowned and demanded concrete numbers. The Gamma Iseyek quickly chirped something out, and his assistant translated the answer:

"Tuki-tuka-de-sa, the total purchase price in Tesse would be three hundred forty million credits. Delivery and unpacking would take four days. After that, we would be able to produce up to sixty drones per day at a production cost of two hundred forty credits per unit."

"I give you three days to get it up and running. And also, get enough to make one hundred twenty drones per day. If you need two production lines to do that, buy them. In thirty days, I need no less than three thousand new drones for a full fleet refit."

"Such extreme conditions for an order will bring the total costs to simply gigantic numbers." The Gamma

Iseyek started thinking for a few seconds and said, "One billion three hundred million credits, and your fleet can have the number of drones it needs one month from today."

In silence, with no emotion, I transferred the total to the laboratory-manufacturing complex's account. After that payout, I had two billion credits remaining.

"Your order will be completed on time, Crown Prince Georg," the Gamma Iseyek bowed, imitating a human gesture. "Would you like to see our other laboratories?"

Unfortunately, the scientists had yet to make any inventions that were as epically groundbreaking as that one. They didn't figure out the *Sledgehammer*'s shield recharging system. The Alien communication system also remained a seven-seal mystery. Cannons, producing antimatter, thrusters, Alien fabrics... none of the projects had yet to bear fruit. Only in the hangar, where a large group of specialists was poking around in the mobile-warp-beacon-equipped frigate, was I given some hope of certain success being made. The scientists had figured out how to turn some of the frigate's systems on, and had carefully even piloted the Alien starship, once taking it out of the hangar into space.

"If that little ship can jump invisibly between systems and open a mobile warp beacon in four weeks, I will shower gold on all of you," I promised, but it became apparent by their confused faces that even they didn't think they could do it.

"Your Highness, Count Avalle royl Anjer ton Mesfelle has arrived to *Emperor August* with some companions," my communications officer told me.

To be honest, I was a bit confused. My sister had said she would get a meeting together with the second man in the Orange House, but I wasn't expecting it to be so soon. I had to leave the orbital laboratory complex and return to my flagship.

The Count did not arrive alone. And even if I personally was no match for twenty guardsmen armed to the teeth, there were enough of my soldiers on the heavy cruiser to make sure my guests wouldn't think they could let too loose. But then, the young looking companion of the Count set me right on guard as soon as I read the information in her popup hint.

*Marian Sabati*
*Age: 91*
*Race: Human*
*Gender: Female*
*Class: Mystic*
*Achievements: Master Psionic, Kills with a Glance, Punisher, Child Killer*
*Fame: 41*
*Standing: -74*
*Presumed personal relationship: Unknown*

Mother of my wife! What kind of monster had the Count brought with him?! I couldn't even understand what to be more surprised at here: the abundance of terrifying achievements, how young she actually was at ninety-one, her high fame or her standing, which was so ghastly that I wouldn't even have reached it in my darkest moments in the game... It might be time to call Miya in as a counterweight to this monster.

"Look who's talking about monsters..." said Marian, clearly offended. "You got close to a Truth Seeker whose conduct makes normal people afraid to so much as greet you. I'm not talking about the paralyzed girl sleeping on this cruiser, either."

The Truth Seeker didn't even hide that she was shamelessly digging around in my brain, despite the fact that such behavior is considered very uncouth. Ah then! I didn't try to hide my mocking smile. Go ahead, read more of my thoughts. Marian's eyes first grew wide in surprise, then the woman laughed uncontrollably:

"Georg, that's enough! I'm obviously flattered that I cause such fantasies in you, but you are seriously embellishing reality. And also, the last position you were imagining just wouldn't work. Just believe my almost century of experience."

The Truth Seeker turned to her master and said something matter-of-factly without a drop of joy in her voice:

"Your radiance, the Crown Prince has some doubt that he is capable of defeating Duke Paolo's United Fleet. And another important thing: somewhere nearby, probably here on this cruiser, Miya is hiding. That is precisely why Crown Prince Georg has no fear of me and isn't even taking this seriously. He is sure that Miya is capable of appearing here at any second."

"Miya is the last thing we need here," the Count said, bristling as if from cold. "Marian, you are free, let the Crown Prince and I talk one-on-one."

When the Truth Seeker was still in the door frame,

she stopped sharply and turned to me:

"Your comparing me with a monster seriously affected me, Crown Prince. I saw a girl on your ship who hides her disfigured face behind a mirrored helmet. I would like to see her. Differently from Miya, I sometimes do nice things for people."

"Marian, if you can help Valian's burns heal, you have my word as a Crown Prince that I will publicly apologize to you and give you a gift worthy of an heir to the Empire."

After the door had just barely closed behind the ninety-year-old beauty, the Count declared:

"Alright, now we can talk, *tet-a-tet*. If you want my support in this conflict, my price is fifteen billion credits. I know that you do not have that much in money, Crown Prince, but I am not picky about how you pay. I'd be willing to take ships, star systems, or other property as well."

To be honest, I was quite caught off guard by him starting the conversation that way, and didn't even make an effort to hide it:

"Actually, I was seriously thinking of asking your Grace for an approximately similar sum in exchange for the Duke's title and post as Head of the Orange House, which I could bring you on a silver platter."

"Don't be stupid, Georg. You have thirty-five days left before the Emperor's deadline for making peace is up, and everyone knows it. And, though perhaps my brother is no military strategist, he's no dummy either. He's planning on simply holing up in the Orange House Capital for the next few months and gathering all the forces of the United Fleet there with the warp beacon turned off. That is why there is no way for you to keep your promise to the Emperor without my help."

I smiled and took out a small jewelry case I'd brought with me, opened it and showed Count Avalle the Emerald Star inside.

"This star is one of five issued to me by the Emperor to award to the worthy. This one is for you, Count Avalle. I'm describing the situation as it will be in a month. My fleet, operating from the Unguay system, will take the Ulia system, which belongs to you, Count. Duke Paolo won't give the order to split up his huge fleet and send ships to help you out. The United Fleet will remain in the Orange House capital, as your Excellency will even order."

The Count frowned in consternation and wiped down his sweat-covered forehead. Clearly, the strike on his system I'd described wasn't at all to his liking. Though there was no way to avoid it. An infinite stream of transport ships flowed through the Ulia system, which linked the Imperial Core with Sector Eight. The Emperor had clearly forbidden that warp beacon from being turned off long term. Having seen that my thought had reached him, I continued:

"After the fall of the strategically important Ulia system, the three stations cut off, Bren, Asti and Rea will come over to my side voluntarily, though they won't have much choice in the matter either. After that, a strike on the Nessi system and the Orange House Docks will follow. In theory, I could even attack Fastel and Varan. I have more than enough forces, though I don't especially see the point of doing that. And so, what will the Emperor see a month from now? Sector Seven fully supporting my side, Sector Nine doing the same, Sector Eight completely under my control other than a couple of isolated systems under total blockade. The outcome is obvious. August will declare me the victor. And if the Emperor doesn't want to personally intervene, the next deputy council will raise the issue of a voting to censure the Orange House Head, and will make that decision whether or not there is any resistance, given that over ninety-five percent of votes will be in my favor. The Duke is doomed to lose one way or another. Everyone understand that now. But I would prefer a clean, unconditional victory without any votes or debates."

Count Avalle royl Anjer ton Mesfelle threw himself back into the armchair and wondered what exactly I meant by a "clean victory."

"Your Truth Seeker is not wrong. I really do want to wipe the United Fleet out. No matter how dumb that idea may seem, I can win. Yes, technically I do have one fourth the ship power of Paolo's United Fleet, but..." I turned the Count's attention back to the Emerald Star. "This is the last of five given to me by the Emperor to distribute to the worthy. The last four medals have already found owners, though their names will become known to society only after the Orange House split is over. That is precisely why I know the basic picture that your Grace has yet to perceive, and know that my fleet will win. As you see, Count, I am being quite open with you. I have other allies and other options as well. And with them, we do not discuss whether I can win or not. It's a totally different question: what role are you going to be playing in the forthcoming events, Count? I offer you to become a knight of the Emerald Star and the new

Head of the Orange House."

The man stayed silent for some time, throwing himself back into the chair and looking at the rivets in the heavy cruiser's armored wall. But then he lurched forward and took the jewelry box that was lying on the table. After that, we discussed nothing but purely technical issues. When Count Avalle and those accompanying him had left my flagship, I made a call to Admiral Kiro Sabuto:

"Admiral, all signs point toward our guest being on his way to the Orange House Capital. The warp beacon will be turned on for the Duke's younger brother to let his ships out of Tesse. Make sure a couple of cloaked spies and at least one division of stealth bombers sneak into our enemy's lair unnoticed. They'll have to wait quite some time once they get there, so make sure they're stocked up to stay around for the next month."

"I'll get it all done, Crown Prince. By the way, I am now in the fleet headquarters. An orderly is telling me that a Kingdom of Veyerde diplomatic shuttle wants to dock on *Emperor August.* The ambassador says that he has valuable diplomatic cargo on board from the Kingdom of Veyerde that must be delivered directly into the hands of Crown Prince Georg royl Inoky ton Mesfelle. Should I give them permission?"

I gave my permission and went to the hangar to receive whatever diplomatic cargo Astra had sent. Walking down the resonant corridors of the heavy cruiser, I tried to guess what my former favorite had sent. To be honest, the right answer was the first thing that sprang to mind, but it seemed too unbelievable. The ambassador's shuttle had already managed to fly away. In the center of the huge hall, Astra was standing right there in the flesh, wearing a light-pink dress with a bunch of suitcases and boxes next to her. Already expecting something was amiss, I read the character information:

*Astra ton Veyerde*
*Age: 18*
*Race: Human*
*Gender: Female*
*Class: Aristocrat/Artist*
*Achievements: Iseyek Mating Dance, Former Queen*
*Fame: +8*
*Standing: -4*
*Presumed personal opinion of you: +100 (completely faithful)*

"The Crown of Veyerde did not allow me to be next to you, so I abdicated in favor of my older sister Rosa. Aren't you happy that I came?"

I took a seat on one of Princess Astra's boxes, completely wiped out... Maybe she wasn't actually a Princess anymore, but just a high-born "ton" without a title... Without looking toward the girl, I said:

"My cousin Katerina will kill you when she finds out. She put so much effort into ordering your coronation robe, but it turns out all that effort and money just went down the drain..."

"Don't worry, Georg, I'll ask my sister Rosa to send the robe back to Katerina!"

All I could do was wave my hand helplessly. Astra hadn't changed at all. With her naivety in some things, she was capable of putting anyone in an awkward position.

"I had a good reason to return. Your Highness promised me a romantic evening, and I still haven't gotten it!"

To be honest, I didn't know whether to laugh or cry at her considering that a good enough reason for refusing a Queen's throne. Astra kept silent for a bit longer and, looking somewhere past me, added, much quieter:

"And also... the doctor said that I'm having a boy."

# THE LAST PIRATE

I F ASTRA THOUGHT that I would jump in joy after such a declaration and carry her off in my arms, she was seriously wrong. A whole stampede of thoughts began stomping through my brain, one darker than the next. In just a little over a month, I would be leaving the game, and Mr. G.I. would be replacing me and, to him, Astra was simply a sound, and her child was nothing but a shameful misunderstanding in the carrying out of a substitution contract. Worse than that, Miya would return, and she had her own views about exactly which of Crown Prince Georg royl Inoky ton Mesfelle's children were worthy of rights to thrones.

Miya's next steps were not at all difficult to predict: The Truth Seeker was preparing to officially marry Crown Prince Georg before her daughter's birth and, after that, their legal daughter would automatically become a Crown Princess with all the privileges and rights to Orange House and Imperial thrones that came with it. Likanna, my underage daughter from a previous spouse, after Crown Prince Georg's divorce with Marta royl Valesy ton Mesfelle-Kyle, would drop significantly in throne-succession position, though she would remain a Crown Princess. If Likanna were already of age, no position loss in rank tables could threaten her. All the same, Likanna was a child, and her rights directly depended on the legitimacy of both parents. By the way, I figured out why Princess Marta was so patient all that time. Despite all her negative feelings toward her spouse, she was waiting and bearing it until Likanna's sixteenth birthday.

Which of Crown Prince Georg's two daughters would get priority in inheritance and rights was something I could not figure out all on my own. There were a ton of different aristocratic code subparagraphs intersecting, and I had to consider all of the factors. Of course, my advisor Katerina ton Mesfelle could help in this issue, though I was afraid of getting my cousin involved in such a delicate and dangerous topic. One day, Miya might read the information that Katerina ton Mesfelle is aware of her plans, and predicting the dangerous Truth Seeker's reaction to such a potential threat was something I did not want to do.

Besides that, it wasn't good to forget about the fact that my sister, Crown Princess Violetta also had her own plans, which got in the way of our brother Roben and his illness-addled child. Violetta still did not have children of her own, so all of Crown Prince Georg's children born earlier could also be an obstacle in my twin sister's path to the throne for her own children. In addition, there were the many offspring of Duke Paolo, his younger brother Avalle and their two second cousins... And then, on the backdrop of this toxic, deadly hornets next, my former favorite, the ex-Queen of Veyerde tells me she's expecting a son. I breathed a heavy sigh.

"Astra, let me just name a list of those who now have a motive to kill you," I began counting on my fingers for illustrative purpose.

When there weren't enough fingers left on my hands, and I started naming another ten names, Astra finally recognized how serious the situation was, and the smile crawled off her face.

"And what should I do then, your Highness?" obvious fear could be heard in my former favorite's voice.

"To start out, don't even hint to anyone about your secret. Act natural, be happy and weird like normal. Make frequent appearances in public, be dumb and play out the careless, satisfied life of a Crown Prince's companion. We've got about another month before your pregnancy will be obvious. In that time, the curious journalists will get used to the fact that you're back with me, and lose interest. After that, you'll start making less appearances in public until, at the end, you spend all your time under guard in my palace on Unatari, not leaving without very good reason. And finally, I'll hide you in a place where our foes will never find you."

Astra's usual carelessness returned. She smiled and looked at the pile of boxes.

"Thank you, Crown Prince Georg. Could your Highness call servants to bring my things to my cabin?"

"No, Astra. From now on, I will not be risking your life by taking you on military campaigns. For now, let your things lay here. This evening, I'll be flying to Unatari and taking you with me. I have important business to attend to in space, so just sit here in the cabin with my bodyguards. Although... I have a better idea. I'm about to fly out to accept the *Uukresh* carrier into the fleet, and next in line is the battleship *Princess Astra*. You can christen the starship named in your honor."

The girl clapped her palms in joy and said:

"I want to express my gratitude in the normal way, but my opinion of your Highness is already at maximum. Instead, Prince Georg, I can do the interior decorating on the starship *Princess Astra*! The ship won't know its equal in the whole galaxy!"

I seriously considered the possibility for a few seconds, but still decided to protect the battleship crew's mental health. It isn't the soldiers fault, after all, that the artist has a depressing, abstract style. Instead, I suggested that Astra spend the few hours I'll be on the *Uukresh* making a design to go on the outside of the battleship named in her honor.

The *Uukresh* impressed with its dimensions and brought joy to the eye at the perfection of its sleek surfaces, characteristic of all Swarm starships. The ship's energy shield was capable of taking the full brunt of five battleship cannons at once. Heavy energy neutralizers threatened serious problems to any enemy starship in the eighty-kilometer range of this giant. In just a few seconds, any enemy ship would be brought to a halt with its main thrusters, energy shields and cannons all turned off.

But the *Uukresh*'s main feature was its huge number of hangars made to store four hundred combat drones, as well as repair bays for eighty small ships. Of the many set-up options available, I had chosen eighty heavy, short-range *Legionnaire* corvettes. These ships had lightweight warp-drives, which allowed them to only move inside of a star system, however they made up for that with their stronger energy shields, pair of light cruiser cannons and, the especially awesome twenty-combat-drone-capacity bays. In fact, the *Uukresh* was capable of releasing eighty corvettes into battle at once, which could then release a total of two thousand combat drones. And if you consider that all the drones would be swapped out for nastier ones in a month, then I did not at all envy the ships of the United Fleet, who would be the first to have this awesome power tested on them.

Of course, there are effective countermeasures to any tactic but, all the same, I couldn't hold back the ear-to-ear smile when *Uukresh* captain Clay ton Avelle took me on a tour of the huge starship and showed me all this devastating force. Former first assistant Oorast Pohl had been overseeing the restoration of the *Uukresh* for the last four months. In that time, Clay ton Avelle had simply embraced the ship. He could tell you about every compartment and every restored armor sheet, as well as having done a fairly good of job learning how to speak and even swear in the Iseyek language. The gigantic starship's crew was mixed and was made up of twenty thousand people and eight thousand Iseyek of various varieties, the very same ones who had been able to save the dying ship during the Alien defeat of the Swarm in the Aysar system.

At first, I was a bit unaccustomed to seeing a member of my fleet without a Black Star on their Orange House ceremonial uniform. Every participant in the campaign in Alien territory had received this sign of having overcome death, and the black medal was a kind of "symbol of quality" in its way, and a confirmation of bravery and loyalty. Clay ton Avelle had not, in fact, participated in our campaign, and I thought to myself for some time about the option of appointing one of the captains who had distinguished themselves in the distant campaign to pilot the *Uukresh*. However, when talking with Clay ton Avelle, I formed quite the positive opinion about him and decided to keep him on. The brave officer was not at all bothered by the fact that he didn't have a Black Star. Instead of a medal, he had the largest and most dangerous starship in the Orange House under his command and one of the most powerful ships in the whole Empire.

"Captain, how well acquainted are you with the Iseyek under your command?" I wondered to Clay ton Avelle.

"I know all of the intelligent ones by name. There are around sixty of them. They are all capable of making complex decisions on their own. The rest of the Iseyek on my ship had their self-teaching genes deactivated at birth. They are diligent, tireless, and unreservedly loyal workers, but no more."

"Are there any intelligent small Alpha Iseyek here who also wear armored suits over their shells?" I wondered, asking a long-ago-formed question.

The captain thought for a few seconds before giving his answer:

"There definitely aren't any intelligent ones like that, Prince Georg. Though... let me think... I have seen one like that among the normal builders, who I put on the sixth deck of the interior partitions. Small in height, just six feet. Inexpressive, tiny eyes, and, as it were, an armored suit. From some old genetic line, I suppose. Modern Alpha Iseyek are bigger. Should I call that worker here so your Highness can look on the dwarf in the flesh?"

I agreed and said to bring the worker to a separate office. In five minutes, the guards had brought the subject to me. He was wearing an old, scratched armored suit with no helmet. I asked all the guards other than Phobos to leave the room and wait in the hall.

"Phobos, translate for me. Ask this Alpha Iseyek to remove his armored suit. If needed, I'd be happy to help him."

He didn't need any help. The insect unbuttoned the magnetic buttons and carefully lowered the heavy metal plates to the floor. Under them, as I suspected, there was a pair of dark-blue wings folded up.

"Who is that?!" shouted the surprised Clay ton Avelle, who even reached for his laser pistol holster.

"Do not shoot, cap-i-tain. That is Iseyek Prime, male," said Phobos, stating the obvious.

My bodyguard delivered a long trill, and the Iseyek Prime answered him, at first unconfident, but then growing braver with every word. Finally, Phobos turned his body toward me and said:

"He really is Iseyek Prime. But only he is deactivate gene intelligence. Such to be make when birth. Swarm Progenitors to make many experiment with gene of many Iseyek, including they kind, Iseyek Prime."

"Phobos, what do you think, would such a male be acceptable to Swarm Queen Nai Igir? Or should we search for an intact one?"

"My Princcce, thisss one is intact. He is capable of fertilizing a clutch. But don't solve any question. Take decision of leader. He is very much value for Swarm, and Iseyek Prime to give for sssuch male all that Princcce can want."

"Captain Clay ton Avelle, I am taking this one. He is capable of doing more than simply turning bolts and shifting weight loads. Put your armor back on. The secret of the wings is too valuable to tell to everyone we cross path with."

When my soldiers had taken the Iseyek Prime away, I turned to the mothership captain:

"As it turns out, I have promised the Purple House to name one of my fleet's ships 'Joan the Fatty' in honor of the Duke's granddaughter, Joan royl Reyekh. At first, I supposed that my downed flagship from the Sector Eight Fleet would be reborn in the form of a battleship, and I even ordered one for that purpose. But, after touring this carrier, I realized that no other ship could be more worthy of the name 'Joan the Fatty' than this bulbous Swarm mothership. What do you say, captain?"

Clay ton Avelle took a bow and said:

"Crown Prince, it would be a huge honor for me to pilot a ship with the same name as the glorious former Sector Eight flagship."

"That is great, captain. Change the ship's name in all necessary documents. From this moment, the flagship of the Perimeter Sector Eight fleet will once again be *Joan the Fatty*, though to be honest, she's put on some weight."

I was already on a shuttle on its way to the battleship *Princess Astra* when the news about the new flagship reached the Purple House:

**Standing change. Joan royl Reyekh's opinion of you has improved.**
**Presumed personal opinion of you: +27 (friendship)**
**Standing change. Purple House (Empire) opinion of you has improved.**
**Present Purple House (Empire) faction opinion of you: +14 (warm)**

Insofar as I understood, this meant that I had received the highest possible jump in opinion from both the little Crown Princess and the whole faction. But I hadn't been able to enjoy that fact yet before I got a hate-filled letter from my daughter:

"Dad! I'm really mad at you! Joan is being a bitch again, and her and I aren't friends anymore. Why'd you give that fatass such a big ship, but I just got a normal one that you've got a ton of?"

**Standing change. Likanna royl Mesfelle's opinion of you has worsened.**
**Presumed personal opinion of you: +85 (faithful)**

\* \* \*

When we were landing on the planet, two thirds of the interior space in the shuttle was taken up by boxes and baskets of things for my old-new favorite. My only question was how the Veyerdean diplomat had been able to fit all this so neatly into his little ship.

Astra was in quite the elevated mood and was even singing something to herself as she stared at the surface of the endless Unatari ocean we were fast approaching. The girl had a good reason to be proud of herself. The crew of the battleship *Princess Astra* had accepted her with enthusiasm, and an image of the nude green-haired dancing beauty became the official emblem of the combat starship. Astra spent two hours there having her photo taken with anyone who wanted. She was dancing, autographing pictures of herself, and receiving compliments and confessions of love. She was even gifted a five-star admiral's uniform, which she then had to get adjusted to her size, all the while laughing infectiously. I suspect that over the approximately two hours Astra spent talking, she pumped up her personal relationship with all crew members from zero to maximum.

"Over there you can see my island now," I pointed to a small piece of dry land in the purple-blue ocean that stretched out to the horizon. "There are no forms of life dangerous to humans on Unatari, so the sea is at your complete disposal. I have purchased a small pleasure submarine to replace the ones the pirate king's guard hijacked, so tonight after a romantic dinner, we can go out on the open sea and even scuba dive if you want. The bioluminescent seaweed, endless fields of all kinds of amazing shells and corals, flashing transparent fish... Suffice it to say there is something to see."

"I have only swum in an ocean once in my life. On Tesse, near Lika's palace," Astra admitted. "On my homeworld, Veyerde, there is a small Internal Ocean, but it is lifeless and too acidic for humans. The only thing on its shores are boulders and fields of compressed volcanic ash. So, it will all be very interesting for me, but I do ask that you arrange the submarine excursion for before the romantic dinner, so that later I won't have to rush anywhere, and can simply enjoy life."

I couldn't find a reason to object. When the shuttle had set down on the pad before the palace, I pointed my favorite to her room and ordered my servants to carry her things there. I was met in the hall by the blonde Bionica and carefully inquired whether it was Bionica herself or the Arite.

"The Arite," she said, turning into a ship technical worker for a second, before returning to the form of my secretary. "Popori de Cacha and her subordinates are still working on Bionica. Copying all the android's files and calibrating her systems takes a long time.

At that moment, Astra showed up in the corridor, already having managed to change into her swimsuit. After seeing the Arite, the girl gave a shout of joy and threw herself to embrace it:

"Bionica, I'm so happy to see you back in your normal body! We're going for a trip on the submarine right now. Come with us!"

Confused at such a stormy confession of emotion, the Arite shot me a sideways glance, clearly asking for my advice on what was happening. I gave a barely perceptible nod in response.

"Astra! I'm so glad you came back to us! I need five minutes to get dressed and I'll be ready."

I couldn't detect even the slightest trace of artificiality or overacting in Bionica's behavior. The Arite had learned very quickly and, I suppose, could already exist in human society without giving itself away at all. After a quick change of clothes, I started making my way down to the bay accompanied by the green-haired Astra and the Arite mimicking the synthetic blonde. The small silver pleasure submarine was already waiting for us. Two crew members I didn't recognize in Orange House uniforms were standing near the ramp.

"Welcome to your submarine, Prince Georg," the tall man with old-fashioned mutton chops pointed me to an open hatch invitingly. "Come into the central hall. From there, you'll get the best view of the underwater scenery. Would you like me to serve you some wine?"

I nodded "yes" and went down a very steep stairwell into the submarine below and... stopped sharply as the barrel of a sawed-off assault rifle poked into my chest. Bionica and Astra, standing nearby in fear, stretched their hands to the sky.

"So we meet again, Crown Prince," a strangely familiar voice rang out from behind my back.

I turned sharply. The man with mutton chops started tearing a thin latex mask off his face with obvious strain. Under it was Velesh the First, Pirate King of Unatari, still on the run from the law. Just then, his assistant closed the heavy metal door and said, turning to his capo:

"Captain, we should get out of here fast before the routine patrol discovers the corpses and deactivated security systems."

Velesh the First took a look at the screen of his communicator and said with a self-satisfied look:

"We've got time. There's still another two and a half minutes. Our ship will leave the lagoon and be hidden in the depths of the ocean before anyone even notices."

**\* \* \***

"So, that's the story, Crown Prince..." Velesh the First ended his long story about how he had been able to escape detection with the help of old friends, how he had gone from city to city, and star system to star system, changing names and documents along the way, as well as getting plastic surgery done, and ordering different masks. "You ruined my life, and I am simply returning the favor. An authorized representative has already gotten in touch with the Orange House Head and told him about my valuable bounty. Duke Paolo is thirsting to have your Highness in his capital as quickly as possible. All the same, we are in no rush to be guests of the Orange House Head. First, we need to get ready to make sure we don't get caught by customs when flying out of Unatari. So, you and your charming companions will be spending the next couple of days under lock and key in my underwater lair."

Velesh suddenly laughed an unpleasant overacted "movie villain" laugh.

"To be honest, I expected more from you, Crown Prince! The cops here were never the sharpest knives in the drawer, even when they were serving me, but now under a Prince and heir to the Emperor's throne with unlimited abilities... How could they have let me leave the spaceport here on the very day of your coronation on Unatari?! Why didn't anyone check the underground freight lines?! How could you hire people for a merchant fleet without a full background check?! It wasn't at all difficult for me to disappear in peace after getting to Tesse on a fake document saying I worked as an assistant on a superfreighter. To be honest, I was fully convinced that it was some kind of power play. I was being released on purpose in order to capture me later in a more grandiose fashion. But no, I was simply let go. And that was why I decided to return to Unatari, as such a slovenly security service deserves to be punished."

"So then, maybe you'll let this all go like a normal person? I'll give you full amnesty and make you leader of the planet's police force or whatever you want," I offered, dropping a hint, but Velesh shook his head no:

"No, it's too late, Crown Prince. Even yesterday I might have agreed. But not today. There's no reason to negotiate with you. Duke Paolo will still give me much more, no matter how much your Highness might offer. Also, it's a matter of principle and revenge."

I was sitting on a chair with my hands bound behind my back. The kidnappers did not tie Astra or Bionica's hands, though they did have a gun trained on them. Velesh the First was strolling nervously about the hall, turning around sharply and darting from one end to the other and back.

"No, I cannot understand," the pirate began airing his grievances once again. "How could you not have stopped to think where the hijacked submarine had gone? So much time had passed, and it still hadn't shown up in any port. It can't have been so hard to figure out that there was a secret base, right? And where could you hide a base on a planet such as Unatari? Only underwater or in the spacious caves under the islands. I ordered three storage facilities and laboratories that were in such caves evacuated, but no one even came looking for them! How is that possible?! My companion Janis the First was discovered by beachcombers near the entrance to that very underwater lair. The police shot him down, the unlucky bastard, but no one, I repeat, NO ONE, questioned the fact that a Pirate King just happened to be walking around on a tiny, uninhabited island! The place he died was no more than 200 feet from the entrance to an underwater crystal lab. But the police weren't smart enough to find it!!! Tomorrow before noon, we will be arriving to that very laboratory, and your Highness can see for himself all the amenities the underwater base has to offer. And for now, just relax. The road ahead is still quite long."

The pirate captain ordered his guards to lead the captives into a lock-up accommodation at the stern of the submarine. They started to push me there as well after finally removing my handcuffs. When the door closed noiselessly, the Arite sitting next to me whispered:

"I could leave through the ventilation or the crack

under the door and take the form of any of the guards. But the pirates are all armed. I cannot copy weapons, so that may arouse suspicion. And their blasters and laser rifles are capable of harming me."

I thought over the Arite's proposition, but refused all the same:

"No, there's no reason to take that risk for now. I've got another way of getting us out of here in view, I just need to think it all out really well."

My way of getting out was Miya. The most powerful Truth Seeker had said that I could call her into the game. It may seem that one pregnant lady wouldn't be able to do much against six armed killers... But, in specifically Miya's case, I had no doubt whatsoever in her ability to deal with the pirates. The only thing holding me back was the fact that Astra was also in the room. It wouldn't be hard to imagine that Miya wouldn't like that, especially if the Truth Seeker were to uncover my favorite's pregnancy. Yes, Florianna had assured me that Miya was incapable of going against the will of her master, but all the same...

We sat in silence for another half hour. The tiny room was no larger than the end compartment of a train and contained two fold-out cots, a folding table, and a bright lamp on the table. Finally, Astra broke the silence:

"My sister Florianna has had the ability to find me since her early childhood. So, Flora will find us soon!"

I thought on the girl's words and shook my head in doubt:

"Flora went into a crystal sleep only today. For the next three or four days, your sister will be inactive. In that time, they will be able to take us off the planet.

Alright, I'll have to risk it..."

I closed my eyes and decided to call Miya in any case. I had no idea how to actually call the Truth Seeker in the game from a technical standpoint, but I decided to try a few methods.

*"Miya, I need you now!!!"* I mentally called.

"Finally! I was already starting to think you had forgotten about my request." At first, I thought the voice was in my head, but a second later I realized that the person talking to me was a big-bellied lady sitting on the bunk opposite mine in a bright red, free-flowing dress.

Miya?! It was that easy? I suspect that at that moment I had an impossibly stupid and surprised look on my face, as the Truth Seeker started laughing in delight:

"All you had to do was call. All the rest of the work I did on my own, and believe you me, it was no small feat."

The woman with a huge belly stood up with difficulty from the cot and looked around the small room with measured curiosity. It was just then that I noticed that Miya was barefoot.

"Prince Georg, who is she and how did she get here?" Astra asked, with notes of hysteria in her voice.

Ugh. I wish my favorite had kept quiet... Miya stopped looking at the metallic walls and slowly turned toward the girls, who were sitting with their legs on the bed. I saw the Truth Seeker's eyebrows shoot up in surprise when she saw the Arite in Bionica's form. For no less than a minute, Miya looked at the interplanetary being before moving her gaze to Astra.

"Now that's a surprise..." the Truth Seeker even got a bit lost herself, having managed to read the information in the space of a few moments and see who exactly it was before her. Miya turned toward me. The expression on her face was one of extreme displeasure, looking menacing:

"Georg, have you lost your mind? Have you forgotten our contract? It was written there in black and white: no children, not with Marta, and especially no bastards! It looks like you've created another problem I'll have to deal with on my own..."

The Truth Seeker cracked her fingers, flexed them with a snap, and turned to my favorite. I realized that if I didn't interfere right away, something terrible and irreversible would happen. The only thing I could do was hope that Florianna hadn't been wrong about Miya.

"Miya, stop! Don't you dare touch Astra, that is an order!" I screamed and, jumping up from the bed, grabbed the Truth Seeker by the shoulders and turned her toward me.

Miya's eyes were burning with a rabid flame. The metal walls began resonating from the sound of her voice.

"How dare you stop me! Have you lost all fear?!"

I looked Miya right in the eyes and understood clearly that I was staring Death herself in the face. All the same, it was too late to take it back.

"You dare raise your voice to your master?!" I tried to copy the intonation I heard in the Truth Seeker's voice. "On your knees, scum!!!"

The lightbulbs in the small room began flickering. The air started spinning in electric sparks. I even heard some small explosions. In the dark gray murk that had begun to descend on me, Miya's eyes shone back like two orange demonic bonfires. Their flames were at once alluring and terrifying. You either wanted to bow before her unlimited power, or run without looking back. I felt a heaviness that threw me to the ground. With every passing second it became harder to resist. And suddenly, it all passed at once. The lights returned to normal, the heaviness fear and strain all disappeared at once. Miya, kneeling on the cold metal floor, was touching my hands with her forehead:

"Forgive me, master. Your faithful servant forgot her place," babbled the bowing beautiful woman with bright crimson hair in an apologetic tone.

At the same time, I heard a soul-chilling voice in my brain:

*"Ruslan, you have just signed your own death warrant. And I don't give a damn what Georgiy says about it. You will die right after your contract is up, that is my promise to you as a Truth Seeker!"*

The thought flashed by that I should force Miya to swear an oath that she would not harm me. All the same I did not manage to bring that worldly thought to action, as Miya had already answered:

*"That is utterly useless, Ruslan. Here in the world of* Perimeter Defense, *I was in no way thinking of touching you. I really cannot bring harm to you. I do not know who told you that secret, but I assure you that person is already as good as dead. But then, everything outside the* Perimeter Defense *world, my oath would have no bearing over. That's why you'll die as soon as you leave the game."*

"I very much recommend against rushing into making those kinds of promises, Miya. I would be very surprised if you could survive even a month without me!" I said out loud.

"Alright, we'll see," the Truth Seeker agreed, standing from her knees with obvious strain. "If only you knew, Georg, what kind of bloody rage is boiling in me! I'm gonna have to kill someone now! Maybe it won't be this pregnant dummy, but at least someone!"

"So then, why is this an issue?" I pointed at the locked door. "On the other side of that door are six armed pirates that have captured me and my people. Miya, they're all yours. Do with them as you wish, but please leave just the one who can help bring the submarine back to port."

The Truth Seeker laughed an evil laugh, throwing her long hair back and cracking her fingers as she said:

"You three stay here. There's no reason for you to see what's about to happen on this submarine."

Miya went up to the metal doors and put her palm on the lock. I heard a gnash and a snap as if something had just broken inside the thick armored doors. With a terrifying tooth-chattering shriek the four-inch-thick door opened, letting the red-headed beauty out, before it closed again right behind her.

"Can you drive the submarine?" I could hear the Truth Seeker's muffled question through the wall.

The guard's answer, I could not. All the same, I suspect that it was a no, given that I could hear a scream of pain and fear. Shots thundered out. The shooting, swearing and yelping continued for two minutes, at which point everything suddenly grew quiet. The doors screeched open once again, and Miya came into the cabin holding Velesh the First's decapitated head.

"Georg, why did you lie to me that there were only six pirates?" the Truth Seeker said with reproach. "There were fourteen! One recognized me and screamed that there was a huge price on his head," the woman said, pointing to the ghastly trophy. "Only he managed to surrender, but while that was stopping me... another remained alive after the slaughter. He'll take the submarine wherever you want."

The Truth Seeker flung the pirate captain's head under my favorite's legs. Astra immediately doubled over to vomit. Miya, clearly pleased with the effect it had had on her rival, commented with a sideways evil grin on her face:

"Still a snot-nosed punk, and yet you crawl into politics... Very well then. I can let you go, just this one time and as a very big favor to the Crown Prince. But if you ever cross my path again, there will be no more quarter. Do you understand?"

Astra gave a very fast nod, after which the former Princess vomited again. Miya frowned in disgust and left the room. I followed after her.

The inside of the submarine looked like something between a slaughterhouse and a horror movie set. Dead bodies, bullet holes on the walls. There was even blood spatter on the ceiling. The Truth Seeker walked to the dirtiest part of the large hall and sat down in the chair with strain.

"Georg, I barely had enough power to finish them off," Miya admitted, inviting me to take a seat next to her.

Now, the person in front of me was a normal woman in the late stages of pregnancy. Awkward, vulnerable and very tired from the constant burden.

"I need crystals very badly. You promised to get them. Where are my crystals?"

"Well, as luck would have it, the submarine is on its way to a secret underwater crystal lab," I said, quickly finding my place. "We'll be at the base in a few hours, and you can take as many crystals as you can carry."

"You are telling me, an official Mystic from the list confirmed by the Emperor himself, to make do with the crap those illegal drug traders produce?" Miya flared up artificially.

All the same, the glint that appeared in her eyes gave away the mystic's craving for crystals, and she knew it.

"Alright, I agree. Ask this strange being to prepare dinner. And tell your girl that there is a normal bedroom here too. Let her go there. There's no reason for her to sit in such an unbearable atmosphere."

It was a crazy dinner, so much so that it would make tea-time with the Mad Hatter seem like the very height of normalcy. Miya and I were sitting at a small circular table in the central hall of the submarine. We were drinking some wine that the Alien creature had warmed up, and eating something I didn't recognize that pseudo-Bionica had managed to prepare from what she could find on the submarine. There were dead bodies lying all around, and the floor was slippery from all the spilled blood, despite all that, we did our best not to focus on the mess and had a completely peaceful conversation. An outside observer would never have guessed that it was between a ghoulish woman murderer and her future victim.

Astra absolutely refused to go into the bedroom and fell asleep with her head on my knee. Miya, at least externally, had lost all interest in my favorite and was making a show of not noticing the sleeping girl.

"I haven't seen my employer in quite some time. Usually Mr. G. I. isn't gone for so long," I said, finding a new topic for conversation.

"He broke his collar bone. He was fighting in a bar with some biker and had an unlucky fall on a bar stool. Now he's sitting at home trying to drown out his mental and physical scars with alcohol."

"He always had the pair of bodyguards with him," I said in surprise, remembering the morning I signed my contract. "How did they let that happen?"

The pregnant woman shrugged her shoulders:

"I don't know. You should have a better idea than I do. As an Imperial Crown Prince, you have the same bodyguards, yet your face is covered in fresh scars... By the way, you disfigured the body of my future husband!"

I guffawed, as I could sense that her grievances were totally contrived.

"It's almost already back to normal. You should have seen me a day after the Alien battleship explosion. I was lucky not to have lost an eye! And as for the body, you couldn't be more wrong. I'm even taking very good care of it. On my first day in the game, it was even hard for me to walk. My gut would swing around, practically banging on my knees when I walked. I couldn't go five steps without a breather. My legs hurt like a bitch. My blood pressure jumped all around. Every time I would take off or land on a shuttle, I practically died. But, over these five months, I've lost eighty pounds, built muscle mass in the gym, and I can swim a kilometer without a break. I can almost already do a pull up!"

Miya looked at me as if for the first time, somehow smiling mysteriously as she took a small gulp of wine from her glass.

"No one asked you to change the Crown Prince's lifestyle, Ruslan. These aren't just pluses. They do have their downsides, but thank you all the same. You've done your main mission: you held off the Alien attack, you got the Sector Eight Fleet in shape, and also got him sorted out financially... You have done even more than we were expecting you to. I admit, I didn't believe right away how powerful the glow of glory and admiration surrounding you had become. I couldn't hold back from such a rare delicacy and drank all that power to the last drop. I'm still drunk on the energy overload. I haven't had the like in thirty years, and maybe longer. I must thank you."

"Think nothing of it. The paralyzed Flora has often admitted that she feels a stream of power after serious victories and nourishes herself on them."

"Yes, that is precisely why the girl is progressing so quickly. But she also understands that as soon as your contract is up, there will be no more victories. She fears for the future. I can sense it. By the way, on the subject of deadlines, you started that conflict with the Duke to no avail. Mr. G.I. is no soldier and will not be able to handle it himself, so you must solve the problem before the end of your contract. I am prepared to help you in this matter. I cannot simply kill Paolo royl Anjer for a whole number of reasons. But now I am full of power and capable of a lot. Tell me, what do you need to win?"

Geez! The most powerful Miya was offering to help me! This was a once in a lifetime chance! What did I really need? I thought for some time. There were too many wishes to sort through. Finally, I singled one out and said what I considered the most necessary:

"Miya, I need the Orange House Capital warp beacon turned on in a month, just for a couple seconds."

The Truth Seeker laughed in response:

"Alright. I don't yet know how, but I'll make that happen for you."

# Taking Down the Boss

T HE SHEER ENORMITY of the Sector Eight Fleet's new flagship allowed me to not have to think about being economical with interior space. I suppose that only the yacht *Queen of Sin* could compare with *Joan the Fatty* in terms of comfort. There were gyms, pools, entertainment centers and spacious greenhouses for the crew members to psychologically decompress. There were ultramodern medical centers, comfortable bedrooms and a great deal of dining rooms. There was even a zoo on board with exotic creatures from dozens of worlds. Yes, the complete overhaul and updating of the *Uukresh* had forced me to spend a nine-figure sum, but all the expenses had been worth it, in that I had succeeded in adapting another species' starship to allow the mixed human and Iseyek crew to co-inhabit for a prolonged period.

All the same, despite the comfort, the flagship remained above all else a combat ship. There were huge data screens in the fleet headquarters, a surprisingly detailed holographic tactical map and a projection of the current star system the size of a five-story building, all of which allowed me to see everything on the battlefield and around it in detail. The staff officers needed almost two weeks to stop gasping in delight every time they sat down at their console.

"All ships, at the ready in five minutes! Begin acceleration toward the Orange House Capital. We expect the warp beacon to be turned on," I was behind the huge semicircular console, somewhat reminiscent of Savasss Jach's workstation.

"And the observer? Maybe shoot it down anyway?" Space Captain Nicole Savoia said, expressing uncharacteristic bloodthirstiness today.

A suspicious container ship had been circling not far from the Sector Eight Fleet in the Tesse system for two days already. My ships would regularly report that the freighter was scanning them for different things, determining energy shield capacity, nuclear arsenal, and other combat characteristics. Of course, we could destroy the spy ship, but why?

"No, let it keep sending its data. Duke Paolo royl Anjer should see that my fleet in Tesse has just five hundred ships. That is very important. If our enemies from the United Fleet are not convinced that they still have a four-to-one advantage, they might flee before we get there. I'm pretty worried for our enemy's psychological condition when they see the unknown beacon pop up in their capital system..."

Nicole laughed. The Alien cloaked ship capable of installing mobile warp beacons was a military secret. I'm not sure if Miya had fulfilled her promise that way, or the scientists on Unatari had really made a real breakthrough, but my specialists were able to figure out the main systems of the Alien frigate. Getting the cloaker into the Orange House Capital turned out to be a not-at-all-trivial mission. The beacon was turned off practically all the time. But we were also able to overcome that problem. When my "crystal balls" on enemy territory discovered reinforcements for the United Fleet in the Varan system preparing to leave: five light cruisers, six destroyers and around forty frigates. The Orange House beacon blinked on for just half a second, but that was all my soldiers needed to get the warp-beacon carrier into the enemy lair.

"Call Crown Prince Roben royl Inoky ton Mesfelle," I demanded from the communications officer, and ten seconds later, my brother appeared on screen.

The huge Roben was sitting right on the grass in a light, free-flowing robe. Next to the big corpulent man on the blanket, lying on a bunch of pillows, the little smiling Georg was flexing his legs.

"I knew you'd want to talk, brother dear. And that was why I ordered a portable screen brought out to the glade here, so I could tell you my answer right now: no! My decision is firm as ever. The Tesse Fleet will maintain neutrality and will not take part in the battle, neither as part of the United Fleet of Duke Paolo, nor on your side."

"The Tesse Ships would be a great help to me, brother..." I said, making my final attempt to convince Roben, but he remained uncompromising.

"No, and don't keep asking, Georg. My decision is firm to stay on the sidelines of all this squabbling. Understand me: my conscience won't let me go against my brother. But elementary caution won't let me join your side either: supporting someone with a more than one-to-four ship disadvantage doesn't look like a good investment in a peaceful future to me. I already almost left my son fatherless when I helped you financially, arousing the Orange House Head's unhappiness. I am not preparing to repeat that horror again."

I shook my head in reproach. I had a whole bunch of arguments on the tip of my tongue, but I didn't tell them to him, for some reason knowing already that none of my reasons would work, and I would never convince my brother. Crown Prince Roben royl Inoky had made a serious political error with his inaction, and I also had no doubt in that. The new head of the Orange House, whoever that may be after the fall of Duke Paolo, would hardly be likely to have a positive view of the ruler of Tesse's inaction at a time when many aristocrats had helped him get on the throne. And also, my sister Violetta would definitely view my older brother's neutrality as a sign that he is unreliable and would return to his scheming. But I also didn't reveal these arguments, and signed off.

"The Sector Eight Fleet is ready for attack. The ships are ready to warp, waiting for the beacon," reported Admiral Kiro Sabuto.

"All ships in the Docks are also accelerating toward the Orange House Capital and are ready to jump to the beacon when it appears," my assistant Nicole Savoia pledged.

The second fleet, which had managed to sneak by unnoticed by the Orange House Head's observer and get to the Docks, was my trump card. Even Count

Avalle, who had promised to join my side immediately before the general battle, didn't know about the Sector Eight Fleet's backup ships. I didn't have much faith in the Count. He was clearly trying to sit in two chairs at the same time, and would only make his choice in favor of the stronger side at the last possible moment.

I definitely knew from several independent sources that the Orange House Head's security service had been searching very actively for which of the aristocrats I had given the four remaining Emerald Stars to. The Duke's bogeymen had subjected all United Fleet captains to lie detector and Truth Seeker testing for possible collaboration with Crown Prince Georg and the possession of an Emerald Star. The only way Duke Paolo royl Anjer could have known about my giving out the medals was from his younger brother, which characterized my ally as extremely unreliable. Fortunately, Count Avalle had interpreted my words wrong, so the spooks were looking in the wrong place, and the true recipients of the four Emerald Stars had still managed to avoid suspicion.

"New warp beacon detected!" several staff officers' voices rang out at once.

"Nonstandard indicators. It's something strange!"

"Beacon located. It's the Orange House."

It worked! I felt like a weight had been lifted from my shoulders. The step of opening the new portal to the blocked system was the most difficult part of the whole operation. We had only run through warp beacon opening scenarios one time in training in the little-visited Sigur system. We figured out that opening a hole in space and keeping it there required a huge amount of rare radioactive isotopes.

Fortunately, I had the Tivalle system at my disposal with its ice asteroid fields, so we could collect the materials we needed.

"Attention Sector Eight Fleet and allies! Enter new beacon coordinates, set warp tunnel exit point at three hundred miles back. I'm waiting for Admiral Kheraisss Vej to confirm."

"My Princcce, all Swarm ship is to understand order and to be ready!"

"Excellent. Send a message to the cloaker: turn off the beacon in thirty seconds and leave! All ships, fifteen seconds to warp! Nicole, countdown! WARP!!!"

It seemed simply impossible, but my ships didn't find anyone there when we arrived to the Orange House Capital system! I was expecting to see the terrifying United Fleet when I came out of the warp tunnel at a short distance, and was psychologically prepared for the battle to begin immediately. But my enemies hadn't noticed the beacon in their system!

"My Prince, this is Major Mike Geroni, captain of the *Portal*. In accordance with you order, we put out the beacon and went invisible. We're at three hundred miles from your Highness's fleet."

"Tuki-tuka-de-sa, this is the captain of *Surprise-1*. My bomber division has been waiting six hours at full preparedness, but the United Fleet has not shown up in the area of the flashing warp beacon."

I turned to my assistant, Nicole Savoia in confusion.

"I don't understand a thing... The beacon was on

for almost a minute and a half, but none of Duke Paolo's ships came to destroy the Alien ship!"

The space captain smiled happily:

"Your Highness, you and I know that the Alien warp beacon frigate is fragile, and should be shot down immediately. But the United Fleet's admirals, I suppose, are still in shock from seeing an Alien starship in the Orange House Capital."

Our conversation was interrupted by a message from the communications officer:

"My Prince, incoming call from Duke Paolo. The signal is coming from this system, most likely the battleship *Orange Majesty.*"

"Alright, put him through. Let's see what the Orange House Head has to tell us."

However, instead of Duke Paolo royl Anjer, who I was expecting to see, an unfamiliar, middle-aged woman with a black robe and a hood thrown back appeared on screen. She had dark hair with a touch of gray, proper facial features, and was wearing no makeup. The woman met with my gaze, smiled in happiness, stretched her right pointer finger out at me and said in a tranquil tone:

"Die!"

*"My Prince, you are under attack by Selena ton Bist, Duke Paolo's Truth Seeker! I have taken the strike with my body!"* Despair and pain came through in the message sent by Florianna.

"Turn the screen off now!" I ordered, but the officer who ran in hesitated for some reason.

"It's useless, Crown Prince," the woman on screen smiled again. "The line is open. You have received my greeting, and now the result is in no way dependent on the monitor being intact. As soon as the little Truth Seeker grows weak, you will die. And so your little girl won't suffer any illusions, I'll show you the real balance of power.

At the very bottom of the small screen, seven additional windows opened in a row, and each of them containing the strained face of a different Truth Seeker. All the women were in identical dark clothing and I didn't recognize them... However... Marian Sabati, Count Avalle's ghoulish Truth Seeker I did recognize.

*"They are all attacking together! It is very hard for me, Georg! I can't hold out much longer!"* I heard clear panic in the paralyzed girl's thoughts.

One of Florianna's minions gave a sharp creak of pain and collapsed onto his back, appendages twitching. Just three Beta Iseyek remained around the flying chair. The insects placed their many hands on the little paralyzed girl, causing them to shake in perfect synchronization. Florianna needed help, but how?!

The red-headed Bionica, serving in my headquarters as a second translator together with the real Bionica, suddenly stood from her place and went to Flora's room, changing shape along the way. In two steps the Arite already looked like the red-headed Miya, and took a few heavy steps toward my Truth Seeker. The arrival of a new participant was immediately apparent, though the slight confusion in the ranks of the enemy lasted just a bit longer than a second.

"Very funny," Selena ton Bist waved her hand carelessly, and the Arite dissolved into a whitish cloud before trailing off in a long line into the ventilation.

*"Miya, I need you right now!!!"* I thought, calling her mentally, all the while watching the Arite's strained escape attempt: my bodiless acquaintance was rushing to hide from the Truth Seekers' rage.

The new participant's arrival I first heard, and only later saw. But first I noticed that all the noise in the room immediately ceased. The officers in the headquarters went silent at once. Even the instruments started buzzing more quietly, and the light in the room dimmed noticeably. I saw Nicole Savoia's eyes grow wide, having seen something scary behind me, and I turned sharply.

Miya was walking unhurriedly between the staff officers' work stations. The Truth Seeker was wearing a long crimson robe that went down to the floor this time. On her head, a hood was obscuring the pregnant woman's red hair. Miya came out into the middle of the hall, stopping three steps from Florianna's chair and said, looking at the big screen with eight enemies.

"So then. I recognize all these faces. The party's at full swing, but no one invited me. That's not very polite..."

It was as if Miya was smiling and joking, but the sound of her voice made your hair stand on end, and gave you the feeling of ants crawling on your skin. I noticed a dribbling sound coming from Florianna's flying chair onto the floor. The paralyzed girl, who had been fighting bravely against eight more experienced enemies bravely until that point, suddenly panicked at the sight of her tormentor. Miya turned to the girl she had paralyzed and said:

"Don't worry, little girl. I'm not here for your soul today. We're even going to have to spend some time side by side... By the way, dummy, what are you doing?! Why are you letting all the pain go to you? Give it to others! Not me, bird brains! Just others."

"I pass!" Count Avalle's Truth Seeker suddenly declared, and one of the windows went dark.

And suddenly, I stopped caring about the screen of enemies. I was struck by such pain that I wanted to howl and climb up the walls. It felt like my skeleton was being ripped right out of my body.

*"Sorry, Prince Georg. There just wasn't anyone else to give my pain too. I am only connected to you, my sister and your main Truth Seeker. Astra is too far away, and I cannot share my sensations with her."*

"No problem, I'll deal with it," I squeaked out, trying not to lose consciousness and fall on the floor.

"The Crown Prince needs your help!" Miya explained to the officers, worked up by what was happening. "The enemy Truth Seekers are attacking Prince Georg royl Inoky. The commander needs your support, your respect, your love."

"Georg! Georg! Georg!" The team began chanting in unison.

At the same time, Miya's cold voice rang out in my head:

*"Ruslan, hold on, it's about to get easier. Share your pain with your subjects. There's thirty people in this room, so you can totally rid yourself of all unpleasant sensations. And even if one of your subjects doesn't survive, it's no tragedy. I sense that the attack's intensity has already begun to fall."*

"No, that's not right, Miya!" I said decisively,

standing to my feet. "Get me a direct broadcast immediately to the whole Sector Eight Fleet!"

The cameras had just managed to turn on when I began speaking into the microphone. At first, it was hard to move my lips, as I had bit them until they bled, but then the consternation and pain began to pass gradually. I told my captains about the depraved attack, and about how little Florianna had held it off all on her own. And how Miya had come to the rescue just in time. How seven frightening enemy Truth Seekers were now working together, stretching their abilities for all they were worth, but could not do anything. I said with a confident smile that our enemies had made a miscalculation. Crown Prince Georg royl Inoky had better defense than any armored suit or energy shield could provide: the adoration of the Sector Eight Fleet. And the pain being sent could be shared between tens of thousands of crew members and wouldn't be felt at all.

"My Prince, add four hundred thousand Alpha Iseyek from the *Tria* to your calculations. My assault troops are used to bearing any pain and are also prepared to die for you," Bionica said, translating General Savasss Jach's trill that had interrupted my speech.

*"Our enemies have begun to weaken. The intensity of the attack is on the decline,"* Florianna reported, already completely coming back to and radiating confidence.

Miya did not agree with Flora:

*"Little one, you give in too early. I sense that the Crown Prince's mental block has been broken. Our enemies may read something from Ruslan's memory,*

*and that is not permissible. As such, we cannot allow any of the seven to get out alive. And when the Truth Seekers figure out that the jokes are over, and this battle is to the death, they will fight with extra abandon. For now, we're just grinding them down. Let them think that they're just attacking me, you and your overgrown cockroaches. And as soon as I gather the energy, we'll go on the counter attack. I'll teach you to kill properly."*

"My Prince, the United Fleet's starships have started showing up on our radar systems! They're getting closer! A huge number of markers!"

Oh well, it was unavoidable. My ships' coordinates had been calculated, and Duke Paolo had thrown his armada into battle, wishing to take us down in one fell swoop. I glanced at the timer. There were fourteen minutes left until the reinforcements from the Docks would arrive. I just needed to hold out. I readjusted the microphone on my uniform, and said:

"All ships, attention! Begin acceleration toward the sun. Realign into battle formation. Heavy guns and *Tria*, stay by *Joan the Fatty*. Light cruisers and electros, at the ready. Let's see where the enemy comes out of warp and choose our formation based on that. Frigates and destroyers, hold course forward. Keep two hundred in front of the flagship."

The fleet began maneuvers. The ships realigned and started accelerating toward the local star. Suddenly, the tactical map grid took on a red color. The United Fleet came out of warp near us in several long hot dog shapes, clearly having set prewarp from different directions.

"Multiple targets. Two thousand four hundred

thirty marks. One hundred miles to the nearest group. The enemy has a total of forty-four battleships on the battle field, and one hundred ninety heavy cruisers..."

"My Prince, incoming call from the heavy assault cruiser *Marta the Harlot*," the communications officer interrupted the tactician's report.

What I wanted to do was sharply object to my subject's very untimely message, however, the ship's familiar name stopped me. *Princess Marta* appeared on screen, though I hardly recognized my own wife. In the last months, she had clearly gotten some work done on her face, and also intensively worked on her figure, losing a few spare pounds and turning her somewhat horrific hippo's body into a much more presentable one. No, Marta hadn't become skinny, but now her body's slight plumpness and roundness looked natural and even pleasing to the eye.

"Georg, please show my ships their place in formation," Marta requested.

What is this: enemy trickery or an honest desire to help? Should I give the exact coordinates of my fleet to ships in the United Fleet? The risk was huge as, in the case of error, I would have two thousand enemy ships prewarping "to zero" and a fast battle. On the other hand, what if Marta really did want to support her husband in this general battle? To believe or not to believe? Looking for a hint, I glanced at Miya and Flora, but they were clearly not thinking about me at that moment: the battle was raging with a renewed fury between the nine Truth Seekers. I would have to solve the dilemma myself, so I risked it:

"Admiral Kiro Sabuto, accept the Kingdom of Fastel

ships, give them coordinates for prewarp, communications passwords, and show them their positions in formation.

On the tactical map, fifty red dots jumped right into the middle of the green ball and instantly turned to green. I waited in anticipation of what would come next, but nothing bad happened. The coordinate data did not leak out to the enemy.

"Heavy cruisers *Marta the Harlot*, *Fastel Hero*, and *King Valesy*, hold tight on the edge, 30 miles from *Joan the Fatty*. And also, Marta, thank you!"

"There's a group of enemy ships right in our fleet's path!" Nicole Savoia pointed out, and I also saw it myself.

Around sixty fast frigates and destroyers from the United Fleet were outstripping the Perimeter Sector Eight Fleet and were now on in my ships' path. Of course, I could send out my frigates and destroyers to mop up the path for the heavy cruisers. But the main difficulty was in the fact that Duke Paolo's other ships could warp out to the small group of starships at any moment. Exchanging fire with such an obvious numbers advantage and the enemy having more reserves was not at all in my interest. Though, there was no reason to rush...

"Attention, all ships! *Joan the Fatty* is to stop. All the other ships are to take an orbit around the flagship. Destroyers, on high alert! An attack on our fleet by enemy stealth bombers is possible."

* * *

Time passed, and nothing changed. The Sector Eight Fleet now looked like a swarming bait ball or a curled-up hedgehog. The enemy's many ships were circling at an unreachable distance, still not risking approaching. Earlier, some excessively self-confident cruisers and destroyers of the United Fleet had been turned into a collection picturesque fragments. That was what happened to the Duke's stealth bomber division, for example, which was completely wiped out together with the bombs it released. But the most illustrative example was the enemy *Varan* battleship's attempt to get into firing distance. My fleet released four thousand drones at once, and the enemy battleship was no more. No shield recharging from any number of *Surgeons* could have saved them. By the way, the remains of twenty-five *Surgeons*, bitten down by the drones, made a harmonious addition to the huge remains of the exploded battleship.

After that, the enemy starships stopped making active attempts to approach my fleet. No one was in a rush to end up the same as their fallen comrades. I was also not rushing the events, drinking vitamin-enriched energy drink to restore my strength and looking from time to time at the countdown. There were just a few minutes left until our reserves showed up. The battle, de facto, had already been won by the Sector Eight Fleet, though our enemy had yet to suspect as much. I took another look at the time, and decisively swigged the drink down. It's time! This war in the Orange House needed not only to be won, but to be won with style!

"Connect me with Duke Paolo royl Anjer," I demanded to the officer.

No less than a minute went by before the head of the Orange House appeared on screen. The Duke was trying to put on a brave face, and had clearly just been using the services of a make-up artist, but I still saw that the man before me was old and extremely tired.

"I've been expecting your call, Georg!" the old man on screen smiled. "The Sector Eight Fleet has wandered right into the dragon's den, but clearly didn't know our forces. Your ships are surrounded and doomed. I have retransmitted our conversation to all ships in the United Fleet just for the occasion, so all of the Orange House crews could be witness to your capitulation."

"Excellent, Duke Paolo. Now that our conversation has become public property I, as Imperial Crown Prince and Perimeter Sector Eight Fleet Commander, officially suggest that you surrender."

"What???" on my last words, the self-satisfied smile crawled off the Orange House Head's face. He was clearly counting on the exact opposite ending to my sentence.

"I repeat my words once again. Give in or be annihilated! Duke, you have blackened your name with many dirty deeds: embezzlement, blackmail, forgery, extortion, threatening to kill Crown Prince Roben royl Inoky, and repeated attempts to kill two other Crown Princes: Georg royl Roben ton Mesfelle, and Georg royl Inoky ton Mesfelle. Also, you betrayed the Orange House by signing a treaty with the Swarm to destroy the Perimeter Sector Eight Fleet..."

Miya appeared behind my back, and walked on screen, speaking into the camera with her one-of-a-kind icy voice:

"I officially affirm the truth of each of the accusations made by Crown Prince Georg royl Inoky ton Mesfelle. I swear on my abilities as a Truth Seeker, that everything he said is accurate!"

Miya looked spectacular and convincing, but the Head of the Orange House objected with his creaking old-man's voice:

"Georg, you cannot call your own Truth Seeker as a witness. She is too dependent on you and would say anything you order! I could just as easily call Selena ton Bist, and she would say the exact opposite!"

"No, Paolo, I'm afraid that would not be possible," Miya smiled, demonstrating her flawless white teeth. "Selena ton Bist is dead, as are all the other Truth Seekers you poisoned against my master."

I turned the camera back on myself and continued my speech:

"Duke, you scoundrel, you have earned yourself the harshest of punishments. But you could at least have the decency to spare the lives of your loyal fleet. After all, it isn't their fault that they joined the wrong side in the Orange House conflict. Your fleet is doomed, but I will give the United Fleet's ships one minute to give up and save their own lives."

Duke Paolo looked somewhere past the cameras in surprise, clarifying something from someone off camera, and gave a powerful laugh:

"That is a bluff! I still have four times as many ships as you! The United Fleet is strong and will be able to wipe your ships out without even noticing!

Georg, your attempts to win over my people have failed. No one has joined your side!"

"Are you sure about that, Duke?"

I looked at the timer. Eleven seconds until my ships showed up. Everything had come together perfectly!

"Well, I'm sorry to be the one to disenchant you, Duke Paolo. I don't know who your security service caught, but now it's time to meet the people who really did come over to my side. The Perimeter Sector Seven Fleet and its commander, holder of an Emerald Star, Svetlana ton Mesfelle! The Perimeter Sector Nine Fleet and its commander, holder of an Emerald Star, Marat ton Mesfelle! The Damir system fleet and its commander, holder of an Emerald Star, Crown Princess Violetta royl Inoky ton Mesfelle! The Swarm Fleet and holder of an Emerald Star, Swarm Queen, Iseyek Prime, Nai Igir!"

The tactical map became overcrowded with green markers. Three hundred fifty Sector Seven starships. Two hundred sixty Sector Nine starships. Three hundred Damir system starships. One thousand five hundred Swarm ships. When you added my ships to that number, the total size of my fleet came to three thousand.

"And, the last holder of an Emerald Star, Count Avalle royl Anjer ton Mesfelle!" the Count's voice rang out. The Duke's younger brother had finally decided on the stronger side in the conflict, and joined it.

Four hundred ships on the tactical map changed color from red to green. After that, it even got through to the most pig-headed United Fleet captains, which force on the battle field was dominant. Chaos erupted.

Some enemy ships fled, others sent surrender messages, a third tried to come over to my side. Just five minutes later, there were no more than forty red dots left on the tactical map. They were the battleship *Orange Majesty*, and the other soldiers most fanatically loyal to Duke Paolo.

The Head of the Orange House stood on the screen, weighed down with impotence and shame. It seemed he tried to say something through his shaking lips, but couldn't bear it and waved his hand in shame, turning away from the camera. A system message came in immediately:

**The Head of the Orange House, Duke Paolo royl Anjer ton Mesfelle has resigned.**

**ATTENTION! A Great House of the Empire cannot be without a leader!**
**Election for new head of the Orange House must begin immediately.**

**You have the right to cast 41.3% of the votes in the Orange House. Would you like to support the first in the line of succession: Count Avalle royl Anjer, or would you like to vote for a different candidate?**

I froze for several seconds. More than forty percent of Orange House aristocrats with the right to vote had entrusted their votes to Crown Prince Georg royl Inoky. And what would happen if I voted, not for Count Avalle, but... for myself? It was very tempting... All the same, I decided to uphold my agreement with

Count Avalle and agree to his candidacy.

**ATTENTION! The new head of the Orange House will be Duke Avalle royl Anjer ton Mesfelle (80.3% of votes)**

Just for curiosity's sake, I opened the table with more detailed results of the election already in for the Orange House head. The second in the list was Crown Prince Georg royl Inoky ton Mesfelle, with 14.6% of the votes. If I were to add the 41.3% of the vote at my disposal to that result... I could make myself head of the Orange House, though I gave the historic chance a pass...

"Crown Prince Georg, I am grateful to you for making the right choice," the new Great House Head appeared on screen, glowing in happiness. "I promise that I will not forget your contribution to my victory and will review your bids for star system ownership as soon as the coronation ceremony is over."

Cries of glee could be heard all around. My officers were happy at the end of the civil war in the Orange House. Miya, barely able to stand, approached me, looking either drunk or dead tired.

"Crown Prince, for the first time I do not know what to say. When you called me into such a critical situation, I was ready to tear you to pieces with my bare hands, as you had put not only my life in danger, but also the life of my daughter. But now... that was magic, honest! Even my previous master Inoky was never able to achieve so much adoration from his subjects. I got fuller on energy than I ever have before. I can't even take any more. I'm still shaking and rocking back and forth. But tell me, Georg, why did you refuse to become Head of the Orange House?"

It was senseless to lie to the Truth Seeker, so I answered honestly:

"First, because I promised the Orange House throne to Count Avalle, and I am accustomed to keeping all my promises. Second," here I lowered my voice to a whisper, "do I have to remind you when my contract ends? What do I need all these problems for? I'm not getting paid for this. Also, what if Mr. G. I. doesn't want to be Duke?"

Miya smiled, somehow tortured and tired:

"Perhaps my master does want it... somewhere in the depths of his soul. It's just that he would never get this much recognition in the Orange House himself, so he wasn't counting on this chance even arising."

I dedicated all the next days to preparing for the end of my contract. Above all else, I was trying to mentally prepare those close to me for a potential character change. According to my version, I hadn't gotten rid of my narcotic crystal addiction. It was really hard, and from time to time I felt that I could just rip in half. I also warned them that, due to the effects of the narcotic withdrawals, my abilities as a fleet commander had become unstable and may even disappear for some time, though also not forever. I explained it by saying that, at those moments, I lost confidence in my abilities.

They heard me out carefully and nodded in sympathy. My personal doctor, Nicosid Brandt, summarized my complaints and confirmed that these were possible side effects from trying to quit a strong psychological dependence, and he was totally surprised I had been able to hold out as long as I had. The doctor offered to replace the medicine in the capsules sewed into my arm, and I agreed to the procedure.

After that, I tried to make sure all the people and nonpeople close to me would be provided for during my absence. I supposed that my return to *Perimeter Defense* was inevitable. The Aliens were still a threat to humanity, so an Imperial Fleet Commander capable of fighting against them was necessary. Also, I had no doubt that Mr. G.I. would have a positive evaluation of my work and would want to offer me a new contract. As such, all I had to do was cover the people near me for a few weeks, a month at most. That was exactly how much time I thought that the real Crown Prince Georg and Miya would need to realize they would have to call me.

The easiest of all was with Popori de Cacha. My bodyguard leader had asked for five months off on her own, on account of the strong necessity to continue the species soon. As far as I knew, Popori de Cacha herself had checked possible grooms for suitability at the large tournament on Sss, however none of the Chameleon males had been able to win over the overly sassy female in the hand-to-hand fight. As such, my bodyguard head had simply pointed to several cavaliers she did like, and none of the Chameleon males dared refuse the honorable role.

Astra, her sister Florianna with her minions, and also Bionica, Phobos, Valian ton Corsa, and the Arite, in the company of a group of Chameleons set off to the scout ship *Star Mutt* on my order. At first, I wanted to send Nicole Savoia there as well, but I had a better idea come to mind.

"Nicole, tomorrow you'll fly to the Throne World, here's your ticket for a star liner. I made an agreement with the Imperial Joint Staff for you to give a month-long course on Alien ships, military tactics against them, and other intricacies you figured out in the Perimeter Sector Eight Fleet.

If my subject was also surprised at Crown Prince Georg making such a decision, she made no effort to express it out loud. I gave the girl time off and a bonus for her excellent work, then sighed in relief.

It turned out harder with Katerina. My cousin had equipped her recently-purchased island with a palace, and as such all her thoughts were engulfed with furniture, statuary and art choices. I was not able to figure out any reasonable pretexts to send Katerina ton Mesfelle away anywhere for a month. All that was left to do was hope that the real Crown Prince Georg wouldn't hurt his cousin.

The most problematic in the list was my wife Marta. Her unexpected help during the general battle, and desire to talk closely with me after the battle was so unexpected and untimely that I completely lost myself. Marta was expecting gratitude from her husband, and couldn't understand why I was acting cold. I just simply couldn't tell my wife about the reasons for my behavior without breaking the contract. The only thing I was able to do was extract a promise from Marta that she would be more careful in the next few months, and would not talk closely with Miya.

Afterwards, I had to solve the ownership issues. It was possible that the real Georg wouldn't appreciate the full value of some discoveries, so I tried to shore up my most important assets. I ordered the research laboratories and drone production facilities packed up and moved to the Fia star system, one of my former Swarm systems. There, at the docks, I ordered a second *Uukresh* outfitted in complete secrecy. I spent almost two billion credits to buy materials and equipment for the future giant. The first *Uukresh*, with a convoy of Admiral Kheraisss Vej's ships I also sent away to Swarm territory, as I was not prepared to entrust such a valuable ship to my replacement.

My last evening in the game was spent in my palace on Unatari. At first, I just wanted to sit on the sea shore, listening to the sound of the waves breaking and taking in a beautiful sunset. But, as bad luck would have it, new space battle tactics just kept coming to mind. The idea of a raid on Alien bases with a fleet of light ships without big guns. The idea of luring the enemy to the flagship and sending out my thermonuclear fireboats from the depths of the *Uukresh*. The idea of gravity bombs to destabilize the *Behemoth*'s ammunition storage systems...

After realizing that I wouldn't be able to turn away and relax in nature, I returned to the palace, and sat up until the depths of the night working away at a computer screen, calculating in detail all possible space fleet configurations and their applications. Only when my work efficiency had fallen to zero due to my eyes closing in tiredness did I sit in bed, looking at the clock and waiting with curiosity for my exit from the game. Based on my calculations, there was a bit less than a half hour until my contract was up. I resolved firmly not to let my eyes close until that very moment...

"Wake up, sleepyhead!" Mr. G.I. was leaning over me and smiling, shaking me by the shoulder. "That's it Ruslan, your game is over. Sit still for a couple of minutes to wake back up and get used to your body again. After that, crawl out of the capsule, but be careful taking the suit off. There are thin wires there. Be careful not to break them. Your clothes are on the chair. Everything is new, bought just for you. I'll be waiting for you in the next room."

As soon as the door closed behind my employer, I sat up sharply and took a look around. It was a small room with no windows, in the center of which was a large elliptical cocoon made of dark plastic. The cap of the cocoon was ajar. My body was lying on a porous elastic sheet inside the cocoon and was being held in a fine mesh of the thinnest wires, attached with suction cups to my chest. I tried to remove the fasteners, raised my arm and realized that something was keeping me from moving. Every joint of my finger had a rubber ring with metallic electrodes on its inner surface attached to it. I removed all these devices from my arms, and then was able to unfasten the suit and crawl out of the capsule.

That meant it was a game after all... I experienced a

very strong sense of disenchantment and shame. Even when, a few years earlier, I had been left by a girl I loved, I wasn't feeling half as shitty as I did now. Everything I believed in, that I loved, and that I fought for was just the plot of a stupid computer game... I quickly got dressed and went up a stairway into a big hall. Georgiy was waiting for me there in a rocking chair next to an open window. There were green trees, summer sun, tweeting birds, and a warm wind. Six months really had passed since the time, on a cold winter morning when I left my house to talk to a potential employer.

"Ruslan, on the table you will find a sealed envelope. Inside it is a bank card, and with it you will find the pin code. Everything is there, as we agreed. There is quite a lot of money in that account, so if you need, my guards can accompany you to the bank, and then to your house."

"No, no, that will not be necessary..." I had been overcome by total apathy, so I could honestly have cared less whether there even was money in the account. "And where is Miya?"

"Miya?" Mr. G. I. pretended to be surprised. "What makes you think Miya should be here? Back in February she ran away from me to some resort down south, and since then I haven't heard a thing."

I knew he was lying. The first thing I sensed when coming out into the hall was the smell of violet perfume, that always accompanied Miya in the game. But as my former employer was not planning on telling the truth, I decided not to insist on it. Also, if I thought it out well, I didn't want to see Miya right now. I was reminded of how she promised to kill me as soon as I went out into the real world...

"I can't wait to get back into the game! Ruslan, you can't even imagine how much I've missed *Perimeter Defense*!" Mr. G.I. began to shiver in impatience and agitation.

"What can I say, it's a good game..." I let out through my teeth, hiding the envelope with the card in the inside pocket of my light jacket and headed for the exit.

"The guards will give you a packet of your winter things on your way out, then they'll take you straight home," promised my former employer, but I just mumbled back indeterminately in reply and went outside.

My employer was not lying. The full amount we agreed on really was on the card but, for some reason, that didn't make me happy at all. I was sitting in my stuffy rented apartment looking dumbly and dully at the New Year's wreath still hanging from the curtain rack. No one had removed it in the six months I had been gone, and I also wasn't feeling up to climbing up on the window sill and unraveling the pine decoration. I didn't want anything at all...

On the table in front of me was a mug of my favorite kind of unfiltered beer. The foam had long since faded, but I hadn't even taken a sip of the amber drink. Depression, apathy, despondency... In my head, I was trying to work out the word that best captured my state. By the end of the six-month contract I no longer had any doubt that I was in the real, fantastic world of the future, that I had a wonderful daughter, great friends and advisors, as well as status and recognition in society, I was making grandiose plans for the future. How could I have been so deceived?

I pushed away the still untasted beverage and gathered my strength and thoughts. It was already time to get back to the real world. I took a look around, already with my head screwed on better. On the table there was a thick stack of unpaid bills that I had dug out of the post box. The highest bill for the apartment had a threatening stamp on it: "If unpaid by the 20th of May, will be subject to legal action." Based on the fact that it was already July out the window, all these deadlines had long passed. At least I had the money to solve this issue. By the way, I should put the bank card away in my desk drawer so I don't accidentally lose it...

I placed the card with other valuable things and documents, and tried to close the drawer, but for some reason it wouldn't move. Of course, it's off the roller again, some part of the drawer has fallen off and is stopping the thing from moving. It was something that happened from time to time. I took the drawer all the way out and stuck my arm in to get the obstruction out. It was a transparent plastic box, inside of which was a brightly colored ball, overflowing with reflected light. And the strangest thing was that I understood perfectly that what I was holding in my hand was crystalloquasimetal-cis-isomer valiarimic acid, or in English narcotic crystals

I was probably the first person in history to give a big belly laugh after finding a dose of drugs that could get you the death penalty in their apartment. I started laughing, and just couldn't stop. A game? Well, well! Of course you made a pretty set for my awakening. Too bad I didn't think to check if that virtual reality capsule was even plugged in.

All that was left to do to make sure was to take a trip to the medical clinic. An hour later I left jumping for joy with an X-ray in hand showing a fracture to the collar bone beginning to heal. Everything came together. When I found a few empty bottles of cognac and vodka under the couch as well as a used needle, it only served to add to the totality of the picture. My body wasn't in a virtual reality capsule for half a year. Georgiy was playing me "in reality." He had sucked down vodka, taken drugs and partied it up in nightclubs.

I decided to voice my grievances to my former employer and set off for Mr. G. I.'s house, as I had luckily remembered the way perfectly. Imagine my surprise when, instead of the luxurious villa with a large, well-groomed park around it, I found a ruined, long, long abandoned building, filled with trash and old rotten leaves. The trail had gone cold. The hateful messages I sent to Space_General123 in the game we had once met in were also to no avail.

The only thing left was to wait and hope that my talents as a fleet commander would really be needed by Crown Prince Georg royl Inoky ton Mesfelle and his ghoulish Truth Seeker. I figured it would take at most ten days. That was as much time as I supposed my employer could spend in the game without my help.

However, a week passed, then two, and then three... I turned out to not be needed at all. No, I didn't forget about Perimeter Defense, but reality gradually put the fantasy world I'd left behind further and further from the front of my mind.

A call to my cell phone from an unknown number rang out at the very moment I was undergoing the next planned procedures in the medical clinic. That... bad man Mr. G. I. had been taking not just crystals, but heroin, and even three months after using, I still had to go to the medical center three times a week to get an injection of glucose with vitamin mix to cleanse the liver and blood, and fight the effect of drug withdrawals.

"Yes?" I said, pressing the accept button on the cell phone with my free hand.

"Ruslan, I have a serious proposition for you."

So much time had passed, but I would have recognized that voice from among a million others. Miya! So maybe I was needed after all.

*"You're right,"* the Truth Seeker's voice rang out in my head. *"Mr. G.I. will be waiting for you in the same place in forty minutes."*

My feelings were mixed. On the one hand, I desperately wanted to dive head first into the fantasy world of *Perimeter Defense*. On the other, my last experience had come at too high a price. The money I got in the first contract had barely been enough to pay all the fees and fines that Georgiy had left behind for me. My friends had turned away from me, I had fought with close relatives, and that's to say nothing about the hard drug torment and alcohol binges.

"After what you did to me last time, I don't even know what arguments could possibly make me go back into *Perimeter Defense* and give my body back to you to keep ruining!"

She kept silent for a few seconds, then said:

"The Alien *Queen* at the head of a three-thousand strong fleet has captured Hnelle. Your capital, Unatari is cut off from the Empire and we are preparing for a hopeless battle. The local soldiers have no chance of winning. The people's only hope is that Crown Prince Georg will personally return to lead the fleet.

I kept silent for a few seconds, digesting the worrying information.

"This time, the contract is on my terms," I declared decisively.

"I agree," Miya said, for some reason not even asking her master's opinion on the matter.

"Alright, I'll be there in ten minutes," I ripped the needle from my vein and headed for the exit of the operation room.

# END OF BOOK TWO

# About The Author

Michael Atamanov was born in 1975 in Grozny, Chechnia. He excelled at school, winning numerous national science and writing competitions. Having graduated with honors, he entered Moscow University to study material engineering. Soon, however, he had no home to return to: their house was destroyed during the first Chechen campaign. Michael's family fled the war, taking shelter with some relatives in Stavropol Territory in the South of Russia.

Having graduated from the University, Michael was forced to accept whatever work was available. He moonlighted in chemical labs, loaded trucks, translated technical articles, worked as a software installer as well as scene shifter for local artists and events. At the same time he never stopped writing, even when squatting in some seedy Moscow hostels. Writing became an urgent need for Michael, driving him to submit articles to science publications, news fillers for a variety of web sites and a plethora of technical and copywriting gigs.

Then one day unexpectedly for himself he started writing fairy tales and science fiction novels. For several years, his audience consisted of only one person: Michael's elder son. Then, at the end of 2014 he decided to upload one of his manuscripts to a free online writers resource. Readers liked it and demanded a sequel. Michael uploaded another book, and yet another, his audience growing as did his list. It was his readers who helped Michael hone his writing style. He finally had the breakthrough he deserved when the Moscow-based EKSMO - the biggest publishing house in Europe - offered him a contract for his first and consequent books.

Want to be the first to know about our latest LitRPG, sci fi and fantasy titles from your favorite authors?

Subscribe to our NEW RELEASES newsletter:
http://eepurl.com/b7niIL

Thank you for reading *Beyond Death!*
If you like what you've read, check out other sci-fi, fantasy and LitRPG novels published by Magic Dome Books:

**Reality Benders LitRPG series by Michael Atamanov:**
*Countdown*
*External Threat*
*Game Changer*
*Web of Worlds*
*A Jump into the Unknown*
*Aces High*

**The Dark Herbalist LitRPG series
by Michael Atamanov:**
*Video Game Plotline Tester*
*Stay on the Wing*
*A Trap for the Potentate*
*Finding a Body*

**Perimeter Defense LitRPG series by Michael Atamanov:**
*Sector Eight*
*Beyond Death*
*New Contract*
*A Game with No Rules*

**League of Losers LitRPG Series
by Michael Atamanov:**
*A Cat and his Human*

**The Way of the Shaman LitRPG series
by Vasily Mahanenko:**
*Survival Quest*
*The Kartoss Gambit*
*The Secret of the Dark Forest*
*The Phantom Castle*
*The Karmadont Chess Set*
*Shaman's Revenge*
*Clans War*

**The Alchemist LiTRPG series by Vasily Mahanenko:**
*City of the Dead*
*Forest of Desire*
*Tears of Alron*

**Dark Paladin LitRPG series by Vasily Mahanenko:**
*The Beginning*
*The Quest*
*Restart*

**Galactogon LitRPG series by Vasily Mahanenko:**
*Start the Game!*
*In Search of the Uldans*
*A Check for a Billion*

**Invasion LitRPG Series by Vasily Mahanenko:**
*A Second Chance*
*An Equation with one Unknown*

**World of the Changed LitRPG Series by Vasily Mahanenko:**
*No Mistakes*
*Pearl of the South*

**The Bard from Barliona LitRPG series
by Eugenia Dmitrieva and Vasily Mahanenko:**
*The Renegades*
*A Song of Shadow*

**Level Up LitRPG series by Dan Sugralinov:**
*Re-Start*
*Hero*
*The Final Trial*
*Level Up: The Knockout* (with Max Lagno)
*Level Up. The Knockout: Update* (with Max Lagno)

**Disgardium LitRPG series by Dan Sugralinov:**
*Class-A Threat*
*Apostle of the Sleeping Gods*
*The Destroying Plague*
*Resistance*
*Holy War*

**World 99 LitRPG Series by Dan Sugralinov:**
*Blood of Fate*

**Adam Online LitRPG Leries by Max Lagno:**
*Absolute Zero*
*City of Freedom*

**El Diablo by G.Zotov**
(a supernatural thriller)

**Mirror World LitRPG series by Alexey Osadchuk:**
*Project Daily Grind*
*The Citadel*
*The Way of the Outcast*
*The Twilight Obelisk*

**Underdog LitRPG series by Alexey Osadchuk:**
*Dungeons of the Crooked Mountains*
*The Wastes*
*The Dark Continent*
*The Otherworld*

**An NPC's Path LitRPG series by Pavel Kornev:**
*The Dead Rogue*
*Kingdom of the Dead*
*Deadman's Retinue*

**The Sublime Electricity series by Pavel Kornev:**
*The Illustrious*
*The Heartless*
*The Fallen*
*The Dormant*

**Citadel World series by Kir Lukovkin:**
*The URANUS Code*
*The Secret of Atlantis*

**You're in Game!**
(LitRPG Stories from Bestselling Authors)

**You're in Game-2!**
(More LitRPG stories set in your favorite worlds)

**The Fairy Code by Kaitlyn Weiss:**
*Captive of the Shadows*
*Chosen of the Shadows*

More books and series are coming out soon!

In order to have new books of the series translated faster, we need your help and support! Please consider leaving a review or spread the word by recommending *Beyond Death* to your friends and posting the link on social media. The more people buy the book, the sooner we'll be able to make new translations available.

Thank you!

Till next time!

www.ingramcontent.com/pod-product-compliance
Lightning Source LLC
Chambersburg PA
CBHW071632260626
47170CB00001B/64